The Resistance

Jack DuArte

REVISED EDITION

Cloud 9 Press

The Resistance Copyright © 2012, Jack DuArte

Book Design by Cloud 9 Press

Cover Design: Chris Inman, Visual Riot

DEDICATION

To my parents, Antoinette and John, who always believed in me.

And with loving thanks to my wife Susan for her great encouragement and undying enthusiasm that I could finally pull this all off.

To my son John Duarte, for his encouragement and marvelous help in researching and verifying many aspects of this work.

To Steven and Susan DuArte who also stayed behind me all the way.

ACKNOWLEDGEMENTS

To the many others who helped in one way or another make *The Resistance* a reality:

Daniel "Rusty" Staub, Sharon and Mark Rodi, David and Linda Chesterfield, David and Kimberly Wilson, Sharon Rosenblum, Margaret Wollums, Chris Inman, Kay Hoffman and Dale Albers, Rich and Pat Scelfo, Dick Francis, Richard DeAgazio, Ricardo Diaz, Jules Epstein, Timothy Capps, Patricia Maxwell, Mary Ann Mitchell, Jack Saux, Doug Cauthen, Jack Millikin, Jo Merriam, Mrs. Bill Atkins , Marilyn and Ron Smedley, Yvonne and David Seagrave, Marsha Ann Trobaugh, Michael Suscavage, Scott Rion, Joell Finney, Cheryl O'Brien, Sharon and Mark Rodi, Jane and Archie Casbarian, Lisa and Rick Hart, Ricardo Diaz, Jack Guthrie, Pamela Levy, Barbara Curry, Bill Bazzell, Marilyn and Ron Smedley, Emily Fluhrer, Don and Zee Kurfees, Steve and Cathy Snowden. Bill and Ellen Uzzle, Rev. Thomas Farrell, Rodney Le Blanc, Barb Greene, Katie Donovan, Tim and Marsha Cone, Mark and Linda Mattmiller, Linda Lamphere, Melanie Del Zompo, Barb Lesco, Peter Thompson, Katie Mahaney, Ben Kuchera, Joe Lewis, Anthony Jones, Catherine Hudson and Justin Skeens.

In France: Cecile Marie, Isabella Fransesci, Marc D'Bergougnoux, Cecile Senard, Felicity Maunder.

Forward

December 1941

A pair of shadowy figures paused briefly as a passing cloud cleared the three-quartered moon causing their silhouettes to be highlighted. The larger of the two, Guillaume Picou, motioned for his accomplice to wait. After a few moments, another cloud appeared shrouding the moon. Picou nodded and the pair proceeded forward.

Twenty yards ahead, their path was blocked by a ten foot high stone fence ringed by clusters of small bushes, which had long since dropped their covering of leaves. Guillaume hoped the bushes weren't roses and that the branches were free of sticky thorns that would impede their progress. Brushing the bushes aside, he mounted the wall with minor difficulty and paused on top, motioning for his partner to follow. Felix Noel followed Guillaume's lead, scaled the stone barrier without problem and came to rest in a squatting position some ten yards beyond the stone wall.

Guillaume fixed his attention on the chateau itself, spread silently before them. A faint light emanated from a second floor room on one corner of the structure. Other than the weak glow emitted by the second floor opening, the entire place seemed peaceful and empty in the cold December night. The men made their way around the building to the chateau's backside, which dropped off perceptibly. Guillaume estimated the descent at another twenty yards, which had the effect of placing the entire building atop a small hill. The two made their way carefully down the decline and to a spot beneath a squared window two floors higher. It was here that Picou was able to perceive the outline of a door. If his estimations were correct, Guillaume Picou surmised this portal would lead to the chateau's cellar, and to the contents within.

Guillaume whispered to his smaller friend, "Quiet now, someone might be awake inside."

Felix Noel nodded, but doubted Guillaume's warning. The pair had been in this type of situation many times before and Felix knew that people living this deep in the country were always asleep at 2 in the morning.

The cellar door was made fast by a bar across its entrance, secured in turn by a large rectangular lock that lay flat against the door. Felix reached for the wire cutter he carried inside his small bag. He carefully snipped the lock and pulled back the bar. Guillaume lifted the door and looked down. He removed a flashlight from the bag and pressed its button, but nothing happened. He shook the instrument, which finally emitted a weak beam. Guillaume glanced at Felix, silently rebuking his partner whose duty it was to have checked the flashlight, and took a first step downward. The chiseled stone steps produced a faint sound. The crunching of accumulated pebbles beneath their feet and broke the silence. The two descended six more stairs and stepped firmly onto the stone cellar floor of the old chateau.

They proceeded forward, rounded a corner, and entered a much larger chamber covering a good deal of the actual floor space of the building. Guillaume danced his light off the ceiling and around the room. He settled the light on a series of wooden crates, neatly stacked on both sides of the underground chamber.

He motioned for Felix Noel to lift the crate nearest to him, and removed a small crowbar from their sack. Noel held the crate firmly and Guillaume carefully pried loose the wooden strips holding the crate together. He then removed the contents, which were tightly wrapped in a soft cotton cloth.

"What is it?" Felix murmured his words barely audible.

"I'm not really sure, something in a frame I think."

A sudden sense of vulnerability engulfed Guillaume. It was a sixth sense possessed by members of his profession who suddenly they realize that they are dealing with a very delicate situation in a particular place where they really shouldn't be. He pointed the flashlight down to examine the outside markings of the crate, rearranged the cloth wrapping and returned the rectangular object back to its original resting-place.

"We need to leave here fast," Guillaume intoned faintly.

"But, I do not..."

The eerie quiet was interrupted by a clicking sound as the entire room suddenly became bathed in light. It took the Guillaume and Felix's eyes several seconds to adjust to the brightness.

"Stand where you are," a deep, authoritative voice commanded from behind the pair.

The twosome did as ordered, dropping the sack containing their tools. It clanked heavily to the stone floor.

"Turn around."

They turned and found themselves facing an array of long guns in the hands of three serious-faced men.

"Who are you, where are you from?" the deep throated man asked. He was dressed in a purple satin robe and held a handgun with an elongated barrel. A second man, dressed in normal clothes and wearing a beret and an overcoat, eased his way from behind the speaker and took up a position some eight feet from the speaker's side. The final figure remained in a partial shadow thrown by one of the beams that extended from the cellar's ceiling with only the barrel of his rifle showing.

Guillaume thought for a moment. He guessed it would be better to tell the truth.

"Thieves," he blurted out, summoning up his courage. "We are but simple thieves, Monsieur."

The robed man inspected the intruders, and their bag of tools. He eventually returned his gaze to the taller of the two perpetrators, both of whose arms were still fully raised. He looked balefully into Guillaume's eyes.

Guillaume sensed the man's intention, and pleaded.

"Please, Monsieur, we meant you no harm. We just intended to rob you. Turn us over to the police if you must, or just let us go. You will never see us again. I promise you that. Please."

"I am afraid I am not in a position to do either."

Terrified, Felix Noel leaned slightly forward. He was concentrating on the partially hidden man standing in the shadows. Something about the person was vaguely familiar. He suddenly realized the connection and uttered.

"Jean-Jacques, is that you?" The shadowy figure remained silent.

"Surely you recognize me. It's your cousin Felix. Do you not you remember the times we spent together when we were young, and all the trouble we used to get into? Why do you not say something? For heaven's sake man, speak up," he pleaded."

Silence enveloped Felix Noel's futile request.

Guillaume returned his view to the first man, the only one who had thus far spoken. He looked into the man's eyes and saw that it was too late.

"But surely, Monsieur, in the name of God..."

Felix started toward his cousin, almost crying. "Please Jean-Jacques, I beg you..."

Before he could complete the sentence, the man stepped out of the shadow and fired his rifle. The first shot hit its mark in the middle of Felix's chest, throwing him backward, a crumpled mass on the stone floor.

The distraction was all that Guillaume needed. He turned and abruptly made for the stairway around the corner from where he stood.

The other men reacted and fired in his direction. The wall that extended out and divided the cellar saved Guillaume's life. The bullets buried themselves in the plaster wall as the three men scrambled to follow Guillaume.

The thief reached the stone stairs and bounded up into the blackened night. His pursuers were right behind and reached the opening several seconds later. Guillaume continued his desperate flight and headed for the same side of the building from which he and Felix had originally emerged. As he approached the corner, his frame was silhouetted against the building's lighter color. A single shot rang out, causing Guillaume to clutch his chest as he fell heavily to the ground.

The pursuers rushed to the fallen body and turned him over with the barrel of the rifle held by the shooter. Guillaume's eyes were wide open, the only sign of life in the crumpled body. The figure relaxed his rifle and turned back in the direction of the chateau, nodding to the robed man who was still standing at the cellar door entrance.

The robed man turned his back on the carnage and descended back into the cellar. He approached Felix's body slumped on the stone floor and checked it for any sign of life. Finding none, he walked away toward a second set of rough stone stairs located at the other end of the large room. He ascended the stairs and entered the main corridor of the chateau. As he reached the top, he flipped the light switch and the cellar returned to darkness, a cellar now accented with the acrid smell of gunpowder and death.

*   *   *

A cold, numbing dampness penetrated the meeting room in the London offices of Britain's Special Operation Executive, chilling the participants who were forced to spend long hours sifting through the myriad information being offered by allied intelligence. A small heater in the room proved futile and produced only minor relief from the numbing cold for the men gathered there.

Jean Moulin, 42, was involved in more serious matters than the inevitable unpleasantness of his chilly surroundings. He was able to put such a minor distraction as being uncomfortable completely out of his mind. When he was a child in the France's southeastern coastal city of *Beziers*, Moulin's mother had cautioned him about such things.

"When you grow older, Jean, make things that matter important to you, and only things that matter."

Jean Moulin heeded his mother's advice, and often reflected on the many life values that she had instilled in him early in his life.

Moulin elected to study law at the nearby university in Montpelier. Immediately upon graduation he entered the French civil service. Jean possessed an excellent head for such matters and in 1930, became the youngest *subprefect* in France when he was given charge of an *Arrondissement*, a specific area of civil responsibility. Seven years later, the likable and well-respected country administrator was made *Prefect* of the much larger *Eure-et-Loir Department*, just southwest of Paris, whose *department* seat was the ancient and beautiful city of *Chartres*.

When France first assented to the Nazis, the country was divided into two zones. The first included the City of Paris and was occupied by the German Wehrmacht, which had absolute power over anyone residing within the occupied zone. The second zone was placed under the administration and protection of a government sympathetic to the Germans and was governed by Nazi-chosen leaders. The headquarters were located in the Central France spa town of Vichy. During this political turmoil, many French *department* heads fled their positions. Jean Moulin, however, remained at his job and catered to the steady flow of refugees who passed through his *department*. As his reputation spread, the Germans began to fear a potential problem with Moulin.

About this same time, a number of quasi-political organizations sprang up located within both occupied and unoccupied France, dedicated to preserving France's ultimate sovereignty. Included were splinter groups of the French Communist Party, disenchanted with Germany's sudden invasion of Russia. The problem with such organizations was simply that each acted in its own interest, with little national cohesiveness. The Free French government in exile, led by Charles de Gaulle, determined to establish unity within the splintered resistance political groups. The ultimate aim was to organize a single entity that would attack the basic problems associated with the Nazi occupation of their country. Such a goal was not an easy thing to accomplish.

At one fortuitous point for the Resistance, the German commander in *Chartres*, no doubt attempting to rid himself of a troublesome figure, authorized Moulin a pass that permitted him to cross into unoccupied Vichy territory. The pass proved to be Moulin's authority to travel throughout the borders of France relatively unimpeded, and greatly aided his continuing efforts to establish a coherent Resistance movement.

Moulin's reputation and bravery, as well as his past actions in the French civil service, were already well known to de Gaulle. The Free French leader was charged with organizing a group within France that could aid any sustained military actions undertaken by the Allies in the reclamation of France. Most importantly, de Gaulle was acutely aware that a splintered Resistance action had little chance of doing anything without a singular leader. Under Jean Moulin's leadership, de Gaulle felt the fledgling organization had a realistic chance for success.

De Gaulle saw in Moulin the adhesive he was seeking and gave him unrestricted responsibility for converting the loosely structured French Resistance into a cohesive political entity. Equally important De Gaulle was his confidence that Moulin could also develop the quasi-military force necessary to provide much needed disruptions to the everyday functions of the German army of occupation.

In a little over a year, Moulin's tough stands with local leaders and his ultimate persuasiveness and incredible administrative ability accomplished the job de Gaulle had mapped out. France now had a secret underground movement designed to enable the Free French, to disrupt German activities.

Jean Moulin was the key political figure in the entire network.

At this time Germany was nearing the apex of its military prowess. Its armies were finding little resistance and the plight of its enemies seemed ill fated at best. Even with the United States' entry into the war, the outlook in France was bleak and French sentiment constantly wavered as to whom win the war, a quality still would found in the French populace to this day.

In the early days of 1942, Moulin was summoned to Lisbon to meet with de Gaulle. There, it was decided that he be flown to London to assist in planning Resistance activities for the foreseeable future. London was the base for the SOE, which had been given allied control of most Resistance activity. A sub-branch of the organization, tabbed SOE-RF, was given control of Resistance activities in both occupied and unoccupied France. Great Britain's Special Operations Executive would later be renamed the British Secret service and is still charged with clandestine activities of the British Crown. Both offices worked closely with the Free French *Bureau Central de Renseignements ET d'Action (Militaire),* the BCRA, which was charged to get the Resistance up and moving in the right direction.

Moulin arrived in London, where he would be occupied for several weeks. During his extended stay, he was briefed with the information the combined allied intelligence networks were able to piece together.

While Moulin was somewhat familiar with events occurring in Europe since Nazi aggression had started years ago, he was unprepared for the depths of depravity to which the Germans had sunk. Even though Germany's ruthlessness and incredible disdain for human life and culture touched him personally and also his own *department,* Moulin realized the world he knew and loved would never be the same.

The intelligence sessions produced varying effects on Moulin, but a particular briefing rang true to the new head of the French Resistance. Former curators of national museums who had managed to escape from Austria, Czechoslovakia, and Poland gave this specific briefing. With great compassion, Moulin listened to factual accounts of pillage and the rape of their countries' historical places. The speakers firmly believed it was the intention of the Nazis to exterminate every trace of their country's history and culture.

The Polish spokesman in particular, painted a devastating picture of German officials parading through the National Museums in Warsaw, Krakow and Katowice. They pointed to specific paintings or sculptures that attracted their fancy. These treasures were soon packed and sent on the next available train for Berlin or to other German destinations.

"I saw with my own eyes, the corruption of so many German officials. The entire event happened so quickly; we were all at their mercy. There was no time for anyone on our staff to take any action," the Polish curator explained.

"One day, a group of high-ranking officials --- I believe both Goring and Goebbels were there --- visited my museum in Krakow. Each had an assistant with a notepad. As they passed through the paintings and statues, each pointed out the pieces that caught their fancy. It was as if they personally owned the museum. The very next day, Wehrmacht and Luftwaffe soldiers came and forced us to crate up all the articles that were on their lists. Trucks arrived and took the crates directly to trains, which carried them back to Germany. It was incredible how few of our Polish treasures the Nazis left.

By doing this, the Germans robbed us of our culture and heritage," the shattered Pole slowly continued. He inadvertently glancing toward Moulin, whose eye contact with the Pole caused the man to pause for a second.

Moulin felt a rush of genuine empathy for the man, whose eyes were filled with desperation and anguish.

The Pole lowered his head and continued almost inaudibly. "The fact is, we are now left with very little of our Polish culture. It is as if our country has all but ceased to exist. The Germans have left us with only the barest shreds of hope," he said.

Silence ensued, not a single person in the room wanting to disturb the speaker's solitary moment.

Moulin stared blankly. He was totally absorbed by the horrendous tale and its indisputable dire consequences to the country involved.

He made several notes on the pad in front of him and returned his attention to the remainder of the briefing, which continued its intelligence mission.

But a seed had been planted in Jean Moulin's mind, and he knew that he would require more detailed information if the seed were to germinate.

A few days later, Moulin made his way to the office of the Free French *BCRA*, the agency that assisted allied intelligence activities in London. His purpose at *BCRA* was to submit a request for information concerning France's national art treasures, and Moulin was immediately referred to the ranking French officer in the agency, a major named Andre Dewavrin. Moulin soon learned the man preferred to be known by his code name "Passy," which he had taken from a *Paris* metro station.

"Your request for information," questioned Passy, who remained across the room from Moulin intently studying a set of papers in his hand, "For what purpose do you want to know about the art treasures and their locations?" Moulin considered the question for a moment and carefully replied.

"An SOE intelligence briefing I attended a few days ago concerned the looting of other countries' museums. Much of what the Polish speaker said rang true to me. I started wondering if France was really prepared for the same eventuality.

I have been apprised of just how well the war is going for the Germans at this time. I have also been made aware that there is a realistic rumor in circulation among the intelligence agencies here in London regarding the fact that the Nazis possibly intend to occupy the remainder of France. It is quite possible that this action could take place in the very near future. I would like to ensure that Poland's unfortunate situation not be duplicated in France."

Passy continued to concentrate on his papers but motioned for Moulin to sit at a table in the center of the room. He picked up a chair for himself from along the wall and settled directly across from Moulin.

"From what I know about it, France prepared itself for such an eventuality several years ago. A set of contingency plans was drawn up by the *Comite des*

Musee and implemented even before Germany declared war. The contingency plan was a big undertaking, but most of the art treasures were safely removed from their homes. Even the stained glass from a number of the historic cathedrals, *Sainte Chapelle*, for instance, was removed and moved to a safer place."

"Where was it all taken?" Moulin asked.

"At first, everything was taken to *Chambord*, in the *Loire*. Then, certain officials began to worry that the location was too close to *Paris*, even considering the traditional historic protection the *Loire* River itself offered," replied Passy.

Moulin reflected on Passy's statement and asked again.

"What happened then?"

"Well, according to my sources, several events occurred. The paintings and sculptures were subsequently disbursed to a number of different hiding places. Some were transferred to *Louvigny,* near *Le Mans*, and others went to *Brissac*, the *Chateau* of *Sourches* and also to *Chervenay*.

Then, in the summer of 1940, several of the greatest paintings, including the Mona Lisa, were taken to an old abbey in the Midi called the *Abbey du Loc-Dieu*, not far from the town of *Villefranche-de-Rouergue*. I think those in charge reacted to political events that occurred and did what they believed to be best to protect the *objet d'art*."

Moulin nodded, but did not speak.

"And later, another decision was made to place the *finest* pieces in an even safer location. These works were sent to a secret hiding place, a semi-deserted castle, somewhere in the *Midi*. I do not know the exact name of the place, but I could probably find out. From what I understand, for security purposes, only a select number of people were told the location of the old castle. Unless I am mistaken Monsieur, the castle in the Midi is the current location for our country's most treasured works.'

Passy continued his explanation, but Moulin's attention had already waned.

His mind had already begun to develop the seed of an idea that could have deep, symbolic implications.

Moulin knew his plan would affect many French men and women. It would require a great deal of coordination and would utilize many of the resources at the disposal of his organization. He silently prayed his idea would prove worthwhile to everyone involve.

Chapter One
Paris - February 1942

When he accepted the position of chief curator of the *Louvre*, René Huyghe realized his new role as the top historical guardian in the French art world would change his life. While he had known early on in his career that great attainments were in store for him, he had even surprised even himself with his rapid rise to the very pinnacle of his beloved profession. Huyghe was blessed with an unusual knack for studies even when he began at his primary ecole, a gift he believed emanated from his scholarly mother. While his businessman father peered up over his daily paper at the morning table, it was always his mother who took real interest in young Rene's studies and accomplishments. It was she who prodded him into fields of endeavor that she herself had always longed to pursue. As he reached his twentieth birthday, his handsome combination of mature good looks and a formally piercing demeanor provided him professional communication tools usually carried only by a more seasoned veteran of the artistic arenas.

By the time he reached 36, he had occupied the chief curator's position for several years and was warmly accepted by both friends and adversaries as the best person in France for the celebrated job. As in most posts of such high statue, certain elements of the old guard considered the museum their personal art treasure and considered him young for such a job. Their protests were typically met with Huyghe's usual stiff resolve. Rene Huyghe accepted these apprehensions as part of his responsibility. He set out to prove to his detractors that their reservations had no basis in fact. He accomplished this over time with a staunch penchant for hard work, and a savvy political sense that told him when and where to make a stand on critical issues and when to acquiesce to an opposing point of view.

His efforts were nearly always successful. He was and at all times focused on the welfare of the *Louvre* and her incredible treasures. With the aid of his devoted staff, many of whom worked for what Huyghe considered barely livable wages, Huyghe finished the reclamation and restoration of many artistic treasures lost or stolen during World War I, or the Great War as it was typically referred to in casual conversation. It had taken the *Louvre* and a number of the other great European museums nearly two decades to accomplish this task.

In 1938, René Huyghe began to realize that the approaching Prussian menace that was threatening all of Europe would cast dark heavy clouds over the artistic landscape of Europe. He quickly set out to develop plans that would protect the *Louvre's* masterpieces and history from any eventualities.

By the middle of 1939, he masterminded a preventative course of action for the great museum. A decision was reached by the Louvre's governing body that was based on the deteriorating political situation throughout Europe and the suddenly impending threat of war with Germany.

Huyghe's plan was simple. He directed most of the museum's treasures be immediately sent into exile to one of his favorite old castles named *Chambord*, an imposing, storied citadel located between *Orleans* and *Tours* in the Loire Valley. When the political situation worsened and questions were raised as to whether the paintings could really be protected at *Chambord*, René Huyghe's plan went into its second phase. This important second stage called for moving a number of the most valuable art pieces to new, less obvious hiding places that he considered safe. A detailed schedule of works and their new hiding places had been drawn up in advance. Rene Huyghe kept the *only* complete copy of its contents.

The young curator frequently glanced at his list, taking pride and care with one particular work. As a schoolboy around the age of thirteen or fourteen, he had fallen in love with this masterpiece the first time he was given the opportunity to see it with his own eyes. As he stood in front of the work gazing upward, his mind was filled with a wonderment he had never before experienced. His heart pounded with the pure joy of realization that he was standing in the presence of something almost ethereal. From that moment on, René Huyghe was conscious of the fact that the *Mona Lisa* would bring special meaning to his life.

His position as curator of the *Louvre* was quite naturally one of the most important artistic posts in France. His political views made him a natural target of the occupying Germans. He joined The Resistance when he was first approached, considering it not only patriotic duty, but truly wanting to contribute to his country's cause and make a difference in the French struggle. His upper level contacts with the Resistance soon provided him accesses to a myriad of quasi-intelligence and information from sources throughout France and other occupied countries. This flow of information became the basis for his plans and strategies to thwart German attempts to subjugate artistic France. In his mind and in the minds of a great number of the leaders of the Resistance, Huyghe's presence and confident control insured the secrecy and safety of the treasures of the *Louvre*.

In late February 1942, an event occurred that Huyghe, Jean Moulin and other Resistance leaders felt called for immediate action.

One of Huyghe's minor subordinates at the *Louvre* was detained and roughly interrogated. From the questioning, it was apparent to Huyghe's employee that the Germans were attempting to locate the masterpieces that had been removed from the museum. Fortunately, the man arrested was a minor level employee who was not involved with the movement of the artwork. He survived the brutal questioning and was eventually released. The freed man had the good sense to immediately seek out René Huyghe and impress on him his feelings toward the German interrogation.

Huyghe listened patiently as his worker related the story. There was no doubt in his mind as to the Nazi's intentions.

He knew he would be next. There was no time to waste. He calculated the risks to himself and his beloved wife and children along with a small group of trusted friends and decided that he should immediately go underground for the remainder of the war. He immediately directed the two other Louvre employees who knew details concerning the locations of the *Louvre's* priceless pieces to do the same.

*   *   *

The cold Northeast wind cut through the partially exposed cobblestone street adjoining the *Place de la Bourse*.

As the solitary figure approached the corner and turned left onto the wider *Rue Vivienne*, he glanced quickly to both sides to assure himself he was completely alone. It was nearing ten o'clock and with new Nazi regulations in effect, it was chancy to attempt to cross even small sections of *Paris* at this time of night without running into a patrol along the way.

A thought crossed his mind as he slowed his pace.

Good thing it never occurred to the Germans that the sound of their steel-toed boots echo precisely through Paris' labyrinth caverns, always giving fair warning to anyone on foot. Maybe such sounds are just what the Bosch intended anyway. The sound of steel boots reminds the remaining French in Paris of Germany's presence and dominance.

He returned his attention to the present and another fifty yards ahead turned right onto the *Rue 4 September* and then quickly crossed the *Rue Richelieu*. He spotted the worn red canopy protruding from the front of the Brassiere Fouchant and quickly ducked into the tiny adjoining alleyway. The side door would be open as always, and his journey would be completed, at least for the present.

*   *   *

The nightly *Luftwaffe* bombings had become an unpleasant fact of life for most Londoners and were now accepted as a part of each evening's foreboding hours. Each night, ominous wails of air raid sirens would be followed minutes later by sounds of heavy bombs reverberating throughout the city. As long as the whistling accompanying the bombs was faint or non-audible, one's particular hiding place was considered safe. If the sound reached shrilling proportions, you knew you were close to a bomb's detonation site. The city's bomb shelters were always crowded and smelly since water service was spotty at best and most Londoners weren't accorded the luxury of bathing frequently.

To combat the problem caused by such massive bombing and to minimize the risk of direct bomb hits on vital areas, British High Command dispersed as many of its key departments as possible to locations that provided some measure of safety in the face of the incessant bombings.

Special Operations Executive (SOE) Section RF was just such a unit and was headquartered on the third floor of an undistinguished building at 64 Baker Street, in the northeast quadrant of Central London near York Circle. Section RF was manned by a number of British officers and staff plus several civilian employees. Its primary duties consisted of gathering and disseminating allied intelligence activities within France.

In the largest room on the building's third floor, three British officers sat around a small circular table in the sparsely furnished room. A number of maps of France and a detailed map of the English Channel decorated two of the walls. Numerous color-coded pins and flags were prominently displayed on each map. On the other wall was hung a poster depicting the heraldic British lion with a German soldier held within its mouth. The poster was a particular favorite of the British press as well as many young and even older British citizens who identified wholeheartedly with the message portrayed by the poster and sought solace in its definitive message.

The ranking officer at the table was Brigadier General Percy Barclay, a youthful 50-year old, lightly silver-grayed hair with a boxed chin and striking good looks. He was immaculately tailored as befitting the titular head of SOE. The Barclay family had been bankers in Britain for over two hundred years and was a pillar of the British financial community. General Barclay was a career army officer who had opted for the glamour and action of the armed service rather than a tranquil family position within the banking community. During his twenty-five year career in the British Army, he had never regretted his decision.

"Gentlemen," Barclay began in a precise diction developed during his student days at Oxford, "it seems that SOE has given RF a new project to sink our teeth into. I've studied it for the past several hours and it looks like this could be a bit of a whopper."

Both officers raised their eyebrows slightly as Barclay continued.

"Major Passy, who, as you are aware, is head of the Free French Secret Service under General de Gaulle, has asked us to get involved with an undertaking which would require some very precise planning on our part. The mission will involve military and Resistance operations both here in England and also within the unoccupied zone of France. This is another of those special missions that will probably go unnoticed by most of the world. If we are successful, and there's no reason to assume we won't be, then the mission's potential effects are quite enormous. And, before I forget to mention it, the operation's success will mean a *great* deal, both to General De Gaulle personally, and also to the French people. When you hear all the pertinent details, I am sure you will understand why I have agreed for us to participate."

He paused, took a few short steps in the direction of the wall containing the maps of France and turned to face his subordinates.

"Once this briefing has been completed, it will be totally up to us in this room to see that this operation is successful."

*   *   *

With the *Louvre* Museum practically closed and his beloved workplace deserted of viewers, these cold mid-winter days were particularly difficult for Andre Faboul, assistant curator for older paintings at the museum. From the time he was a student at the *Sorbonne* in the late 20's and until he realized that his life's work would involve *caring for* and *not producing* great works of art, Andre Faboul approached his vocation with a fixed dedication and resoluteness, emotions that he found effortless in such lofty environs.

By 1935, his career was proceeding nicely as an assistant curator at the smallish *Musee Jacquemarte Andre*, on the *Boulevard Haussmann* near the *l' Arc de Triomphe*. An associate in the museum informed him about an assistant curator's position that had recently opened at the *Louvre*. Even though the pay was roughly the same, Faboul considered the status and pull offered by the *Louvre* irresistible, as he had always considered the *Louvre* to be the apex of museum hierarchy. Like many visitors to the old, somewhat magical historical edifice, Andre had been enthralled with its elegant rooms and *salles* since first accompanying his mother at the age of eleven to see an exhibit of the first great French impressionist Camille Carot. Carot's brilliant use of light in both his landscapes and figures produced an incredible effect on the youthful Faboul and directed his entrance into the world of art.

Ten years later, while a student at the *Sorbonne*, and during Andre's first unfruitful attempts at painting, Faboul and his classmates made frequent trips to the museum and were always among the last to leave when it closed. Inside the Louvre's walls Faboul found that there was so much to absorb, and so little time to do so considering the number of hours the *Sorbonne* required from each of its fortunate students. When it became apparent to Faboul that he possessed insufficient talent to survive as an artist, he immediately sought an arrangement within the art world that would associate him with his precious artworks. His classic training and general attitude toward his chosen career had impressed the curator at the *Musee Jacquemarte Andre* and Andre Faboul's curator career in museums had begun after his first interview.

When he was initially interviewed for the assistant's position at the *Louvre*, Faboul had not even considered wages when the subject was brought up. He mused to himself the sheer incredibility of a situation that found him actually being paid to work every day at the greatest museum in France, if not the entire world.

Andre Faboul was initially assigned to work in the *Louvre's* Antiquities Department, the sector that procured older paintings for the *Louvre*. As time passed and Faboul became accustomed to his assigned duties, he found his newfangled pursuits and surroundings immensely rewarding. He had become decidedly talented in the fine art of negotiating for rare works. He was successful in acquiring a number of older paintings that became available through estate sales. Less frequently, he successfully obtained paintings and sculptures through outright purchase from owners who suddenly needed to turn family heirlooms into much needed cash. Instead of feeling sorry for those who sold out of cash needs, he felt that the objects he was acquiring were bound for their best possible home and would now be shared by the *Louvre's* countless visitors from across the globe.

Faboul quickly became one of René Huyghe's top ministrants when it was decided to move the *Louvre's* treasures for safekeeping. From the beginning of Faboul's employment, Huyghe had been impressed with Faboul's personal work ethics; his fondness for detail and over time favored his younger assistant more than some of the older curators with more seniority but less enthusiasm for their work. In time the two became close personal friends, a scenario that brought satisfaction to both parties on a number of occasions. So when the ultra-secret occasion arose when Huyghe decided it was time to act in secreting away the Louvre masterpieces, it was Andre Faboul who was given the charge of personally supervising the packing and drayage of nearly all the important works that were the property of the museum. Two other trusted assistant curators helped Faboul who decided it best to work day and night to accomplish the task. It took the trio three days and nights. They slept for short periods on wooden crates in the rooms where the paintings had been amassed but accomplished their task to their own and Huyghe's satisfaction.

During the long hours of packing, Faboul recalled to his mind the time not so long ago in 1940 when the Germans marched unopposed into *Paris* to begin their occupation of his beloved city. That same day, Andre Faboul watched in disbelief and later horror, as the hated invaders descended on the venerable old museum. He winced as a German officer gathered the museum's staff together for a lesson in Nazi Germany's particular brand of propaganda. The speech extolled the fact that the *Louvre* and its contents were now German property and should be treated as such by all employees. He shifted his weight uneasily as the German officer eyed him directly as if daring the young Frenchman not to follow his ordersAs with most loyal Frenchmen, Andre Faboul was appalled at the German's dogmatic tone. His open regard for the beloved museum and his love for his country's future went far beyond the boundaries of his job and circumstances.

As he stood among his fellow employees, old feelings and patriotic thoughts filtered through Faboul's mind. To pass the time, Faboul tried to recall facts about the museum from his school days.

Was he right when he recalled that the great buildings of the *Louvre* were officially designated by Francoise I in 1527 as his courtly residence, and as such became the housing for his incredible collection of Italian Renaissance masters?

I am probably right about the date, he mused, *one doesn't forget such important a date if one is going to be successful in the museum business.*

And the old place is still in pretty good shape. Even though more than four centuries have passed; the museum and its contents remain basically intact. What will now happen with the Germans in control? His mind wandered as he again heard the drone of the German officer creep into his mind.

Andre Faboul sighed and collected his thoughts. He knew deep inside that his beloved museum might never be the same.

*   *   *

Obersturmbannfuhrer Kurt von Heltscherer of the Waffen SS was delighted with his assignment in Paris. He knew the special assignment was a great boost for his career, which, before this latest relocation, seemed headed for nowhere.

Von Heltscherer truly looked the part of a Waffen SS officer. He possessed an almost photogenic German face, set off by high cheekbones and a thin aquiline nose. His once blonde hair now possessed traces of gray, which added to his allure. At 51, he was the correct age for a career officer colonel, but he privately questioned further advancement even considering his family was descended from nobility. With the Nazis in power, family lineage was often construed as a liability. A great uncle, two generations past, incurred the wrath of the Kaiser with underhanded business dealings and the von Heltscherer family fortunes had been compromised from that point on. Von Heltscherer's more recent hopes were buoyed by the fact that his first cousin, Helga, became engaged to Reichsmarschall Hermann Goring's nephew.

At the wedding that followed a few months later, von Heltscherer met and conversed for the first time with Goring, the Nazi Party's second in command. Since there were few military men at the wedding, von Heltscherer was delighted to be introduced early to the Reichsmarschall who was standing next to a table filled with champagne and wines from the Moselle. Goring took note of von Heltscherer's Waffen SS uniform and decorations and initiated the conversation.

"I find the events here totally boring," the regally white uniformed Goring began, turning his head as he spoke and gazing around the room. "But family is family and Frau Goring would be livid if I didn't make an appearance. She so likes to show me off to her friends."

"I do understand fully, Reichsmarschall," von Heltscherer replied. "I am in much the same position. Women enjoy weddings much more than men do because they can gossip about each other to their hearts content."

"Ya, ya, you are right," Goring agreed, taking an immediate liking to the fit younger officer who seemed unfazed in talking to a true hero of the Third Reich. In actuality, the pair offered a great contrast to anyone observing the conversation, both physically and mentally. Goring was grossly overweight and his sweeping white and gold-laced Reichsmarschall's uniform did little to accentuate his portly physique.

Von Heltscherer was trim, his uniform manicured to his athletic build and stood at a semi-rigid form of attention even as he talked. Interestingly, Goring did most of the listening while von Heltscherer provided most of the banter between the two. Von Heltscherer was immediately taken with the Reichsmarschall and understood why his Luftwaffe subordinates often called their leader "Uncle Hermann," as a genuine show of fondness.

Goring also appreciated the fact that his presence did not intimidate the lesser officer in the least, and made an immediate decision to utilize this dedicated Obersturmbannfuhrer if the occasion should ever arise.

When Hermann Goring's Luftwaffe adjutant called three months later inquiring as to whether a certain Waffen SS Obersturmbannfuhrer would possibly be interested in a special posting in Paris, von Heltscherer leapt at the opportunity. Von Heltscherer's present unit had been involved in combat in Poland but the Panzer squadron to which he was assigned was only involved in mopping up scattered bits of resistance, which Poland's undermanned and antiquated Army could provide.

He was duly amazed when, at one point, a few straggling Poles actually attacked his tanks on horseback. The attack was quickly dispersed when the tanks methodically pelted the attackers and their mounts with machine gun fire. The resulting carnage left an incredible mute picture in the mind of the German officer.

Von Heltscherer was also very aware of the real possibility of being sent with his panzer unit to duty on the Russian eastern front, the prospect of which he discreetly dismissed from his mind. He had visited Paris several times before the occupation and always found it a charming, most alluring place. To be posted there even for a short period of time was certainly a most marvelous stroke of luck.

*　　*　　*

René Huyghe enjoyed the musty, almost vinegary smell of the Brassiere Dauphine as much as he admired its ambiance and old-fashioned provincial décor. It was one of Huyghe's preferred pre-war watering spots, and its location made it a perfect rendezvous for top-level Resistance meetings. His mind savored the curious mixture of beer, wine and cognac vapors mixed with the heavy spices of *Provence*, the convergence of which awaited Huyghe's arrival. The thought of such fondness warmed his senses and provided for a welcome respite from the bitter cold February night.

As he has rounded the corner on the *Rue Vivienne*, Huyghe felt the flecks of snow which had begun falling and which would afford a nice covering by morning.

The fact that the snow would present a small hazard to the German vehicles that would be driving the next day comforted Huyghe. The only real motorized vehicles to be seen these days were either German military vehicles or delivery trucks bringing produce and goods into Paris to be sold. French cars were becoming practically non-existent, and the gasoline ration coupons to run them were nearly impossible to acquire, even on the black market. Out of a possible three hundred fifty thousand parking spaces in *Paris*, Huyghe knew that less than 4,000 driving licenses had been issued. More and more frequently, horses were used to pull a number of petrol-less automobiles, a fact Huyghe considered an ironic aspect of the absurdity of the present times.

From his vantage point approaching the storefront, no movement apparent in the brassiere at this hour, and black curtains were drawn covering the street side windows.

Huyghe descended a small flight of stairs immediately around the corner from the front entrance that led into the brassiere's *caves* where the restaurant's supply of wines and spirits was stored. He opened an unlocked door that creaked as it turned. His eyes focused on a small barrel that sat in the center of the room, its shape visible from a candle flickering in the near blackness. Huyghe made out the outline of two figures seated around the barrel.

He recognized one of the men by his round, stubble face as Jacques Bitoun, the Brassiere Dauphine's cheerful, rotund proprietor.

"*Bonjour,* he offered. "*Ca va?*"

"All is okay," came the reply. "It is good you made it safely. It is not the best of nights to be out."

"Yes, even the Boche does not enjoy these snowy nights. The patrols stay indoors as long as possible to try and keep warm. It makes for crossing *Paris* a little easier."

Huyghe took a chair and looked at the other participant. He was obviously French and well dressed.

Bitoun handed the newcomer a small crystal brandy snifter. He lit a second candle, which provided the cave with a great deal more light.

"Here is some nice Calvados I just received from my old friend who makes it in Normandy. A really good brandy is becoming harder to get all the time. I know the *Calvados* is your favorite so I thought you would enjoy some," Bitoun smiled at Huyghe as he handed the smallish glass to him.

Huyghe took the snifter and swallowed a little, letting it slowly round into his mouth.

"Nice," Huyghe agreed, "very soft and delicate. The fruit is not compromised a bit." He drank another sip.

Bitoun glanced up from the bottle and spoke again to Huyghe.

"René, the main reason for you to come here is to meet with Jean Moulin, the new leader of the Resistance in France." He looked at the other man seated around the barrel.

Huyghe looked into the man's face and broke into a wide grin.

"I was never sure you actually existed, *monsieur*, that is, until now that I have a chance to see you in person. I have heard a great deal about your efforts on behalf of the people of France."

"And I, in turn, have been told of your work in our cause," replied Moulin, observing that the younger Huyghe blushed slightly with the compliment.

Good sign, Moulin thought. *A most sincere man.*

"Now, if we can get down to a little business, please let me tell you exactly what has brought about our meeting," Moulin said. He eased the tight scarf around his neck, exposing a large scar. Huyghe took note of the wound, recalling the stories that had circulated in resistance circles pertaining to Moulin and his sessions with the Gestapo.

Moulin spoke slowly and distinctly, his gaze directed solely at Huyghe.

"Something has been bothering me for the past two months since my intelligence visit to London, and I think the time has come for us to do something about it. Several Free French intelligence officials in London have informed me that our wonderful German liberators have taken it upon themselves to systematically loot the historic museums of each country they have overrun. In a few instances, this looting has been done piece by piece, with some of the artwork actually finding its way into museums throughout Germany. Other times, priceless pieces went directly into the collections of high-ranking Nazi figures, most of who have suddenly developed great taste in classic art. Hitler and Goring among other Nazi swine have received confiscated pieces, and, I should not have to tell you what this means to the character and culture of the countries involved."

René Huyghe nodded his agreement, glancing across the table. The events of the past few weeks passed through his mind, bringing a measure of meaning and understanding as well as the rationale for this meeting.

"We are all aware that the German occupation of France will probably be a long, drawn-out affair, and may last for several years," Moulin started again. "There exists a current feeling within the intelligence community that Germany could easily extend its occupation to the remainder of France, regardless of the agreement with Vichy. This further occupation could possibly occur as early as the end of this year or the beginning of the next. Such an action could pose additional problems for our French national art treasures, which thankfully *you* and your staff were responsible for moving to safer hiding places. If Germany does indeed succeed in occupying *the rest of* France, I am sure you will agree there will be *no* truly safe hiding places in our entire country."

"Yes, I most certainly agree with you," Huyghe replied, a bit tentatively, "but what can we do about it? After all, the paintings have already been moved several times and are now in the most remote locations I was able to find."

"I believe I might have an idea that might help, but understand my friend, that the idea will be implemented only if you agree after what I tell you now." Jean Moulin looked at Rene with a solemn glance.

"But first, I must let you know that I think it is going to take a great deal of effort if *any* of us are going to survive the remainder of this bloody war. We are all wanted men and as such, the Gestapo is going to apply even greater pressure to find us, even if it were possible for them to be any more relentless. Each of us must carefully plan our Resistance work and involve as few of our confederates as possible. Only those who have a real *need* to know will be informed or involved. To that end, I have just finished developing a three-point pyramid system whereby one resistance member is responsible for two additional members and only two. Each unit becomes an individual cell and limits the exposure of each person to only three. If we are infiltrated by anyone from outside, I strongly believe my pyramid system will, in theory, minimize our losses. I am already beginning to suspect that the Gestapo has penetrated parts of our movement. You must realize what that means."

Huyghe acknowledged Moulin's comment in silence.

Moulin continued. "While I was in England, an idea came to me that I feel might be workable. If you agree to help and it proves to be successful, the plan will insure the French people a ray of hope at the end of this terrible ordeal. I want you to listen to all the details. Certain aspects of the plan have already been initiated in Great Britain. If you concur with its concepts, we will put the remaining details into motion. I believe with your support and assistance, we would have a means to make the plan successful."

*   *   *

The three Englishmen brought diverse backgrounds to the planning table at SOE. In addition to Brigadier General Percy Barclay, two additional British officers were present; British Colonel Maurice Buckmaster, a 25-year career British army officer, operations specialist and section head for SOE's French operations RF, and Flight Colonel Barclay Smith-Reeves, a 1926 Sandborne graduate who had opted for wings upon the advent of military glider flying. For the past year, Smith-Reeves has been considered the Royal Air Force's premier powerless flight expert and commanded its Glider Pilot Regiment, Great Britain's only existing combat ready glider unit.

"Because of its very nature, this promises to be a most exhilarating operation," intoned General Barclay as he laid a detailed map of Central France on the table in front of the pair. "As a matter of fact, if this mission is successful, and there seems no reason it should not be , I think it will definitely provide us a basis for even more involved Resistance activities in the future.

I have had a series of meetings with the new leader of the French underground, a chap named Jean Moulin. I'm sure Colonel Buckmaster remembers him well from his time spent here with us late last year. Jean has requested our help in pulling off a sham. If successful, this operation could provide major achievement regarding for our ongoing relations with the Free French movement."

"A sham Brigadier?" Colonel Buckmaster questioned his superior quizzically, recalling the ever-serious Moulin he knew. Buckmaster and Moulin had become friends during Moulin's brief stay at SOE. Buckmaster himself had stepped in and personally coordinated the Frenchman's successful parachute jump back into northern France. Colonel Maurice Buckmaster knew already that he was interested in anything that involved Jean Moulin and he intended in playing as active a part as possible in making it happen.

"Give me just a minute, Colonel, and I will explain everything.

Our intelligence has verified that the Nazis have repeatedly plundered the national museums of each country they have occupied. What's more, a good many of the best pieces have been spirited away by the Nazi's party top goons, which is particularly disgusting to just about everyone involved. The long-term effect of seizing such items involves more than mere thievery, it touches each country's artistic heritage and culture. When the Germans effectively remove such national treasures as I have just mentioned, the countries involved are left with very little on which to rebuild. Besides, there's no telling what will happen to such priceless pieces during wartime.

The French and Jean Moulin in particular, are determined not to let Germany get its hands on *any* of their artistic treasures, or at least the *crème de la crème* of the *Louvre's* paintings that have been relocated to an ancient castle in the middle of France. We also have scattered reports beginning to surface that the Germans are intent on finding the paintings, a fact that adds a time factor to our problem.

This scenario is the basis for our mission, and where I intend to fix the focus of the RF Section. The initial plan that we have developed calls for cooperation from each of your units, as well as a great deal of interaction with the French Resistance itself. The operation is quite complex and involves a great deal of pre-planning and precise timing. I think we have all the necessary ingredients to make it happen. However, we will probably need a little visit from dame Lady Luck at some point during the plan's implementation to make everything mesh.

That said, in keeping with the spirit of the operation, I have designated the entire sham with a name drawn from antiquity. Henceforth, the entire operation will be coded, Operation Angerona."

"Angerona?" asked Colonel Buckmaster, unable to place the term in his memory.

"Angerona. The Roman Goddess of Secrecy," General Barclay immediately replied.

*   *   *

Brian Adams Russell's boyhood had always been filled with the premise that he would one day fulfill some special purpose during his lifetime, something out of the ordinary, as was the tradition in his family since Colonial times. He was told early on that both his parents' families were directly descended from some of the earliest American settlers and were responsible for a number of historical accomplishments throughout the years.

Even as a child, Brian Russell took particular delight whenever such stories were told in front of the family's fireplace or over a family meal on the Russell's huge dining table.

His mother, Sarah, was a great-great granddaughter of President John Quincy Adams. Her family had continued the political traditions of their early ancestor in Massachusetts and throughout New England during succeeding generations. Brian's father was William Russell, whose early relations were mostly teachers and printers. Such men and as such were always in the background of historical happenings. William Russell followed his family's early tradition easily earning his doctorate in English history and selecting several jobs in academia, always moving up the ladder first at Williams and later at Tufts. His big break occurred in 1930 when he was named Dean of Fine Arts at Yale University, passing up a number of more senior applicants in the process. As such, Dean William Russell carried considerable weight amongst the scholarly elite of the United States. He had even attracted a sizeable following on the European Continent after publishing a number of highly praised scholarly studies during his early tenure at Yale.

Brian Russell inherited his father's strict attitude toward schooling, and was inwardly relieved that his studies came easily to him at even the youngest age. As he grew and matriculated, his schoolwork improved. Young Brian Russell excelled in practically every aspect of scholastic endeavor. He sailed through high school and entered Yale in the footsteps of his proud father. In New Haven, Brian Russell was found to possess unusual aptitudes for both language and literature, was fluent in French and by the end of his sophomore year, moderately adept in Spanish. Russell was open-minded about his future but, as he was about to begin his junior year, he was still undecided on the exact direction he intended to pursue regarding his career and life.

For several months he allowed his mind to vacillate on the matter of his future, but Brian finally sought his father's counsel. He has always shared nearness with his Father but felt a bit uncomfortable about approaching his father for advice on a personal matter he thought he should be able to figure out for himself.

"Dad," he started awkwardly, reaching for the correct words. "I am a little undecided about what to do with my future. I thought I would have some notion by now, but everything comes up blank. I enjoy just about everything I do, but so far nothing jumps out at me. Shouldn't I know what I want to do by now? Some of my friends are already sure of what they want, but I just seem to vacillate to whatever I am doing at the moment."

Brian paused and continued. "I hope you can help me, you always seem to know the right thing to do."

The older Russell listened attentively to his son's plight, smiled and replied. "I've been watching you lately, Brian, and I knew something was up. As a matter of fact, I half expected something like you've just described."

Brian peered inquisitively over at his Father, unsure of what was coming next.

"Same thing happened to me about your age and I had to speak to my Father about it too."

Brian doubted that his father had ever been unsure about anything in his life, but allowed his father's words to seep into his mind.

"For me everything worked out after a while and the path of education opened its doors," Dr. Russell smiled again recalling his quandary more than two decades before.

"But you are different from me in many ways, even though we are from the same stock. I have always felt that you possessed unlimited horizons, some sense of adventure that would take you far away from your Mother and me. Anyway, I've already made a few calls on your behalf and I have a proposition for you.

My old friend and colleague of many years Guy Paissant, teaches the humanities at the Sorbonne. I've explained your aptitude for French and the wanderlust that seems to be lurking in your soul. He recently wrote back that he would be delighted to have you for the next year in Paris. How does something like this sound to you?"

It took Brian Russell all of ten seconds to agree to his father's suggestion.

La Belle France was an awakening for Brian Russell and one year turned into two, then three. He received his degree and stayed on to pursue graduate studies. He fell in love with the country, the City of *Paris*, and most importantly, the French language. He excelled in practically every aspect of the French tongue and by his third year spoke French *sans* any trace of an accent.

This ease of speaking proved invaluable to Brian, particularly when young French ladies were introduced to him in *Paris'* smoky bistros and clubs. Brian's boyish good looks and playful attitude made him extremely popular with all his friends. He took full advantage of his linguistic ability and a number of lovely, young French mademoiselles succumbed to his charm and wit.

He spent his summers at the homes of his university friends' families, frequently in the *Dordogne* and also in *Alsace*, and gleaned for himself as much French history and culture as was possible. He knew in his mind that he would spend the rest of his life in his adopted country.

He developed a liking for the French game of *footbol* or soccer, and was soon considered a better than average player. On Sundays, when soccer matches were contested in *Paris*, Brian was usually a willing participant.

In 1939, he had just finished a term at the *Sorbonne* and returned to *Paris* from a late August holiday with some friends to the wine country, some eighty miles from Paris around the hilly town of *Chablis*. After returning to Paris the following day, he awoke in his small apartment off the *Rue Sequier* near *Notre Dame* to a newspaper hawker's cry.

Germany invades Poland!

Two days later on September 3rd, France joined Britain in declaring war on the aggressor.

For the next six months, Brian had carefully assessed the changes France was undergoing. He was worried that the France he knew and loved might not survive. Most of the news trickling into the Paris papers was increasingly negative.

On June 17, 1940, Marshall Petain issued a proclamation to the people of his desperate nation, an address that was repeated hourly on *Radio France*.

"Frenchmen! Called by the President of the Republic, I am taking over the direction of the government of France as from today. Certain of the devotion of our superb army, which is fighting with a heroism worthy of its long military tradition against an enemy superior both in numbers and in arms; certain that by its magnificent resistance it has fulfilled our duties to our allies; certain of the support of our old soldiers, whom I have been proud to command; certain of the confidence of the entire nation, I offer myself to France in order to lessen her suffering.

It is with heavy heart that I tell you today that the fighting must cease. Tonight I will contact the enemy and ask him if he is prepared to discuss with me, as between soldiers, after fighting the battle and defending our honour, the steps to be taken to end hostilities."

Prodded by a call from his worried parents back in the United States and unsure of his status in politically murky France, Brian Russell booked on the first available airplane to Lisbon and then on a freighter that landed him back in Boston two weeks later.

The solitary figure quickened his pace as he approached the *quai* that bordered the river's edge. This was the roughest section of *le Puy en-Veley* and Pierre Bonde thought it wise not to loiter here when there was no good reason to do so. He checked both sides of the path leading to the *quai*, and found them both deserted.

His Resistance responsibilities had increased in recent months. But along with the added duties came a dogged feeling of frustration that weighed heavily on his partisan shoulders. As head of Resistance activities for the entire *Midi*, Bonde was irked for two main reasons.

First, he felt that his local partisans were ill equipped and generally untrained for their mission Secondly, and even more important in Bonde's mind, a number of his men had been recently arrested and detained by officers of the Vichy Government.

The Vichy Government! What fools the French leaders were in getting themselves into such a mess. Could not anyone see what was happening? Did anyone really believe the Germans wanted to be France's friend and ally? How absurdly stupid we were what with the last war, the Great War, only over a mere twenty years. What happened to our collective memories and the strong voices that promised not to let such a thing happen ever again? If it were not for de Gaulle and the ex-patriots, there would not be even a ray of hope for France.

The distasteful thoughts chagrined him and Bonde forced his mind to revert to the real world. In doing so, the idea of Vichy infiltration of his organization crossed his mind again. Bonde made a silent note to alter his group's reporting system in order to simplify the level of command. He correctly reasoned that the fewer people he involved in decisions meant much less chance of detection and possible capture.

He turned the corner and strode onto the *quai* itself. He disliked having to come on foot to this part of the city at nighttime, where the old warehouses and buildings provided excellent locations for a myriad of clandestine activities.

The building he sought was now less than a block away, and jutted out near the street. He was focusing on its outline when a shadow stepped out of the darkness and grabbed him from behind.

The assailant flashed a long knife, which gleamed in the moonlight as its holder turned his hand.

Bonde was turned around by the assault, and now stood face to face with his attacker.

"Careful, monsieur, this knife can do serious harm to your face."

Bonde regarded the man, whose age he guessed to be about thirty, with small, thin lips and a vulpine face. The man appeared nervous, his features clearly masked with concern.

"What is it you want from me?" Bonde asked openly, taking on an almost aggressive tone.

"Everything you have, and do not take your time in giving it to me. No more words."

"And what if I am not prepared to give you anything?" Bonde chided his attacker.

"But, I have a knife. Are you crazy?"

"Possibly. But maybe that is what is wrong with France right now. No one wishes to stand up and be counted. We are like sheep, willing to be lead wherever our leaders say."

The assailant studied Bonde's impassive features, suddenly realizing that he was confronting a problem that assuredly was growing by the second. "You are talking crazy, I do not know what you mean." He raised the knife and swished it in the direction of Bonde's nose. "Now, your money," the robber wailed his voice ascending.

"If you insist." Bonde took a step backward and opened his coat as if to hand over something inside. The flaps opened as his hands parted the material.

The assailant watched him closely and peered inside the coat. Holsters for two pistols hung snugly inside.

Bonde expertly removed one of the pistols before the surprised man could react. He cradled it in his right hand and pointed it squarely at the knife.

"Now, what was it you wanted?" Bonde teased.

The assailant flushed and stammered. "N…N…Nothing, Monsieur, it appears I have made a mistake." All truculence had left the robber's suddenly woeful eyes.

"Such an attitude is something that is all too common in our country right now. We have made too many mistakes."

"Please, Monsieur. I only meant to threaten you." The demoralized man started backing away from Bonde attempting to shrink away in the process. "I will leave you alone."

Bonde watched as the man turned and started to run. He lowered the gun slightly.

Bonde's mind raced as the distance between the two slowly lengthened. He had not really heard the assailant's parting words. His mind's consciousness was somewhere between the uncomfortable and the intolerable.

Too many Frenchmen were satisfied with just existing.

He frowned as he quickly considered his next move.

Slowly he raised his pistol and pointed it at the fleeing man. He squeezed the trigger evenly and watched as the tiny missile sought out the diminishing figure.

Pierre Bonde did not bother to go over to check the crumbled form lying face down on the cobbles. He knew before the bullet hit that the individual was already dead.

Main Gestapo headquarters in *Paris* was located in an undistinguished older building at *93 Rue Lauriston*. A small office on the top floor of the fourth story of the building was set aside for SS Obersturmbannfuhrer Kurt von Heltscherer's office. Arriving in Paris without specific orders, von Heltscherer was assigned a few general duties. These often included the harassment and interrogation of a number of Jews, a duty he soon found that he could enjoy.

On one such occasion, while on a raid at a home suspected of harboring Jews, von Heltscherer perceived an uneven wall within a large room of the targeted house. He tapped around the protruding wall area, until finally his efforts produced a dull thud indicating a hollow space behind the baseboard. When the accompanying Gestapo agents finally succeeded in prying loose a false door, two families of Jews that included twelve people were found trembling behind its walls.

Von Heltscherer was delighted with his role in the proceedings, and took some pains to insure the action was included on his personal record.

Less than a week later, an official dispatch was dropped on his desk. Von Heltscherer opened the document and carefully read its contents. He could hardly believe his eyes.

The official communication from the German High Command was brief and to the point. The letter stated simply that Reichsmarschall Hermann Goring would arrive in Paris *in two days. It also informed the SS Obersturmbannfuhrer that he should make himself completely available at that time.*

* * *

General Percy Barclay was entirely satisfied with the ongoing tone and progress of the morning meeting. Both his military subordinates were in agreement that their respective portions of the mission were mostly achievable but Barclay still harbored a few lingering doubts as to Operation Angerona's overall feasibility. He realized his plan involved specific coordination; a helpful dosage of Lady Luck along with another calculated and broad effort on the part of the fledgling French Resistance. It was an awful lot to expect from such varied participants. All Percy Barclay's prior military experience suggested the entire situation was at best a huge gamble that could easily go astray.

He glanced at the map of Central France that lay on the nearby table and studied it closely for the better part of five minutes.

Satisfied with the information he gleaned from the map, Barclay picked up the phone from the nearby desk. His assistant in a nearby room immediately came on the line.

"Sir?"

"Please ring Professor De Jean for me"

"Right away, Sir."

He glanced at the map and within seconds the phone next to him rang. He picked it up.

On the line was Professor Philippe De Jean of the French *Ecole des Beaux-Arts,* a classic example of a person caught in the right place at the wrong time. When news of the German Army's entrance into *Paris* reached De Jean, the celebrated artist/teacher was in London fulfilling a speaking engagement. Even though he repeatedly tried to return to *Paris* and his family, the German occupation of France simply made such a happening impossible. Luckily, the same colleague who had extended the invitation for him to speak proffered De Jean the opportunity to stay at the colleague's family's large Victorian home in one of London's classiest suburbs. The place was spacious and his friend and host most gracious, but Philippe De Jean longed for his unhappy family and friends back home.

Each passing day found him pouring over each scrap of information he could secure about the war in France. De Jean glued himself to the Victorian's sole radio, where he listened for hours to the broadcasts from *Radio France* for news about his homeland. Even though the broadcasts were identifiably biased and undoubtedly screened by the Germans, De Jean was comforted by the fact that he could hear the French language spoken on a daily basis. Such daily access brought him a surprising bit of satisfaction even if he didn't believe more than a fraction of what was being reported.

De Jean's spirits perked up immensely when he received a call early one afternoon inquiring if the visiting professor would be interested in a project which was being put together by an element of the mysterious sounding Special Operations Executive.

Philippe De Jean jumped at the opportunity. An initial meeting was held in the SOE's offices nearly a month prior, where De Jean had been introduced to a number of officers including Brigadier General Percy Barclay.

"Hello Philippe," Barclay opened the conversation.

"*Mon General*, it is nice to hear from you."

"I was wondering how everything was progressing with our little project?"

"It is coming along quite well. I think two, maybe three more weeks and we will be completed."

"I have already started the wheels in motion," the General imparted.

"*Bon*. Everyone on this end is quite enthused. Our part will be finished, and sooner than expected."

"Thank you Philippe. I knew we could count on you. Good bye for now."

General Percy Barclay replaced the phone into the cradle and glanced again at the detailed map on the table. He continued his concentration for several minutes.

Chapter Two

SS Obersturmbannfuhrer Kurt von Heltscherer assured himself for the third time that morning that all preparations had been made to guarantee his illustrious relative's visit would take place without a hitch.

Von Heltscherer had recently been assigned an assistant, a veteran SS Scharfuhrer (staff sergeant) from the Southern German region of Franconia named Mueller. Mueller was a blocky individual complete with hardened facial features. His service time in the army as a regular soldier along with his natural veteran's knack of interpreting orders quickly and correctly made him instantly indispensable to von Heltscherer. It was immediately evident to the Obersturmbannfuhrer that Mueller was a master at unwinding and circumventing military red tape, a fact that von Heltscherer realized could prove quite helpful to him if the situation warranted.

The Colonel was surprised and curious when Scharfuhrer Mueller knocked on his door early the following morning as he sipped his morning *tasse* of rich, aromatic coffee. He made a mental note to find out where the coffee originated, since Germany had not seen any coffee of this quality for at least the past two years. Von Heltscherer motioned for him to come in.

"Herr Oberstrumbannfuhrer, I have just received a note by courier."

"Yes, go on with it," von Heltscherer replied, somewhat stiffly.

"The Reichsmarschall has changed the place for your meeting. He now wants you to meet him at the main entrance to the *Louvre*. It is to be at the same time."

Von Heltscherer took the paper from Mueller and glanced at its contents.

"Of course, I will be delighted to oblige the Reichsmarschall."

Von Heltscherer folded the paper neatly, placed it inside his tunic pocket and turned again to Mueller who was still standing at attention. "That is all for right now, you may go."

Mueller saluted smartly extending him arm outward and departed.

*   *   *

Professor Philippe De Jean replaced the phone in its cradle and immediately returned to his duties. The work area assigned to him was a spacious, well-lit room with several oval windows. During daylight hours they were uncovered from the heavy double layered curtains that fulfilled Britain's nightly black out regulations. The stately old ivy-laced Victorian manor home in which he and his artists lived and worked was about twenty miles outside London in the small town of Derbyshire. This area that was relatively free from the merciless bombings that were inflicted daily by the Luftwaffe on the City of London.

Recently however, a misdirected German bomb had actually fallen in a neighbor's pasture less than a mile away. The event was closely attended by a small group of neighbors who actually ventured into the field to see for themselves. It was common consensus among the residents that the area had happily been spared from any real Luftwaffe bomber assaults. Everyone there made a pledge to continue praying that their village's luck would continue for the future.

When first approached by the SOE's representative, a light colonel from London, De Jean wasn't completely confident about the Operation Angerona's ability to succeed. He was unsure that he could gather together a group that could produce the quality of paintings the plot needed to succeed. He was also uncertain of the SOE's ability to put the plan into effect.

In the months that followed, De Jean's perspective on the operation had changed and he now found his little group had grown very close to one another. They were now imbued with a shared goal, a fact that tended to further inspire their individual work. Weeks later, after carefully assessing the partially finished paintings, Philippe De Jean realized that he was now convinced that the plan's chance of success was greatly increased.

When he formed his little group, De Jean had selected a trio of artists; each chosen by De Jean for a specific reason. The first artist was one of De Jean's former students, a promising young woman from *Nice* named Noelle Lejeune. She had applied herself to her work and received high praise from every one of her teachers, graduating with highest honors. Noelle's art reveled in the works of the classic Italian masters and she was considered by everyone concerned to possess a bright future as a classical artist.

Not long before graduation, she had fallen in love with another young painter; a Scotsman named McBride, and followed him to Scotland where they were married. That was several years ago and De Jean had not been in contact with her since that time. When Operation Angerona was detailed to him, De Jean fondly remembered Noelle Lejeune and her classically correct painting and urgently sought to find her.

Luckily, Noelle was still living in Scotland. She still used her maiden name in her painting, and so was easily found by the vast resources of the SOE. Once De Jean explained to Noelle the role she would play in the operation, Noelle Lejeune agreed to help. In two days, the southern Frenchwoman was in London and had immediately started on her work.

Hubert van der Root was another part of De Jean's collection. His story had taken a different bent. One of the most recognized Dutch artists of the late 20's and 1930's, van der Root had joined the Dutch underground as soon as Germany had overrun Holland. His artistic status around Europe allowed him to serve the Dutch Resistance in the role of an international courier. Van der Root moved freely in and out of Holland, and for over a year his efforts as a courier proved quite successful. Then, an unfortunate break in the chain and betrayal by one of his underground colleagues rendered him useless as a courier.

It was by sheer coincidence that van der Root was in Stockholm when he was notified by the Dutch underground that the Nazis were on to him.

While relieved he wasn't in Nazi custody as could easily been the case, the patriotic Dutchman also yearned to return to his clandestine underground activities. The actual rush such actions provided his relatively placid life had started to provide van der Root with a new outlook and sharpened his sea-blue eyes to an extent that he hadn't felt in years.

Several weeks after his near miss with the Nazis, an old friend of van der Root's at the British Consulate in Stockholm was asked to initiate an inquiry on Hubert van der Root's behalf. The query involved the gifted artist's possible value to the Allies. The probe was a boon to both Allied intelligence and the SOE, both of whom reacted quickly to the query. In a matter of hours, van der Root was flown to London where he was immediately dispatched to Derbyshire and Professor Philippe De Jean's cozy Victorian accommodations.

The final member of his little group was an enigma to Professor Philippe De Jean.

He was an Englishman named Jake Barton, and he had been by far, the easiest member of his band to locate.

Barton, it seemed, was resting quite uncomfortably on the Isle of Wight. His surroundings included an unpretentious and windowless cell of his Royal Majesty's Albany and Parkhurst Prison.

In a case familiar to the British art world, Jake Barton was, in 1936, convicted in an art scandal that rocked not only Great Britain but also the entire European continent. The calumny involved the forgery of several classic masterpieces and was the talk of the British art world, not only for its importance in uncovering the dastardly act, but also for the sensational manner in which the deed was first discovered.

A noted London art dealer/collector bought the forgeries knowing full well their history. The unfortunate gentleman then decided to divorce his wife of many years in order to marry a much younger woman. During the civil proceedings, the dealer attempted to sell the forgeries, not realizing that he had confided to his wife the fact that the pieces in question were fakes. His wife took full advantage of the situation and repaid him handsomely for his infidelity.

During the ensuing investigation, which was carried out daily in numerous British tabloids, Barton was identified as the forger and subsequently landed in British prison for a period of some ten years. Barton's sentence was widely discussed and was generally conceded as not nearly long enough in the opinion of true British collectors who valued the integrity of their art industry.

As with most principals in the art word, Philippe De Jean had followed the scenario closely. When he first saw Jake Barton's work in British art magazines, he realized the man's forgeries bordered on the fantastic. He studied the paintings carefully and was at a loss to explain why a man with such talent would stoop to such depths to convey his natural gift of expression. He was inwardly delighted when Barton's name was mentioned for his project. He couldn't wait until he could meet Barton in person.

It didn't take more than five minutes for Jake Barton's basic wholesomeness and engaging personality to completely envelop the French professor. Once he was comfortable with the talented Englishman, De Jean went all out to assist him in gathering the necessary supplies to begin Operation Angerona's delicate work.

Barton insisted on several key items. First, canvasses must be obtained that were relevant to the time period involved. A number of old paintings were brought to him and Barton selected three that were comparable in size to the paintings De Jean's artists were to copy. Barton carefully ground the images of the existing paintings off the canvasses, taking care not to remove the original ground from the works. Once the paintings finished, Barton would apply own particular form of age crackle that would closely approximate the original patterns found on the canvasses.

Jake also paid close attention to the oils and brushes he secured for their work. He chose a classical approach and sought out several shops that continued to sell traditional older materials and supplies. He recalled how important specific colors were to Italianate works and would not settle for any oils that did not contain exactly the ingredients that he desired. After three weeks of searching, Jake Barton assured himself that he had the correct components for his two associates and himself to begin.

Philippe DeJean had given each of his artists the assignment closest to their own natural style.

Two weeks later, it appeared to De Jean that his project was progressing in the right direction.

*   *   *

After three years in the glider service of His Royal Majesty, Colonel Barclay Smith-Reeves figured he had taken just about all the abuse his fellow officers had to offer. His stiff upper lip had been put to the test so often that he considered their good-natured jabbing as second nature.

Most Royal Air Force pilots scoffed at the thought of gliders as a wartime instrument, but their talk did nothing to dissuade the motivated aviator.

Somewhat tall for an aviator, Smith-Reeves carried his slender, yet well-proportioned frame perfectly upright. He enjoyed the expression of a handlebar mustache, which he waxed daily with deft care. He realized he cut a rather dashing figure in his flying suit that he adorned with a purple sash that matched his Glider Pilot Regiment cap. He enjoyed the effect of such minor theatrics on his fellow aviators and played their attention for all it was worth.

He enjoyed flying and considered himself able to fly any aircraft that happened to cross his path. Before the war, a friend and fellow RAF pilot bought a sport glider and offered Smith-Reeves an opportunity to try it out. He was amazed with the sensation it provided and fascinated with his first powerless ride. The glider experience touched his spirit in a way that transcended his feelings about flying.

The commune with nature was unimaginable. Gentle thrusts through thermal currents and the resulting gravity forces were simply too fulfilling for Barclay Smith-Reeves to describe. He had found his niche in the air and began to spend more and more time in gliders.

When Great Britain declared war on Germany, Smith-Reeves jumped at the chance when it was announced that a RAF glider unit was being formed. As a Colonel in the Royal Air Corps and with his dedication to gliders well known to senior RAF officers, he was quickly placed in command of the newly designated Glider Pilot Regiment.

Initially, the dashing colonel wasn't totally sensitive of his Glider Pilot Regiment's ultimate value to the war. When Winston Churchill ordered that the Army Air Corps be spun off to house the glider program, Barclay Smith-Reeves felt totally vindicated as to his choice of duty.

*   *   *

Andre Faboul was quite surprised when he received a communication requesting a meeting from René Huyghe, whom he knew was in hiding from the Germans. Even though their ages were practically the same, Faboul had always admired Huyghe, both as an impartial, sensitive person and also as the *Louvre's* highly motivated curator.

Huyghe was a bit older, and Faboul always sensed a sincere spirit of camaraderie when dealing. He always felt that his superior seemed to enjoy his work at the same intensity, as he did.

Huyghe chose an isolated spot for the meeting; a small park in a residential area, near the *Sacre Coeur,* called the *Square Wilette.* Huyghe was already seated when Faboul arrived.

"Andre, it was nice of you to meet me."

"With great pleasure, curator. Everyone at the museum wondered what had happened to you."

"The Nazis were becoming suspicious and sooner or later they would have come for me. I thought it was time I became less obvious. I have been hiding in a number of places, mostly with friends who have extra rooms. It is not very glamorous, but it beats being in jail. Andre, the reason for our meeting is not about me at all. A matter has come up and I immediately thought of you."

"Thank you curator, it is a great honor."

"Wait until you hear what I say before you thank me, I think this will be a most important mission."

"I am sure it is. All you need do is ask."

"I knew you would react this way Andre. We all need to do our part to save France. We must all act collectively and the sheer force of our actions will ultimately persevere. Our country will remain intact if we all pull together. But, enough of my heartfelt rhetoric. What's really important is that I need your help on this important matter."

Faboul listened; his attention riveted on Huyghe.

"I have always admired your work, the determination and pride with which you approach your vocation. I have become active in the Resistance. It has developed a plan that, if successful, will directly affect the people of France. I have been asked to select some people I am personally familiar with to carry out the plan. I would like to be able to do this myself, I consider it *that* important. Alas, I am too well known, too easily identifiable. I think you would be perfect for such a mission and I would like you to go in my place."

"I would consider such an assignment an honor, curator."

"I must first warn you that a great deal of danger is involved, probably more than you have ever faced in your life. If you decide to help, you must be prepared to leave *Paris* whenever you are notified. I cannot provide you any more details at this time, for your own good. Your mission will be on behalf of the *Louvre* and the beneficiaries of your actions will be the people of France. Beyond that, I can tell you nothing."

Faboul blinked, trying to absorb everything that Huyghe said.

His heart, however, had already answered his associate's call for help.

"I will do whatever I can to help you, curator."

"I had a feeling you would, Faboul." He stepped close to his subordinate and kissed him on both cheeks.

"Go for now, you will be notified when we need you."

The Monday morning after the unwarranted Japanese attack devastated Pearl Harbor, Brian Russell was among the thousands of patriotic Americans who flocked to enlist. His natural aptitudes and schooling propelled him into officer category and he was immediately assigned to the next available scheduled Officer Candidate School class. The urgent military buildup of the United States Army required that actual Officer Candidate School (OCS) training time be cut in half and shortly thereafter, Brian Adams Russell was commissioned a second lieutenant in the United States Army. His proficiency in French and his proximate familiarity with France landed him Washington and a slot in Army Intelligence. The slot also included an immediate wartime promotion to first lieutenant.

For the next few months, Brian Russell busied himself with basic jobs involving translations of communications originating in France and passed on to Washington. He was then transferred temporarily (TDY) to another unit which interpreted information received from various French sources by British SIS in London. This was later passed on to their American Allies.

Russell was unaware that his name had been placed on a prospective acquisition list submitted to the attention of Colonel William J. "Wild Bill" Donovan, who commanded the Office of Strategic Services (OSS) in Washington. Donovan's group was in the process of selecting certain highly qualified candidates for his clandestine operation that was the American equivalent of the British Special Operations Executive. Russell's fluency and former residency in France prompted his inclusion on the list submitted to OSS for immediate consideration.

One day Russell was called into the office of his commanding officer, a regular Army colonel who had been very helpful to Brian since his assignment had begun.

"Lieutenant Russell, we've been asked to provide British SOE with someone who is both fluent in French and has also lived in France within the past three years, and who still has friends and contacts living there. I've reviewed your file thoroughly, and it looks to me as if you fit the requirements to a "T". I hate to lose you, but this is a top-priority request."

"Can you tell me anything more about it, sir?"

"I don't know much more than I've already told you, except for one thing."

"What's that, sir?"

"The slot calls for a captain-level officer or higher. You can consider yourself temporarily promoted to that rank. Do you understand everything?"

Russell nodded. In less than six months, he had been promoted to the rank of Captain, at least temporarily. He was delighted with the prospect.

"Yes sir, I think I understand."

"Then you leave for London immediately."

"Yes, sir," Brian Russell saluted, repressing a smile. He knew it would be in bad taste to show his pleasure at such an assignment, and besides he admired his commanding officer and enjoyed his work within the unit. He wasn't wholly familiar with the Special Operations Executive or its workings, but it didn't matter. He was now on his way to London and would be involved in the war on a first hand basis.

*   *   *

René Huyghe's decision to leave his home and live underground was proving to be a difficult task. The Resistance provided him with a new set of papers, but travel in and out of the occupied zone was becoming more and more difficult. Checkpoints were everywhere, and it was not unusual for Huyghe to travel miles out of his way to get from one point to another.

René was relieved that he had the foresight to send most of his key associates to various locations throughout France to physically accompany the museum's prized artworks. In the *Loire* and elsewhere, his men were able to remove themselves from the maelstrom of activity that surrounded the occupation. All of Huyghe's *Louvre* employees were also provided with fake identities that had proven effective to this point.

The underground newspapers circulating through *Paris* and elsewhere throughout France began to call for local and vocal demonstrations on certain issues, but Huyghe opted not to get involved.

A confidential source of René Huyghe, an employee of *Paris Match*, confided to Huyghe that the Germans were actually enjoying much success in their Russian campaign, and that realization struck a basic key with Huyghe.

When originally contacted by Jean Moulin, Huyghe admitted to himself that he found Moulin's proposal to switch a few of the greatest masterpieces somewhat far-fetched. Current events and a changing political situation were beginning to change René Huyghe's perspective. He now conceded that Moulin's plan possessed a great deal of merit and determined see that the plan reached fruition. Huyghe would do everything he could to make it happen.

*   *   *

US Army Captain Brian A. Russell had been waiting for nearly an hour at SOE– RF Receiving Office and he was starting to get fidgety. The trip from America on the dilatory DC- 3 had been both long and tiring and the weather through which the transport had flown was downright brutal. He decided his new job must carry some degree of weight because his flying priority allowed him to bump two Colonels from the flight who were also trying to make it to London. The colonels in question had shrugged when given the bad news, looked him over several times, and finally returned to the airport lounge to renew their liquid intake.

A uniformed British Woman's Royal Army Corps clerk seated behind a desk by a typewriter and phone that hadn't rung since he arrived, had greeted Russell politely. In fact, the busy woman behind the desk was the only person Russell had seen thus far.

He was deep in thought when a British Army Colonel emerged from a side door and approached him.

"Captain Russell, happy you have finally made it here. I am Colonel Buckmaster."

"Thank you sir, it's nice to be here."

"Please follow me, the general is waiting."

Russell trailed behind the officer and the pair soon came to a small planning room. Two additional British officers stood and greeted him as he saluted.

"Here now, no need for all that. We are quite relaxed at RF Section about that sort of stuff," General Percy Barclay mentioned pleasantly, motioning Russell to take an empty chair.

Russell nodded and sat.

"You have already met Colonel Buckmaster," Barclay continued, "I am General Barclay and this is Colonel Smith-Reeves of the Royal Air Corps' Glider Pilot Regiment."

Russell nodded and General Barclay started again.

"Captain Russell, the reason for your presence here is that SOE is presently involved in a rather daring mission. It is a plan that has need of some special personnel with unique capabilities and a certain degree of familiarization with central and southwestern France."

"I studied in *Paris* and I lived there until the war began," Russell interrupted. "But, as far as other parts of the country, I'm not sure…"

"We are well aware of your resume, Captain," Barclay said abruptly, without glancing over at Russell. "We understand from your record that you spent some time at a place called *Brive-la-Gaillarde*. Is that information correct?"

"Well, yes, Sir. I did spend some summers at a friend's family chateau outside *Brive-la-Gaillarde*. But the house was actually in a tiny village called *Turenne*. It's so small it's probably not on anyone's map."

Barclay consulted the map in front of him and continued.

"Well, it seems to be right here on this map," he noted, pointing to a spot. "Now, if I can continue…"

Russell blanched at the comment and returned his gaze to the General.

"The Free French Government, through the French Resistance, has asked for our help in pulling the wool over Jerry's eyes. The mission has to do with some of France's most precious national art treasures. We are calling this whole spectacle Operation Angerona.

Our main intention is to substitute forgeries of some of the world's greatest paintings in place of the originals, which are all property of the *Louvre* Museum and of the French nation. What's more, we are going to perform this operation in manner that requires utmost secrecy and delicacy."

Russell blinked, attempting to grasp what he had just heard.

"This mission will require most specific timing and will involve our department as well as one of Colonel Smith-Reeves' aircraft. His glider regiment will provide us with an aircraft that will fly undetected directly into South Central France with the forged artwork.

And, more importantly, Captain Russell, you are to be the *pilot* of *this* craft!"

Von Heltscherer arrived at the *Louvre* an hour prior to his meeting with Reichsmarschall Goring. It was a cold and blustery day, most typical of *Paris* in late February. Since most of the important artwork was missing from the museum, the *Louvre* was considered *unofficially* closed since the beginning of the German occupation. Von Heltscherer was surprised to find a pair of Luftwaffe corporals standing guard at the front entrance. Von Heltscherer was not entirely sure what the show of military force at the old place meant.

The guards saluted crisply as the SS Obersturmbannfuhrer approached. One stepped to the door and quickly opened it. Von Heltscherer entered and surveyed the long corridors extending to each side of the building. It had been several years since he had visited the Louvre, so he decided to spend the remaining few minutes before Goring's arrival reacquainting himself with the historic building.

Von Heltscherer strode the elongated corridors in silence, his steel boots clicking noisily in the high-ceilinged hallways. He paused in certain sections, casually reflecting on the bits of history that he could recall that involved the paintings still displayed, and also the silent magnitude and inspiring ambiance of this great palace.

His thoughts engrossed him for some several moments, until he thought to check his watch.

It was nearly time for Goring's arrival. Von Heltscherer abruptly turned and headed back to the main entrance. Everyone who knew him considered Hermann Goring a most punctual man. A man who was never ever kept waiting.

Chapter Three

In the past, flying was always an exhilarating experience for Brian Russell. It was also true that he had never tired of his infrequent rides in passenger airplanes. What really bothered Russell was the simple fact that he had never before actually *flown* an aircraft. When it came right down to it, Brian Russell had never even *considered* piloting an airplane on his own.

Colonel Smith-Reeves, whose confident, self-assured and benignly professional manner had impressed Russell on their first encounter in a way that Russell couldn't exactly explain to himself, comforted him.

"Your craft is very special, more of a sail plane than a glider, Captain. It is completely constructed out of wood and, in terms of size, you could correctly say it is the shortest that Glider Pilot Regiment uses. It is, in fact, a miniature version of the Hotspur Mark II that is manufactured by our General Aircraft Company."

"What exactly *is* a Hotspur?" Russell asked blankly.

Smith-Reeves paused for a moment, raised his hand to his mouth to cover a slight cough and continued. "The Hotspur was named after a soldier from antiquity and the smaller model you see here can carry one or two pilots, depending on its use. And, don't worry, old chap, there is really no need to be a skilled pilot in this type of craft. Fact is, all one really needs is a good sense of balance and a stomach that will handle the change in thermals." Noting Russell's skepticism, he added in a frank tone he hoped would ease the younger officer's doubts, "Mind you, takes a bit of practice, but you will definitely get the hang of it. The prototype here was developed in quite a hurry to be used strictly to teach *you* how to fly."

Russell stared at the tiny glider; not yet convinced by Smith-Reeves that his mastery of the fragile craft would be so easy a task to accomplish.

Next, Smith–Reeves showed Russell a circuitous route to the quartermaster's shack where his new protégé was outfitted in a new tan flying suit.

"Looks rather spiffy if you ask me," Smith-Reeves commented with genuine feeling.

"Rather tight in the crotch, if you ask me," Russell replied, admiring the fabric's neat lines as he stretched his arms and shoulders in several directions.

"A rather natural unpleasantness for practically any aviator, but you will get used to it. After a while you will tug at it from time to time, but that is all."

Russell stretched a bit uncomfortably, attempting to make himself snug. He finally gave up and returned his attention to Smith-Reeves.

"Now it's time to get down to the bloody essence of the thing. Are you ready?"

"As ready as I'll ever be," Russell replied weakly.

The pair walked to a spot behind the aircraft and Smith-Reeves beckoned Russell to get into the craft's rear seat. A pair of RAF airmen materialized from the background and held the wings of the glider level as Russell climbed in. After Russell showed that he was buckled in properly, Smith-Reeves adroitly climbed into the front seat and gave the thumbs up to the airmen to proceed. Another pair of airmen came out to help, raising the ground crew to four. The small assemblage then walked the glider to the end of the runway some 400 meters away and attached the towline to an eyehook located at the rear of an older model trainer that served the facility as a tow plane. Once the tow plane's engine was started, the ground crew labored to hold the glider's wings level until the larger craft began its forward movement. The crew expertly guided the glider for the first few yards until the craft caught its balance in the tow plane's air flow. As the ground speed gradually increased, the crew released the wings and the glider gracefully lifted itself a few inches off the ground as it tugged at the towline. In less than seven hundred yards, the process was completed as both aircraft lifted successfully into the air above the runway.

The tow plane slowly gained altitude, changing direction several times in an attempt to stay in the general vicinity of the GPR base. Twenty minutes into the flight, Russell felt a slight pull on the line as the glider was released high above the base, located near the town of Feltham. On the ride up, Russell had been encouraged by the view of the verdant countryside that laid out before him in what seemed like an endless panorama. Reality replaced spectacle as Russell was brought back to actuality as he glanced at his meager instrument panel. His altimeter needle danced steadily around the number 40, which translated to the fact that the glider and its two inhabitants were cruising above the British countryside at slightly above 4000 feet.

Smith-Reeves hadn't said much during the climb, but now began chirping instructions to his new backseater.

"In a minute, I want you to take the stick, and see how she feels. She will react quite distinctly to any pressure on the stick, so I suggest you take it slowly at first. Rig-g-hh-tt...Are you ready?"

Brian Russell wasn't at all sure he was, but clamped his jaw bravely in an attempt to overcome his internal misgivings.

"I'm ready." The words hung thickly in the thin English air.

"O.K. then...you may take her at any time. She's all yours."

Russell felt his grip tighten on the control stick. The nose suddenly dropped and the craft began plunging forward.

"Easy does it, old boy, "Smith –Reeves softly cautioned from the front seat. Loosen your grip on the stick and gently bring the nose back up. Feel how smoothly she answers your touch."

Russell pulled slowly upward on the handle and the craft slowly returned to near level flight.

"The control stick is much like holding a woman's hand," Smith-Reeves chirped. "Squeeze it too tightly and she reacts negatively. Caress it with feeling and understanding, and she will practically follow you anywhere."

Russell considered his instructor's advice and slowly eased the stick from side to side. Each movement sent the glider heading in the direction he desired. After a while, Russell was pleasantly pleased with himself as he felt his confidence increasing each minute the glider cut silently through the thermals. A few minutes later, his confidence had increased enough to permit him to try a basic vertical maneuver that Smith-Reeves had suggested. This feat required Russell to ease the nose up, then down and then from side to side. The plane answered the inexperienced pilot's every request, a fact that brought a rare grin to the face of Smith-Reeves.

The experience of such suspended flight opened an incredible new vista for United States Army Captain Brian Russell. The feeling enthralled him immediately. Once he had overcome his initial fear of weightlessness and understood the theory encompassing the flying of a craft with no power, Russell's original dire concerns were swiftly replaced by an all-rewarding euphoric sensation.

Russell could now imagine the phenomenon birds enjoyed whenever they flew, the pure joy of careening through the air with effortless abandon. He was thoroughly immersed in such a thought when he was awakened from his idealistic reverie. Smith-Reeves yelled back that he was reassuming control of the glider so that they could land. Brian quickly released his grip on the stick and watched as the plane quickly lost altitude.

Smith-Reeves coaxed his way through the thermals with a skillful hand and finally set the glider down on a small grass airstrip adjacent to Feltham's regular landing strip, which was used by propeller-driven aircraft. Landing on the grass was necessary, Russell was told before the flight, because it was inconceivable to anyone connected with the glider program that the gliders would ever land on normal airstrips during actual missions. The explanation made complete sense to Russell.

'There you go, sport," Smith-Reeves said, unbuckling his safety belt. He alighted quickly from the craft. Seconds later, Brian followed him out "A few more of these training bouts with me and you will be ready for a solo flight."

Still infused with his recent accomplishments as a virgin pilot, Brian nodded and glanced back reflectively at the small craft.

"Safest aircraft ever built," Smith-Reeves injected, noticing Brian's concern. "Very little can go wrong once the glider is airborne. It just takes knowing which way the winds are blowing and being sure of where you can land. Rest is, as they say, duck soup!"

"Right," came Brian's reply, which lacked a tone of real assurance. The fledgling aviator wasn't at all convinced it was going to be *quite* as easy as his instructor indicated.

A few days prior to Huyghe's meeting with Andre Faboul, French Resistance Leader Jean Moulin (code name Max) had sent a message to an old ally in the City of *le Puy en-Veley,* a town about two hours' drive southwest of *Lyon.* The message reached Pierre Bonde the following day.

Jean Moulin and Pierre Bonde had been friends since their days as law students at Montpelier. Bonde was Moulin's first choice to lead the French Resistance in the interior part of France, a vast and wonderful region influenced by the majestic rivers, the *Dordogne & Lot.*

Bonde was also aware of Moulin's past experiences with the German army of occupation and in particular the circumstances surrounding Moulin's rise in status. Moulin had been propelled into the role of leader of Free France's vast network of resistance activities.

Bonde reminded himself, with the spirit of an old friend's fondness, the fact that Moulin's *Department* was strategically located for Resistance activities within the German-occupied zone. In June of 1940, Moulin's status had grown rapidly, prompting the German military to attempt to reduce Jean Moulin's role within his sphere of influence.

A number of people in the community of *Saint-Georges-sur-Eure,* a village within Moulin's *Department,* had been suspiciously killed. Moulin was prompted by the Germans to sign a paper accusing French-African soldiers of the deed. Moulin immediately investigated the incident and surmised that a bombing probably caused the deaths. The leader also realized the importance of the paper he was being forced to sign was a crude attempt to dishonor the French Army without any proof. It was no surprise to Bonde that his old friend Moulin, a man of great personal integrity, refused to sign the paper of accusation.

The Germans immediately arrested and beat Moulin and left the battered *prefect* overnight in a room along with the body of one of the victims of *Sainte-Georges-sur-Eure.* Growing more and more impatient for results, the Germans finally moved him to a private house in *Chartres* that served as a prison and resumed the daily beatings. As he lay on a decrepit mattress in dingy anonymity after another bloody battering, Moulin sensed that he was close to cracking. He realized that his mental state had deteriorated and he felt helpless and detached from all he held sacred. He knew in his heart that he could not withstand another day of interrogation and beatings without signing the accusatory paper

In despair, Jean Moulin reached for a shard of broken glass and cut his own throat.

Moulin was found the next morning near death, but his attempt had only nicked an artery, not severed it. He was taken to a hospital and slowly began the process of recovering his bodily functions. Incredibly, the German attitude toward him changed. His captors were now fearful of Moulin's actions. He had become an instant hero in the eyes and hearts of his constituents. The German posture toward Moulin was altered for the foreseeable future.

Upon his recovery, Bonde was delighted when informed that Jean Moulin had been allowed to return to the *prefecture*. There he continued the reinstitution of both pride and patriotism for his beloved country. Both of these were key aspects of French culture that Moulin felt his people had lost when accepting the humiliation of the German take over.

Some months later, however, Moulin's actions as prefect became all too overt and the Germans subsequently removed him from his position. From that time on, every waking minute of Jean Moulin's time and all of his efforts were spent in the cause of the French Resistance. It was altogether fitting that Moulin's good friend, Pierre Bonde, share the important responsibility as Resistance leader in his region.

Since beginning operations, Bonde was given the code name Victor by Moulin who had chosen the name Max for himself. Code names were used to insure confidentiality and protect each other, Bonde's group had been responsible for a great deal of sabotage throughout the entire region, as well as the transportation of numerous refugees through their centrally located area.

Max's message was simple and to the point. Sometime in the near future, a very special traveler would need the Resistance's help in escaping France. The responsibility for this traveler was given directly to Victor and his partisans. Victor was directed to formulate a plan along with an acceptable escape route. No date was specified, the terse message simply stating that further instructions would be sent in the near future.

Bonde took the note and lit a match to one of the corners of the paper. It ignited quickly and Bonde held it carefully until it almost burned his fingers. He sighed as he recalled the warmth and personality of his dedicated old friend.

He weighed the contents of the message carefully in his mind and immediately started to develop a plan.

*   *   *

Daily flying lessons had progressed to the satisfaction of practically everyone involved in the operation. Captain Brian Russell had even surprised himself and actually survived his first solo flight. According to Colonel Smith-Reeves' report, the young pilot flew greenly during his initial flight aloft and was justifiably critical of his own performance, a fact that earned Russell a few extra points with his instructor.

Russell was airborne for about thirty minutes before he decided to make his first solo attempt to land. Russell had observed Smith-Reeves land a number of times from the back seat and was even allowed to land the glider himself on several occasions, but always with the imposing figure of Smith-Reeves buckled in the front seat, his hand a split second from the controls.

Now Russell was *alone* in the front seat of the glider and was about to land the craft on his own. During the descent everything went smoothly as Russell adjusted the wings until he reached an altitude twenty meters above the ground. A sudden updraft caught the airframe and it jerked wildly, reacting to the new rush of wind. Russell overcorrected the glider, which had the net effect of deleveling the wings. Although slowed by the movement of the spoilers, the aircraft hit the grass and bounced at an abrupt angle to its right in a near cartwheel movement. After a second bounce, the right wing staked itself and the entire craft flipped over.

Russell was left upside down in the cockpit, held in by his seat belt. Within moments, the ever-present ground crew members arrived and flipped the glider onto an upright position. A craggy RAF sergeant lifted the unbroken canopy and tried to help Russell out of the cockpit, to no avail. Russell either couldn't, or wouldn't leave the plane.

Momentarily Colonel Smith-Reeves arrived at the crash site after a short jog from the control tower. He had witnessed the entire episode from the nearby operations tower. Smith-Reeves was relieved to see that from first appearances, his American pupil was unhurt.

Brian Russell sat there staring straight ahead, mortified beyond his wildest imagination.

"That might just be the worst landing in the history of aviation," Russell blurted out in the general direction of Smith-Reeves. "It took real talent to land like that."

"Ri-gg-hh-tt," chirped Smith-Reeves, surveying the damage. "Wonder if we could see that again?"

Russell glared at his superior but held his tongue. All he could muster was a weak "I…"

"Happens to the best of us," Smith-Reeves added cheerily.

"Remember, you are *always* at the mercy of the wind and with no motor to compensate. Frankly, sometimes the landing is downright difficult to control."

Russell ingested his Colonel's lexis and gloomily agreed. He shakily exited the glider's cockpit and looked at the battered wing and fuselage of his glider. He wouldn't be flying this plane for a while, in fact, from the looks of it, the glider might never fly again.

He scratched his head and turned to follow Smith-Reeves who was already heading in the general direction of the Officer's Mess.

A Scotch right now isn't such a bad idea. Maybe even five or ten would help even more.

Andre Faboul was relieved when he finally received his instructions from Pierre Huyghe.

He was instructed to go to the *Gare de Lyon* on *Paris'* southeast side on July 7th, at 8 o'clock in the morning. He was further directed to find platform fourteen where he would wait until contacted. His contact would provide him with new papers, tickets and further instructions.

Faboul would initially be asked directions for the train to *Vichy* and would reply that he did not know the train's platform, and would ask in return for a *Gitanes*. Along with the cigarette, the contact would also hand Faboul a package. Faboul was to then proceed to the WC, and immediately read the package's instructions.

*   *   *

The Glider Pilot Regiment's Officer's Mess at Feltham was a traditional Royal Air Force basic structure that afforded its officers a brief respite from their duties. Equally important, the place banned most visitors from the outside world. By British military tradition, the bar area was always well stocked with various highest quality spirits, was generally noisy and always highly animated. Since Feltham was relatively isolated and located in what was considered the country, its officer compliment spent many hours within the Mess's walls.

Smith-Reeves gestured Russell to follow him inside. He realized the best elixir for someone who had just had a near brush with death was undoubtedly a stiff drink followed by a full plate of unimportant conversation and diversion.

The senior officer wasn't sure Russell realized just how close he had come to serious injury or even death, and he knew better than to harp on the subject. It would be helpful to make light of what had just happened, a beginning of the task of renewing Russell's confidence. It would be interesting to see just how much reassuring Russell needed, a measure of his real flying ability. Most pilots escape close brushes with death at one time or another, and, as a pilot's experience increases, such close calls are often considered commonplace. Smith-Reeves hoped silently that Russell would be such a flier.

"So, you have perfected the new technique of cartwheel landing," Smith-Reeves said facetiously, turning his head slightly to conceal a half-smile. "I thought such a phenomenon was only in the planning stages."

With his head bent downward, intently regarding the iceless scotch in front of him, Russell replied. "Easy for you to say, I don't suppose you've *ever* cracked one up?"

"As a matter of fact, old sport, I most certainly have."

"Really?" Russell looked up feeling a tinge of relief at the base of his neck. "When did it happen?"

"About a year ago, while we were practicing some night work. I came into the landing much too fast and tried to correct at the last second. The nose hit and the entire craft splintered itself into anonymity."

"Were you hurt?"

"A whole lot of bumps and bruises, and a dislocated shoulder. The force of impact was so great that the bolts holding my seat belt separated and I was thrown sideways against the canopy. I was out of action for nearly two months."

"I guess we are both lucky."

"Quite." Smith-Reeves relaxed in his chair and fingered his handlebar mustache, gently stroking its edges. " Such an event always serves to bring one back to reality. When flying and landing, one must be always prepared for anything, ready to take action even before the problem occurs. It is much like a sixth sense, all good pilots have it. It becomes second nature after a time, much like when one is first learning to drive. In your case, you have progressed nicely, not counting today's little episode of course."

Russell grinned sheepishly, accepting his mentor's barb.

"And now, it's time for our scotches." Colonel Smith-Reeves hailed a middle-aged woman near the bar, who came directly to their table.

"My dear friend is in great need of a large amount of our Scottish cousins' best whiskey. We'll have two Glenfiddich's and don't stop refilling them until I tell you."

"Right, Governor. I'll be back in a sec."

* * *

Under the pretense of settling some legal matters, Pierre Bonde made his way into *Paris* for a meeting with Jean Moulin. It had been some time since the two had seen each other and Moulin selected an outdoor encounter on a bench near the *Arc de Triomphe* at which to meet.

As Bonde arrived, he noticed that Moulin was already waiting. He was seated on the bench with his coat wrapped warmly against the cold February wind that chilled down to the bone. He acknowledged his compatriot and took a seat next to him. Upon closer inspection, Bonde realized that Moulin had aged a good bit since their last meeting.

"My dear friend, it is good of you to meet me," Moulin began.

"It has become much more difficult to travel," countered Bonde. "I was stopped six times on my way here and my papers checked."

"I would hope that means our activities are becoming more successful," Moulin responded.

"Since we do not have much time here, and we are both probably very cold in this harsh weather, let me get to the point. I will need your help sometime soon for a most important mission. You must assign your best people to do this, this mission is *that* important. I will give you as much notice as possible, but, by necessity, the message will not be sent very far in advance of the actual time.

Your part in the mission involves a young man on an important assignment who must be escorted out of France and into Spain. What he will be carrying is of extreme national importance, both to the Free French Government and also to the French people themselves. You must insure that this person reaches his destination safely, at all costs. I would like to give you the exact details, but that would not be wise. What I have told you is all you need to be aware of at this time."

"I understand," Bonde replied. "I will start to work on it at once."

"Thank you old friend. I knew I could count on you and your organization."

"You can always rely on us. You have only to ask."

"I know. There are many like us in France right now. We are all working toward a common goal. Once the Nazi brutes are expelled from our country we can all go about our business again. Until then, we must *all* do what we are asked."

"Always. But, you already knew that."

"*Oui*. I thought as much. Be careful on your return home." Moulin paused a moment, and smiled warmly at Bonde. " I enjoyed having the opportunity to see you again."

"*Moi aussi*."

Moulin stood up, adjusted his *beret* and started off in the direction of the huge tower.

After a few minutes, Bonde got up and crisply walked down the opposite path.

*   *   *

The precise hour of Hermann Goring's visit to the *Louvre* continued to be nasty and cold. A fierce wind blew off the western coast, pushing the ripples of the *Seine* into small waves. Along with the wind came moisture in the form of heavy snowflakes, which soon became pellets in the teeth of the wind, ripping the face and generally keeping everyone indoors as much as possible.

Von Heltscherer was on edge and pacing, for Goring was a few minutes late in arriving.

"Something must have happened," he remarked as he stood next to the Luftwaffe guards at the entrance to the *Louvre*. While Luftwaffe guards at the *Louvre* seemed a bit out of place to von Heltscherer, he assumed that the

Reichsmarschall's keen interest in the building's contents had something to do with the choice of guards. Von Heltscherer also correctly concluded that, as Commander in Chief of the Luftwaffe, Goring personally saw to the institution's security.

"He is always so prompt. The Third Reich prides itself on being prompt."

Momentarily, the guard stiffened and von Heltscherer turned his attention to the driveway. A long black 1940 Mercedes Cabriolet A with its top in place pulled up and a Luftwaffe Major stepped out. He turned back to the car and the huge form of Hermann Goring alighted in his lavish white Reichsmarschall's uniform.

Von Heltscherer and the guard saluted crisply but Goring brushed by them quickly and entered the building.

"Too cold to stand outside for formalities," the Reichsmarschall stated flatly.

"Kurt, you are looking well." He extended his hand. "Let us begin. I do not have a lot of time to spend here."

*   *   *

"Gentlemen, if I can have your attention, we should be getting started."

All conversation stopped and the officers gathered together fixed their attention resolutely on General Percy Barclay.

It was evident to everyone involved that Operation Angerona's myriad of details was starting to come together. Barclay and Colonel Buckmaster had begun fine-tuning some of the more important aspects of the plan and both agreed the timetable initially set for the mission would probably be met.

Both officers were also pleased with Brian Russell's progress, his resolute American spirit and dogged willingness to learn. Soon after Russell had reported to SOE-RF, Barclay had introduced him to a French friend and Russell had conversed with the man in French for a long time. Afterward, Barclay had inquired of his friend as to Russell's level of linguistic competency. Barclay was assured that Russell's command of the French language was nearly perfect and that it would be impossible for anyone to tell him from a native *Parisienne*.

One detail of the operation was still unsettled. That fact resulted in Colonel Buckmaster summoning Captain Brian Russell to this particular meeting in General Barclay's smallish private office. A detailed map of the *Dordogne* Region laid spread out on the table. Barclay pointed to the map.

"Captain Russell, we have been having the damnedest time selecting a landing place for your glider in France," Buckmaster began once everyone was seated around the table. The actual area we need to pinpoint is not far from the place you are familiar from your summer visits. But, it is somewhat mountainous and presents some special problems. We must find an open site that would permit the glider's landing and one that would also be easily identifiable from the air.

Remember, this will be a nighttime operation in a part of France that employs dim-outs. There will be few lights visible to help you navigate. Our meteorologists will attempt to select as clear an evening as possible, but there's only so much one can identify from the air under such primitive conditions. The Resistance has agreed to attempt to light the way with ground fires, but that will only help you for the last few miles. Even if the Resistance is successful with the fires, there is a question as to just how apparent these lights will be to you and to what degree they will help. I must tell you most realistically, that, at this point, we are still somewhat in the *dark* if you don't mind the pun."

Russell smiled at the witticism, and attached his gaze to the map. His mind mulled over his options and the room remained in silence. Russell bent closer to the map, studying its detail. His finger touched one spot, then another. Finally his index finger settled on a particular spot and Russell spoke.

"This just might do," he said, pointing to a tiny dot the map.

The others looked closely; their attention focused on the minuscule speck on the map

"It's the ancient mountaintop city of *Domme*, which rises nearly straight up from the area around it. It is located practically alongside the *Dordogne* itself, and it should stick out even in an unlighted, dim out environment. If I remember correctly, it's about ten to fifteen miles from the main road between *Limouges* and *Toulouse*. Directly to the north of the city are some incredible open hayfields that could serve as a natural landing site. We went there to fly kites when I was on holiday and the fields were thousands of meters long. The meadows were composed of some type of long grass, which is very similar in height to the landing strip here at Feltham. If I could locate the main *Limouges/Toulouse* road and use it as a guide, I could turn at the *Dordogne* and make my way to the long hayfields. Best of all, the area will be probably deserted since there's no reason for anyone to be there. There was never anyone around when we flew our kites."

General Barclay studied the map for a while longer, and then raised his head.

"Gentlemen, I *do* believe our American friend is on to something. Let us hope Captain's Russell's recollections are correct and the place still exists as he remembers it. I will notify the Resistance that this is our choice and also find out how they intend to illuminate the road leading to the river, and quite possibly, the landing space itself. Any further questions?"

Seeing none, he turned, exited his office, and motioned for Colonel Buckmaster to follow.

Brain Russell returned his gaze to the map. His mind returned to the carefree times of years ago in that particular area. He soon realized such times were now gone forever. An unanswered thought also entered his mind for the first time. Just how much has his beloved France changed under the Nazis?

He also realized that it would not be long until he would find out for himself.

The walk through the *Louvre* with Reichsmarschall Hermann Goring was inspiring to Kurt von Heltscherer. Even though Goring's huge statue seemed larger than he remembered, von Heltscherer was delighted with the sense of intimacy the meeting provided.

He learned that the Reichsmarschall visited *Paris* often, and was even considering moving to *Paris* and making his main office here. Goring disclosed that he took great pleasure in visiting the *Louvre*, was most impressed with the paintings of seventeenth century Flemish artist Johannes Vermeer, and still enjoyed the *Louvre* even though in its present status it contained few painting of real note. He hinted that it was entirely possible that the status of the *Louvre* might change and it was because of his own special interest in art that he had chosen the Luftwaffe to guard the historic building. He subtly reminded von Heltscherer that his responsibilities as Reichsmarschall included being the head of the Luftwaffe for the National Socialist State.

Goring paused at certain sculptures and paintings, but seldom commented. It was as if he was assessing each work in his own mind.

At one point, he stopped in front of a painting by the 17th Century Dutch artist van der Helst. He paused for several minutes and whispered directly into von Heltscherer's ear. The latter stiffened, snapped his heels in a Nazi salute and shook his head affirmatively.

Goring then motioned for von Heltscherer to follow him across the room. He held his hand up as a sign to the others in his party to remain where they stood.

"Kurt, it is time for you to know why you are here."

"Certainly, Herr Reichsmarschall. Whatever you..."

"I will explain," Goring interrupted brusquely. "I need someone for this job in whom I have absolute trust. The French have pirated away many of the great treasures of this museum along with many other masterpieces from throughout the country. I guess they didn't expect many visitors during the war. But, as spoils of war, these pieces rightfully belong to the Third Reich. It has always been that way throughout history. Whoever wins the war gets to keep the other country's prized possessions. I am determined to retrieve as many of these great treasures as possible and send them to Germany for safekeeping.

I want you personally to locate these treasures, and you must work quickly. With bombings and sabotage rampant throughout the country, something might happen to them, which would be horrible for everyone involved.

From today on, your *only* mission will be to determine what the French have done to hide the artworks and find their exact locations. I will put my full authority at your disposal to insure your success. You are aware of what that means and of the immeasurable resources of our country. All of these assets are now available to you. You will report directly to me and to no one else. You might begin by locating and interrogating the curators of the museum. They will be the ones most likely to be aware of where their little treasures are currently kept.

And, Kurt," Goring concluded confidently. "Your success in this will assure you of an even higher position with the Third Reich. Heil Hitler!"

Von Heltscherer felt the blood rush to his temples as he snapped to attention and practically shouted, "Heil Hitler!"

Goring noted his subordinate's enthusiasm, and turned to face the group. He peered down at his watch. It was a signal to everyone that he would leave immediately.

Von Heltscherer followed Goring back to the entrance where the Reichsmarschall again shook hands with him, this time with added fervor. Goring reentered his Mercedes whose motor was already running.

Von Heltscherer again saluted "Heil Hitler!" as the Mercedes pulled away.

He turned and preceded back into the museum, motioning to another of the Luftwaffe soldiers, an Unteroffizier (sergeant), who had joined the procession during the visit.

"Take the picture that the Reichsmarschall enjoyed and have it crated immediately. The Reichsmarschall will be taking it back to Berlin when he leaves. Have it brought to my office at Gestapo headquarters when it is crated."

The Unteroffizier snapped at the order.

Chapter Four

Throughout the entire return trip to his home in le Puy en-Veley, Pierre Bonde contemplated the undertaking Jean Moulin had outlined to him. Bonde was riding in the cab of a truffle delivery truck. It had dropped off a small load of choice underground fungi for which the Dordogne is so well known to several top restaurants in Paris. The real reason for the truck's trip was to insure Bonde had a safe way to return to his home.

It was becoming more and more difficult for Bonde and his partisans to pass people through the Midi Region and ultimately out of occupied France. With the bombing of Germany by the Allies now rumored to be underway, it was even more conceivable to the Resistance, and, to regional leaders like Bonde, that the flow of refugees and downed airmen would increase in the future. And, Bonde had ceased to be amazed at the steady flow of Jews attempting to flee Nazi tyranny by traveling through France in search of freedom and an end to their harassment.

Recently, his entire region had witnessed a significant increase of German patrols on roads. There was also a renewed military presence in a number of larger towns as the Germans attempted to block the seemingly endless flow of Jews. Even as the war began, and France was partially occupied, it was apparent to Bonde and the Resistance movement that the means to which the fanatical Nazis would resort to accomplish their goals would never be satiated. It was also understood that the Bosch would undoubtedly resort to the most despicable means possible in their attempt to seize Jews.

Bonde also wondered about the rationale behind his journey all the way to Paris for the meeting with Jean Moulin. He was recently made aware that agents planted by the Gestapo and their Vichy equivalent, the Milice, had recently infiltrated the Resistance. Some Resistance fighters had already been betrayed. Even more importantly, his close relationship with Moulin allowed him to gauge the upcoming mission's level of importance. That fact was decisive enough for Bonde to attach his own priority to the mission at a much higher level than he would have normally.

The delivery truck lumbered southward on the winding, wet country road. Already, a few unconnected ideas had begun to form the rudiments of a plan in Pierre Bonde's shrewd mind that would accomplish his directive.

His thoughts settled on several of his key operatives, including one particular female partisan in which he had the utmost confidence. Her name was Christine Allard, and Bonde was well aware of her capabilities.

He smiled to himself, taking a measure of pride from her past actions. Christine Allard had proven herself many times over. She had far surpassed Bonde's expectations on several different occasions. If he was correct in his initial assumption concerning the upcoming assignment, Bonde was confident that he would again be able to call on Christine for help.

I am fortunate to have such people working with me, and France is indeed fortunate to have such people who are so willing to risk their lives in her cause. God willing, we will all persevere!

*　*　*

On days when the chilly, wet English winter weather permitted, Brian Russell spent most of his daylight hours attempting to master the art of powerless flight. He learned from Smith-Reeves some of the inside tricks of glider flying, which included exploiting the thermals until the very last moment in order to achieve maximum altitude and distance. In his own mind, he was also nearing expert status in landing. This was a goal he had imposed upon himself after his abysmal first attempt. In reality, any status change was mainly due to the sheer number of landings he attempted. These were frequent, a multi-day occurrences that kept both the tow plane pilots and members of the RAF ground crew hustling throughout most weather-permitting hours.

Colonel Barclay Smith-Reeves took more than a personal interest in Russell's progress and monitored every moment of Russell's flying. Early in the process, Smith-Reeves admitted to himself that Russell possessed the rare aptitude of a truly *natural* pilot, a rarity in someone who had never flown before. Smith-Reeves was delighted when he observed that his prize student had even developed a smidgen of glibness toward his job. This attitude was a prerequisite, in Smith-Reeves' opinion, for any really expert pilot. Smith-Reeves had observed, somewhat sadly, that many fighter pilots lacking this tenacious approach didn't last very long in the crowded, deadly skies over England.

On a particularly clear day after one of Russell's more successful practice flights, Smith-Reeves signaled his charge to follow him into a small hangar that adjoined the glider landing field.

Once inside the building, the senior officer reached into a pocket of his flying jacket and produced a maroon beret decorated by a Lion with blue wings. It was the hat worn by members of the select Army Flying Group. Smith-Reeves patted the hat into its circular shape and handed it to Russell.

"Here, Old Boy, you've earned them."

"But," came Russell's reply, "I don't know…"

"Nothing official, mind you. It's just I figured you've more than earned the right to wear them. And everyone connected with GPR agrees with me. We would all be honored if you agree to wear them."

"Well, it seems as if I don't have much of a choice," Russell smiled, taking the beret and fitting it squarely on his head.

"And, I have another surprise."

Turning away from Russell, Smith-Reeves stepped over to a large canvas cover, draped over a rectangular form on the floor of the hangar. He pulled the canvas off and uncovered a long, angular glider, a longer, more streamlined type that Brian Russell had never seen before. The craft bore French markings and French identification number.

"So, exactly what is this?" Russell asked, admiring the swept wings and rubbing the smooth fuselage with the palm of his hand.

"This, my good fellow, is your new best friend! I told you before the craft we've been using was a prototype. Well, Captain Russell, this one is the real thing. The people at our General Aviation Company just delivered it to us."

Russell observed the glider's sleek lines, noting it was single-seated and wondered how it would handle in the air.

"This is the one of the most advanced single seat gliders in the entire world," Smith-Reeves informed Russell. "Work on its design began as soon as the plan for this operation was developed. We've wanted to produce a glider like this for quite some time. Your mission was all it took for everything to proceed along. Interestingly, we have been able to change a few things in her design to give you as much range as possible. Her wings were altered a bit, but not enough that it should deter her aerodynamic performance. Her designers at General Aviation also lengthened the fuselage to compensate. The net effect gives her the capabilities of a much larger craft."

"I can't wait to get her in the air," Russell blurted out, unable to control his genuine enthusiasm.

"Tomorrow, Captain Russell, if the weather is as agreeable as it was earlier today."

"And she bears French markings."

"Quite observant of you. Wouldn't do to have His Majesty's royal markings all painted up if the craft is somehow discovered once you are on the ground in France, would it? Better to keep everyone guessing. Hope the Vichy characters haven't changed markings on their planes. Somehow we weren't able to find out about that."

Russell acknowledged his leader's words with a shrug of his head, and returned his attention to the elegant airframe. Even to an inexperienced, irregular pilot such as himself, the new glider really was the most beautiful and delicate piece of equipment that he had ever seen.

SS Obersturmbannfuhrer Kurt von Heltscherer took the crated painting immediately to the Gestapo offices where he was informed that Reichsmarschall Hermann Goring was involved in an important meeting. He decided to give the crate to Goring's personal driver who was waiting outside the office, along with specific instructions that the Luftwaffe sergeant hand the crate to Goring himself. The Oberstrumbannfuhrer also insisted that the driver make Goering aware of the fact that he had personally delivered the painting.

Von Heltscherer left the Gestapo's *Paris* offices secure in the knowledge that he had provided a valuable service for both Hermann Goring and the Fatherland.

He couldn't wait to tell Sophie about the events of his day.

*   *   *

For most of her twenty-seven years, Christine Allard enjoyed her role in life. Born to a middle class watchmaker and his wife in the mountain city of *St. Flour*, Christine was watched and talked about since the age of fifteen, mostly by young men. She enjoyed striking good looks capped off by a wonderful head of long, flaming red hair and a pair of azure green eyes that pierced the shells of almost every person she encountered. Early in life Christine developed an often-fiery temperament to go with her good looks. Her disposition eventually caused everyone around her to treat her as an equal. Additionally, Christine was considered a natural tomboy. She genuinely preferred the outdoors and stringent activity to most activities considered suitable for young women. During her school days, Christine excelled in most sports, often competing with the boys in games and on outings. She seldom lost a contest, and it took the heartiest boys to beat her in an even match.

As she reached full womanhood, Christine matured and even attempted to tone her competitive nature, to no avail. At the insistence of her parents, she even tried to make herself more passive, again with no success.

Christine gave up and then decided to be herself, opting enjoy her life as it was rather than for the sake of those around her.

At nineteen, she had offered her virginity to her first real love. She soon came to the realization that neither she nor her lover were mature enough for a lasting relationship. She quickly broke off the affair. After her schooling was completed, she worked in her family's watch business with her father. It was immediately apparent to everyone concerned that Christine Allard yearned for more challenges and adventures than the small shop could provide.

"Christine, you are a most restless girl."

It was a phrase her father Leo had often repeated in her presence. "And one day that restlessness will get you in trouble. You are not content with what you have. Not everyone in the world is offered what you have here at home, and still you are not satisfied. Think of your mother and me and what we have in our lives."

"You just do not understand, Papa. For some reason, I know there is a great big world out there, and I believe I can make some contribution to it. If I stay here in *St. Flour* with you and Mama, I will never be able to experience anything beyond what I have already experienced. And, for some reason I cannot explain, that is simply not enough for me."

"But Tine, you help us a great deal," her father used his pet name for Christine. "And, I hope you realize how much we appreciate it."

"It is not a question of appreciation, Papa. It is what I want to do with my life. I want to amount to something, " her green eyes beginning to tear as she spoke.

Christine saw the hurt her words brought to her father's eyes, but was unable to say anything to ease his distress. After the incident, she continued with her daily duties at the family's shop and silently hoped that something extraordinary would occur to help her in her search for a more meaningful existence.

What happened next was a blessing for Christine Allard. Like many Frenchmen and women, she suffered through the intolerable agreement the Vichy Government made with Germany. When whisperings of the French Resistance first reached her ears, she soon realized that here, at last, was the vehicle for which she had been waiting her entire life. The Resistance offered Christine a dramatic outlet for her pent-up energies and passions. In the beginning, mostly through underground newspapers, Christine was able to follow Charles de Gaulle and his Free French cohorts' early exodus. Their patriotic vocal stands against both the Germans and the Vichy government stirred her inner spirit. Christine was careful to make her support of the movement known to certain influential citizens in *St. Flour,* one of who was a distant cousin of Pierre Bonde. Once introduced to Bonde, Christine Allard was quickly incorporated into Bonde's still fledgling organization. Bonde realized her personal attractiveness and purposeful dedication to the true values of the Resistance could be invaluable to him in setting up his network. From the first mission she was assigned, Christine Allard proved to be the type of passionate fighter who excelled in every regard.

Neither the degree of danger nor the difficulty involved in what she was assigned to do mattered to her. Bonde saw to it that Christine became an excellent marksman and even assigned her to certain missions that required precise and accurate shooting. Bonde also presented a new carbine to her for use on those specific occasions, a weapon that Christine became expert in its use and one that she valued tremendously. From her first operation on, Christine was keenly aware of the internal excitement that would build up inside her that would last until the mission's conclusion. While she was at a loss to explain such feelings, she knew the impact they had on her psyche and outlook. The French Resistance and its gallant cause was exactly the elixir Christine Allard had hoped and prayed for her entire life.

The passionate woman soldier also displayed an aptitude for leadership. Once Bonde saw Christine in action and assessed her accomplishments, the alert leader quickly assigned her leadership tasks for undertakings in which his partisans played a key role.

The day after returning from his meeting with Moulin in *Paris*, Victor summoned Christine to a meeting at a rendezvous point in a small town not far from *St. Flour*. They met inside a small café that served as a meeting place for members of Victor's group. Christine listened attentively as her leader spoke.

"Jeanne," he began, referring to her code name, "you will prepare yourself for an extended visit to your cousin Lucille in *Cahors*. You will leave within the next few days, but, unfortunately, I am not definitely sure when that will be. This is not altogether bad since we need the additional time to prepare a new set of papers for you.

By the following week, or perhaps longer, you will be met by one or more Resistance members. These individuals will be involved in a most important operation."

"What type of operation?" Christine inquired softly. She knew a feminine approach often softened up the weary Resistance leader.

"It is not important that you know the details at this time, only the role that you will be expected play. The less you know about the particulars, the safer it is for you and everyone involved."

Bonde (Victor) paused, collected his thoughts and continued. "The person contacting you will use the code name Georges, and he is the one who will provide you with more information. It will be your job to help get the person who will accompany Georges, and whatever that person is carrying with him, out of France. I have considered an escape route for both of you to use. This one is slightly different from the one that we have been using. This route will also end up going through the mountains into Spain. Do you understand?"

"Yes, but why the change in route you mentioned? The old one has been successful so far, hasn't it? "

"Unfortunately, I just received word that parts of our old routes have been compromised."

"Ah, I suspected something like that," Christine replied, shaking her head. "I guess we had to expect something like that at some point."

"Unfortunately so, my dear Jeanne, and there will probably be more to come. The Gestapo and *Milice* have made infiltrating our organization one of their top priorities.

And Jeanne, you need to know one more thing." Victor's tone toward her became almost parental.

"And what is that?"

"This is a very particular type of operation, more important than most. I've been told a great deal is at stake here so you must be quite careful and use your most prudent judgment. You must not take chances beyond those that are absolutely necessary."

"Victor," Christine chided, " I understand perfectly. You already made all that clear. I will be ready." She winked in a manner that practically melted the hardened Bonde.

*   *   *

Von Heltscherer returned to his comfortable apartment off the *Boulevard Haussmann*. It was located not far from the *Opera*, and was considered by the German military to be one of *Paris'* most fashionable neighborhoods. The apartment had been confiscated from its Jewish owners who had fled the city immediately prior to the Germans entering *Paris*.

At the hallway entrance stood Sophie Michel, who had moved in with von Heltscherer soon after they had first met. She met his eyes and warmly embraced him.

Sophie was 28; her bright auburn hair was set in a permanent bun and was quite attractive in a flashy sort of way. von Heltscherer had first noticed her inside a little bistro near his flat and boldly struck up a conversation. Sophie was immediately impressed. She was smart enough to know the Germans would remain in *Paris* for some time and the prospect of having an attractive German officer nearby seemed quite sensible. She went home with him the first night and was delighted with the immediate intimacy they were able to share. The couple spent each succeeding evening together and by the end of the first week, von Heltscherer insisted Sophie move into his spacious quarters.

"You can bring with you as many of your things as you like," von Heltscherer offered. "I have more than enough room for everything. In fact, several people could move in here and be perfectly comfortable."

"Will I have to cook for you?" Sophie asked a bit naively, more out of desperation than a desire to please him. Sophie's mother had never bothered to teach her to cook and the thought of such an ongoing task could present a formidable obstacle to her ongoing peace of mind.

"Not if you do not enjoy cooking," von Heltscherer answered, not wanting any impediment to her presence. "There are more than enough good restaurants around for us to eat."

Sophie extended the conversation a bit longer to impress on von Heltscherer the magnitude of her decision. In reality, she had made her mind up several days ago. Her own living area was nothing more than a room and tiny kitchen, with a shared W.C. that was often cold and smelly. The German officer's kind offer also brought promises of monetary support, a thought that pleased Sophie immeasurably. Such an arrangement would mean that she would no longer have stand long hours with the other girls on the street corner near the *Square St. Lambert,* a choice spot where she offered herself to the varied clientele who happened along.

Von Heltscherer kissed Sophie passionately, producing a sense of familiarity he had rarely felt in any of his former female relationships.

From the first time he had visited France, von Heltscherer had enjoyed the ardor of French women, but, in truth, his infatuation with Sophie was much more.

Tonight, he felt it was important to make Sophie immediately aware of the achievements of his day. "It all went quite smoothly," he crowed excitedly, flattering himself with the compliment as the pair moved slowly out of the hallway.

"The Reichsmarschall was very impressed. I am sure a note will be placed in my records that will have a positive effect later in my career. He even wanted one of the *Louvre's* paintings to take back with him. He intends to give it to the Fuhrer himself."

Sophie nodded but continued nibbling on his ear as the SS Colonel gently tried to push her away.

"I want to tell you about my new assignment," he added feebly, realizing he was fighting a losing battle. Sophie paid little attention and continued exploring his ear with her tongue. He sighed and gave in to her. Sophie had already started unbuttoning his pants.

"Sophie," he gasped as her tongue smothered his mouth.

*   *   *

When Captain Brian Adams Russell, United States Army, was released from the tow plane on his first flight in the new airframe, he became conscious of the fact that his new glider possessed greatly expanded capabilities over the former plane he was used to flying. The knowledge that the airframe had been developed specifically for Operation Angerona added to his growing appreciation that his particular mission was considered important enough to the overall war effort to elicit such time and energy from all involved.

On his new aircraft's initial test flights, Russell was cautious to take extra care for its safety and even fussily cleaned it himself upon his return to Feltham. He was fast becoming familiar with its handling. The glider surprised Russell as to how it cleanly gripped the thermals and how its extra length and extended wing space actually proved beneficial to its landings. Glider Pilot Regiment Intelligence was also able to obtain some detailed information through resistance sources in Belgium. This new intelligence data made him aware of the success of

German gliders in an operation in Belgium, a fact that for some obtuse reason reassured him concerning his own dangerous mission.

U. S. Army Air Force Captain Brian Adams Russell continued to set stiff parameters for himself.

First, he ordered some of his assigned GPR ground personnel to place pieces of cloth in the shape of an X at random locations on the grass landing field whenever he went aloft. He subsequently tried to hit the cross with his wheels on touchdown. At first the feat proved difficult, but after several attempts he was able to get within a few yards of the target. Unfortunately, from time to time a strong gust of wind arose that lifted the craft at the last moment nullifying his attempt. Nonetheless, the "X Game" as he preferred to call it around the field, was a game of his own invention. Brian Russell excelled at its achievement.

He had now flown over twenty-five test flights and was sure he could handle most circumstances that might arise during his mission. It also became apparent to Russell that the other officers and men of the Glider Pilot Regiment were delighted with his progress and general flying ability. They appeared to take a certain regimental pride in his accomplishments.

Immediately after his twenty-seventh test flight was completed, Smith-Reeves summoned Russell him to the regiment's operations room.

The Colonel spoke first. "From what I have observed, it seems like everything with your new aircraft is going along quite nicely. At least I haven't seen you cracking it up yet," he smiled.

Russell beamed proudly. "Yes, sir. I'm hoping you won't have to order a new one anytime soon."

"It is time for me to show you another important phase of our mission. Why don't we go into my office?"

Russell followed Smith-Reeves and another officer into his office, where he was offered a chair.

Smith-Reeves motioned to the third officer who produced an elongated cylinder.

Smith-Reeves pointed to the object. "This will be attached to the inside of your glider for the mission, to protect it from any possible harm in case you are forced to crash upon landing. The cylinder is made from extraordinary materials and is practically indestructible. When its contents are loaded, it is controlled by a special spring lock, which compresses a second, inner tube. To the untrained eye, the contraption appears practically empty. It will eventually contain several objects which must never leave your side."

Russell studied the cylinder and twisted the top, locking the canister in a similar manner as Smith-Reeves had demonstrated.

"I think I've got that down, sir." He handed the cylinder back to Smith-Reeves.

"Then, I suppose you are prepared for the next step?"

"The next step?"

"Why night flying test flights of course. You didn't think for a second we were going to send you in over France in daylight, did you?"

*   *   *

The morning following Goring's visit, von Heltscherer went directly back to the *Louvre*. He wanted someone there to provide him with a list of the pre-occupation curators of the museum and more importantly, their home addresses.

When he found no clerical workers present at the museum, von Heltscherer detailed SS Scharfuhrer Mueller, who had accompanied him to the museum, to gather the information he needed from the personnel files. von Heltscherer had indicated that expected information would be located in the museum's administrative offices.

The offices were closed and locked, but those facts presented little impediment to SS Scharfuhrer Mueller. He expertly forced the lock and quickly entered the offices. Von Heltscherer had foresaw the need for a French/German dictionary and after a period of one hour, the pair was able to locate the records pertaining to personnel of the museum. Most were contained in older wall cabinets that ringed the large room.

It took von Heltscherer and Mueller another full hour of searching through the drawers and shelves of the cabinets to locate the files they were seeking, that were contained within museum's antiquated system of filing. Finally, von Heltscherer was able to withdraw the names and addresses of ten individuals whose job description he felt matched his needs. He glanced over at Mueller who waited expectedly.

"I think this is exactly what we need, Mueller. Now we can finally get down to business."

"Certainly, Herr Obersturmbannfuhrer," Mueller replied, unaware of the next step, but completely willing to proceed. "The names weren't all that difficult to find. I don't think the French expected us to be so thorough."

"The Third Reich is *always* thorough when it pertains to matters of national importance," von Heltscherer offered. "It is one of the facts that separate us from the rest of the world."

"Yes, Herr Obersturmbannfuhrer. I think you are perfectly correct. The fact is that no one bothered to hide any of the personnel files for employees of the museum. Once we were able to find the section where the upper level records were kept, it was quite easy. I hope everything else is equally as easy."

"There is no reason to think it won't be," von Heltscherer added, almost arrogantly. Von Heltscherer was truly amazed that the information was so readily available. Maybe the French were not as smart as everyone considered them to be.

As the pair departed the museum, von Heltscherer was glowing in his early success. He offered his subordinate a rare plaudit for his efforts.

"Well done, Mueller. This is exactly what I needed. I now have something substantial upon which to base my investigation. I will see that a note is placed in your record."

"Jawohl," the hardened sergeant offered a hint of a smile. " I am pleased that you are happy, Herr Obersturmbannfuhrer."

Von Heltscherer complimented himself on his good fortune.

With the information contained on the list, it would be no time at all until he would be able to interrogate the *Louvre's* top employees.

His search for the great treasures of the *Louvre* had begun in earnest. More importantly, he knew Reichsmarschall Herman Goring would also be satisfied.

* * *

When all three artists under his control started complaining and criticizing, Professor Philippe De Jean correctly summarized their work was approaching completion. The fact that each individual was a gifted artist in their own right made it that much easier. He was confident that he had successfully matched each of his artist's styles with that of the original artist selected for Operation Angerona. Philippe De Jean felt this bit of artistic insight lent more credibility to the remarkable undertaking he was assigned to complete.

In fact, gazing at the nearly finished works, De Jean reveled in each artist's accomplishments.

He appreciated that it would take careful scrutiny by top notch experts to tell that any one of the paintings inside the room was not the genuine article.

Hubert van der Root was putting the finishing touches on his canvas, and both Noelle Lejeune and Jake Barton were close to finishing their paintings. From time to time, each scrutinized the other's work and was duly impressed.

The paintings would be finished the next day and then would be turned over to master forger Jake Barton. It would then be Barton's responsibility, and thankfully his dominant forte, to further doctor the paintings so that each would approximate its respective age.

The process of art aging was an art within itself, and within its celebrated confines, Jake was the acknowledged eminent artist in residence.

The process of quick art aging was known professionally as art crackling.

From the very beginning of their efforts Barton had seen to it that all three artists utilized a synthetic resin compound known as Bakelite, developed several decades earlier in the United States by an American chemist named L.H. Baekeland. The substance also contained phenol and formaldehyde. Bakelite had the ability to withstand heat, provided hardness and imperviousness, and was perfect for Jake Barton's process of quick aging for the forgeries. Barton simply included the phenol and formaldehyde to their pigments and olive oils to provide the desired effect.

When the three forgeries were finally handed over to Barton the next day, he immediately began the process known as art crackling. The three canvasses were placed in an oven and baked for several hours at 105 degrees C. He next applied a light coat of varnish and wrapped it around a metal cylinder to induce the age crackle.

Then Jake Barton covered the entire surface with India ink, and allowed the ink to penetrate the cracks within the paintings. This was an attempt to replicate the centuries of fine dust that accumulates in the cracks of older canvasses. Once this facet dried, the ink and varnish were removed and an additional coat of light brown varnish was applied.

As a final signature detail, Jake Barton took the three canvasses and damaged each one, minutely and purposely. He even produced a small cut on each to portray wear and tear and eventually reattached the canvasses to their original stretchers, using the old tacks that he had been most careful to save. Jake felt that all these factors were important in the event that the paintings were ever closely scrutinized.

When he was finished, master forger Jake Barton carefully surveyed his handiwork. Each piece glowed with lively colors which approximated to a large degree the original dyes crafted centuries before. Barton was sure the forgeries would withstand scrutiny, and could only be truly identified under close analysis by world-class experts under laboratory conditions.

Professor Philippe De Jean stood with him and admired his finished work.

"I now understand why everyone thinks so much of you, my dear Jake. The job you've managed to complete here is almost too much for words."

"Thank you, Professor. Coming from you, that's a truly great compliment. I do not expect to fool everyone, but we will certainly give them a run for their money."

"I just hope it never comes to that, Jake," De Jean replied, realizing full well the consequences that would precipitate such an action. "The best thing would be that no one would *ever* find out."

Jake Barton did not respond, but intently continued to study his creations.

Chapter Five

Brian Russell had never flown the glider at night and Colonel Barclay Smith-Reeves wasn't about to send Russell up by himself on his first flight. True, it would be necessary to return to the old two-seat model for the flight, but Smith-Reeves wasn't overly concerned.

Night flying, the experienced British flier explained, was vastly different from flying during daytime. Smith-Reeves' personal keys to successful night flying were what he termed *useful* references; a horizon that was visible during day was practically indistinguishable at night, and, buildings, trees and mountains that aided you during daylight were also all but invisible at night.

During nighttime, a pilot can only see by the luminosity of the moon and any illuminations from the grounds that are visible. Smith-Reeves was also quick to point out that during Russell's upcoming flight, even when the aircraft would be in the vicinity of larger cities, it was entirely probable that the German imposed dim-out would most likely render ground sightings practically useless. Russell was happy to acknowledge his veteran instructor's precepts, but didn't realize the extent to which his mentor's insight would affect him.

His first night flight with Smith-Reeves provided him with an incredible revelation.

When the training glider popped free of the tow plane at about 4,000 feet, Russell looked down and gasped!

Nothing was visible from the cockpit. The entire terrain below, and, to both sides of the glider, was pitch black. He glanced upward, reassuring himself of the presence of the moon, stars and the myriad of elements that compile the Milky Way. He was also glad that a large part of his ground training had focused on a crash course in navigation, which he presently found most helpful. At least the basic night sky components seemed up above were where Russell assumed them to be.

Smith-Reeves sensed a quiet apprehensiveness in the cockpit and sought to steady the young Captain.

"Okay, now, old boy, we will take this all very easy. When I let you assume the controls, I want you to feel the difference in the thermals. At night, they aren't as active and therefore aren't nearly as helpful. You must pick and choose the ones that will be useful to you."

"I understand. You want me to take it now?"

"Yes, but go easy when you do."

Russell squeezed the control stick slightly and immediately felt the plane's nose dip.

"Easy does it," Smith-Reeves assured him. "Lift her gently upward. Also pay attention to your instruments. They could conceivably be all that you can count on."

Russell corrected the nose and turned slowly to starboard. He eased his grip on the wheel and took a deep breath, realizing it was his first mouthful of air in some time.

"I'm beginning to get it," he exclaimed in relief, glancing at the altimeter. Russell gasped as he read the dial, illuminated by a small night-light.

The glider had *fallen* almost 1000 feet during the maneuver.

* * *

Sophie Michel was delighted with the attention Kurt von Heltscherer lavished upon her during the past few days. Even though the German officer was a bit older than she would like, Sophie accepted the reality that her new lover genuinely knew how to treat a woman. Moreover, there were certainly more unpleasant options facing her at the present time than her present situation. She envisioned the prospect of returning to her former nightly activities around the *Square St. Lambert*, and immediately forced the unpleasant notion from her mind.

Since the Reichsmarschall's visit a few days ago, Kurt had remained in truly high spirits. He assured Sophie, on several occasions that his career would soon move forward to bigger and better things. Sophie listened as von Heltscherer repeated a second time what this new assignment in *Paris* meant to his career.

"The Reichsmarschall himself selected me for this mission, a mission that is very important to him personally. By all appearances, it should not be all that difficult an assignment, finding where the French have hidden their finest masterpieces. The Reichsmarschall has assured me of his total support and that means I have unlimited resources to draw upon. With a little luck, it should only be a matter of time."

Sophie wasn't sure of *which* masterpieces von Heltscherer was referring to, and didn't really care. She was for the most part a very basic woman. Her attitude toward most daily occurrences was strictly one of survival A similar feeling was held by many French people during the period. Her street-wise character also allowed her to surmise that the high-ranking German officer she had recently chosen to live with seemed perfectly capable of protecting her in the future.

The one thing that surprised Sophie the most about her recent good fortune was her own acknowledgment that she was actually capable of having certain basic feelings for von Heltscherer. In Sophie's line of work, such feelings were extremely difficult to experience.

Sophie took to presenting von Heltscherer with little gifts he didn't expect, including a scarf from one of the fashionable shops on the *Rue St. Honore*. Its cost was more than she could afford at the time, but she felt the gift was well worth it.

And, their lovemaking became incessant and filled with copious passion. Sophie felt herself gratified and content even though she ignored the fact that von Heltscherer suffered from the quickness of release that affected a great number of her past clients. She decided early on that her own immediate satisfaction was not at all important, and should not develop into a detriment to their happiness. Sophie speculated in her mind as to just how long she would persist in feeling this way about their relationship.

*   *   *

Jake Barton couldn't believe his incredible good luck. Even considering the sordid experience with his former customer that brought about a prison sentence, Barton presently felt like he had been given his life back.

All he had ever wished for during his lifetime was to be able to paint, and by the time he was ten or eleven, it was apparent to practically everyone that Jake Barton possessed a special gift. Born to working class family in London's South End, young Jake spent most of his free hours painting. He gradually found his way to oils, which developed into his favorite medium. But the oils themselves proved exceedingly costly to Jake and his family.

Jake's father wasn't particularly keen of spending his hard-earned shillings on canvasses and oils when there wasn't enough food to provide for his family. When his father was injured while constructing a building, it was decided that Jake would assume his father's job to provide money for the family's upkeep. Jake's creative painting would have to wait. Even so, Jake found time to paint after finishing his labors even though he was often bone tired at the end of a shift.

At one point in his late teens, Jake began copying a beautiful old picture of a painting that he had found in a magazine. He soon realized he possessed a remarkable knack for rendering each detail, each color combination precisely the way it appeared in the magazine. He pilfered a book from a neighborhood bookstore that contained hundreds of classical works of art and started copying each one from the beginning. The project took him almost two years to finish, but by the time he had finished the book, Jake Barton's copies were as professional as any other artist in the world.

He began replicating fake paintings in a small way, encouraged by a gallery owner to whom he had taken some of his earlier works.

The street-wise gallery owner advised Jake to stick to the lesser-known artists. Theoretically, the gallery owner pointed out, collectors of that variety of art wouldn't pay as much attention to authenticity as to artwork attributed to the masters. Jake took the advice and slowly built up a steady clientele. In no time at all, the young artist started to earn an excellent living.

The money his copies brought in was much more than Jake Barton could ever expect as a laborer, not to mention the fact that Jake was being paid for doing something he actually enjoyed. Jake was assiduous and patient with his forgeries, which by then were in strong demand. Over the next few years, Jake's business grew until he was finally able to consider himself financially secure. He even bought his family a better home and regularly sent money to his mother to help in his family's upkeep.

But Jake regularly wrestled with an ongoing question. Why would anyone be willing to pay good money for a particular piece when they *knew* it was only a *copy* of the original?

Even though he was unable to answer his own question, Jake always thanked the heavens for his good fortune. That being able to produce his work in an environment that continued to make him happy and satisfied. That is, until Jake Barton finally got caught!

Jake's downfall was absurdly simple and really had little to do with Jake himself. One of his best customers wound up in a scandalous divorce. The mud-slinging and financial settlement eventually involved Jake and some of his fake artwork that his customer had claimed as genuine art. It was in late 1938, and Jake Barton's warmly coated world came crashing down. He was arrested for painting art forgeries and handed a stiff sentence by the royal magistrate who firmly stipulated that, in addition to his period of incarceration, Jake Barton would not be allowed to paint *inside* His Majesty's Albany and Parkhurst Prison on the Isle of Wight.

Jake Barton had become an international celebrity during the trial and his case was followed by practically everyone in the European art world. Professor Philippe De Jean had also followed Barton's case in the French and British art journals. De Jean's first priority, after agreeing to become involved in Special Operations Executive's delicate scheme, was a visit to Jake Barton at his prison quarters on the Isle of Wight.

When Barton was brought from his cell into a private room for their initial meeting, De Jean made sure he was armed with a powerful arsenal of possibilities concerning Jake Barton's future that he felt would be of interest to the renowned inmate.

"I am in need of an artist who possesses certain, well, *highly specialized* ability, "De Jean began, carefully choosing his words. " I am familiar with your work and I feel certain you are the person for my project."

"So you're lookin' for a bloke to forge some paintings for you, right?" Barton's accent was decidedly more cockney than De Jean was expecting.

"To get right to the point, yes. You are mostly correct. There is much more to what I need than plain old forgeries, but your interpretation is basically correct."

"And what might you be offerin' for my services, considerin' those services are *highly specialized*?"

"For starters, you would be released from here in the prison and would work with two other top-caliber artists I have already contacted at an estate outside London."

"And what else? Just gettin' out of here don't exactly thrill the pants off me."

"Oh. Yes, Monsieur Barton. I just had not reached the other part of my offer as of yet. At the end of the war, I have convinced the British Government to grant you a full pardon for your past discrepancies. How does that sound to you?"

"It would sound better iffin' I didn't have to wait 'til the end of the war to get my pardon. I have my career to think of ye know."

"I will see what I can do," Philippe De Jean added, "and, I do not think it will take me too long."

The too long De Jean had mentioned had turned into less than a day a day. Within hours on the day following his visit to Barton, a pair of constables neatly deposited Jake Barton in Professor De Jean's hands.

Upon arriving at the estate where De Jean and the other artists were already at work, Barton went immediately to work. At the present moment, the bespectacled artist intently scrutinized the painting resting on the easel in front of him. A pair of pebble glasses, given to him inside the prison by another inmate, aided his myopia. Jake had noticed his vision slowly eroding, but was powerless to do anything to correct the problem. His new cheaters helped his vision immeasurably.

The painting on Jake Barton's easel was his rendering of Titian's masterpiece *Francois I*, a portrait of the 16th Century French King, the first eminent patron of Italian Renaissance painting. Jake had learned a number of years ago from a book he was copying, that in 1527, the insightful king was also responsible for allowing his personal collection to become the framework for the modern collection of the *Louvre*.

Francois I instantly became Jake Barton's favorite work of art, and his public trial had announced that fact to the entire art world. Barton's high regard for *Francois I* did not escape the attention of Philippe De Jean. It was also the significant feature tying Jake Barton to Operation Angerona, since De Jean felt the piece to be one of the *Louvre's* greatest assets.

Titian's original *Francois I* was highlighted with incredibly rich red tones but it was the painting's sublime elegance that had attracted Jake's senses early in his career. The masterpiece aroused in Jake an artistic passion superior to any other work Jake had ever seen. Jake immediately realized his favorite painting was much too famous to ever copy for profit, but his admiration for the work had continued unabated since he first saw it reproduced. When Professor De Jean made Jake aware that it was *Francois I* that he was to copy, Jake was left with little to say for the first time in his artistic career. He silently thanked God that his prayers had finally been answered.

Now as he surveyed his new copy for the umpteenth time, Jake knew that his work was finally nearing completion. Jake would next treat the painting with his own formula that contained certain aging chemicals. When these chemicals were treated with heat from a hair dryer and given sufficient exposure to light, the resultant artwork attained an aged mien, enhanced sufficiently to meet Jake Barton's exacting standards.

The process was all part of the Jake Barton chronicle. Years before, Jake somehow encountered a research chemist who soon became his friend. The chemist worked closely with Jake and taught him various tricks, a few of which allowed Jake to age his paintings in a matter of days. It was all incredibly simple and vaulted Jake Barton to the top of his profession.

Barton had two additional paintings to put through his aging process before his job for the Special Operations Executive would be complete. He had been able to observe the Noelle Lejeune and van der Root paintings almost from their inception, and grudgingly longed for either one of his associates' classical abilities with a paintbrush.

Jake found himself enjoying watching each artist's smooth, effortless style take form on canvas. In turn, Noelle and van der Root were equally astounded at Jake Barton's uncanny ability to replicate the painting of *Francois 1*. Their common work has united the three artists and the trio had become close friends during the time they were together. Each, in turn, was vocally supportive of the other's efforts on canvas.

*   *   *

After several days of futility, Klaus von Heltscherer was only able to locate one person who was on the list he developed with the help of SS Scharfuhrer Mueller. It was apparent to von Heltscherer that the top museum officials had either fled *Paris* or were in hiding away from their homes and known associates.

The SS Obersturmbannfuhrer used some of Goring's promised resources help and issued high priority wanted bulletins through the Gestapo and other military agencies. He singled out Head Curator René Huyghe and all his top four assistant curators, but not a single lead was developed.

The one employee von Heltscherer was able to find was a lower level management custodian named Jules Retif, whose responsibility had been the ongoing restoration of some of the older, damaged paintings that were the property of the *Louvre*.

With little else to go on, von Heltscherer ordered Retif brought in and questioned by one of the Gestapo's most skillful interrogators at the Gestapo's *Paris* headquarters.

After more than a day of questioning, it became apparent to the interrogator that Retif knew nothing. He related to the interrogator that in 1938, he was part of a large group of workers that helped pack a great amount of the museum's superior artwork. He also assisted in loading it onto trucks supplied by the *Comedie Francaise.* Retif was questioned intensely as to where the trucks were sent, but the scared man insisted he was never aware of their destination

Von Heltscherer observed the Gestapo grilling and reluctantly gave the order to have Retif released, opting to have Retif placed under surveillance. On his way home from the interrogation, Retif sensed he was being followed and weighed his next course of action.

On his wife's next visit to the *boulangerie,* Retif managed to send word to his former employer Rene Huyghe who was hiding in a borrowed apartment not far from the establishment. Within two hours, Rene Huyghe was made aware of the Gestapo's efforts to locate him and his top assistants. Retif's news was not completely unexpected by the head curator of the *Louvre* who had allowed for such a contingency within weeks of the paintings leaving the *Louvre.*

* * *

At about the same time on the opposite side of *Paris,* von Heltscherer was in the process of paying a visit to the offices of the *Comedie Francaise.*

He stopped to quiz several employees he initially encountered upon entering the building. He was directed to the executive offices of the company located on the old building's second floor. Von Heltscherer found the company's *Director General* in his office and quickly demanded to know the circumstances concerning the movement of the *Louvre's* paintings and statues.

Yes, the man related, it was certainly true that the trucks for such an undertaking had been loaned to the *Louvre,* but their destination was kept from himself and everyone in the *Comedie Francaise.* Upon further questioning, the general manager also remembered that the vehicle use request originated within the government, at the very highest levels. No matter how much von Heltscherer pushed and bullied, the terrified man provided no help as far as the place of his trucks' final destination.

But von Heltscherer remained skeptical of the man's veracity, noting a subtle undercurrent between them. He decided to have the man brought in for further questioning when he returned to his office at Gestapo headquarters. The SS officer rose abruptly from his chair and left the director's office without a word.

As von Heltscherer made his way down the hallway, a small, beaked-nosed man motioned him outside, and into a small alley that divided the nearby buildings. It was obvious that the man intended that no one see him talking to the

German officer. von Heltscherer noted that the man appeared to be in his sixties and was slightly hunched as he walked.

"I believe I might know where the trucks went," the old man whispered mellifluously, so as not to be heard. "I was talking to some of the men you first questioned inside the *Comedie*. But, I must explain something to you first, and you must listen to what I have to say."

Von Heltscherer nodded approvingly to the much smaller man . "Go on, I am listening."

The old man summoned his courage and started again. " I support Marshall Petin and our country's loyal Government in Vichy. A pact has been signed and we are Germany's partners in this horrible war against the Soviets. I think it is my patriotic duty to help you."

Von Heltscherer shifted his weight and nodded his agreement as the man continued.

"When the trucks returned after moving the paintings, one of the drivers was upset about all the traffic around the city of *Vincennes*. The congestion was very bad and his truck was involved in a minor accident. He complained loudly to everyone who would listen about what had happened. He didn't want to be held responsible for the damage to his truck. He went on and on about the fact that none of the trucks had been able to get through to *Chambord* without enormous difficulty…"

The stooped man's words hung as the fading footsteps retreated down the hallway. The SS Oberstrumbannfuhrer was already on his way out the building.

* * *

Nearly 350 miles away from *Paris* was the interior City of *Montauban,* within the unoccupied zone of France. Senior *Milice* Inspector Raymond Soward busied himself with his final preparations for the raid he had scheduled later that day on the home of a suspected Jewish family. Of all his *Milice* duties, Raymond Soward enjoyed arresting Jews the most. He was always very careful to arrange and coordinate his daily duties accordingly.

The particular family he was following on this occasion was recently exposed by one of Soward's best informants, a man who specialized in ferreting out suspected members of the Jewish faith. The Germans paid informants the sum of 200 francs for each Jewish family unearthed, so Soward was kept busy with a string of potential leads.

It was also Soward's responsibility to coordinate the actual raid on the suspected family's home. The inspector normally scouted the residence of the alleged persons well in advance of the actual raid, hoping to establish a specific time when all family members would be in attendance. If the raid proved untimely, and the suspects were spooked into hiding, Soward had learned from his prior mistakes that rounding them up would be a most laborious task.

Tonight he had assembled a force of ten Vichy militia at his *Milice* offices to accompany him and his assistant, who held the rank of a *Milice* sub-inspector. Even though the targeted family consisted of but two adults and three minor children, Soward was a person who took no chances. Besides, Soward firmly believed that a demonstration of brute force always had a positive effect on neighbors and witnesses.

At about seven in the evening, the *Milice* force gathered in the dark outside the main *Milice* building and loaded the militia into an elderly truck, a ragged old Peugeot diesel. The ancient vehicle was the type with hoops in the back and a canvas top. From its exterior appearance, it was improbable the venerable old machine would ever start, but its asthmatic engine first sputtered, then caught and wined into life. Senior Inspector Raymond Soward and his band of *Milice* thugs were on their way.

Nearly two miles later, the vehicle screeched to a halt in front of a modest single story building, just off the town square. Soward wore his black leather Gestapo-style coat and drew his police issue Walther from an inside holster. He signaled the militia to disburse and walked toward the building's front door. When he felt all were ready and in position, he signaled again, A burly militia sergeant put his shoulder into the door, splintering it immediately.

The militia rushed in to the screams and cries of people inside. A minute later, when the premises were considered under control, the sergeant in charge called for Soward.

Inside, the terrified family held each other closely, trying to console the two smallest children who appeared to be four to five years old, and who were both crying noisily.

With the tense situation was under control Soward advanced boldly.

"I have reports that there are Jews in this house."

"No, no," a man in his early forties replied, holding his wife and one of the children tightly. "There must be some mistake. My family is not Jewish. We have lived here for many years, everyone knows us."

"Can you provide any evidence to me that what you say is true?"

"I am not sure what kind of evidence you wish," the man answered uncertainly. His children continued to bawl.

Soward withdrew a small notebook from one of his pockets that contained the notes he had transcribed from his informant. He turned to the woman who was holding the other children.

"Was your grandfather named Emanuel Lefarge?"

"Why yes, but he has been dead for…"

"And is not Emanuel a Jewish first name?"

The woman hesitated. "Yes, Monsieur, it might well be, but in my grandfather's case…"

"Enough of this." Soward cut her off abruptly. "It is just as I suspected. There is definite Jewish heredity here. Take them all to the truck."

The father stepped forward, in the direction of Soward.

"Please Monsieur, there…"

Soward raised his pistol and cracked it against the man's face. The man fell backward, as his wife tried in vain to break his fall. The children shrieked again as several more militia stepped forward with rifles pointed at the family.

*   *   *

Von Heltscherer felt a sense of elation as his open-air Mercedes sedan made its way across the *Loire* River. Even though it was still quite cold and the wind ripped his face, von Heltscherer was pleased with his progress. The trip to the southeast had only taken two hours during which von Heltscherer was able to ponder his next move. If the old man's information proved accurate, one could reasonably assume that he was getting closer to the location of the French masterpieces. It would be quite rewarding to be able to upgrade the Reichsmarschall on his mission's progress.

His thoughts returned briefly to the individual who had confronted him at the *Comedie Francaise* and who had given him the first real lead to the location of the paintings.

Poor misguided idiot. The man was not unlike so many of the other Frenchmen von Heltscherer had encountered. *Does the average Frenchman not grasp the absurdity of his situation? Is he not aware of the fact that the Third Reich has **conquered** France? Does anyone really believe Germany is an ally of France? No wonder it was so easy for the Wehrmacht to simply march in and occupy as much of the country as it wished. The French are like sheep…*

The vehicle pulled up to the elegant front gate of the rambling chateau, which von Heltscherer instantly established was closed. Upon closer inspection, von Heltscherer saw that a chain was looped across the gate and secured by a sizable lock. He motioned to his driver, SS Scharfuhrer Mueller, who reacted swiftly.

"Right away Herr Obersturmbannfuhrer. It will only take a second."

Taking out his Luger, Mueller expertly aimed at the lock and fired. The lock burst into pieces and fell to the ground. Mueller removed the chain and flung open the gate, then helped von Heltscherer back into the car. They drove up the road toward the breathtaking chateau that was *Chambord*.

As the car approached the structure, it was apparent that the entire place was deserted. The great chateau's windows were boarded up and the door was closed in the care of a huge padlock. Von Heltscherer walked to one of the nearby windows, but was unable to see anything inside. He muttered something under his breath and returned his gaze to the old building. He had traveled all the way to the *Loire* Valley only to find his objective deserted.

Remounting their car, von Heltscherer decided to return to the small village they had just passed through before arriving at *Chambord.*

* * *

Once he perceived the real feeling of night flying, Russell determined it wasn't all that difficult. After his second flight with Colonel Smith-Reeves, he had soloed the craft, With the exception of a rather nasty bump on landing, the flight proved uneventful. It was true that the aircraft handled in a different way at night, but the necessary adjustments came naturally. Both Russell and Smith-Reeves were satisfied with Russell's progress.

The lack of familiar ground landmarks, not to mention a void of any directional lights, proved to be Russell's biggest problem. But when considering the fact that a complete blackout of England was in effect, Russell realized he must cope with what was at hand. When it was available, he used moonlight and his familiarity with local terrain to get him safely back to the base each evening. To his credit and the relief of Smith-Reeves, Russell's homing instinct proved to be unerring.

While aloft one particular evening Brian Russell even encountered some British fighters, a pair of Spitfires, flying higher than him at medium altitude on a scouting mission for German bombers. Russell heard and spotted the Spitfires first and quickly realized his predicament. He jerked his glider away from the fighters' flight path and prayed that he had not been seen. It wouldn't pay for him to be discovered by a set of eager British fighters with his aircraft bearing French markings.

Once clear of the Spitfires, Russell banked the glider neatly to port and soared in the general direction of the base at Feltham. He relished flying in this manner and resolved to continue flying gliders if his future circumstances would ever permit.

He followed his compass heading and was aware that his craft's altimeter confirmed a gradual decent as he began to make out some dark objects on the ground. An old bridge that served as his primary approach landmark appeared on his left and he was aware that the field lay about three miles directly ahead. He extended his flaps, further reducing his speed, and looked forward off the glider's nose. He pushed a button on his console that emitted a radio signal that was received on the ground.

Ten seconds later, a half-dozen pairs of headlights appeared in front of him. Russell lined up the nose of the aircraft as best he could with an imaginary line down the center of the headlights. He continued descending and seconds later felt a familiar thud when his wide wheels hit the soft grass of the airfield. Russell's glider encountered another softer bump and another successful night flight was completed.

His mission was getting closer.

* * *

Upon their arrival, von Heltscherer noted that the tiny village of *Chambord* contained a small hotel and little else. von Heltscherer and Mueller pulled in front of the small, well-kept building and Mueller shut off the motor.

The sergeant walked around the rear of the Mercedes and opened the door for von Heltscherer. He then followed at a respectful distance behind his superior up the small stairway leading to the front door.

Before they reached the top, the door opened and a diminutive, well-dressed woman in her sixties emerged to greet them.

"I am Madame Pinot, the proprietress," she announced firmly. "Do you wish rooms?"

Von Heltscherer snapped to attention, a move that made little impression on the small woman who stared down at his shiny boots and then raised her head.

"No Madame, not at this time. I am simply seeking some information about the nearby chateau," he explained, politely and softly. He also pointed in the direction from which he had just come.

"The chateau is completely closed, Monsieur, as you must have seen. As it has been for several years."

"Yes, I saw the way it was left. But, I need some additional details. I wish to talk to someone who knows about what happened there. I need to find out if there is anything left inside. And, if there is anything remaining there, I want to know what it is."

"To my knowledge, *Monsieur, Chambord* is quite empty. There was a large amount of activity out there two or three years ago, with a number of trucks coming and going. It was the first time in several years that *Chambord* had any occupants at all. A number of people came and went. It was a good period for my business here at the hotel. Some of the visitors spent the night, particularly when the weather was bad and it was raining. Then, about a year ago, different trucks came and removed everything from inside. Once they were finished, the place became empty again and the boards were hammered up again."

Von Heltscherer studied the small, assertive woman and posed a final question.

"Were you aware of what the trucks were hauling, *Madame?*"

She dropped her head a little and thought for a second.

"Everything seemed to be in crates, *Monsieur,* and the backs of some of the trucks were open so one could see the crates quite clearly. But, if I am not mistaken, many of the crates contained paintings, works of art. The reason I believe this to be true that is I overheard some of the drivers who ate here at my hotel talking about paintings. Beyond that, I really have no idea…"

"And do you know where the crates were taken?"

"No, *Monsieur,* I would have no way of knowing such things."

"Thank you, *Madame,* for your time. You have been quite helpful." von Heltscherer clicked his boots again, gave a half salute, turned and walked back to the car.

He sat rigidly in the rear seat deeply immersed in thought as Mueller turned the vehicle and headed the automobile back toward *Paris.*

Maybe the French were a bit smarter than he had originally thought!

Chapter Six
The Mission - July 1942

Colonel Maurice Buckmaster, head of RF Section of the Special Operations Executive, called the meeting to order at SOE's crowded Baker Street offices. Attending this particular meeting were General Percy Barclay, Colonel Barclay Smith-Reeves, Captain Brian Russell and Antoine Thierry, of the *Bureau Central de Renseignements et d'Action, BCRA*, representing Major Passy, the head of Free French Intelligence in London.

Tall and angular, Buckmaster stood as he began the meeting.

"Gentlemen, I am pleased to say that our meteorologists have given us a three day window of opportunity for Operation Angerona. The three days occur in early July, and RAF data estimates that a huge high weather system will dominate most of Europe on those days. Barring changes, it is expected to extend all the way from Norway to Southern Europe. The weather experts feel it will contain some favorable upper level winds that will benefit our project considerably.

After studying our options, I propose that we set Operation Angerona's glider release time to somewhere between 2300 and 2330 hours on July 7th, two days hence. I think we should also consider extending the release period for an additional three hours to allow for uncertainties."

"Uncertainties?" It was the Frenchman, Antoine Thierry who spoke. "We like to provide a cushion for missions that are extraordinary such as Operation Angerona. One can never tell what might happen. The tow plane could have problems, an air raid might disrupt things, there are a number of things that could crop up. At any rate, we consider it wise to provide a supplementary time window for most missions." Buckmaster paused for a moment, looked at each of the officers around the table, and finally asked,

"Any other questions concerning the additional release time?" After another quick glimpse around the table, Buckmaster consulted his notepad and was about to continue when the accented voice asked.

"Have the forgeries been delivered?" It was the thorough Frenchman, Thierry. He was again checking another detail. "And, will they be safe?"

"Yes, all the paintings are here. SOE received them earlier this morning, and according to our people who know about such things, they are quite remarkable. I want to add another note you might not yet be aware of. One of our chaps suggested we add a special lightweight, non-destructible, self-closing cylinder to the operation. It has already been attached to the inside of the glider. By use of a special wall inside the cylinder, the forgeries are enclosed within that wall. The special wall is only apparent to the designers and practically invisible to anyone else. From a safety standpoint, the design of the cylinder is such that, even if the craft crashes, the paintings will be safe."

Colonel Smith-Reeves cringed at Buckmaster's allusion to crashing and checked to see Russell's reaction.

The American captain had not flinched.

"And, oh, yes. After some discussion with the Royal Air Force, we have changed the tow plane for the mission to one of the Lancaster Bombers that will also participate in an actual early morning bombing mission. After discharging Captain Russell's glider, it will continue on and participate in bombing the high tech German radar-building works located at Friedrichshafen."

"What about the local Resistance. Have they been notified and are they prepared to assist?" Thierry asked again checking off another important aspect of the mission.

"Quite so. The Resistance has agreed to light a series of fires to show Russell the way to the landing site just north of *Domme*. They have also agreed to meet the aircraft when it lands. As you are probably aware, *Domme* is a city that sits atop a steep hill and can be seen from a great distance. The Resistance has promised to have most of the city lights on the northern face of *Domme* itself turned on for an hour-long period or as long as they can pull it off. If our timing is anywhere near accurate, the lights from *Domme* should provide the most noticeable beacon Russell could ever utilize. The crucial element of the entire mission will be Russell's ability to recognize the exact road our plan specifies and turn his aircraft at the prescribed time. The Resistance will also dispose of the glider once it has landed. As you are doubtless aware, this glider was expressly designed so as to be able to be dismantled very quickly."

"If the weather experts are indeed accurate and this will be a cloudless night, how is it that Russell's aircraft will be able to fly all that way undetected?" It was evident that Thierry had come to the meeting well prepared.

"That is precisely why we decided to use a glider in the first place. There is practically no nighttime aircraft movement over France at this time except for the intermittent bomber mission or the Germans' own night patrols. Aircraft engines would bring attention to our mission. And the glider itself is our best ally. Compared to conventional airplanes, its frame is quite small and we have taken the precaution to paint the glider black to blend in with the nighttime. One would have to be looking directly at it to see it, and could only observe it for a few brief seconds. We feel the chances of the craft being detected are almost negligible."

"And the landing site? Is it safe?" The Frenchman seemed to be getting to the last of his questions.

Buckmaster answered quite assuredly. "Given the mission requirements, it is the best we could find in the entire vicinity. Besides, Russell himself first suggested the landing area north of *Domme*. He spent some time there before the war and feels quite confident that it will work for us."

Satisfied, Thierry glanced around the table and rose to leave.

"Good day, gentlemen," he half saluted as he left the room. When the door closed behind him, the British officers could barely manage to suppress a chuckle.

"It sometimes amazes me just how confident our French friends are," General Percy Barclay ruminated, alluding to Thierry's rather abrupt departure. "One would think they are doing us a favor in allowing us to partake in this little scheme to protect some of their national treasures."

"Yes, it certainly seems so," agreed Colonel Buckmaster.

"Maybe it has something to do with the fact that the man is presently nearly devoid of a country," Russell popped into the conversation. "And, there is very little he can do to change the way conditions are going to be in the foreseeable future. To me it would seem to make even minute events and issues seem more important."

"I see your point," Buckmaster responded with typical British indifference. "But there are certain standards by which one should conduct one's self. Thierry is not the first frog I have encountered with such a supercilious attitude."

"And he undoubtedly won't be the *last*," General Barclay stressed, signaling an effective end to the discussion.

"That will do us until tomorrow," Colonel Buckmaster concluded, trying to regain his control of the meeting. He nodded to General Barclay who had already stood up. It was a signal for the group to file out of the room and begin the final preparations for Russell's mission.

*　*　*

It was extremely close and humid in *Paris* when one of the Gestapo agents von Heltscherer knew by sight eagerly burst into the SS Obersturmbannfuhrer's office three days after von Heltscherer's unproductive car trip to *Chambord*.

"Herr Obersturmbannfuhrer," he began, his voice obviously keyed up, "I think our office might have uncovered something that will interest you."

Von Heltscherer gestured for the square-jawed man to sit down. He observed the Gestapo agent was still wearing his black leather coat indoors even though it was already early July.

"During our investigations, we often routinely question a number of French civilians whose ancestry is in question for one reason or another. One of the persons we recently interrogated could not provide us with enough detailed answers, so we increased our examination."

Von Heltscherer said nothing, but was acutely aware of the fact that increased interrogation generally meant torture or the use of the drug scopolamine, or something equally ominous.

"After a while, we were able to extract some helpful facts from the suspect. Before he unfortunately died, he was disposed to tell us everything we wanted, including some information we did not anticipate."

"Get to the point," von Heltscherer insisted, becoming a bit annoyed with the scenario.

"Well, among other things, the man gave us the names and addresses of some members of the underground. One of them is a name included on your museum curator's list, a fellow named Pierre Sassy. We know where he is staying and believe we can apprehend him very quickly."

"Well then, by all means go and do it," the SS Obersturmbannfuhrer barked at the Gestapo agent. "In this matter, time is of the essence."

"Jawohl. I assure you, we will pick him up. He is unaware that we are onto him. Heil Hitler!" The Gestapo agent turned and left von Heltscherer's office.

*   *   *

Christine Allard was not used to sitting and waiting, but there was very little the slender, evenly proportioned, ravenesque woman could do about it. After arriving at her cousin's home in *Cahors* nearly a week ago, she was yet to receive any further communication from Victor, who had cautioned her to be patient. Christine was determined to make the most of the situation and genuinely enjoyed the opportunity of again seeing her favorite cousin Lucille.

Close friends since childhood, the pair spent the first few days of her visit reacquainting themselves with each other's lives. Christine considered telling Lucille about her activities on behalf of the Resistance, but realized she dare not for fear of her cousin's future safety.

Christine was aware that her impending mission was far from normal, and dismissed any minor resentment towards Victor for sending her to *Cahors* so early.

Her mind drifted unproductively for the umpteenth time that day as innumerable possibilities passed through her thoughts.

How much longer must I wait and what will I be asked to do? Is the mission as dangerous as I have begun to suspect? Am I simply too anxious for my own good and should I just sit back and relax? Her thought process was interrupted when Lucille finally returned home

"Any word yet?" her cousin cheerfully inquired. "I would have thought you would have received some word by now." While Lucille suspected something was unusual about her cousin's current situation, she too had prudently avoided the subject of precisely what Christine was involved in.

Christine shook her head in mock frustration as Lucille came over and hugged her tenderly.

"I am tired of just sitting around and doing nothing, Luci. All the waiting is actually starting to get under my skin. I guess I am not very good at being idle and doing nothing."

"The world does not work for our convenience, and we live in most confusing times. I know it seems to you as if you could be doing more..." Lucille tried to comfort her cousin.

"But that is just the point. I am quite sure I could."

"Soon, *Cherie*, soon." Lucille stroked her anxious relation's hair with her fingers. "You will receive what you have been expecting soon."

*   *   *

By a stroke of sheer luck, the Gestapo was able to keep its promise to von Heltscherer.

Pierre Sassy, along with other assistant curators from the *Louvre*, had been adequately forewarned about the consequences of remaining in *Paris*. Sassy had initially opted for a hiding place with an old school friend in *Deauville*, on the West Coast of France. He had not returned to *Paris* for the more than six months. He unwisely decided to chance a visit to his former home to retrieve some important documents he had left behind.

The place was under surveillance and several Gestapo agents who observed his entrance waited a few minutes and simply knocked on the door. A startled Sassy opened the door himself and produced a set of forged papers. The Gestapo agents carried an old photograph of Sassy with them and quickly arrested him.

Sassy was a thin, pock-faced man, around 50, and totally unsuited for the rigors of Gestapo grilling.

He was able to endure the severe questioning about four hours, with von Heltscherer present during the latter part of the interrogation.

Even though the *Louvre* and its contents were precious to him, Sassy considered all consequences and decided his life was even more valuable.

An exhausted and emotionally spent Pierre Sassy then blurted out to his captors a number of pertinent details concerning his activities for the *Louvre*. Foremost of these disclosures was the fact that Sassy admitted to being one of the curators. He admitted that, in the summer of 1940, he helped move a number of the pieces from the storage site at *Chambord*.

He also acknowledged that the artworks' next destination was an old abbey located somewhere in the middle of France, to his knowledge some 500 miles from *Paris*. He was then able to recall that the place was named the *Abbey du Loc Dieu*, and was near a town called *Villefranche-de-Rouergue*. Finally, he believed the town's location was on or near the *Aveyron* River.

Sassy's painful admission elated Von Heltscherer and improved his spirits immensely. He returned to his upstairs office and wasted no time in sending a top priority, coded message to Reichsmarschall Hermann Goring. In it, he detailed his actions up to the present and included his intention to proceed immediately to the *Abbey du Loc Dieu*. The SS Obersturmbannfuhrer concluded with a personal note to Goring that he truly believed he would be in possession of the masterpieces within a relatively short time.

* * *

It was shortly after midnight when Pierre Bonde finished coding notes assigning several of his men to another Resistance project that would help disrupt German military rail service in his region. Bonde had just put down his pen when the early morning silence was interrupted by one of his female Resistance followers. She opened the door to the room where Bonde was working and walked quickly inside. Her ongoing job for the Resistance involved monitoring transmissions from London by the British Broadcasting Company.

The partisan woman had just identified an urgent message and had been instructed to notify Bonde whenever a message of this type was received. Germany had been successful in blocking a number of transmissions into certain regions of France, but in the *Dordogne*, the BBC signal was usually received loud and clear. Bonde studied the paper he was handed, which included a list of phrases. One specific line caught his eye.

"Feed the rabbit his morsels."

The locution was the signal from England that Operation Angerona was about to begin. Two days prior, Bonde had been notified of the exact details of the mission, and Bonde was on the lookout for the signal that it would begin soon. Due to the fact that its planning was so detailed and also because Jean Moulin himself emphasized its importance, Bonde knew that Operation Angerona was one of the most significant missions he and his group had ever been assigned.

He also was aware that the mission contained key ramifications for his beloved France. The gist of the encoded message informed Bonde of the fact that, thirty-six hours from the time of the broadcast, a glider would be set free above France. It was time for Bonde to notify the rest of his fighters.

For several days, Andre Faboul found difficulty in sleeping. However, on this particular night he was quite content and comfortable with his wife Marie reclined in the bed next to him, complete with her occasional snore of contentment. He was used to Marie's choppy nasal sounds, which usually occurred when she slept on her back.

Faboul had tried hard to make himself fall asleep when he and Marie first went to bed but there was simply too much occupying his mind for him to doze off. For the fiftieth time Faboul reviewed the directives he had been given and silently prayed that all the details he had memorized would come together as planned.

He gently rolled out of bed so as not to disturb Marie and crossed a small hallway into their home's tiny kitchen. Reaching inside the pantry, Faboul extracted a pre-war bottle of *Camus Cognac Napoleon* that he had treasured for some time. Finding a small glass on an inside shelf, he poured a small amount of the precious golden liquid into the glass. He partially filled his mouth with the glass's contents and rolled the cognac around, savoring the delicate caramelized flavor for several moments. His palate totally gratified, Faboul poured another similar amount and repeated the swilling motion.

He felt himself begin to relax as he rolled his neck and finally returned to bed and his place beside Marie.

With the aid of the cognac, Andre Faboul's mind relaxed and he finally managed to close his eyes. It was now *his* turn for some sleep. He sighed deeply and was fast asleep within a few seconds.

Faboul's covert assignment on behalf of his museum and his country would begin tomorrow.

*   *   *

Earlier that same afternoon, the Wehrmacht Mercedes staff car that von Heltscherer had requisitioned sped steadily southward toward the interior French city of *Rodez*. The Wehrmacht detachment commander in *Rodez* was alerted through von Heltscherer's Gestapo contacts to have a number of men ready to support SS Obersturmbannfuhrer von Heltscherer the minute he arrived.

Once the car had left the environs of *Paris*, SS Scharfuhrer Mueller had been able to make excellent time. The only real drawbacks were German checkpoints along the way. The car needed a fresh tank of gas, which von Heltscherer had been able to appropriate from a moving German armored column they had encountered along their route.

The lengthy trip became tiresome and von Heltscherer was eventually forced to relent in his effort to persuade Mueller to join him in conversation. It was obvious to the senior officer that his sergeant was uncomfortable conversing idly with him. Mueller mostly limited his answers to one or two words to the various questions von Heltscherer posed. Von Heltscherer decided quite correctly that the rigid Mueller was a true product of the structured German military environment where the role of a non-commissioned officer was always to be seen and not heard. He decided to let well enough alone.

At long last, scattered houses and a few commercial structures alerted von Heltscherer that the staff car was finally approaching the outskirts of *Rodez*. He consulted the map that the Gestapo had cheerily provided him along with directions to his ultimate destination. It was nice to be on Hermann Goring's side, a fact that the Paris Gestapo office took very seriously.

Mueller succeeded in correctly navigating the historic, hilly city and pulled up in front of the *Rodez* German Wehrmacht headquarters, The offices were officially located at *6 Boulevard Gambetta.* The old building was part of the downtown section of the old city, immediately adjacent to the ancient 13th Century *Cathedrale Notre Dame.* The Wehrmacht workplace was one of a handful of administrative military offices the Germans maintained throughout unoccupied France, and was primarily intended as a focal supply point should wartime fortunes make it a necessity for the German war machine.

Mueller again popped out of the driver's seat and opened the door for his Colonel. Von Heltscherer stepped down and adjusted his uniform from the long journey. He brushed himself off just down from the neighboring cathedral's huge front doors, carefully regarding the huge church. What impressed him most about the weathered structure was its massive, spiritual presence and clean classical lines. It was by far the most magnificent edifice of its kind he had seen outside *Paris.*

Von Heltscherer suddenly took note of the guard still standing at attention and crisply saluted with a distinctive, "Heil, Hitler."

The guard clicked smartly and von Heltscherer went inside the old building. The SS Obersturmbannfuhrer was immediately shown into the office of the Wehrmacht officer in charge.

The aforementioned officer held the rank of an Oberstleutnant, the Wehrmacht equivalent of von Heltscherer's SS rank. His name was Dieter Hoven and he crisply walked toward von Heltscherer and offered his hand.

"Welcome to *Rodez*, Herr Obersturmbannfuhrer. My staff and I are at your service."

From his general demeanor, von Heltscherer sensed that Hoven was sufficiently impressed at the prospect of an SS officer paying him a call. Such a reaction could come in handy and von Heltscherer was careful to store it in his memory for later use.

Von Heltscherer seized the opportunity to illuminate the situation. "I am here on a most unique mission, under the personal approval of Reichsmarschall Hermann Goring."

Oberstleutnant Dieter Hoven was even more impressed by the reference to the high-ranking Nazi's name and nodded excitedly.

"My immediate duty involves identifying and recovering a large number of paintings and artwork which were removed from the *Louvre* and other museums by the previous French government. Under their government's orders, the former curators of these museums have placed a large quantity of these priceless museum pieces in hiding. The rights of war can now consider these artworks as property of the Third Reich. The Reichsmarschall is a true art lover and has decided that all these important works be located as swiftly as possible, to save them from any harm.

Herr Oberstleutnant, I have information that a large number of these paintings and sculptures were sent to this very area sometime last year, to an old abbey not too far from here. The place is called the *Abbey du Loc Dieu.* Are you familiar with its location?"

"Yes, Herr Obersturmbannfuhrer. It can be found about forty miles from here, not far from the *Aveyron* River. I have never been really close to it but I have passed signs indicating its existence during some of our motorized maneuvers."

"Good. I have a good feeling about this place. We will need at least a platoon of soldiers and I would like to be able to depart as soon as possible."

"Certainly, Herr Obersturmbannfuhrer. My men have already been placed on alert. It will only take a few minutes to get everything ready for our departure."

Hoven called outside the room for his adjutant who issued orders for two armed personnel carriers to be brought to the front of the building. Within ten minutes, a column led by von Heltscherer's staff car and consisting of two armored personnel carriers and three mid-size trucks containing soldiers was mustered and quickly pulled away. The column turned westward and slowly made it way toward the city limits of *Rodez.*

The trip to *Villefranche-de-Rouergue* took almost one and one-half hours, during which Wehrmacht Oberstleutnant Hoven outlined a simple plan to von Heltscherer. The armed personnel carriers would take up strategic positions at the front and rear of the buildings while the soldiers would completely surround the place thereby theoretically capturing everyone inside. Von Heltscherer agreed. Hoven's strategy was uncomplicated enough and if it proved successful and the paintings were found, von Heltscherer reasoned he could then call the Reichsmarschall and relay to him the good news.

Upon reaching the town of *Villefranche-de-Rouergue*, which von Heltscherer estimated about half the size of Rodez, he watched intently as Hoven discreetly sought out the most direct road to the Abbey It proved to be about 10 miles north of the city. The column was first directed to the city's *Poste*, where a narrow road intersected that led out of the city. The vehicles followed that road for another twenty minutes through sweeping, rolling hills and farmlands until the procession finally approached the group of buildings that comprised the Abbey.

The staff car with both von Heltscherer and Hoven in the back seat slowed down as it drew near the Abbey complex. Von Heltscherer noted at once that the *Abbey du Loc Dieu* was itself a most impressive complex of buildings complimented by well-tended grounds. Set back in a grove of trees, with an exceptionally stunning reflective lake as a background, the main building was four stories high with three prominent towers, each with a large cross protruding from the top. An ancient ten-foot high stone fence covered with various types of ivy and plant coverings surrounded the entire complex. At the north end of the development sat three brick buildings. These were offset by an ornate wrought iron spear gate that blocked passage onto the manicured gravel road leading to the Abbey.

The column stopped and one of Hoven's junior officers, a Hauptmann (captain) named Franz, alighted from one of the personnel carriers and approached the staff car. Hoven quickly explained his plan and issued a set of orders to cover his action. The captain saluted smartly and returned to the trucks to disperse his men. Each of the armed personnel carriers assumed authoritarian positions along the road leading to the complex while the soldiers fanned out in columns directly in front of the gate.

When everyone was in place, SS Obersturmbannfuhrer von Heltscherer and Wehrmacht Oberstleutnant Hoven stepped out of the car and drew their service revolvers. They approached the imposing iron speared gate and rang the antique bell.

After a few moments, a solitary figure emerged from one of the brown brick buildings and approached the gate. She was a habited nun, a diminutive woman in her mid-fifties. She surveyed the amassed display of vehicles, soldiers and their drawn guns. She turned and faced the two German officers.

"Well now, exactly what is it you want, my sons," she said in perfect German.

For the first time in a long time, von Heltscherer found himself speechless.

"How is it you speak such excellent German, Mother," Hoven asked, attempting to gain control of the moment.

"It's all quite simple, my son. Our Abbey is part of the Order of Reformed Cistercians, and we have abbeys and convents throughout Europe. Before the war, I spent a great deal of time in one of our order's German convents," she replied. "There, it was much easier to speak in German than in French. I thought you would be more at ease if we spoke in your mother tongue."

The two German officers looked at each other and then back at the nun.

Recognizing this confrontation with such an astounding nun was not progressing favorably, von Heltscherer picked up the conversation. He quickly decided on a more compassionate approach. Sensing no danger from the nun, he replaced his *Walther P-38* and motioned to the rest of the soldiers to lower their guns.

"We are here for the *Louvre's* paintings, Mother, to take them to another place for safekeeping. I have been told that the paintings are here and I expect your full cooperation."

The old French nun surveyed von Heltscherer's striking SS uniform while assimilating his words. Even within the cloistered walls of the convent, the reputation of the Waffen SS was well known. She glanced about again at the massed group, and replied with a neutral expression on her face.

"Then you are much too late, my son. Well over a year ago, some trucks came and took away everything that had been stored here. I overheard some of them talking and the ones who seemed to be in charge thought that our Abbey was too exposed and leaky. For all I know they might have been right. After all, our old Abbey was constructed hundreds of years ago."

Von Heltscherer blinked, hardly believing what he had heard. Even though his present position was more than a quarter mile away from the main building, the place seemed in excellent shape. He found himself in the middle of an immediate quandary. He was himself raised as a Catholic and was taught as a youth never to question the word of a nun. It was always explained to him, sometimes in the company of a stick or cane that nuns *never, ever* lied.

"And, Mother," von Heltscherer proceeded cautiously, "I am sure *you* were informed as to where the paintings were moved?"

"Oh no, my son. The movement of the paintings was all completed quite reticently. For much of the time they were here at the Abbey the men talked in hushed tones. At the time I was not sure if it was out of reverence for our Order and the sanctity of the Abbey or the fact that they did not wish to share any information with us."

With frustration beginning to set in and only partially convinced by the nun's abject sincerity, von Heltscherer whispered to Oberstleutnant Hoven to insure that the soldiers thoroughly search the venerable *Abbey du Loc Dieu.*

After all, the Mother in question was a *French* nun.

The extensive search by the Wehrmacht soldiers through the premises took more than two hours to finish and produced no results.

The old Mother remained next to the two officers until they ultimately prepared to leave.

"Thank you, Mother, for your hospitality," Oberstleutnant Hoven said politely as they walked through the gate.

"Hospitality *is* the home of the Lord," she replied in an equally civil tone, again in flawless German.

The officers glanced at each other blankly and stepped back into their car. A signal was given and the soldiers remounted their trucks. The staff car's engine purred, then started forward as the remaining vehicles quickly fell in line for the long return trip back to *Rodez.*

Chapter Seven

On July 6th, the day previous to the mission's proposed commencement, Brian Russell determined it was the perfect time for him to attempt to put his personal life in order.

He had already checked over his black glider several times earlier in the morning. Shortly after noon Brian sat down to write a grossly overdue letter to his parents. It was intended to bring them up to date on his perceptions of England. He was forced to omit any reference to his mission or even a mention of its significance, not only because of censorship but also with the full realization that his parents would just worry about his safety as all parents surely would.

As he reread his letter's contents before mailing, Brian Russell was a bit surprised at how much his new interest in flying literally leapt out of the two pages. Brian wondered if his parents were even aware of the role of the glider in the war effort.

No way, he thought, few *ordinary citizens are even aware of the craft's existence.*

He was glad that his letter mentioned the potential importance of the glider in the future of the war. He was aware the part about the glider's importance probably would not make it past the censor's scissors, but he was willing to take the chance. He hoped his letter would let his parents know that flying had become an important aspect of his life.

Adams also mulled over the prospect of writing additional letters to several other old friends, but found the idea a bit morbid. In the end the young officer decided against it. He could write his friends whenever he returned from the mission. No one would be the wiser.

Brian also had the foresight to commit to memory telephone numbers of several of his former close acquaintances in France in case communicating with them became necessary during the mission. During the process, his mind drifted. *How have those who lived in and around Paris fared during the German Occupation. Are most still alive?*

*   *   *

Not more than ten minutes after the German column departed from the *Abbey du Loc-Dieu,* Mother Therese Santenay scribbled a detailed note that was hurriedly handed to another nun, Sister Jeanne-Marie Altouse. Among Sister Jeanne-Marie's daily responsibilities at the Abbey was the caring and handling of a large homing pigeon colony. The colony was located in an area behind two small buildings just off the main gate of the Abbey.

The nuns originally used the pigeons as a means of communicating with the Order of Reformed Cistercians' network of convents and abbeys throughout Europe. Realizing the extended value of such a network, Resistance leaders had early on made use of its capabilities for certain messages. These were deemed too sensitive to travel by telephone or other ordinary means.

Sister Jeanne-Marie placed the note in a tiny canister fastened to the leg of one of the birds and released it with a sweeping motion.

The bird rose quickly made a wide turn to the northwest, and continued its flight in the direction of *Paris*. As it rose to a comfortable altitude, the pigeon passed over the rear echelon of SS Obersturmbannfuhrer Kurt von Heltscherer's motorized convoy that was slowly winding its way back to *Rodez*.

*   *   *

On the bright, sunny British morning of July 8ᵗʰ, Colonel Smith-Reeves summoned Russell to the hangar where his glider was situated. Russell noted with pride that an armed RAF airman stood guard beside his aircraft.

Noting Russell's reaction, Smith-Reeves spoke first. "Can't be *too* cautious," pointing in the direction of the guard. "Besides, something new has just been added to your aircraft."

Genuinely interested, Russell felt an elongated box-like contraption that had been fastened near the left rear side of the fuselage to the rear of the glider.

"It is something our designers have been working on for the larger gliders, but I had this one especially rigged and fitted to yours. It is controlled from here. " He pointed to a small handle just inside the cockpit.

Russell glanced at the mechanism and looked back at Smith-Reeves for enlightenment.

"The gadget is intended to serve as an added safety device. Inside here," he continued touching the rectangular shape made of wood , "is a small parachute that is attached to the end of the glider. You are able to deploy the parachute by pulling a handle inside the cockpit. It is intended for use in the air to stabilize the aircraft during an emergency landing. It should keep the craft from spinning, but I think it might also be an effective help to you as a drag chute if you are forced to make a rapid landing. Unfortunately, there is not sufficient time left to allow you to try it out Too many other things on your plate before you push off tonight. Hell, chances are you will not even need it."

Brian examined the small rectangular object that was affixed to tail of his glider. A small wire was attached to a hole drilled into the plane's fuselage. He traced the wire inside the cockpit and found that it attached to a small lever on the left side of the panel, immediately adjacent to the control panel.

"All you need to do is give the lever a tug," Smith-Reeves continued his explanation, pointing to the handle. "But, be careful, it is liable to give you a nice jolt when it deploys."

Russell continued to examine the contraption, envisioning its use in the air.

"It seems relatively uncomplicated. I agree, the contraption might just come in handy," Russell concurred as he fingered the mechanism. "With something like this to stop my momentum, I could conceivably land in a shorter space."

"Quite, old boy. That's what first came to my mind. I just wish we had time to try it out."

"No such luck, I'm spoken for the rest of this afternoon and evening," Russell added jokingly. "As long as I remember it's there, that's what counts."

Colonel Smith-Reeves departed the hanger area and Russell returned to his pre-flight preparations. Operation Angerona was scheduled to lift off in fewer than nine hours.

* * *

For nearly twenty years, Bernard Masson operated his cheese production and sales business in the picturesque southern French City of *Pau*. He loved the wooded areas and enjoyed its proximity to the majestic *Pyrenees* Mountains, France's majestic natural boundary with Spain. Around *Pau*, all the ingredients for his cheese products were plentiful, and skilled labor was readily available. Masson's natural business sense soon caused his cheese business to flourish. For several years prior to the outbreak of the war, demand for Masson's distinctive *fromage du Pyrenees* soared affording Masson and his family the ability to live well beyond their needs.

Given his business success when the war began, it was altogether quite unlikely that 47-year old Bernard Masson became the first businessman in *Pau* to join the Resistance. A loyal Frenchman whose father had served with the French army in the Great War, Masson firmly believed the French people were sold out by Marshall Petain and the unpopular Vichy government. Moreover, Masson was a keen supporter of Charles de Gaulle and passionately felt it his patriotic duty to help the Free French effort in any way possible. Bernard quickly grew to despise the Vichy puppets that he felt always buckled under to the Germans and found himself cringing whenever anyone mentioned the pact that bound France and Germany together. Initially, he seriously considered leaving France and joining Free French forces outside the country, He came to a more reasonable decision that he could do more good staying in *Pau* where his business contacts and professional experience were without match. Once he made the initial overtones, the Resistance accepted him enthusiastically. The group promptly accorded him responsibility for most Resistance activities within his local area. In the beginning, German presence in and around *Pau* was light and Bernard Masson found it absurdly easy to accomplish whatever jobs the Resistance directed to him.

To further his military skills, Bernard Masson also took it upon himself to learn about the use of firearms. He enlisted the help of his oldest and most trusted friend who was an accomplished marksman. Masson told his friend that he was not in a position to say why he needed to learn about guns. Without question, his friend agreed to help. He took Bernard to a secluded area outside of *Pau* and taught him how to fire a number of different weapons with great precision. Bernard was a fast learner, and as time passed, a highly proficient natural marksman. What's more, as his friend's political viewpoints became evident and paralleled those of his own, Bernard Masson brought his old friend into the service of the French Resistance.

On one occasion, after the pair had been practicing for several months, his friend confessed to Bernard.

"If I teach you much more and you get any better at shooting, you will be more proficient than me."

Bernard took the comment to heart and continued his progress. He soon found that he was able to produce excellent results with most guns, but particularly with a special pistol. The gun was an older French *Lebel M1892*. The gun rapidly became Bernard's favorite firearm.

Bernard's instructor was a former member of the French Foreign Legion and the pistol had been his issue while on duty in Equatorial Africa. It was an 8mm weapon that carried six bullets in its chambered cylinder. It weighed an ounce over a pound and was slightly over 9 inches long. Produced at the *Manufacture d'Arms de St. Etienne,* the *Lebel* had been a mainstay of the French military for over fifty years.

"This is a trusty weapon Bernard," his mentor initially explained. "It might be old, but it is always reliable. Ammunition is plentiful and as long as you keep it well oiled, it will never let you down."

Bernard Masson remembered feeling the weapon in his palm and realizing at once that he had found an instrument that was completely comfortable to his touch. The first time he fired the *Lebel M1892* he hit his target squarely. He felt a level of comfort that was lacking in other guns he had fired. Masson also decided to become an expert in the handling and firing of the old *Lebel*.

When his instructions were completed, Bernard's old friend made the weapon a graduation present to his star student. From that point on, the weapon was always in Bernard Masson's immediate possession.

He had begun carrying the pistol with him whenever necessary. This was a result of the intensification of Resistance activities in *Pau* and throughout the entire region.

The Germans became aware of the fact that many refugees, downed fliers and allied agents were passing through *Pau* and the surrounding region attempting to reach Spain. The Wehrmacht dispatched active German troops to the locale and greatly increased security precautions throughout the region. Even though this area was part of unoccupied France, German troops became actively engaged in attempting to stop the flow of refugees.

Masson worked diligently to expand his Resistance network and eventually became the final link for many in the long road to freedom. It was a road that began as far North as Belgium and Holland and for some as far as Germany itself.

From his first contact with the Resistance, Bernard Masson rarely considered the danger involved, considering as he did the work to be the patriotic duty of any true Frenchman.

He had met Victor several times and always came away impressed by Bonde's assertive personality. As his group's activities escalated and his own role became more essential to the entire movement, Bernard Masson ineludibly developed a deep fondness for his leader. Infused with his initial success, Masson had confided to Victor that he was prepared for any assignment offered him. The degree of difficulty was secondary.

Victor was equally enthused by Bernard Masson. When Operation Angerona first came to Bonde's attention, the Resistance leader immediately recognized that a large amount of the final responsibility for the operation would ultimately be placed upon Bernard Masson's broad shoulders.

Bonde was confident that Bernard Masson could handle the job.

* * *

Brian Russell wasn't fully convinced he was able to absorb all of the mission's detailed pre-briefing, but conceded to himself that he was completely caught up in the broad spectacle of the event. It was mind boggling to Russell that so many people had been involved to see that Operation Angerona went off without a hitch. The fact that he *was* Operation Angerona didn't occur to him in the least.

Having never participated in a wartime operational operation, he admitted to himself he was part petrified and part exhilarated, and was experiencing both sensations at the same time. The feeling brought to Russell's an old movie. Gary Cooper as Sergeant York flashed by Russell's recollection, a film in which the actors reassured each other that it was best to be scared going into battle. Russell felt his current situation would fit neatly into the plot lines of any old movie.

Operation Angerona's pre-flight briefings reassured everyone that the Allied meteorologists were right on the mark. The weather this July evening was proving to be next to wonderful.

Russell also took note of the fact that the crew of the Lancaster bomber that would tow his glider was also in attendance from their home base at Fiskerton. Russell observed the crew's interaction with each other, and was pleased by their loose, casual attitude and seeming indifference to the job ahead.

The Lancaster pilot, Royal Air Force Flight Lieutenant Byron Master, came up to Russell at the conclusion of the meeting.

"So you're the bloke everyone's talking about, the chap we are to pull all the way into Central France."

"Yes, sorry to put you to all the trouble."

"It's not actually all *that* much trouble."

"I didn't mean it that way."

"I know you didn't, I was just having a poke with you," Flight Lieutenant Master smiled.

Russell felt a bit foolish. "Sorry, I guess this whole thing has me wound up tighter than I thought."

"It is probably better that way. What, with the God-awful crap we all go through on a daily basis, we are always searching for a way to loosen things up a bit. My crew has seen it all and has witnessed a number of our chums go down in flames. The more missions we fly, we know the closer *we* get to that eventuality. Each mission becomes a fine line between the uncomfortable and the intolerable. My job is to fly the plane and try and keep everyone in one piece, both physically and mentally."

"I didn't realize..." Russell's voice trailed off.

"But things are looking up," Master looked Russell in the eye and grinned. "We have a long overdue leave after tonight's mission. I will be able to go home and spend some time with my family. It will be the same for my entire crew. They are all pretty excited."

"I hope you all enjoy your time off." It was all that Russell could think to say.

"Right. And Captain. I will try and take it easy on your glider tonight. No sudden stops or anything like that." They shook hands as Master laughed again and headed off.

Russell watched in envy as the blonde aviator rejoined his crew. It was only then that Russell noticed that every one of the fliers surrounding Master appeared to be younger than the aircraft commander.

Three hours later, Operation Angerona commenced in earnest. After a discussion with GPR Operations, it was mutually agreed to have the pilot cut back on the takeoff power as much as feasible so as to assist the glider in lifting off cleanly. The fact that the bomber was at less than full power meant that there would be less turbulence in the bomber's wake.

This action would be no simple undertaking since the Lancaster was fully loaded for its bombing mission. Considering his options, Flight Lieutenant Master felt he could do it safely, even if it meant pushing his bomber's flying envelope further than normal. In the end, the decision was the young officer's call to make, and was left at that.

Russell was greatly reassured after his encounter with Master. He felt a great deal of respect for the English pilot's professional approach, to both his job and his crew.

As Russell made his way out of the briefing, a familiar face in the person of Colonel Maurice Buckmaster was waiting.

Russell saluted, and Buckmaster returned his salute.

"Captain, there is one last piece of business before you go."

"Yes, sir?" Russell questioned.

"We just received these details a few hours ago. I felt they were important enough that I wanted to deliver them to you personally."

Russell was impressed with his superior's gesture but remained silent.

"When you land near *Domme*, you are to place the paintings in the hands of a Resistance fellow whose code name is Georges, and no one else. It is Georges' responsibility to see that the paintings are later exchanged for the real ones. He is very knowledgeable in these matters and will be personally known to the people at the *Chateau de Montal*. We felt it would make more sense to the individuals at the Chateau to see someone they already knew. It all seems to fit together a little tighter. Do you understand?"

"Perfectly, sir."

"Well then, is there anything else I can do for you?

"No sir. I think you've just about thought of everything."

"I certainly hope so Captain Russell. Best of luck to you all and God's good speed."

"Thank you, sir."

*　*　*

René Huyghe examined the note from Mother Therese-Santenay, the Abbess at the *Abbey du Loc Dieu*, which had finally found its way to him. From the information contained in the note, Huyghe was now aware that his earlier premonitions concerning the Germans and their interest in the *Louvre's* paintings were indeed correct. Ever since he had made the initial decision to place the museum's art treasures in hiding, Rene Huyghe knew the Germans innate greediness would not allow them to give up owning the treasures. Huyghe had considered this from the beginning, and the note in his hand held practical proof that the Germans were presently involved in a specific attempt to locate the paintings.

What still bothered Huyghe was the degree and quality of information about the treasures the Germans actually possessed and the means they intended to employ to pursue it. His mind raced through a number of improbable possibilities without reaching a conclusion. Rene Huyghe scolded himself for harboring such non-productiveness in his thoughts. Such thinking on his part was a waste of time, since he was now unable to control even one of these eventualities.

He thought back to Jean Moulin and his fervent plan, a scheme that René Huyghe had initially believed somewhat unnecessary. He admitted to himself that he was now greatly relieved that the operation called Angerona was scheduled to begin shortly. In this case, René Huyghe was genuinely pleased to admit he was wrong.

* * *

The first object Russell checked when he arrived at the plane on mission night was the rounded cylinder securely fastened to the inside of the aircraft. When Russell adjusted the cylinder top, he assured himself the forged paintings were included within the tube. Next, he completed the checklist given him by the GPR Regiment Operations Officer who had been waiting for him near the hangar entrance. Deliberately and carefully covering the list, U.S. Army Air Force Captain Brian Russell was ready to embark. He was sure the adventure would be the most exhilarating journey of his still youthful life.

He wanted to board the craft immediately, but too much time remained prior to his mission's actual departure point to render that wish inopportune. Russell's eyes swept the airfield. An unusual amount of lively activity was apparent throughout the area. He quickly reminded himself that his mission wasn't the only one scheduled for this night. Another Glider Pilot Regiment mission, one that would utilize a great deal more manpower than Operation Angerona, was also approaching readiness.

Russell sighed inwardly and resigned himself to having to wait. He glanced pensively at the operations officer who was still standing alongside his glider. The older RAF officer, realizing Russell's anxiety to get going, shot back a sympathetic glance.

The southbound train arrived on time into *Sarlat-la-Caneda*, a fact that Andre Faboul considered a good omen. Like most Frenchmen, Faboul was aware that most trains operated by the French national railroad SNCF, were routinely late. Faboul recalled the Resistance instructions he had been given, planning to follow them to the letter. He descended from the train and moved to an area dominated by a small platform immediately outside the station. He lingered there, browsing through a newspaper he had brought with him, for about ten minutes. At length, an older, slightly bent woman, holding a knitted handbag on her arm, approached Faboul.

After exchanging the appropriate passwords, he accompanied her for two blocks where she stopped in front of a small plaster fronted building that appeared to be a house. The woman motioned Faboul around the back of the structure while she entered the front door with a brass key that she produced from her handbag.

Faboul walked around the dwelling where he encountered a small stone barn with double doors ajar. Faboul looked back over his shoulder at the first structure just as the old woman appeared at the rear door and motioned Faboul to go into the barn.

He approached the open barn door somewhat apprehensively. He made out the figures of four men standing inside the dimly lit enclosure. Faboul nodded to the group and was beckoned closer by one of the figures. As his eyes became accustomed to the lighting, Andre Faboul was able to see the interior of the barn more clearly, including a rectangular form immediately adjacent to the four men. He focused on the spot and was somewhat startled as he identified the object. Resting alongside the four men was small brown wooden pine casket, propped up from the ground by a pair of crudely fashioned wooden horses!

One of the men stepped forward and extended his hand.

"Welcome, Monsieur, we are your colleagues for your journey. My name is Antoine."

Faboul smiled and shook his hand. He remembered to use the code name he had been given before he mounted the train in Paris.

"It is a pleasure to be here," he said a bit awkwardly, hoping to sound as positive as possible. "You should call me Georges." He next took care to shake the hands of the other men standing in the barn.

"We had better get started," Antoine spoke up, gesturing at some nearby bicycles leaning against the barn's inside wall along with a small four-wheeled cart. "The road toward *Domme* is fairly demanding and will take us some time to reach our destination."

Antoine reached inside his jacket and produced a small piece of fabric.

"Here, we must all put these around our arms." He handed Faboul a black cotton armband, which Faboul rolled up and around his left arm. "After all, we are all in mourning for our departed friend."

Faboul shot a quick glance at Antoine and then back at the casket, but said nothing.

After a moment, the group started on its journey, with Antoine assuming the lead. The procession departed *Sarlat-la-Caneda* and in a few minutes reached the outskirts of the town. They pedaled almost due south. Their final destination was the verdant fields alongside the *Dordogne* River just north of the elevated city of *Domme*.

According to Russell's dimly visible watch it was nearly midnight and the steady drone of the Lancaster's big engines diminished Russell's ability to concentrate. According to the pre-briefing, this period was the critical part of the takeoff. It was the point in time when the bomber actually started rolling down the runway and commenced picking up speed. Nighttime, along with the associated lack of light made the situation all the more difficult. Fortunately, Russell had experienced nighttime take offs before and knew what was coming.

His glider had been towed to the end of the runway by a small lorry specially equipped for the task, and then attached to the rear of the bomber. The glider's position was therefore out of the prop wash unless the Lancaster's nose drifted to one side or the other. Since this was a known problem, Flight Lieutenant Master had assured Russell that, as the bomber's pilot, he would definitely keep his aircraft's direction as straight as possible.

Russell felt a sudden jerk as the short towline stiffened and the glider started forward directly behind the Lancaster. The pair slowly picked up speed and Russell experienced a series of bumps as air slid under the glider's wings and the glider attempted to lift itself. For what seemed like an eternity to the young pilot, the full-throated wind buffeted Russell as he wrestled with the glider's yoke to keep his craft as close to the ground as possible. Finally, with engines straining and rubber screeching, the earth released its hold on the lumbering machine and the Lancaster began its rise.

Russell gradually allowed his glider to lift in tandem along with the bomber. It had been agreed that Flight Lieutenant Master would manage the Lancaster's slow ascent as much as possible, a notion that would further reduce the drag on the glider.

The Lancaster painstakingly increased its altitude and some twelve minutes later leveled off at two thousand five hundred feet and initiated a slow turn to the northeast.

This guy is really good, thought Russell. *With all the extra weight he is carrying his plane must steer like a stiff old truck, but thank God he's managed to make it quite easy for me.*

He turned his attention to the nighttime sky and to the total absence of any ground lights. He tapped his control panel compass and was happy to see the needle pointing to 090, the pre-briefed course for the flight.

Another ten minutes passed by and suddenly Russell was delighted to see a pair of Spitfire Mark II's join their formation's left wing as fighter escorts. The lead Spitfire gently rolled his wings and gave the thumbs up sign to Russell, and then another comparable sign to the Lancaster pilot. The escort would stay with the Lancaster and its passenger as long as possible. Hopefully, that break-off time wouldn't arrive before Russell's glider was situated well into central France.

An incredible sentience engulfed Russell with the appearance of the Spitfires. He was now part of a proficient military operation involved on a mission that his superiors felt was crucial to the core and character of the French people. A successful completion to his undertaking would arguably assist the French nation in beginning its cultural healing at the conclusion of the war.

While Russell was fully aware of the positives involved in his impending adventure, he was also astutely conscious of the task's hazardous potential. The youthful pilot knew he could be called on to die in order to make Operation Angerona successful. Captain Brian Russell was prepared to make that sacrifice.

*   *   *

For the third night in succession, Christine Allard found it a real challenge to attempt to sleep. She lay in her bed, alternately tossing and turning. She was unable to find a position that suited her comfortably.

Her cousin Lucille slept in the same room with Christine in the small apartment, and, at one point during the night woke up. Lucille perceived Christine's restlessness, and spoke to her younger relative. More than a year ago, Lucille's husband Claude had left to fight with the Free French. Christine was the first guest who had slept in Lucille's house since Claude's departure. Lucille had decided the event was most enjoyable. Having another person around her home, particularly someone like Christine who had always been one of her favorite relatives, was heartening .

"So, you are having trouble sleeping again?"

"I am so sorry...I did not intend to keep you awake Luci."

"It is all right, would you like to talk about it? Lucille paused for a second. "Is it a man?"

Christine laughed softly and said, "If only it were that simple."

"It is *never* that simple. After all, this war has made a shambles of all our lives. My poor Claude..."

"Yes, I know to what extent you must miss him. You two were only married for such a short time before he left."

"Just over a year. Right now, that does not seem especially long to me. When I look back at it, it seems as if our time together was only a few weeks long."

"Have you heard from him at all?"

"Only once, just after he left. Claude managed to post a letter to me. All the local men who supported the Free French way of thinking were banding together to form an actual army unit. Claude was a bit older and had just been promoted to Lieutenant. He was so proud and I was so happy for him. He was doing what he felt he had to do. Soon after that, the Vichy government issued a decree that censored all incoming mail. I have not heard from him again."

Christine waited as her cousin paused. Lucille was very near tears. Christine stared as a reluctant stillness engulfed the small room.

Christine pulled her cousin toward her and patted her on the back. "Claude will come home and you will have him back," she reassured.

"Yes, I suppose so." Lucille said warily, choking back her emotions.

Christine spoke again. "And, I should stop feeling sorry for myself about something as trivial as not being able to sleep. After all, I have been sent here with specific instructions…" Christine stopped in mid-sentence, realizing she had revealed more than she intended.

Lucille was now recovered and interpreted her cousin's silence.

"Well, whenever you decide, you can always come to me… we have always been able to talk before."

Christine calmed herself and stretched out on the bed next to her relative. Moments later, she was finally able to doze off into a peaceful, deep sleep.

Chapter Eight

The winding road from *Sarlat-la-Caneda* toward *Domme* passed through a number of undulating short hills. Faboul was experiencing more than a little difficulty in keeping up with the others. His normal bicycle trips around the flat terrains of *Paris* had not prepared him for the climbs he was experiencing. His calves ached from the additional strain of constant pedaling up the winding road's sizable inclines.

Antoine signaled for a stop in front of one of the little houses the procession passed on the road. Antoine knew the residents of the dwelling and called the halt just long enough to place a hurried call to another Resistance ally who was waiting in a nearby town named *la Roque Gageac*, somewhat closer to *Domme*. By means of the call, Antoine made sure the additional preparations for Russell's landing outside *Domme* had been started.

Since his group had not been making the time he had hoped for due to Faboul's slowness, Antoine's alternative was to have his other operatives start the landing preparations prior to his band's arrival. Back on the road again, Antoine attempted to keep up a pace that would put them near *Domme* about a half hour later than he first planned.

He looked over as Andre Faboul gritted his teeth once again as the bicycles started another small climb. Antoine admired Faboul's determination to keep up with the group and silently willed his new ally the ability to overcome his aching calves and increasingly sore back.

Antoine's phone contact brought three additional Resistance fighters to help prepare the fields. A series of small fires would serve as beacons for Russell's glider. Their plan was simple enough and required the men to step off twenty-meter intervals. Small fires were placed about thirty meters apart.

The men had brought sufficient firewood with them and cans of kerosene to douse the wood and insure immediate flames. Keeping the distances squared wasn't all that easy in the darkness and the leader of the small group kept moving the piles until he was comfortable with the spacing.

* * *

Hanging suspended from the Lancaster wasn't really that difficult for Russell's glider, even considering the constant buffeting the craft received from the bomber's head winds. The glider's sleek aerodynamics steadied the craft to some degree and accorded Russell a relatively even flight. Russell adjusted the straps on his parachute a little tighter and silently prayed that he would never feel the sensation of a bail out. To his knowledge and that of his compatriots at Glider Pilot Regiment, no one had ever needed to bail out of a glider. Those who had encountered problems in the air choose instead to land the craft rather than bail out. But Russell had been equipped with a parachute to cover any eventuality, a fact that Russell really didn't mind. When the subject of a parachute first came up, Russell decided that the equipment was intended to provide the GPR peace of mind and left it at that. He returned his concentration to his gauges and realized that a change in heading on his compass signaled the fact that the flight had now successfully crossed the English Channel and was now crossing the French coastline.

To Russell's surprise, the Spitfires covering the bomber angled up and Russell mused to himself, *they are probably off in search of a possible intruder. Must be wonderful to fly a fighter like the Spitfire. All that power under your control.*

Minutes later the fighters joined back up on each side of the Lancaster, in a position slightly to the rear. Operation Angerona's mission pre-briefing conceded the possibility of the flight being intercepted by German night fighters, but the intelligence officer conducting the briefing could not specify when or where. If such a condition were to occur, such action would probably force the Lancaster to release Russell prematurely ... and Russell didn't fancy that considering what would happen if that scenario arose. With the salty English Channel safely behind him, Russell breathed a bit easier.

The instrument panel altimeter showed three thousand feet and Russell was positive he could see darker forms below. To his rear, lay the rudiments of a large landfall, as the small formation crossed the coast of southwestern France. The moon was visible in its nocturnal entirety and few clouds were apparent as far as Russell's view to the east and south could see.

Bracing himself upright, he stretched as best he could. There wasn't an abundance of room inside the cockpit and this was the first time since the flight departed that Russell had considered his discomfort.

He reminded himself again of the planned flight path and calculated that he must be somewhere above France's *Normandy* Peninsula. They were in the vicinity of the city of *Nantes*, the first identification point the bomber crew would use as a reference. The Lancaster's heading was now 170 degrees indicating a direction almost directly to the south. His altimeter continued to climb slowly and Russell realized the Lancaster was now approaching the prescribed release level of 4,500 feet.

Minutes later, he was still concentrating on his instruments when all hell broke loose.

A German night fighter plane, a Messerschmitt Bf 110E, that Russell was able to recognize from the briefing silhouettes he had studied, dived and fired at the formation from above and to the port of his glider. Russell was in a perfect position to see the fighter who flashed by. The Messerschmitt's tracer bullets spewed wildly over the entire port side of the Lancaster, spraying it loosely. The firing stream luckily missed the glider as the swift German aircraft chose instead to direct its fire at the trailing Spitfire fighters. At least one of the bullets from the Bf110's 20mm cannons found a home in the engine casing of the lead Spitfire that caused the engine to abruptly start trailing a thin line of smoke. The fighter's pilot labored to keep his craft at the bomber's altitude for several moments until the engine choked. The subsequent larger eruption of smoke caused the Spitfire to fall into a slow downward spiral.

The crippled Spitfire quickly fell below and well aft of Russell. Russell monitored the scene as best he could until the Spitfire disappeared below his field of vision. At the very last instant, Russell thought he caught a glimpse of the pilot struggling to break out of the cockpit in an attempt to parachute to the ground, but he wasn't completely sure.

The other Spitfire wasted no time in turning in an attempt to follow the German intruder who wisely turned away from the formation. In a few seconds the two were invisible, lost in the ebony darkness and boundless reaches of nighttime.

Russell turned his attention back to the Lancaster above him where he decided something was definitely wrong. The left engine of the bomber was producing a thin trail of smoke, which widened itself even as Russell observed. Something seemed awry in the cockpit itself as the huge bird shuddered and shook, struggling to maintain its altitude and heading. Russell rechecked his map and thanked God that the attack had not occurred ten minutes sooner. A few more minutes on this course and he would reach the vicinity of his drop off point.

The smoke trail from the left engine expanded itself further and continued to stream backward, causing Russell to conclude the Lancaster was in really dire trouble. The thought crossed his mind as to how long the plane could continue on. Russell prepared himself for the imminent disconnect from the bomber. He glanced quickly at his map for a final time and hoped he been correct in calculating his position and bearings. He lauded Flight Lieutenant Master and the Lancaster crew who had persevered on course despite their bomber's mounting problems. He checked his altimeter and found he had lost almost three hundred feet.

For another sixty seconds, Russell pondered what to do. He had no way of knowing if the bomber had actually reached the vicinity of the city of *Limouges*, the initial dropping off point for his glider.

Then, almost as if by magic, the warning light on Russell's instrument panel, indicating momentary separation, blinked on. The Lancaster was signaling that it was time for release. Russell counted out fifteen seconds and finally pushed the panel lever that released him from the Lancaster. He looked in silence as the bomber immediately executed a left turn and began dropping altitude. From its general appearance, the Lancaster seemed to be losing its fight to survive.

Russell was again both terrified and exhilarated at the same time. He forced himself to concentrate on his own dilemma and his flight toward rendezvous with the French Resistance. While he was fortunate to have caught a descent thermal almost immediately after release, he had no way of knowing how long it would last. Equally importantly, Russell desperately needed to identify the *Limouges/Toulouse* road that was the crucial identification point for his flight to be successful. If he were able to properly distinguish the road, Operation Angerona's planners felt Russell would then be able to follow it southward and make an accurate turn west. The glider would then expect to follow the majestic *Dordogne* until reaching the landing site above *Domme*.

Russell also puzzled over the German fighter who had fired on them. Had the Luftwaffe pilot had sufficient time to recognize his glider, and if so, what consequences could he anticipate? Happily, Russell had not seen the German fighter since its initial pass, nor had he seen what had happened to the second Spitfire who had left the formation in pursuit of the attacker.

Russell found a new thermal that helped assist his ascent and allowed him to continue along his route. He decided to proceed under the assumption that the point at which he released his glider from the Lancaster was sufficiently near enough to the preset drop off point so as not to adversely affect his new heading.

He peered out into the darkness and then gently pushed the control stick back to conserve as much altitude as possible. Russell was now aware that the most difficult flying function of his flight would begin. He also hoped that the Resistance would be able to help him along by lighting signal fires along his route.

* * *

At his company's small warehouse in *Pau*, Bernard Masson assisted his employees in finishing crating a large order of cheeses that would be shipped tomorrow to a customer in *Bordeaux*. Prior to the war, he employed any number of workers who would have handled a menial task such as this, but recently he had been forced to perform the chore himself. In the past months, many of Bernard's workers had left *Pau* and other similar cities in France to fight for the Free French or in one of the numerous para-military groups that had arisen within the country. An equally large number of the best men had been unlucky enough to be conscripted by the Nazis to work in Germany's war factories. A smaller but growing number had left the area and had never been heard from again.

Considering the circumstances, Masson really didn't mind boxing the cheeses that insured the continued survival of his family business.

In addition, another crucial event transpired earlier in Bernard Masson's day. Early that same morning, the Resistance notified Masson through a coded message that a significant operation was forthcoming and that he should be prepared to act on it in the near future.

The message enthused Bernard Masson. His assignment was about to begin.

*   *   *

Luftwaffe Hauptmann Wilhelm Heintz tapped the shoulder of his radio operator, Unteroffizier Bruno Taubensee, who was seated next to him in the cockpit. He then banked his Messerschmitt Bf 110E back toward his Staffel's (squadron) home base at *St. Dizier*. The twin-engine night fighter was fast approaching its maximum range of 1000 kilometers and, while the fuel warning light on his control panel was still green, Heintz knew it would change to red in the near future. Heintz felt fortunate that his temporary orders had placed him for the past few days at the airfield outside *Château Roux* or he would never have had the opportunity of running into the British formation. By carefully conserving his remaining fuel, Heintz hoped the Bf 110E might just make it home. Running low on fuel was an aircraft flaw Captain Heintz and his fellow fighter pilots in the Luftwaffe always encountered with *any* Messerschmitt fighter. In the pilots' opinions, all fighters were improperly designed for long flights.

His flight had thus far been eventful and Heintz was elated that he had been successful in shooting down one of the Spitfires. He knew his newer E-model Messerschmitt had several advantages over most British fighters. These included new Lichtenstein BC radars and also the revolutionary night color scheme that made his aircraft practically invisible at night. The color scheme involved a light green background crosshatched in darker green lines, making somewhat of a blocked, pattern less shape interspersed with random green blocks.

But his squadron's positioning at *St. Dizier* in Northern France brought him few chances to prove his fighter's superiority. Nevertheless, Heintz would seek his right seater's acknowledgment of the kill, even though their Bf 110E Zestorer wasn't able to stay around long enough for a full substantiation of the incident.

Besides, the whole episode happened so rapidly.

The fires from the Lancaster's engines first attracted Taubensee's attention in the darkened sky. He was quickly able to paint the large aircraft with the aircraft's new Lichtenstein BC. After seeing the target on the radar display, his eagerness to intercept the intruder caused Heintz to nearly commit a serious error. That occurred when an excited Heintz first pushed his night fighter into a steep dive toward the bomber, the Messerschmitt's optimum firing stance.

On the radar, the Spitfires weren't as visible as the larger plane and Heintz was forced to react swiftly when he caught sight of the deadly cover aircraft. Instead of breaking off his pass at a normal interval he continued for another six to eight seconds and kept his fingers on the 20mm cannons that were spewing out as many rounds as possible. He knew his rounds were headed in the right general direction from the tracers he could see, but was amazed when Funker (radio operator) Unteroffizier Bruno Taubensee reported smoke from one of the Spitfires.

It was then that Heintz realized he was extremely lucky to have damaged one of the escorts on a single pass. His initial intent was to get the Lancaster, and only his quick reaction to the presence of the Spitfires escort, along with the additional rounds he instinctively discharged, caused the Spitfire's eventual demise.

Heintz was totally unaware that he had also dealt a deathblow to the lumbering Lancaster. Since the remaining Spitfire was hell bent on evening the score, it took all of Heintz's flying ability and the Spitfire's rapidly worsening fuel situation for the British fighter to give up the chase and return to his base.

Both German aviators were also surprised by the fact that the British bomber was following a curious southerly route when they first engaged the Lancaster. It was the first time either officer could recall a bomber heading almost due south under escort of two Spitfires. Unterofficer Taubensee was also disturbed by another fact that kept resurfacing in his mind. When their night fighter flashed by the bomber and escorts, the young radio operator thought he perceived another craft. The craft was much smaller, flying immediately behind the Lancaster.

The entire episode had happened in a matter of seconds!

Luftwaffe Unteroffizier Bruno Taubensee made a mental note to report the unusual sighting when his Bf 110E returned to its base at *St. Dizier.*

* * *

After flying his prearranged heading for another five minutes, Russell started to agonize. The ground below was pitch black with very few lights showing, even with the luminance available from the moon. Russell was forced to weave and adjust to the available thermals and because of his frequent motion steadily lost altitude. The aircraft was now at 3000 feet and if he were unable to reclaim some altitude, he would *never* make it safely to the vicinity of *Domme.*

Several minor waterways became apparent with the aid of the moonlight, but nothing substantial enough to help the fledgling aviator pinpoint his position. He banked a little in each direction, but was unable to distinguish anything in the darkness.

He looked down and checked his watch.

Even with the Luftwaffe night fighter encounter, Captain Brian Russell saw that he was still effectively on schedule.

* * *

It was well after nine and already dark by the time Antoine and his men finally reached the banks of the *Dordogne,* nearly an hour later than he planned. He searched across the opposite bank of the river and thought he could make out the outline of the mountain top city of *Domme* in the distance. Antoine couldn't be sure, for there were no lights visible to identify the city. He mentioned to a completely exhausted Andre Faboul to keep an eye out in the general direction of the city of *Domme* and Faboul readily agreed.

Antoine was happy with his cohorts' choice of a landing field. They had selected a long pasture about three hundred meters from the road that was rimmed by a tree line highlighted by a long row of small trees. He directed his men to assist the other Resistance fighters who were already preparing the beacon fires for the glider's approach.

Faboul glimpsed at his watch and offered Antoine his silent gratitude for insuring the group arrived at its intended destination.

Antoine acknowledged the gesture and returned to his work. Additional details needed to be dealt with if the landing site was to be made ready.

* * *

Russell was now becoming frantic. Even though he had managed to steal back a little altitude, his altimeter indicated 3400 feet; he also sensed his predicament was rapidly deteriorating. He turned to port to gain visibility and a glint of light near the horizon caught his eye. The light was faint enough in the darkened night sky but to Russell the illumination seemed like a huge fireball in the otherwise black night.

He peered intently and suddenly moonlight illuminated a band of water twisting serenely in the blackened night. It was headed north to south and seemed too small to suit his purpose. A river, perhaps, but too small to be the one he was looking for.

Russell continued his search for the *Dordogne*. It was entirely possible he could cross the huge river without ever seeing the *Limouges/Toulouse* Road. That would present a different set of problems, which Russell chose not to consider at the moment. He must still regard himself as following the proper course, and that prospect meant that the majestic river would still be ahead, silently waiting for him in the moonlight. Russell started to reduce his altitude by pushing forward slightly on the stick. His altitude decreased accordingly.

Russell also altered his course directly toward the light source and held his breath. A minute later, he quietly swished over a series of three distinct fires he was clearly able to see, burning at the widest point of a straight section of what appeared to be a major road. Some 500 yards or so past the fires was a bridge that crossed a relatively wide river.

The fires had been started a half-hour earlier on the *Limoges/Toulouse* road by additional members of the local French Resistance. The bridge Russell just crossed over spanned the *Dordogne* River and was Russell's correct ground mark for his turn to the west. Without hesitation, he gripped the glider's yoke and softly executed a starboard turn. He could now follow the river directly to his intended landing spot.

*   *   *

Inside the City of *Domme*, eighty-year-old Louis Herault made his way into the antiquated building that served as the city's power source. For the past fifty-five years, ever since electricity first came to Domme, it had been Louis Herault's responsibility to insure the mountain top city had adequate electricity with which to operate. Accordingly, Louis took great pride in accomplishing his task.

Due to its unique location, all of *Domme's* electrical power was of necessity channeled from the valley floor below into a single building. It was then subdivided into four main grids, each of which served a particular quadrant of *Domme*. Another piece of electrical equipment separated the city's outside lighting system from the power needed to serve its other needs. The telephone call Louis received several hours ago from his old friend Antoine Bourg was a follow-up to a similar call the old man had received several days earlier.

At that time, Louis had agreed to flip the grid lever that controlled the outside lights to *Domme's* northern quadrant, thereby illuminating that entire section of the city. While Louis understood that his action violated the Vichy government's blackout laws, Louis Herault confided that he was much more interested in doing his part to help his old friend than he was about the Vichy Government.

Antoine Bourg had not informed his aged acquaintance of the reason for needing the lights, nor had Louis even bothered to ask. Besides, Louis knew he would be fast asleep in his bed if anyone came to investigate. He pushed the lever forward that controlled the lights, turned and exited the building, making sure he closed the ancient unlocked door to the building behind him. The door to the building had never possessed a lock since it was initially constructed.

Some two plus miles below the city of *Domme*, Andre Faboul was startled when a number of lights suddenly appeared in the sky, apparently suspended by some inexplicable force. He walked swiftly over to Antoine and pointed out the illumination.

"Right on time," Antoine mused, "that should give our pilot something to really home in on."

Faboul stared back at the lights for several moments more.

The illumination was truly a sign from heaven.

*   *   *

Back at Glider Pilot Regiment, General Barclay, and Colonels Buckmaster and Smith-Reeves waited in the radio room by the side of one of the regiment's radio operators. It was unusual for Barclay to leave London but he felt that Operation Angerona and its consequences warranted his actions. A seated RAF airman finished copying the transmission and handed it to the General.

Barclay glanced at the paper and cleared his throat.

"Bloody marvelous. Simply, bloody marvelous," Barclay intoned, his voice laden with frustration.

The other two officers stared at their leader and glimpsed at each other, consciously aware of what seemed to be dire impending news.

"Bad tidings, gentlemen," Barclay began. "This message says a German night fighter jumped the flight shortly before the glider's scheduled release point. During the engagement, one of the Spitfire escorts bought it and, according to our intelligence, so did the Lancaster. The Lancaster pilot was killed but the co-pilot managed to keep the bomber flying for several minutes.

During that period the aircraft was able to radio back that the remainder of the crew was able to bail out before she went down. They will have a bloody hard time escaping the Germans if they happen to survive the jump.

The only positive note was that the fighter attack occurred well within France and the Lancaster was able to release Russell quite close to his designated drop point.

The officers shot concerned looks to each other, but said nothing.

Finally, Colonel Smith-Reeves broke the silence. He fingered his waxed mustache, which was expertly bent around to produce a perfect circle.

"Considering what we have just learned, our Captain Russell will have to be most fortunate to make it to his precise landing site. Looking at the positive, I prefer to consider what will happen if he somehow *does* make it to the spot.

Then, of course, there is the matter of the following few days. He is, as we are all aware, a very competent young man. But, he must be blessed if this operation is to be successful and we are to ever see him again."

"I have always felt that Russell is the sort of person who makes his own good fortune," Colonel Buckmaster added with a degree of certainty. "And, do not forget he has the complete resources of the Resistance behind him."

"You are both quite correct in what you say," Barclay added lucidly. "I sincerely hope both of your opinions prove to be correct. Will all our efforts be enough? Only time and the dictates of God will tell." Both Buckmaster and Smith-Reeves nodded their agreement in hesitant silence.

*   *   *

Russell's confidence was escalating as he neatly executed a right hand turn to a 270-degree heading, which turned his glider in the general direction of *Domme*. His mental state was much improved over the past few moments, and the luminescence of the moon allowed Russell to follow the course of the river quite easily. The actual landing plan called for Russell to initially fly over the field as a signal to light the fires the Resistance had prepared to aid him in lining up his landing. Russell would bank the glider as slowly as possible in circling the field to allow the partisans below sufficient time to light the fires.

He coasted along silently and was amazed when a series of lights suddenly came into view a distance away off his port side. These lights were different in intensity from the bonfires he had seen earlier and Russell correctly surmised that the Resistance had been successful in lighting some of the outside lights in the City of *Domme*. He adjusted his heading slightly to pass just north of the lights he was seeing.

Russell checked his altimeter. The glider was cruising steadily at 1200 feet It was an altitude Russell felt would allow him as much room as he needed to maneuver.

He looked down as the moonlight danced off several small streams, all fingers leading directly into the river beneath him.

He checked the position of the lights ahead and found they were much clearer now. He eased the glider's nose down to lose altitude and was suddenly able to make out a fairly long row of trees to his starboard. He continued to let the nose drop as his altitude decreased.

At three hundred feet, a dark expanse void of any trees appeared slightly to the port side of the glider's nose. On the ground, the sudden appearance of the eerie sight startled Faboul and spooked Antoine's men. The form streaking out of the blackened night sky straight at them was sufficiently jarring as to produce momentary chaos, but Antoine's men recovered quickly and ran to light the fires. Within twenty seconds, the entire area was blazing and brightly lit.

Russell caught the brief movement beneath him and executed an elongated 180-degree horseshoe turn designed to steer him back toward the spot he had passed over, a move that also served to lower his altitude even further. He was presently approaching 120 meters and holding steady. A tree line off his port side became visible that was quickly illuminated by the fires. Russell carefully surveyed the spectacle in front of the nose of the glider and felt all was ready for him to attempt his landing. He altered his course and slowly turned to port again and finally back toward the fires. He started down and was about 80 feet off the ground when he realized he had cut his turn too short and would probably overshoot the landing. He also lamented the fact that in his desire to line up properly, he had neglected to employ his aircraft's spoilers that would have assisted his descent without increasing his speed. He tried pulling up the control stick but gravity continued to tug him toward the earth. At twenty meters, Russell knew he must make an immediate decision or he would surely crash.

The landing now would be very tricky if Russell tried to set down anywhere in close proximity to the fires. What terrain lay beyond the boundaries of the fires was unknown to Russell, and he wasn't about to chance finding out. He continued his descent and abruptly remembered the emergency parachute device. Russell groped for the handle and grasped in firmly with his left hand. He tried for a moment to gauge its effect on his landing and quickly pulled it back toward the rear. The chute immediately deployed, filling with air.

The extra drag of the deployed parachute worked wonders and succeeded in forcing the craft downward where Captain Brian Russell was able to gently coax the nose down at a point almost a quarter mile past the twin rows of fires.

The force of the glider's unceremonious landing created a large bump as the craft touched down, then several smaller ones as it continued its rapid dance with the pasture land. When the craft finally rolled to a stop and settled unceremoniously on its left wing, Captain Brain Russell and his precious cargo were finally and firmly on French soil.

Faboul ran directly to the glider, which was listing on its left side. He helped right the craft and opened the cockpit.

"Welcome to France, Monsieur," he said beaming at the pilot.

"Can I say I am delighted to be here?" was Russell's courteous reply in perfect French.

Duly impressed, Faboul extended his hand and exclaimed, "Of course Monsieur, with great pleasure."

Captain Brian Russell alighted from the glider and shook Faboul's outstretched hand. He reached back into the cockpit and extracted the cylinder and started to offer it to Faboul.

He stopped, recalling his orders.

"And you, Monsieur. Just who are you?"

"You may call me Georges, Monsieur," Faboul replied officially, taking the cylinder in his hands. The two stepped away from the glider as Antoine and two of his men approached the craft.

Antoine next signaled to the men who were already towing the plane in the direction of the nearest stand of woods, a distance of more than two hundred yards away. His remaining men had just finished extinguishing and disbursing the fires and would soon be able to help.

"*Allons, allons,*" Antoine whispered, always mindful of the time. "We do not have all night."

Faboul glanced around in all directions, but there was no sign of any other activity. The area seemed completely deserted.

After fifteen minutes, the glider's airframe had been dismantled and camouflaged. After insuring his directions were correct, Faboul and Russell set off on foot in one direction, while Antoine and his group remounted their bicycles and started back on the long ride toward *Sarlat-la-Caneda.*

Operation Angerona was now a reality.

* * *

Faboul was relieved that Russell had finally arrived, and equally important, in one piece. He had given the young man a set of new identity papers that indicated his name was now Louis Roussell. The address and documentation indicated he was a resident of *Oloron-St. Marie,* a small town below *Pau* in the *Pyrenees* Mountains. Russell supplied photographs taken in England, which Faboul deftly affixed to the papers. Russell removed his flight suit in favor of a set of clothes that Antoine had provided upon landing. Happily for Brian Russell, the clothes fit reasonably well and made the walk more comfortable.

The pair walked swiftly, Russell thought in a southeasterly direction, attempting to cover as much distance as possible while it was still dark. An hour later, Russell began to experience a problem that no one at Special Operations Executive or Glider Pilot Regiment had remotely considered during Angerona's planning. The trouble involved the canister containing the forgeries. The cylinder proved awkward to carry due to its weight and oblong shape. Russell wondered to himself if the special materials used in making the cylinder that insured its durability also made it incredibly cumbersome to carry.

During mission preparations back at GPR, Russell had lifted the tube several times, but only for a few minutes at a time. Walking for hours toward *Cahors* over darkened French roads cradling the tube like an infant was a completely different matter. He decided to do address the difficulty as soon as the opportunity presented itself.

If time and circumstances permitted, Russell decided to take time out for a shopping expedition in *Cahors* before starting his trek to the south. It was an idea Andre Faboul suggested to Russell soon after the pair began their walk. The more he thought about it, the better Faboul's idea appealed to Brian Russell. He made a mental note to attend to it when he arrived in *Cahors*.

Faboul and Russell passed through two small towns during the night, but neither town showed any visible signs of life or any apparent activity. The road side started to fill with small houses indicating an approach to another town. During the walk, Russell and Faboul took turns carrying the canister. Sharing the chore was the only way the two men were able to carry the awkward object.

They rounded a sharp curve in the road and came face to face with a Vichy checkpoint, comprised of a personnel carrier and two soldiers. It was too late to stop without creating an incident so the pair proceeded forward.

Faboul and Russell stopped in front of the vehicle and reached for their papers. A youthful, acne-scarred Vichy militiaman, who Russell judged could not have been more than eighteen, took Russell's papers first. The young Frenchman looked directly at him, comparing the photograph to Russell. Russell smiled, attempting to lighten the atmosphere. The Vichy soldier reacted casually, and glanced at the cylinder Russell was carrying, hesitating for a long moment. Russell stiffened and his face became serious, unsure of the militiaman's next move. The youth looked into Russell's eyes but finally turned away from Russell. The youth thought better of the situation, turned around and handed his identification papers back to Russell, nodding him through. Faboul turned over his own papers and was similarly ushered through the checkpoint.

By then, Russell was already a few steps ahead of the Frenchman but waited for Faboul to catch up. Russell drew a deep breath.

"Exciting, is it not? Faboul remarked, dryly. "The pigs stop us whenever they wish."

"I wasn't sure if he intended to search the canister. He certainly looked it over for a long time."

"I believe you stared him down and managed to intimidate him a bit."

"He was very young. It wasn't all that difficult."

"It will not always be that easy," Faboul advised, "and, the soldiers might not always be Vichy militia."

Russell nodded his understanding and continued walking.

At least my papers worked thought Russell, who was also suddenly aware of just how tired he had become. *It would be great just to go to sleep if only for a short while. Fat chance of that, we must keep going at all costs.*

Chapter Nine

SS Obersturmbannfuhrer Kurt von Heltscherer conceded the fact he was missing having Sophie around. At times the soldier truly ached to return to her at his cozy flat in *Paris*. However, the German SS officer's basic instincts for survival within his organization bid him to remain in the *Midi* until something opportune happened in his quest for finding the hidden French art treasures.

He admitted to himself that French authorities had been quite astute in moving their prized artworks around *before* the German occupation. That single fact meant locating the concealed pieces would be very difficult for him. He also came to the realization that it was entirely possible that only a minute number of people within the *Louve* hierarchy were aware of the treasures' current location. That reality made his current outlook even bleaker.

It would be very unwise to call the Reichsmarschall at this point with so little progress to report; he wants quick results and so far I have little to show for all my efforts.

For the past twenty-four hours, von Heltscherer had concentrated his attention on the rationale behind the frequent movement of the art treasures by French authorities. He was now aware of how the French cultural system reacted to specific political events outside, as well as inside, its country. As political and military pressures continued to affect their country's future, French authorities had adroitly responded to those proceedings by moving their treasures to locations they believed to be the most unobtrusive. So far the German officer determined the French had been very successful.

Von Heltscherer felt his conclusions were correct and concentrated on what he knew was his most difficult task. He would now narrow down the considerable list of possible storage sites Dieter Hoven had provided him. The list contained several *hundred* locations. If this task could be accomplished expeditiously, then von Heltscherer felt he could properly start to tighten the noose. He could close in on Reichsmarschall Goring's stated goal, confiscation of the art treasures of his country's nearly vanquished ally.

There were two important reasons that caused the SS Obersturmbannfuhrer to remain in *Rodez* at Oberstleutnant Hoven's Wehrmacht headquarters.

Most importantly, the City of *Rodez* was centrally located within the area von Heltscherer hunched the paintings were being stored. The area was far removed from *Paris* and the occupied zone of France that included the close military scrutiny of the German army. The region was known as *Aveyron*. With the exception of Hoven's Wehrmacht contingent and normal Vichy rule, *Aveyron* was an area where French citizens could basically come and go as they pleased. Secondly, von Heltscherer realized that his semi-subordinate Dieter Hoven was seemingly delighted to be able to work closely with him. Hoven considered the mission of great importance to the SS.

It was apparent to von Heltscherer that Hoven went to great ends to provide whatever help von Heltscherer ordered. Such cooperation was expected, yet von Heltscherer found Hoven's attitude even more positive. It seemed plausible that an aggressive Wehrmacht field officer would want to help a high-ranking officer of the SS, but von Heltscherer's former experience in such situations usually found such willingness was often a direct result of fear or intimidation. Non-cooperation between fellow German officers in such matters was usually dealt with swiftly and judiciously.

Hoven's case was different in that it seemed to von Heltscherer that the junior officer was truly enthused about a close working relationship with him. The resulting professional bonding was also very satisfying to Kurt von Heltscherer. If his mission were to eventually succeed, a great deal of cooperation and some pure luck would be necessities.

As to his personal state, von Heltscherer found himself mentally tired and physically exhausted after his frantic travel period during which the officer crisscrossed France several times. Kurt had always felt a need for a reasonable night's sleep and as his age steadily advanced, the necessity became a priority with him.

As he departed Hoven's office, he was just alert enough to remember to bring along the Oberstleutnant's list of old chateaux and buildings in the surrounding region. These were large enough to be possible storage sites for the artwork.

Hoven had even taken the opportunity to invite his superior to join him later that evening for dinner at *Rodez*'s best restaurant, the *Cheval Noir*. But von Heltscherer found himself too fatigued to accept, and respectfully chose to decline the invitation. Von Heltscherer went directly to his room at the nearby *Hotel Le Boney*, just down the street from Hoven's office. As soon as his head hit the soft pillow von Heltscherer went immediately to sleep. He was able to ease his mind by the prospect that Hoven's list was already in his possession. He could begin ferreting it out the following day.

*   *   *

Jean Moulin wasted no time in contacting his Resistance sub-commander Victor about the Wehrmacht's recent appearance and confrontation with the Mother Superior of the *Abbey du Loc-Dieu*. Moulin immediately dispatched a detailed, coded message that reached his long-time compatriot the following day.

The message informed his old friend that he now believed that the Germans had recently set up a special SS military unit that was actively seeking the current location of the stored French art treasures. He also pointed out that the Germans had begun applying pressure on everyone within the French national museum community to acquire that information.

Moulin also warned Victor that he thought the Wehrmacht soldiers that had recently visited the *Abbey Du Loc-Dieu* were probably acting under orders from the same secret unit since the nuns had seen an SS officer with the soldiers. It was therefore highly conceivable, Moulin continued, that the Germans were still within the same vicinity of the *Abbey Du Loc-Dieu*. Moulin ended the message by stating that he was sure the SS would stop at nothing to find the paintings.

Pierre Bonde knew that he must now immediately establish a contingency plan to deal with any ensuing German pressure. Such a plan should be implemented as soon as he felt local circumstances warranted.

Moulin's message gave Bonde direct responsibility for Brian Russell's safety.

As always, Moulin closed the message with his code name, *Max*.

*   *   *

Andre Faboul and Captain Brian Russell spent the better part of the morning in reaching their ultimate destination. The place was the historic 16th Century *Chateau de Montal*. It was located some forty-five kilometers from Russell's landing site outside Domme, near the small town of *St. Cere*. Their journey was made easier during the night when a single delivery truck happened along the road they were traveling. Faboul was able to talk the driver into giving them a lift.

The brief ride allowed Andre Faboul the opportunity to think about the next aspect of his mission. Ever since receiving his instructions at the *gare* in *Paris*, Andre Faboul had pondered over this upcoming part of the operation. Faboul held concern that the actual meeting at the *Chateau de Montal* with the curator assigned to guard the paintings could prove delicate at best. He was deeply apprehensive about it occurring smoothly.

On one hand, Faboul did accept the fact that the original plan developed to protect France's national treasures was simple enough. However, Faboul was afraid that the time and circumstances involving his present mission might be difficult to explain to any man entrusted with his nation's national treasures. It would be even harder to grasp for someone who had lived in total obscurity for more than a year.

When René Huyghe felt the need to initially disperse the paintings from *Chambord* to various secret storage sites throughout France, his original plan detailed certain high-ranking museum curators to accompany the shipments. These curators were given primary responsibility for the artworks for the duration of the war. In the case of certain of the finest pieces from France's top museums, these curators were also assigned to physically remain with the paintings until the war was over.

Faboul learned from his instructions that the curator assigned the *Louvre*'s collection of premier paintings was one of René Huyghe's top assistants, Jean-Pierre Tremain. Huyghe considered Tremain his most reliable employee at the museum. Faboul was aware that Tremain had worked with Huyghe for ten years, was considered exceptionally loyal and wholly reliable. Faboul also recalled from his prior experience at the museum that Tremain's political beliefs were finite. There was never any question as to his stance concerning the simmering conflict between Free French forces and what he considered the misguided leaders of the Vichy government.

Huyghe's original plan also stipulated that from the minute Jean-Pierre Tremain and the paintings arrived at the *Chateau de Montal* in early 1941, no communication with Tremain was to be attempted. This dictate was to allow the Chateau and its contents as much isolation as possible. Equally important to the safety of the paintings, Rene Huyghe made sure that only three people, including himself, were even aware of Tremain's existence.

When Operation Angerona was proposed to René Huyghe, he optimistically reasoned that by ordering André Faboul on this mission, he was sending a person who was already known to Tremain. Faboul was a person with whom Tremain had worked closely for several years. Huyghe also felt that when Andre Faboul was able to candidly explain his mission to Tremain, Tremain would then be agreeable to allowing his former colleague to complete the switch of the paintings. Huyghe did not, even under the compelling current circumstances, break his own rule of communicating directly with Jean-Pierre Tremain.

As part of Faboul's instructions, Huyghe carefully included a personal letter to Tremain briefly explaining the situation. The letter was in Huyghe's own hand and was aimed at verifying Faboul's presence in less than desirable conditions. Huyghe was counting heavily on the fact that Jean-Pierre Tremain would easily recognize his handwriting.

Huyghe also was sure to include a special code word within the text of his letter. This was a symbol that he and Tremain had agreed to over a year ago, just prior to Tremain's dispatch to the *Chateau de Montal*. The particular word, *robin*, was the 1 bird that symbolized the artistic freedom both Huyghe and Tremain ultimately sought for France's greatest paintings. Huyghe knew that without the inclusion of this word in the text of his letter, Tremain would never agree to the proposed switch.

Huyghe was also cognizant of the fact that Tremain's period of isolation had now extended well over a year. Lack of communication and such remote surroundings were not the best companions for anyone, much less a city dweller such as Tremain. Huyghe silently prayed that such negative factors would not prove troublesome to Andre Faboul's task.

Even though Faboul had some minor misgivings of his own about meeting with Tremain, he had chosen not to share any of these thoughts with Brian Russell. Faboul decided to bide his time until he and Russell reached the *Chateau de Montal* itself. Once inside, Faboul hoped to persuade Tremain to meet alone with him where he could then explain in greater detail the importance of his mission. Faboul knew for his upcoming meeting to be successful, a good measure of luck would be involved.

*   *   *

Pierre Bonde decided on his next course of action. He began the task of feeding the Germans a small piece of misleading information, information that concerned the possible location of some of the artworks. His idea was both simple and imaginative and only required a few distorted facts to be leaked to his enemies. He also hoped that the German soldiers at the *Abbey du Loc-Dieu* were part of the Wehrmacht detachment stationed at Rodez, the closed known military assemblage in his region.

For many months, the Resistance had effectively engaged the services of a double agent in Bonde's specific area, a Frenchman named Edmond Dubreil. Dubreil was a minor government official whom the Germans believed was loyal to the Vichy government.

Dubreil was a mousy person. His head was centered with small steel rimmed glasses and was permanently cocked to the right. Dubreil seldom looked anyone in the eye, and had passed on to the Germans bits of information the Resistance wanted to disclose to their enemy. He had become a trusted informer on matters concerning local farmers and their production quotas for the Bosch and was therefore a perfect double agent. Since most French farmers cheated on their numbers on a regular basis, Dubreil's disclosures affected very few. His continued actions made him a favorite mole for the Wehrmacht that sought to control every aspect of French commerce. His speaking manner was barely louder than a murmur, but for some unexplained reason, always contained a certain tone of credibility that the Germans believed.

The Germans were also totally unaware of the fact that Edmond Dubreil was actually a gifted actor who was used to frequent role-playing. He was used to contriving a number of different scenarios that he skillfully and eventually put to good use. He was content with his increased importance to the German military.

Interestingly, the Wehrmacht had acted on some of Dubreil's information during the past week, a fact Bonde hoped he could immediately exploit for the Resistance's benefit. It was Bonde's intention to have Dubreil feed the Germans a mixture of facts and speculation, and counted on the Germans acting on such information expeditiously. If his plan went as anticipated, Pierre Bonde would have a big surprise in store for his adversaries.

Bonde set up a hurried meeting with Dubreil to pass him the bogus information that contained just enough legitimacy to allow the Germans to believe it to be genuine.

* * *

It took Hoven more than a few days to get the information von Heltscherer demanded, and the SS Obersturmbannfuhrer had suddenly become impatient with his Wehrmacht subordinate. The original list of possible storage sites had proven to be of little use and that fact had raised the SS Colonel's immediate ire. Hoven knew that both Central and Southwestern France were filled with many hundreds, and possibly thousands, of old castles and houses. Many of these were capable of storing medium to large quantities of paintings. Hoven had originally tried to select the biggest and best for von Heltscherer to work from. It had taken von Heltscherer less than a day to determine the list was of little help. Those very facts, in addition to the ever-deteriorating spirit of cooperation within the Vichy environment, made it quite difficult for Hoven and his administrative personnel. They were unable to produce a meaningful document that contained accurate information on even a small portion of the possible storage sites.

When Hoven finally placed a number of papers on the desk in front of him, von Heltscherer flipped through the pages and eyeballed his younger compatriot.

"So these are *all* the possible hiding places, Herr Oberstleutnant?" The negative manner of the Obersturmbannfuhrer's tone was disconcerting to Hoven.

"No, Herr Obersturmbannfuhrer, you are quite correct. You are also very incisive. I regret to say the list is significantly incomplete. There is little information available on the type of places you described and it appears there are thousands of them within a 300-kilometer loop of *Rodez*. I regret to say my staff has only been able to document a few of the locations."

"You use the term *regret* too easily my *friend*." Hoven was acutely aware of von Heltscherer's facetious tone. "So, how long will it take you to get me a *complete* list?" von Heltscherer asked testily.

Oberstleutnant Hoven thought for a long moment.

"A month, Herr Obersturmbannfuhrer. I can have it for you within a month."

"I do not enjoy the luxury of being able to wait a month!" von Heltscherer nearly shouted, slamming his fist on the desk. "By that time it might be too late. You must do better, or be prepared to suffer the consequences. There must be another way of getting the information I need."

"We have already tried a number of different methods of securing the information. Many of the local teachers or scholars who might be able to provide such information have either disappeared or are in hiding. Some have even been sent to our factories in Germany to assist us with the war effort. I am not in the habit of making excuses, but such detailed information is simply not readily available."

"I cannot accept excuses," von Heltscherer added icily, "there must be a way to find the information I need."

Hoven cringed; he was suddenly acutely aware that von Heltscherer meant exactly what he said. The informality and agreeableness of von Heltscherer's visit had ended, and the Oberstleutnant immediately envisaged a number of added difficulties for himself and his men.

*   *   *

Faboul and Russell entered the smallish village of *St. Cere* from the north. The area was part of a large valley and it was well after daybreak when they arrived. Russell's first impression was that the area was unusual in that a great deal of the surrounding ground area had suddenly taken on a reddish aura. The color was apparent both in the soils and the buildings found within the towns. He surmised that high clay content was responsible for the coloring of the soil, which tended to give everything within sight a distinctive red-brown color.

Upon reaching the middle of *St Cere*, the pair encountered a craggy, aged man sitting on a crude wooden bench in front of a small soft goods store located on *St.Cere's* town square. They approached the bent figure and asked for directions to the *Chateau de Montal*. The old man regarded them warily, since visitors to *St. Cere* had become more infrequent over the past few years. After he considered the request, he pointed his wrinkled finger to the east. He told them to follow a single lane road to the south from *St. Cere* for approximately 2 miles. The road eventually turned east, and just off the road on the right would be located the *Chateau de Montal*. The old man chortled to himself as he explained to Faboul and Russell that the place was almost impossible to miss. After all, the *Chateau de Montal* was the tallest building in the entire area.

The brief walk toward the *chateau* seemed agonizingly short to Andre Faboul. He had been warily preparing his opening salutation to Jean Pierre Tremain, but realized he was having some difficulty. Arranging all the salient facts of his mission in a manner that Tremain would accept was most challenging.

His perplexed mind was still working through the situation as an intersection appeared in the distance. A very large *chateau* became immediately apparent, set about five hundred yards off the road's right side.

Faboul gestured affirmatively to Russell and the pair turned off in the direction of the *chateau*. They walked down an unkempt path toward the formidable stone building. He noted there was no visible signs of life around the entire place.

The *chateau* itself was situated on a rise in the landscape that could have easily been considered a small hill. Russell observed that it was a classic French structure, with a rectangular shaped main building containing both circular and square towers rising above an impressive top. Several other smaller buildings, apparently of equal age, were set off on the north side of the main structure.

Russell also observed a beautiful shaded outside court area bounded by a perfectly matched row of *Plantane* trees supporting their unusual upended greenery. The trees faced the two main sides of the building's front.

The facade was equally impressive. Six human busts comprised the focal points that were located some thirty feet above the ground. The busts were carved into the stone facings spaced along the second floor level. Their presence prompted Russell to presuppose that they had something to do with the origins of the building. A single ground level door was apparent on the front side of the building and Faboul decided to approach it. A mid-size, rusty copper bell was affixed to the wall next to the door.

Faboul rang the bell twice and waited.

Nothing happened.

He tried again, this time ringing the corroded device harder.

Again, there was no response.

Faboul gestured to Russell and started around the left corner of the building towards the rear of the structure. The lower second floor windows of the place were boarded as if deserted. Before he turned the corner, Russell noticed that large capital letters "R M" were carved high into the façade of the weathered and still astonishingly majestic old building.

Faboul felt a tinge of apprehension and thought to himself.

I wonder if everything is all right inside. After all, it has been over a year since anyone...

They turned another corner and came face to face with a loaded rifle. The gun's holder was a small, rugged man in his 50's, with a rough, weathered countenance set under a black beret. It was not a face that Faboul had ever seen.

"What is it you want?" the gunman said negatively, gesturing with his gun for the pair to raise their hands.

Faboul cleared his throat and tried to assert himself. "Tremain. I must see Jean-Pierre Tremain!"

The gunman stared intently at the two men in front of him for a long moment. With the end of his long rifle, the man gestured in the direction of the house. He stepped back a bit to allow the two men to pass by the back of the building. Without saying a word, he allowed the pair to turn the corner toward the front of the huge *chateau*. The three made their way along the edge of the house and finally turned left toward a door that protruded from the side of the structure. The gunman gestured again and followed the pair as they stepped up a small stairway and into the old mansion.

*   *   *

With the possible exceptions of Bernard Masson and Christine Allard, the brothers Fabien and Jean-Paul Ducrosse were Pierre Bonde's principal operatives within his huge region of Resistance responsibility.

The Ducrosse brothers were twenty-eight and twenty-six, with Fabien being the oldest. Since their youth, the popular brothers had toiled in their family's nursery business, growing flowers and plants for shipment throughout France. Fabien and Jean-Paul had joined the Resistance soon after its establishment and were quickly involved in virtually every significant mission that cropped up within Bonde's section.

Bonde was particularly proud of the fact that the brothers had been able to develop a mastery of explosives near the beginning of their Resistance activities. They had utilized that knowledge to support Bonde in a number of important missions he was given.

The idea that first involved Edmond Dubreil had now begun to reach fruition within Bonde's active imagination. Its complex facets became more explicit to the Resistance leader and he assured himself that the Ducrosse brothers were the keys to the plan's implementation. He summoned Fabien and Jean-Paul to a meeting to explain his concept to them.

"I have a very special job for you to undertake, one that only you will be able to pull off. It is a bit complicated, but not so much that you could not finish within a week or two."

The Ducrosse brothers listened intently as Bonde continued his explanation.

"I am aware of an uninhabited old castle, located in the mountains not too far from here and close to a small village called *Grand-Vabre*. If we bothered to count, the place can't be more than 20 miles from here. I believe it have been vacant for a long time. I want you to go there today and make it appear as if someone has been active there recently, maybe even lived there from time to time."

The brothers eyes met, their interest piqued, as Bonde went on.

"For the next part, you must be extremely clever."

The Ducrosse brothers eyed each other again and grinned.

"I will have gathered and delivered to you a number of inexpensive old paintings. I want you to place the paintings somewhere inside or outside the old *chateau*, wherever it is you think would best suit our purpose. I want them placed in a manner that they will be found if anyone comes looking.

Not completely clear of Bonde's meaning, the Ducrosses' stared blankly at their leader.

"It is important that the place seems to be what it isn't, and that will become clear to you in a minute. You will see what I mean.
Next, I want you to place some booby traps, the kind that wouldn't fool most people. If it is possible, I want you to wire the area in such a manner that will allow any intruders to find the explosives. That way they will believe that they have solved the puzzle. Then, I want you to place a secondary explosive in such a manner that no one would anticipate, the type that would kill everyone and destroy everything in its presence."

Bonde paused, hoping his message was clear. "Is this all clear to you both?"

Fabien Ducrosse felt a surge of adrenaline push through his body. Bonde's idea was exactly the type of skilled mission that he and his younger brother Jean-Paul had secretly yearned for since they had first joined the Resistance. If they were successful, their work would go a long way toward repaying the Germans for the occupation of their homeland.

The Ducrosse brothers nodded their assent and in five minutes were on the road to the old chateau near *Grand-Vabre*.

*   *   *

Faboul led the way and Russell followed behind as they stepped up three limestone blocks leading to the huge building's inner hallway. Additional limestone squares comprised the hall flooring and led into a series of rooms that served as the *Chateau de Montal's* main floor. The gunman urged them into another room, almost rectangular in shape, almost fifty feet long and nearly thirty feet wide. A large stone fireplace dominated the room, marked by a prominent black burn mark indicating extensive use of warming fires throughout the centuries. The great room's ceilings were at least twenty-five feet high. Several walls were covered with huge pastoral tapestries dating from the 16th and 17th Centuries. Directly in the middle was a huge dark brown rectangular table, approximately three inches thick and some twenty- six feet long. Along the back wall, a long angular painting of an earlier French king or aristocrat of some era dominated the room. Faboul studied the work for a moment and whispered to Russell.

"*Henri II*. From its looks it could easily be an original."

Russell studied the painting, impressed with his associate's quick ability to identify the work. Russell knew that Faboul was correct in his recognition of the artwork.

"You could have fooled me," Russell glimpsed back at his friend, attempting to lighten the air. Faboul stood rigidly and said nothing.

Russell saw Faboul's stiffness and decided his wise crack was ill timed. *Oh well, it could be worse...*

Everyone stood silently for more than a minute until an additional figure eventually appeared. Andre Faboul recognized the familiar person that entered the great room.

Jean-Pierre Tremain looked closely at the two men and fixed his gaze firmly on Andre Faboul.

"Faboul, is it you? What in the name of God are *you* doing here?"

Faboul flushed at the sign of recognition and offered his old associate his hand.

"René Huyghe sends you his warmest personal greetings."

Jean Pierre Tremain acknowledged the salutation, but said nothing. It was evident to everyone that he was assessing the entire situation.

*   *   *

The day after Oberstleutnant Hoven submitted his revised report, von Heltscherer decided to chance a visit to the nearest of the buildings that had found its way on Hoven's list.

He drove with SS Scharfuhrer Mueller out into the country and visited an old, weather-beaten *chateau* near *Naucelle*. The staid, aged place was in bad repair. Two farm hands working near the old place's entrance were quite unimpressed by the fact that two outstanding members of the Waffen SS were paying their site a visit. The Frenchmen went about their business and generally ignored the two soldiers' presence.

It was visibly apparent that the old site was uninhabited. More importantly, von Heltscherer saw that the place had not been utilized in any manner in many years and was in danger of falling apart. Irritated, he scratched the address off the list he held in his hand.

Von Heltscherer then ordered Mueller to drive to a second listing; this one located some twenty-five miles away. The new location also proved to be situated in the middle of nowhere, near a tiny dot on the road map called *Verfiel*.

After a half-hour and some difficulty in translating, Mueller was able to enlist the help of some local residents to finally identify the building, located down a diminutive, winding road.

The place was also uninhabited and completely overgrown with weeds. It was obvious to both von Heltscherer and Mueller that, once again, the premises in question had been unused for many years.

It was also increasingly irritating to von Heltscherer that Hoven's revised list still lacked basic credibility and that he was getting nowhere fast. Von

Heltscherer also suspected that his present approach of hit and miss investigation was very inefficient. He realized that he had neither the time nor inclination to spend the next year of his life chasing after a collection of feeble, rotting old French buildings.

There must be a better way.

Von Heltscherer immediately signaled SS Scharfuhrer Mueller to turn the staff car around and the vehicle was soon headed back on the narrow, winding road toward *Rodez*.

*   *   *

The Ducrosse brothers were delighted with the mostly pristine structure that their leader Pierre Bonde had chosen for the mission for several reasons.

First of all, the premises at the *chateau* outside *Grand-Vabre* were not in exceptionally bad shape. They would only require a day's worth of sprucing up to attain the look that Bonde desired, that of offering implied recent usage. A few downstairs windows needed repair and Jean-Paul astutely suggested a fire be lit in the chimney to suggest current use. Fabien nodded his agreement to his younger brother and even though it was approaching mid-July, the fire was set. The Ducrosse brothers had found that being thorough had often rewarded their Resistance activities. This mission would be no exception. With so little to be done in the way of repairs to the main house, Fabien was sure there would be sufficient time for the remainder of Bonde's plan to be put into place.

On their second visit, the brothers also discovered a most advantageous feature of the grounds. The *chateau* backed up to the side of a small mountain, or more exactly, its backside pointed directly to the entrance of a sizable cave. Upon searching the cave, the brothers found that the property's former owner utilized a small portion of the cave for a wine cellar. An even closer inspection showed that a few bottles remained there in crude racks.

As the brothers explored deeper into the cave's limestone environs, a large main chamber opened up into several smaller natural caves, each with an unrestricted amount of storage space.

Fabien Ducrosse immediately realized the cave's inner chambers would provide an enclosure that was *exactly* what Bonde's plan called for.

"This will do quite nicely," the elder Ducrosse brother remarked.

"Yes, I can see what you mean. It couldn't be better for what we want. What better way to control an explosion than to locate it within the confines of a natural cave. Victor will be very pleased."

"For once, we will not have a great deal of rearranging to do."

"Hardly any if my guess is correct. And we will even be finished a bit earlier than expected. Victor will also be pleased with that."

"Most certainly, my brother. The caves will make it all the easier when planting the seed." Fabien Ducrosse stopped talking as he and his brother measured off the exact distance inside the walls of the cave.

Fabien helped Jean-Paul clean up the main house and repair the broken panes in the windows. The brothers' next task was to contact Victor to arrange delivery of the crates that he had mentioned. Once the crates arrived, the brothers could then move them directly into the caves and begin setting the trap for any unsuspecting visitor. This final task would involve rigging and concealing a surprise explosive package that would serve as a sudden surprise for any unwelcome intruders.

Jean-Paul assessed the limestone walls of the huge cavern, turned to his brother and observed, "I would not want to be inside here when the explosion detonates."

"That is the general idea," his brother agreed.

Once again, Fabien Ducrosse found himself enjoying his labors.

Chapter Ten

Jean-Pierre Tremain eyed his new arrivals warily. He weighed the situation carefully in his mind. Andre Faboul was easily identifiable from his time at the *Louvre*, a person he remembered as a loyal and dedicated employee of the museum. But the taller man standing alongside Faboul was a stranger and under Tremain's existing circumstances, strangers at the chateau probably meant trouble.

He took a closer look at the stranger and the circular object the man was carrying. The cylinder was too narrow to house a rifle or gun of any type, but could easily conceal a long knife or similar type of weapon. It was also evident that the object was quite important to the figure that grasped it tightly in his hands.

Moments later Tremain was surprised when the stranger spoke first. The man spoke softly and in a decidedly amiable manner and addressed him simply.

"*Monsieur* Tremain, the *chateau* here is an incredibly stunning place."

Tremain assessed his visitor's remarks and replied uneasily.

"Yes, it most certainly is..." Tremain agreed, unable to find any other words that fit the situation.

What could these men want? Why have they come all the way out here to see me? Wasn't Andre Faboul always considered a respected employee of the Louvre of the highest caliber?

Feeling more optimistic and somewhat relieved about the appearance of the two men, Tremain also decided it was time that he take control of the conversation. He decided on a subtle approach.

"Are you aware of the *Chateau's* history?"

Both Brian Russell and Andre Faboul nodded negatively.

"The building's older records indicate construction on the place was started in the early part of the 16th Century, in 1523 to be exact. The first construction began during the time of the Crusades. The mother of a young nobleman named Robert de Montal decided that she would build him a fine residence for his return from the wars. Before the structure could be completed, his mother, Antoinette de Castelnau, received word that Robert de Montal had been killed. The unexpected news left her completely heartbroken. She ordered the construction halted and the place was left in a somewhat unfinished condition. Later on it was completed and the *chateau* has had a succession of owners until the present. Last year, the King of Belgium and his family stayed here for a period of time after the Nazis forced them to flee their country.

And, if you look closely on the façade of the building, Robert de Montal's initials are carved into the stones that compromise the outside walls. You might have noticed the engraved letters when you were brought around the front to the side entrance."

Russell nodded affirmatively, and Tremain continued.

"*Montal* actually has four floors if you count the cellar underneath, and the old place is as impressive inside as out. Each of the two lower floors has eight rooms, and every room is accented with extremely high ceilings. There are fireplaces at the each end of the house, which also extend upward and heat several upper bedrooms. The *Chateau de Montal* is actually a comfortable place to live as I found out this past winter."

It was obvious to the visitors that Tremain was relishing his position as host and narrator. They listened intently as Tremain continued his narration.

"I am particularly fond of the stairways, because each is made from individually carved limestone rocks and fitted to adhere to the curvature of the stairwell. Three hundred years of usage has not made as much as a scratch on any of the stairs.

Most of the fixtures you see are from the original house with the exception of the rugs, which are oriental. These were added sometime during the last century but the time is not clear. For security reasons, we have boarded up the windows on this ground level of the house. The handmade stained glass windows," he pointed to his left, "are signed and dated from the 16th century."

Russell stepped forward and inspected the window. The date *1535* was inscribed alongside what appeared to be a signature. Russell was unsure of the signature but was in agreement that the scribbling he saw constituted a signature of some sort. He returned his attention to Tremain.

"But gentlemen, enough of this nonsense. It is time we get to the point and find out what you want. Even though you might agree our surroundings are naturally beautiful and steeped in historical facts, I am quite sure you are not here for a lesson in history."

Faboul cleared his throat, and spoke formally to his former colleague, "*Monsieur* Tremain, I had hoped we could speak alone for a moment, but I now see that is not possible. If you will permit me, I will try to explain what we are doing here."

"Yes, by all means," Tremain replied. "We have not received any visitors here since I arrived and I am anxious to hear what you have to say. Please follow me to the living room. We will all be much more comfortable in there."

Faboul and Russell followed Tremain into the adjoining room where Russell's eyes widened. They entered a larger room situated toward the interior of the *chateau*. The *Chateau de Montal's* living room was even more attractive than the room they had just left.

The scene was dominated by a beautiful hanging tapestry depicting a pastoral scene with a number of people engaged in what seemed to be a game of lawn croquette. Several plush sofas were placed in front of the massive fireplace that dominated the far end of the room. The sofas were fairly modern and seemed out of place amid such engrossing objects of antiquity.

A set of six *Pont Angruy* chairs, deep seated with loose cushions, padded backs and arms were spread out throughout the room in *au courant* style. The *Pont Angruy* chairs faced another massive table similar to the one in the first room, but a size smaller. A row of individually sectioned church seats connected together with a carved wood backing faced the table from the backside of the room.

Russell's attention remained fixed on the church seats and caught Tremain's eye.

"That section," Tremain offered, pointing to the connected church seats, "was taken from the old chapel which stands due north of the main house. You passed it when you were brought in through the side door. I am unsure of its exact age, but it too is quite old. Whoever decided the church seat section should be placed in its present position had a flair for the dramatic and it certainly compliments the room. I think I would personally find it quite difficult to sit in it for any period of time. But then, I did not live in that particular time period."

Russell considered Tremain's comment and paused to take it all in. He was positive he had never been in, nor even seen, a room like this in his entire life.

Tremain motioned for his visitors to take a seat on one of the sofas. Both complied, but neither sat comfortably. Each remained on the front of the cushion as Tremain took a position across from them. Russell also noted that the old guard had followed them into the room and stood off to the side with his gun held firmly in a ready position. Jean-Pierre Tremain was taking no chances!

It was up to Andre Faboul to initiate the conversation. He had rehearsed this part in his mind numerous times on the road to the *chateau*.

"*Monsieur* Tremain," he began, choosing to continue his formality with his older associate, "as you must be aware, the political situation in Europe has worsened, to levels even lower than anyone could have expected. The Nazis have become more powerful in the past year. Their armies occupy a great part of France and numerous other countries. Even with the United States entering the war..."

"The United States?" questioned Tremain in total disbelief.

"Yes. Didn't you know? America entered the war at the end of last year, in early December. The Japanese attacked its fleet at Pearl Harbor and caused great damage."

"No, Andre, I had no idea," Tremain mildly expressed his irritation. "My instructions were quite specific. I was told to stay here as inconspicuously as possible. We had an old radio at first, but it has not worked for some time."

"And, no newspapers?"

"None that are reliable. You must remember that the Vichy government controls this zone. We infrequently get their *journals*, and, well, let us say that they forget to include certain facts. You should see one of their *journals* sometime; there are more spaces without printing than you could imagine. After a while, I felt it was practically useless to keep reading it. To me no news was good news," Tremain added facetiously. "But, continue…"

"Through Allied intelligence, the leader of the French Resistance Jean Moulin advised René Huyghe that in several countries the Nazis have occupied, all national museums were pillaged. Much of the highest quality artworks were removed and sent back to Germany. More recently, René had also been made aware that the Nazi Military Headquarters in *Paris* have organized a special unit to attempt to locate our *Louvre* museum treasures our country has taken such care to hide."

"And, what is it you want of me?" Tremain inquired warily, unsure of what would come next.

"Jean Moulin, and René Huyghe have together devised a plan to insure that a few of the greatest of our masterpieces never fall into Nazi hands. Rene selected three of the *Louvre's* greatest pieces and with the help of our British and American allies, have managed to produce a set of exact duplicates of the three masterpieces. My associate here," Faboul pointed to Russell, "risked his life to see that the forgeries were brought into France last night. I was sent from *Paris* to meet him when he landed and bring him here to you. Rene knew you would recognize me and that I would lend credence to the plan. The duplicate paintings are concealed in the cylinder we have with us. It is our plan and the fervent wish of our superiors, that I exchange these duplicate pieces for the originals. The masterpieces will then be sent off to an outside country for safekeeping until after all this current turmoil is resolved.

If we had the time and resources, we would like to be able to do the same for all our great paintings. Of course, that would be practically impossible. The Resistance has devised a specific plan to ensure that my associate can escape from France and make certain the original masterpieces reach a safe place."

"And exactly which paintings did you wish to exchange?"

Andre Faboul paused and took a deep breath. So far Jean-Pierre Tremain seemed to be buying into what he was saying. "The three Huyghe selected are Leonardo's *Mona Lisa*, Titian's *Francois I*, and Raphael's *Belle Jardinière*." He stopped to let his words sink in. Then he remembered the letter he was carrying inside his jacket.

"I almost forgot. I was instructed to bring this with me. It is from Huyghe himself. Faboul removed Huyghe's letter and presented it to Tremain.

Tremain carefully removed the single page from the sealed envelope and read.

My dear friend and colleague J.P. Tremain:

It is under the direst of circumstances that I write this to you. The political and military situations within our country have deteriorated to such an extent that I no longer feel comfortable concerning the safety of our precious artworks. It is entirely possible the Bosch will occupy the remainder of our country, which would put all our priceless paintings at great risk.

I have endorsed a plan that would alleviate the danger to the very finest of our beloved museum's collection. The bearer of this note is Andre Faboul who is already known to you. He has risked his life to reach you and hand you this note. Faboul will explain what I expect of you from this point on.

There is no need to say how much I, as well as the people of France, am in your debt for your dedication up to this point. You and others like you are heroes to our beloved France.

It is only through actions such as the one that Andre Faboul will propose to you, that the robin will finally be set free.

Faithfully,
R. Huyghe

*   *   *

A sixth sense developed over the past several years warned Pierre Bonde that he needed to get personally involved in the operations involving the *Chateau de Montal.*
    There are many strings to tie together and if one remains untied...
He immediately left his residence in *Le Puy en-Velay* and headed south. Another Resistance member was available with an automobile that provided Bonde with a much swifter mode of transportation than he usually enjoyed. With a bit of good luck and the absence of Vichy checkpoints and any major obstacles along his route, Bonde hoped he might still catch Andre Faboul and Brian Russell at the *Chateau de Montal.*
    Pierre Bonde also decided to stop along the way and include the Ducrosse brothers on his present trip.

*   *   *

Edmond Dubreil affirmed to himself his contentment to the current status of affairs in which he was personally involved. The Resistance double agent correctly surmised his usefulness to the Resistance had increased dramatically due to the task Victor had assigned him a few days ago.

This sort of scenario was entirely apposite to Edmond Dubreil. Ever since his youth, when his physical size and appearance excluded him from most youthful games and social situations, Dubreil's thoughts were always crammed with loftier aspirations. His mind produced a number of inherently believable ersatz situations where Edmond Dubreil assumed varying roles. He was sometimes cast himself as a diplomat, adventurer or soldier. In many of his fantasies, Dubreil relished his role in determining the result of particularly dangerous and challenging tasks.

Extremely small in stature, Dubreil's problematic premature birth left him with a permanent tilt to his neck. Over time, shyness related to his appearance caused his head to tilt downward in an almost submissive posture.

When the Vichy government was formed after the signing of the pact with Germany, Edmond Dubreil's skill as an accountant was put to good use. He was given the minor duty of ensuring for the government that local farmers accurately reported their annual crops they harvested. He also developed the reporting system that forwarded that information directly to Vichy.

The appointment proved easy for Dubreil and he was soon given additional responsibilities. His new duties provided him the added flexibility of being able to travel throughout the region without harassment from military or civil authorities.

The fact that Edmond Dubreil was also working under the cloak of the French Resistance brought even greater solace to the partially bent patriot!

His favorite uncle Roger recruited him for the Resistance early in the struggle. Aware of his nephew's intelligence and theatrical aptitudes, his uncle was also conscious of the fact that Edmond Dubreil was the type of person to whom little or no attention was paid on the streets. Dubreil's uncanny ability to blend into his surroundings began to prove increasingly valuable to the Resistance.

Edmond Dubreil received his latest Resistance communiqué from his usual source, his Uncle Roger. Dubreil was instructed to leak certain information to the Germans concerning clandestine truck activity on particular rural roads. The information was supposedly garnered by Dubreil from some local farmers who normally reported to Dubreil. He was told to carefully whet the Germans' appetite, but not to divulge any actual information. Specific times and exact locations would be masked until a certain point, when the Resistance felt comfortable the timing and circumstances could be used to its advantage.

Edmond Dubreil carefully assessed his next move. He knew precisely where he would begin.

Wehrmacht Headquarters on the *Boulevard Gambetta* in *Rodez* was beginning to resemble a madhouse, and Oberstleutnant Dieter Hoven grasped that it was due to the relentless drive of SS Obersturmbannfuhrer Kurt von Heltscherer.

When the two German officers first met, the objectives von Heltscherer outlined seemed quite reasonable. At the time, Hoven could not imagine that it would be too difficult to track down and locate a particular place and afterwards collect its contents.

The sequence of events that had transpired since von Heltscherer's arrival was difficult for Hoven to believe.

After the initial embarrassing confrontation with the feisty old nun at the *Abbey de Loc-Dieu* at *Villefranche-de Rougiere*, in Hoven's estimate, von Heltscherer became unglued. The SS Colonel was seemingly obsessed in his efforts to find the location that he believed would contain the missing artworks. Hoven had detailed a number of his men to assist the SS Obersturmbannfuhrer, but nothing had pleased his colleague.

In Hoven's mind, the task of pinpointing *one* specific building that could serve as a hiding place for the masterpieces was practically impossible. Many hundreds, perhaps thousands, of such places existed throughout his area of responsibility. Unless additional pertinent information fell into their hands, Hoven could not foresee any real progress. As the days progressed, Hoven's regular Wehrmacht duties began to lag behind.

Hoven dared not disclose his uneasiness to von Heltscherer. His prior military training and Germany's current political status convinced him that such a move would not prove judicious to him or his current career objectives.

* * *

Pierre Bonde was relieved that his arrival at the Ducrosse brothers' home was early enough to catch the Ducrosses before their daily morning departure.

"I had a feeling that prompted me to decide to join you for your mission this morning," Bonde greeted the pair.

"We always enjoy your company, Victor," Fabien Ducrosse replied. Both he and his younger brother Jean-Paul both admired and enjoyed Victor's leadership and companionship. The brothers both considered Victor a perfect hands-on leader. "It is good for you to be able to see your instructions put into action,' Fabien added.

"This present assignment is really significant. You might be interested to know that even the *leader* of the Resistance is involved."

Duly impressed, the Ducrosse brothers glanced at one another and nodded.

Fabien spoke again. "We have completed most of the particulars you first gave us; in fact we are presently a bit ahead of schedule. There are only a few details remaining to be finished."

"Good. I knew when I assigned you to all this it would be a good fit. And, oh yes, one last thing. I think it best that you transport the explosives with us now if you haven't already done so. The scheme is coming together much more quickly than I first anticipated. It is better that the final touches are completed as soon as possible."

The explosives were then removed from their hiding place behind a false wall covered by an antique cupboard within the Ducrosse home. The trio quickly set out in the direction of the *Chateau de Montal*.

*   *   *

"**What you** request of me, Andre…well, unfortunately, I am not in a position to make happen." Jean Pierre Tremain looked at the unfolded letter in his hand and finally at the man seated across from him.

Thinking the situation was going well, Faboul was completely unprepared for Tremain's reply. The curator's words included a tone of finality, which ruptured the silence that surrounded the *Chateau de Montal's* living room.

Faboul replied back, "But, I fail to see why. You can see that I am simply following René Huyghe's instructions and…"

"Surely you can understand that I have nothing *official* with which to formulate my decision," Tremain interrupted forcefully. "You arrive here with no forewarning and show me a hand written note and expect me to believe everything you say is factual. And, you tell me about many events that have happened that I have no way of proving.

You fail to take into account the times in which we are living. Many things are not what they seem. Please do not take offense. I do not intend my statement personally."

"But, I…"

"Unfortunately Andre, there is nothing I can do. My instructions were very specific when I last left Huyghe. Under no circumstances was I to let a single painting out of my sight. Now, you come here and ask me to give you, arguably, the *three* finest paintings in the entire *Louvre* collection…"

Tremain sighed, and continued. "I simply cannot do it. The entire rationale behind hiding the paintings in such an obscure location was to afford the paintings the lowest possible profile. Only a *few* trusted people even know the location of this place. Last winter, some men tried to break into the *Chateau* and steal some of the paintings. Even though I harbored some doubts about what they were really after, I was forced to shoot them. The burglars claimed to be nothing but local thieves and one was even related to one of my guards, but, I could not take the chance. My orders were very specific and the two men paid for the break-in with their lives," Tremain paused, thinking to himself.

"And, again, please do not take this personally, but I have no idea where your individual sympathies lie concerning the bastards at Vichy. Your entire story could easily be a grand *charade*, I have no real way of knowing." Jean Pierre Tremain ended his verbal barrage and stared defiantly.

For the first time since Tremain and Faboul started their dialogue, Russell interjected.

"Maybe, Monsieur Tremain, it is time that I spoke up. After all, a great deal of planning has been put into this operation, way too much time and effort to see it fail now. Too many brave people have already risked their lives.

Monsieur, certain officials of the Free French government have watched as the guts were torn out of each country that the Nazis overran. Everything of cultural importance to these countries was destroyed or looted, including practically every important item contained within their great museums. This devastation will affect each country's culture and capability to revitalize that culture when the war comes to an end. Right now, it is true the Germans have most things going their way, and that we cannot help. There is even a great deal of speculation in Great Britain concerning Germany's expanding the occupied zone in France.

Monsieur Tremain, our present mission's intention, and the specific reason Faboul and I are here now, is to insure France has a cultural point from which to rebuild after the war ends. You, more than most, should be able to appreciate exactly what this means. These three paintings are, in the opinion of our leaders, the heart and soul of French art culture. They must not, under any set of circumstances, be lost, stolen or destroyed."

Tremain looked at the young man standing in front of him. Turning, he walked over to one of the rectangular, stained glass picture windows, the only one not covered with outside boards. For a few moments, he remained there, fixed deep in thought.

He turned again, addressing both Russell and Faboul with a lofty indifference.

"And what is my beloved France to do if everything here is *not* as it seems, Monsieur? Where does that leave us? Remember that it was nearly thirty years ago when the Mona Lisa was stolen from the *Louvre*. It quickly became a national disaster for the museum and France. We were all very fortunate at that time to get the painting back. I cannot possibly take another chance."

Brian Russell looked at Faboul. Tremain seemed unmovable and the situation had reached a stalemate. He was unsure as to what would happen next.

Faboul attempted a different approach and appealed to his former associate. "The very reason I was picked to come here was the fact that you know me and worked with me for several years. I assure you, Monsieur, that I have no underhanded intention other than the ultimate safety of the paintings. Surely you can see that."

"These times we are experiencing produce strange bedfellows, Andre. I told you not to take this personally."

"I cannot help but take it personally. Your attitude toward our mission is affecting its outcome."

"For that I am truly sorry. I wish I felt differently."

Faboul stepped away from Tremain and walked toward the back windows. His mind raced to find an appropriate solution to the seemingly insurmountable problem facing him.

*　*　*

Edmond Dubreil's next step involved his forwarding the misinformation he received through his uncle to another member of the Vichy regional government he knew to be sympathetic to the Germans. The person was a fellow worker to whom he had passed several bits of sensitive information before in his role as a double agent. Dubreil accomplished his task informally, when the two next met in the course of their duties.

Dubreil let slip that several of his farmers had recently mentioned seeing trucks on one of the back roads in the section north of *Rodez*. These were large trucks that the farmers knew were not involved in local drayage commerce. Without mentioning any of the farmer's names or any specific places, Edmond Dubreil allowed his Vichy colleague to interpret the information as he saw fit. Dubreil was sure of what would happen next.

Within minutes of the meeting, the other man closed his office, grabbed his coat and hat and left the building.

An hour later, the Vichy informant stood in front of Wehrmacht Oberstleutnant Dieter Hoven at the German Military Office in *Rodez*.

*　*　*

Pierre Bonde and the Ducrosse brothers reached the *Chateau de Montal* in about two hours. Leaving his automobile a good distance from the chateau complex, they silently worked their way around the rear of the huge building and descended the steep hill, splitting up as they moved. Bonde and Jean-Paul turned a corner and were abruptly confronted by a man holding a machine gun that was pointed in their direction. The gun's owner raised the barrel up and down compelling the pair to raising their hands.

As the gunman motioned for Jean-Paul Ducrosse to drop the rifle he was carrying, he was surprised to find a cold steel object nudge the back of his head. Fabien Ducrosse stepped to the front of the man and quietly coaxed the machine gun from the man's grip.

"That is much better, *mon ami*. No need for anyone to get hurt here."

Bonde acknowledged the comment and spoke directly to the older man.

"All right then. Please take us all inside. And be sure to be quiet about it. Understand?"

The man nodded and the four figures made their way to the cellar door and entered. Jean-Paul Ducrosse was ordered to remain at the cellar entrance in case there were any additional guards on the grounds.

Seconds later, the silence in the *Chateau de Montal's* living room was broken by the appearance of the now unarmed gunman, who dejectedly entered the room followed by two armed men. Bonde trained the confiscated machine gun on the old man with the rifle who was also taken aback by the absolute change of circumstances. Fabien Ducrosse walked toward the man and took the aged rifle from his hands.

Tremain was both astonished and shaken, but bravely sought to gain control the situation.

"What are you doing here?" he challenged heatedly. "You have no right..."

"We have *every* right, Monsieur. My name is Victor and I am here on behalf of Free France."

Faboul and Russell glanced at each other, not really sure what the appearance of the two men signified and hesitant about what might occur next.

Tremain motioned for both his guards to leave the room. Bonde nodded his head for Fabien Ducrosse to accompany the men outside the room.

Andre Faboul reacted first, and spoke directly to Bonde.

"Monsieur, can I possibly have a word with you?"

Bonde nodded and indicated to Faboul to accompany him into the next room. Faboul followed and shut the huge wooden door behind him.

"Monsieur, I am unsure of your part in all this, I was not told to expect any additional help." Faboul was excited but tried to control his tone.

"Certainly Monsieur. I will try to explain it all to you. I am called Victor and I serve as head of the Resistance for the Dordogne/Lot. It is an old friend of the mine who planned this entire mission. It was my men who met you at the landing site and it will also be my people who will provide the necessary help to get the real paintings safely out of France. My intuition told me that I should probably be here to insure that everything went smoothly. From the looks of it, I just arrived in time. I listened to the last part of the conversation before we entered the room. I can see you are having a difficult time."

Faboul nodded, breathing calmly for the first time in several minutes.

Bonde patted Faboul on the shoulder and motioned back toward the living room.

"It is well that I decided to come here. If I understand the situation correctly, the curator's position is that he will not allow you to exchange the paintings because there was no official notification?"

"Well, yes. But there is more to it than just that..." Faboul stammered in response.

Bonde interrupted Faboul. "I believe I can change his mind. Please follow me."

Bonde and Faboul returned to the living room.

Bonde stared directly at Tremain, addressing him brusquely while still attempting to maintain a degree of essential civility.

"This gentleman has explained the situation to me, Monsieur Tremain," Bonde began, "and I must say, I appreciate both your position and your dedication. Is it your attitude that you have received no *official* orders to sanction such an action and are therefore unwilling to cooperate?"

"Exactly," agreed Tremain, glancing indignantly in the direction of both Faboul and Russell. "There are good reasons why I must refuse to oblige them."

"Well then, Monsieur Tremain, under the circumstances, I must ask that you consider *this* our orders," Bonde declared flatly, pointing his pistol directly at Tremain's head.

"And if you do not agree to let us switch us the paintings at once, I assure you I will not hesitate to shoot you."

Tremain blanched, feeling his legs tremble under the pressure. It was the first time in his life that a gun was pointed directly between his eyes.

Tremain looked intently at Bonde and studied his eyes. He correctly determined that this new individual was prepared to act in precisely the manner that he had insisted. Tremain slowly lowered his head. He realized that any further resistance on his part would be futile.

*   *   *

Elated at the prospect of some real progress in the search for the hidden treasures, Oberstleutnant Dieter Hoven wasted little time in letting von Heltscherer know about the reports of suspicious truck activity in the area north of *Rodez*.

Von Heltscherer also reacted positively, demanding additional facts. Hoven was prepared for that eventuality and immediately explained that his Vichy informant would soon be able to provide more detailed information.

"Good, at least we have something positive for a change," von Heltscherer uttered, not completely convinced. "This is the first time something has gone our way since I arrived."

Hoven agreed, and silently prayed the forthcoming information would prove beneficial.

"And, oh yes," von Heltscherer added. "When we get the additional information, I want to be sure to personally lead the search. This time there will be no mistakes on our part."

Hoven nodded. His recently developed perception of his fellow officer did not cause him to be surprised by the statement.

*　　*　　*

Faced with a sinking emotion he could not easily fathom, Tremain relented. He signaled the group back into the rectangular room where he had first encountered Faboul and Russell. He walked to a side of the room against the wall, where a medium sized, carved brown chest was situated midway between two windows. A small table stood immediately in front of the chest.

He opened the top of the chest and removed a solitary object. He looked at the object and turned toward Faboul who followed his movements closely. He handed the painting to his colleague. Faboul saw that the painting was Leonardo da Vinci's masterpiece, La Gioconda. The painting was known to the world as the Mona Lisa!

"This is my favorite painting in the entire collection, and I have always kept it close to me," Tremain said wistfully. "Whenever we moved it, I carried it with me in the front seat of the car that transported me. I did not even bother to have it crated; it was too dear to me. I am just one of many who believe it to be the most revered painting in the entire world. It would kill me if any harm would ever come to it."

"We will take excellent care of it, Monsieur," Russell attempted to console the curator, who had now acquired the aura of a beaten man. "I will take it and the other two paintings to a location outside France where they will all be safe. After the war, the paintings will be returned to France and assume their rightful positions inside the *Louvre*."

Tremain was cognizant of Russell's statement but did not reply.

After a few moments, the curator addressed the three men in the room. "Please follow me, the other paintings you desire are located in another room." Tremain exited the living room followed by Faboul, Russell and Bonde who still carried his pistol in full view.

At a smaller side room located at the end of the main corridor, Tremain paused and entered. A number of crates were spread out throughout the room, arranged in neat shoulder-high piles.

"I keep the best paintings here in this room, where they are more protected." He pointed to the rows of wooden crates neatly stacked within the room. The ones that you want are probably in this stack." Tremain moved toward a small pile of objects immediately to his right side. "I will give you the code numbers for the ones you need."

He withdrew a small black book from his coat pocket, encoded with a series of numbers and letters.

"This is my own system," he noted proudly. "To anyone else, the numbers would have no meaning."

Tremain consulted his book and returned his attention to the smaller stack. He pulled out one of the crated paintings and handed it to Faboul.

"That's the Titian," the smallest of the three. "Now for the other." Within seconds, he had produced an additional painting. "This one is Raphael's incredibly beautiful *Belle Jardinière*. Are you aware that all three were from the original collection of *Francois I* which actually served as the basis for the entire *Louvre* collection?"

No one answered, but Russell nodded in an attempt to appease Tremain. As he handed over the last painting, Jean-Pierre Tremain looked wistfully at the crate and entreated Faboul.

"Andre, for God's sake, please take special care of this one." He pointed to the Mona Lisa in Faboul's hands. "You know it was always Rene Huyghe's favorite."

"Mine too. I will be most careful," Faboul assured, and gently removed a speck of dust from the upper side of the painting.

Once Bonde felt comfortable that everything was now progressing as planned, he stepped out into the *Chateau de Montal's* formal garden area. The Ducrosse brothers were waiting along with the chateau's disarmed guards. It was Bonde's first opportunity to study the outside grounds that he now realized were incredibly beautiful. The *chateau's* garden was highlighted by an intricate design of bushes and hedges laid out in spiral patterns and set off by a large trellis area, which protected a part of the garden from the direct sun. Bonde stepped out of the sun light and under the wide trellis covering. Presently, he spoke with the brothers.

"I am satisfied that this part of our plan is under control and I feel that it is no longer necessary for you both to stay here. It would be better if you two departed and completed your work."

"Whatever you say, Victor. it will not take us long to finish what we have left."

"Good. Go then and be watchful of the Vichy militia. It seems like they are popping up everywhere these days."

"We are *always* careful Victor," Fabien smiled at his mentor. In a moment Fabien and Jean-Paul disappeared through the high hedges that led around to the front of the remarkable building.

The final part of Bonde's plan called for other members of the Resistance to gather together a number of basic, older paintings, none of which were considered valuable. Bonde ordered that the entire lot be crated and later dropped off behind the estate house near *Grand-Vabre*. The brothers knew the crates containing the paintings would be waiting for them when they arrived.

Bonde also directed the Ducrosse brothers to apply special numbers and markings to the outsides of the crates. Also, he specified that the word *Louvre* be carefully applied to the crates along with the numerical coding. Bonde knew that this attention to detail would add realism to his plan and make the crates appear to be part of a large collection. It was all part of the bait he was setting.

*   *   *

Back inside the *Chateau de Montal*, the work of exchanging the paintings proceeded along slowly. It took Faboul just about an hour to complete, and involved the process of gently removing the canvases and replacing them with the copies. Afterward, each original was carefully rolled inside the other so that a single round circle remained.

While Faboul worked, Tremain paid particular attention to the forgeries, carefully scrutinizing each one.

At one point, he remarked to Faboul. "Whoever produced these was quite good. Only a top expert could tell them from the originals. The ageing process that was employed was first rate."

Faboul nodded his concurrence. It was the first time he had seen the duplicates and he was genuinely impressed with their quality. While he agreed with Tremain's comment, Faboul privately hoped the new paintings would never have to stand up to scrutiny. Too much could be lost if that scenario would ever take place.

He returned to his work and after Russell explained the lock mechanism to him, Faboul carefully placed the originals inside the cylinder, insuring the special spring lock snapped shut.

He handed the cylinder to Russell who had observed every facet of Faboul's work, admiring his expert patience and benign tenderness with the paintings.

"Now it is all up to you." Faboul sighed and extended his hand to Russell.

Russell pumped the hand several times and replied, "I will certainly do my best."

It was now well past noon, and Faboul spoke again to Russell. It was vitally important that they begin their journey as soon as possible.

Jean Pierre Tremain, whose attitude had slowly improved due to the hopelessness of his position, became more resigned to inevitability of the mission. Moreover, he caught Faboul and Russell by complete surprise with an offer of bicycles for the next part of their trip. Tremain sent for the caretakers who soon produced a pair of older bicycles from a small utility building next to the *Chateau's* old chapel. Drawing upon his remaining fortitude, Tremain spoke.

"If all this is meant to be, then I say, go with the grace of God." He leaned toward Faboul and gave him a kiss on each cheek. Faboul accepted the gesture warmly, and turned toward Bonde and Russell.

Bonde gave Faboul some final instructions that pertained to the next leg of their journey. He then shook hands with both Faboul and Russell and accompanied them to a spot near the front of the *Chateau*. The pair mounted their bicycles and waved back as they quickly descended the hill and started in the direction of the road that would lead them directly to the City of *Cahors*. Bonde watched until they were out of sight and soon walked in the direction of the spot that he had initially parked his automobile. All in all, it had been a good day's work.

* * *

On the way back to his home, Pierre Bonde stopped by Edmond Dubreil's uncle's home and took time to leave Dubreil a coded note.

In it, he ordered Dubreil to arrange for the remaining information to be leaked to the Germans.

At that very moment some forty miles away, the Ducrosse brothers' were putting the final touches to their part of Bonde's intricate plan. The fake painting depository in the cave near *Grand-Vabre* was now expertly rigged for any intruders.

Bonde prayed his plan would work as expected.

* * *

The bicycles Tremain provided for Faboul and Russell were older than Faboul could imagine and more than a little rusty. What's more, as they began pedaling, the countryside surrounding the *Chateau de Montal* in the direction of *Cahors* became hilly with a number of major undulations. This provided both bicyclists, and in particular Russell, who was saddled with the added inconvenience of the cylinder, with a formidable task. They strained as they pushed the grinding machines up the hills. While the bicycles beat the alternative of walking, the reality was that their progress was mostly slow and tedious. Fifteen miles outside their destination of the city of *Cahors*, just beyond the small town of *Murat*, the pair caught a break. An old truck heading in the same direction noisily provided the pair a welcome relief. It was the first vehicle the pair had encountered since leaving the *Chateau de Montal*.

Faboul waved the driver to a stop and managed to talk the fellow into a ride. He and Russell lifted the bicycles on board and climbed onto the back of the rusted vehicle. For the remainder of the trip, Faboul and Russell had the distinct pleasure of traveling in the company of several hundred chickens on their way to market. Amidst the din provided by constant clatter from the poultry, not to mention the constant stream of feathers, both travelers managed to close their eyes for what seemed the briefest of moments.

Chapter Eleven

The morning following his visit to the Wehrmacht offices in *Rodez*, Edmond Dubreil's Vichy government contact was hardly able to contain his enthusiasm until he was able to get the attention of his stooped associate.

He greeted him impatiently at the door to Dubreil's office when Dubreil appeared for work promptly at eight o'clock.

"The Germans reacted quite well to your news," the contact exclaimed. "The officer in charge there thinks you might very well be on to something important. From what I gather, the German soldiers are searching for something significant somewhere in this part of the country and up to now have not been very successful. The officer I talked with wants me to furnish him with all the pertinent details as soon as possible."

Dubreil slowly sat down at his desk, purposely allowing a few extra seconds to elapse before he replied.

"Alright. Even though I don't think there is anything to it, I'll help you if you really think there is something tangible to the reports. I am much too busy to deal with something of this sort right now, but I can tell you what the farmers first told me. But, I want you to keep me out of this completely; you must promise me that or I won't tell you anything. I simply do not wish to be bothered.

"Don't worry Dubreil, I never mentioned you by name ever. I promise to keep you out of it. I really don't mind taking all the credit."

"See that you keep it that way. For now, you need something to write it on."

"Yes, yes. I am prepared for that. I have it all right here," he fumbled with the paper.

"Make sure that you copy the details I give you correctly. You do not want to make a mistake."

"No, no! You can count on me. Everything will be correct."

Dubreil was positive his impatient associate would do so without error. He would bet his life on it.

* * *

Fabien Ducrosse was more adept at physically handling explosives, but his brother Jean-Paul was more versed in planning the use of the charges, an arrangement that worked out well for the brother team.

On this occasion, Jean-Paul opted to attach a single wire across the inner entrance to the cave. He carefully measured the space and finally placed the wire about twenty inches off the cave's floor. He next attached a large amount of *plastique* to the end of the wires, taking time to correctly conceal the wire from view. While Jean-Paul was careful to secrete the wire, he did so with the full expectation that the thin cable would eventually be found.

In fact, Jean-Paul's entire plan for the explosives hinged on the Germans' capability for discovering his concealed trip wire.

Jean-Paul also placed additional charges throughout the second section of the cave, an area that was much more spacious than the cave's entrance.

He also helped Fabien arrange a number of the crates. Fabien had already applied Bonde's coding in addition to the large *Louvre* wording Bonde had also ordered.

Jean-Paul knew the tricky part was still ahead.

He watched his brother as Fabien moved to the first set of crates, leaning one against another and adjusting each one until the crates formed a neat row. It was Jean-Paul's intention that anyone entering the cave would initially encounter this particular row of crates. Fabien then placed a number of additional crates behind the first row, effectively creating second and third rows. Finally, he carefully positioned a hand grenade between the second and third rows, in a dark spot that was hidden to the eye. Now Fabien gently removed the pin from the grenade. He adjusted the pressure between the crates to assure himself that any minute movement of these crates would cause the grenade to topple and fall. On the cave floor area beneath the grenade, he placed additional grenades.

Satisfied, he tapped his younger brother on the shoulder and gathered his weapon.

"This should provide them with a nasty welcome," Jean-Paul smiled, admiring his concept.

"You take too much pleasure in your work, little brother!"

Fabien surveyed the cave and its contents one last time. He was satisfied that their efforts in the cavern would create an environment that he hoped would invite carelessness on the part of his enemies. His past experiences made him believe that their work would prove successful.

As they departed, Jean-Paul considered the consequences of what he and his brother had just rigged. Jean-Paul Ducrosse was pleased that neither he nor his brother would be anywhere near the cave when the explosions came.

* * *

Wehrmacht Oberstleutnant Dieter Hoven informed SS Obersturmbannfuhrer Kurt von Heltscherer of the Vichy informant's report of heavy truck activity in one of the more isolated northern areas above *Rodez* within minutes of receiving the information. These details were expected after the informant's initial visit, and, more importantly, since he had absolutely *nothing* else to go on, the new disclosures immediately sparked von Heltscherer's interest.

"And are you sure the information you have received is entirely reliable?" he demanded in an abrupt manner.

"Definitely Herr Obersturmbannfuhrer," Hoven assured. "I have used this agent several times in the past and his information has always proven to be correct. In fact, I consider him to be one of our better agents."

"Good, very good." von Heltscherer's thoughts were spinning ahead, already developing a plan in his mind.

"And, Oberstleutnant," he added a bit awkwardly, since his rank was only the equivalent of Hoven's, "this time I would like to direct the search myself. If our investigation proves to be factual, I want to be able to report back to the Reichsmarschall at once."

"Certainly. It will be my pleasure to accompany you. My men will be ready within the hour."

Hoven rose silently and departed.

Von Heltscherer waited for Hoven to leave. When he was sure the other officer was gone, von Heltscherer picked up the telephone again and tried the same number in Paris. It rang several times, but still no one answered.

He wondered why Sophie was frequently absent from his apartment and how she was occupying her time while he was away on his investigation. With this new information and the expectation of progress in his present quest, von Heltscherer's mind relaxed and he recalled his brief time together with Sophie in *Paris*. It was a little more than a week since he had left *Paris*, yet it seemed to him much longer.

Sophie. So soft and giving. Always ready to oblige.

His wishful thoughts of Sophie were soon replaced by the uneasy realization of the depth of his current predicament. His investigation's lack of any *real* progress in finding the location of the paintings had made von Heltscherer increasingly apprehensive. He was aware of the fact that Reichsmarschall Hermann Goring always demanded quick action, and in the beginning such a timely and successful conclusion seemed possible. In the past few days, as his investigation's progress seemed to stall badly, his outlook and disposition faded proportionately.

To make matters worse, if Hoven's new information proved unproductive, he would have nothing to report back to Goring, a report that was rapidly becoming overdue. Lack of progress would make the Reichsmarschall furious and Goring's reputation for rage was well known. Von Heltscherer was sure he wanted no part of the wrath of the Third Reich's second most important leader.

Their accelerated ride took more than two hours. Andre Faboul and Brian Russell finally concluded their exhausting trip to *Cahors*, a distance of nearly fifty miles, *arriving* in the city by early evening. Faboul was himself tired from lack of sleep and the stress of his mission. He also noticed that his new companion was nearing exhaustion.

"Soon," he had promised on the malodorous truck ride with the chickens, "you will be able to get some rest." His remark offered the American officer a small degree of hope. Russell was aware that he had become *really* tired. The obliging truck driver dropped off the pair, along with their bicycles, on the eastern edge of the city of *Cahors*.

The river-crescent town of *Cahors* consisted of numerous multi-story structures, arranged on well-attended streets. It was apparent that the outlying section of *Cahors* was primarily residential and that its townspeople took pride in the care of their properties. Many of the building fronts and yards were dressed with deep purple and blue violas, abundant yellow and white raised bushes and red geraniums, which bathed in luxuriant splendor of the waning July afternoon sun. It was as if everything and everyone within *Cahors* was oblivious to the war and its surroundings.

Brian Russell was charmed with what he saw. Even in his weary state the town reminded him of many wonderful times he had enjoyed in France prior to the war. He recalled an aphorism one of his favorite professors at the *Sorbonne* used in describing his own feelings about abstract beauty in France...

"Flowers to the ordinary French man or woman,
Are the expression of art in everyday life."

The candor of the passage struck Russell profoundly and he resolved to one day rediscover the happiness and gratification he had experienced in pre-war France.

The pair crossed the *Lot* River at the *Pont Neuf* on *Cahors'* eastern side, and made their way along the quai toward the center of the city. Most of the buildings in this section of the city were three and four stories, with the ground floor seemingly utilized by a business or office. They encountered an older cemetery to their left that was followed by a succession of small streets and alleyways. They passed an old building that once was the home of a former French King, Henri IV, until finally they arrived at the rear of the 12th Century Church of *St.Vicisse*. The church itself was in an advanced state of dilapidation and a statue of the Madonna with Infant was all that was discernible of the façade. It was the first church building Russell had seen during the course of their journey that was in such a neglected state.

The narrow intersection next to the old church opened into a wider street named *Rue Clemenceau*. Faboul consulted the map he had received the prior night from Antoine, and eventually stopped at the doorway to a four-story white mortar building. The first and third story of the building contained wrought iron balconies, which added a certain charm to the exterior. The number 29 was attached to the front of the building.

Faboul selected a buzzer from an array of eight; each identified by the last name of the tenants. He glanced over at Russell and pushed the button. After several moments, the door next to the buzzers opened and a strikingly attractive dark haired young woman stepped out.

She was of medium height with a boyish, somewhat rectangular face, a perfectly set chin and dimples. Her ravenesque hair was of medium length, swept back from her graceful face by an azure ribbon. Soft brown eyes magnetized one's view to the center of her face.

"Yes, can I help you?" She looked directly at Russell.

Russell was nearing exhaustion and unprepared for such a vision. He was taken aback so Faboul answered instead, carefully recounting the instructions he had received from Bonde.

"My name is Georges, and my friend here, well, you should call him Louis Roussell. We have been sent to you by Victor."

Christine appraised the two, and motioned for them to come inside.

The three ascended a rounded stairwell until they reached the third floor. Christine ushered them inside.

"I am glad that you finally made it here. I am Christine Allard and I too work for Victor. He sent me to wait here at the flat of my cousin, since it was on your route to the south. He told me to expect you, but he was not specific as to when you would arrive. In fact, I have been waiting here for several days."

"Actually, we have made excellent progress," Faboul replied, somewhat defensively, "I believe we are right on schedule."

"I am sure that is true. It is just that I was sent here several days ago, and the time has passed slowly." She indicated for them to sit on a tatty sofa that was situated along a wall in the unpretentious living room, just inside the front door. Russell scrutinized the room for an appropriate resting place and positioned the canister out of sight directly behind the sofa.

"You both look exhausted. Would you prefer to talk about the mission now or wait until you have had a chance to get some rest?" It was evident to both men that her concern for their well-being was genuine.

"Even though we both need a rest badly, it would probably be better to tell you now, in case there are arrangements you need to make. I know you have already been told that it is vitally important that my friend here and the object he is carrying both get out of France safely," Faboul said motioning toward Russell. "What you might not know is that his mission is important to *all* the people of France. I would like to tell you more, but for your own safety, it is probably best you know as little as possible."

"I understand your hesitancy, you are undoubtedly right. But, do not worry, I already have developed a plan."

Faboul listened but was already experiencing a tinge of apprehension about Christine's exuberance.

Was the woman seated in front of him too young and too eager to be entrusted with such a serious undertaking?

As he pondered his own question, Faboul realized that even if his concern had merit, he was faced with few other choices.

Was he simply too tired right now to see things clearly?

He tried to set his mind at ease.

Surely the Resistance knew what it was doing when they assigned her to this important task. Was he now too deeply involved in the mission? Did that cause him to be overly cautious about the paintings and their safety?

Faboul closed his eyes for the briefest moment and willed such thoughts to the back of his mind as Christine spoke again.

"With the Germans increasing their efforts to close France's borders, most Resistance escape routes are currently being forged through the *Pyrenees* into Spain. After discussing the situation with Victor, we decided that your friend would have a better chance of reaching the border if someone familiar with the country escorted him. Victor felt the person should be a woman, which would enable them to pose as a married couple. That way he felt they would attract less attention, particularly if they pretended as if they were going to a family event."

Faboul stared silently as Christine finished her explanation. Christine sensed Faboul's uneasiness and tried to relieve his apprehension.

"So far we have had a great deal of success with similar plans. I know it is a rather long route to travel, but there are fewer and fewer Germans to be encountered as you proceed southward. The entire area we will travel is under the Vichy militia's control. We have found it is generally much easier to deceive them than it is the Germans. Their forces lack any formal military training and are generally performing functions they would rather not do. It is usually not too difficult for our operatives to fool them completely."

Faboul assessed Christine's words his mind and suddenly a thought came to him. "Do you have some sort of map of the south that I can use?"

"I think there is one around here someplace." Christine left and rummaged through a large chest of drawers inside the bedroom. She found what she was looking for and handed the tattered map to Faboul.

Faboul opened the map and checked his calculations. At length he handed the map back to Christine.

"I thought I was on to something, but I wanted to make sure," he said forcefully.

Christine glanced over at Russell who remained silent.

Faboul spoke again to Christine.

"There is only one thing I might add to what you have already mentioned."

"And that is?"

"If you follow through on your initial idea, the one about acting like a family, I think it just might work. What if the two of you should act as if you are on a pilgrimage to *Lourdes*, maybe in thanks to the Blessed Virgin for her part in bringing you together. Such a trip would not be considered all that unusual for a newly married couple. I believe such a cover story would allow you to blend in with others heading toward the sacred shrine. The reason I checked the map is that I wanted to be sure it was on the route to the Pyrenees."

Faboul allowed his words to sink in and hoped that his suggestion added plausibility to Christine's plan. He focused his attention back to Christine while she deliberated the matter in her mind.

Christine replied momentarily. "Georges, I like your idea a great deal. It is very convenient that *Lourdes* is located on one of the main crossovers into Spain. Such a route would make a lot of sense."

Faboul was reassured with her reaction and nodded his agreement. He was ready to proceed with the important instructions that would cover the vital next segment of Operation Angerona.

On a torn piece of paper, he wrote an address that he had committed to memory from the initial instructions given him before boarding the train in *Paris*. He checked the address again for accuracy and handed it to Christine.

"Tomorrow, you must both go to this address and obtain fresh papers for each of you. One of our Resistance supporters owns the store, and he has received instructions as to what to do. I ask you to commit this address to memory as I did and destroy the paper. I'm not sure how long it will take, but you will receive your new documents as quickly as possible. I have a feeling the address is not very far from here, no more than six or seven streets away. The building is supposed to be right near the quai, down by the river." Faboul searched his mind for any other pertinent facts and, satisfied he had repeated everything he had been told, asked Christine. "Do you have any more questions?"

Christine shook her head negatively and observed Faboul as he glanced in the direction of the small kitchen. She realized the two men had probably not eaten in some time.

"Are you both hungry?"

Faboul nodded and turned toward Russell.

He was a bit tardy in doing so. Brian Russell was already stretched out on the sofa, dead to the world.

Christine smiled to herself and studied the horizontal figure. Russell had not uttered a word since she was introduced to him, but there was something about the way the man conducted himself. He evoked a strong and silent aura, which Christine found attractive.

She quickly produced a light blanket from the bedroom, lifted it over him and tucked it around his prone form. From Russell's deep snoring, Christine was sure that her visitor would be in a profound slumber for many hours to come.

Christine turned her attention back to Andre Faboul. Proceeding into the kitchen, she reached into an old icebox and removed a pot containing the remnants of a stew she had prepared for Lucille the night before. She lit the small nearby stove and placed the pot over the open burner. She produced a fresh *baguette* and poured Faboul a glass of red wine from a large, circular jug resting on the rear of the counter. When the stew was sufficiently heated, Christine poured it onto a plate in front of Faboul who had seated himself on one of the two chairs next to the kitchen table.

"Here, I made this last night for my cousin. I hope you like it," she offered, placing it in front of Faboul.

Faboul attacked the stew and nodded his sincere approval. As with most second-day stews, it was delicious and he was starving! In fact, Andre Faboul could not remember anything tasting this good in his entire life.

*   *   *

Pierre Bonde returned to *le Puy- en-Veley* and penned a short, coded note to Jean Moulin. In it, he outlined the details of the mission thus far, informing his old friend of its progress. Barring any problems, the note would reach Moulin's hands within a day or two. He also concluded the message with a final annotation that, in his opinion, the operation was still basically on schedule.

Even though Bonde was personally satisfied with the way Operation Angerona was developing, he realized that the most difficult part of the mission lay ahead. A myriad of possibilities and potential problems still faced Christine and Russell. Their ultimate success would depend upon the efforts of a number of loyal Resistance operatives as well as some help from the heavens above.

Bonde crossed himself and offered a silent prayer for the mission's continued success. It was a gesture Bonde had not performed in several years, and he hoped that the Good Lord would not count his former inactivity against him.

*   *   *

Once again, Wehrmacht Oberstleutnant Dieter Hoven quickly supplied SS Obersturmbannfuhrer Kurt von Heltscherer with a full complement of soldiers to search the location Edmond Dubreil's Vichy informant had pinpointed. Hoven estimated the place was nearly twenty miles from his offices at *Rodez*. Reaching it would require the motorized force to travel on a number of infrequently used back roads.

The German motorcade made for a curious sight as it snaked its way out of *Rodez* and into the lightly populated countryside of southern France.

Von Heltscherer and Hoven occupied the back seats of an older Mercedes touring car while SS Scharfuhrer Mueller was seated in the left front seat. The convertible preceded two personnel carriers and several trucks. The procession's route led them in an almost northerly direction, into more hilly terrain as the narrow road wound around several mountains. Their course included several hairpin switchbacks while it paralleled the banks of a small river. Mueller glanced at the map he brought with him and identified the small waterway as the *Dordou* River. As Mueller studied the map more intently, he saw that the *Dordou* emptied into the much larger *Lot* River. The *Lot* slowly pushed its way southwestward on its ultimate journey to the even larger *Garonne* River and finally into the Atlantic Ocean just above the City of *Bordeaux*.

Almost as soon as the convoy entered the country, a number of low stone fences covered with ground moss began dotting the sides of the road along their route. It was truly a bucolic setting where large black crows and white tailed hawks stood sentry on poles or telephone wires in search of small rodents. Summer in Southern France was at its apex and the sparsely populated surrounding countryside abounded with verdant growth and simple beauty. The entire scene was contrasted by the dull grayness of the convoy's vehicles. The procession turned a curve on the heavily pockmarked highway and entered the town of *Conques*, a quaint hillside settlement that was actually cut out of solid limestone cliffs.

Nearly an hour had elapsed since the vehicles had left Hoven's *Rodez* office and von Heltscherer was amazed that the procession had yet to encounter an oncoming car or truck.

This area would make for an ideal environment for hiding paintings; it is probably the most remote area I have seen since I started searching for the treasures.

A few miles further north, SS Scharfuhrer Mueller's detailed map finally indicated the convoy's approach to a small village named *Grand-Vabre*. A small sign proclaimed its location within the *Grand Gorges* section of the *Massif Central*. A sprawling saw mill dominated the road and approach to *Grand-Vabre* and produced a sweet scent of freshly cut cedar timber as the vehicles drove past.

According to Hoven's informer, the area just beyond *Grand-Vabre* was the scene of the suspicious truck traffic and the area von Heltscherer intended to search.

The line of vehicles slowed perceptibly as it passed through the small town, and finally paused a mile west of the outskirts of *Grand-Vabre*.

Von Heltscherer directed the Wehrmacht driver, an obergefreiter (corporal), to continue forward at a reduced rate of speed. According to the informant, the group should now seek out a small road that cut in from the left. The motorcade proceeded ahead for nearly another mile, and suddenly a roughly cut road appeared around a curve.

"From this point, another smaller road should emerge on the right," Mueller explained, looking at the map and consulting the notes he had received from Oberstleutnant Hoven. "Proceed up the road," Mueller instructed the obergefreiter.

Within a half-mile, a small dirt road appeared on the right, nearly hidden by groves of trees on both sides of its entrance.

The lead car paused briefly at the intersection and turned down the road.

Gazing forward, von Heltscherer surmised that any trucks larger than the ones accompanying their present force would have trouble traveling down this road.

The convoy proceeded another 200 yards, and a medium-sized *chateau* became apparent on their left, partially hidden by a grove of fruit trees.

Von Heltscherer stood up in the back of the old Mercedes, raised his hand and the procession came to a halt. All the vehicle engines were cut and the entire setting was swathed in sunlight. A cloud of eerie silence enveloped the vehicles and soldiers. The only audible sounds were the wind rustling through the nearby trees and the active chirping of busy robins situated in the nearby fields.

*   *   *

Christine tapped Brian Russell gently on his shoulder, attempting to waken him from his deep sleep.

Russell did not move a muscle.

She decided more specific force was necessary and pulled his shirt several times.

His eyes partially opened, attempting to focus on the figure standing above him.

Christine's classic outline came into view. The deep brown pools that held her eyes stared intently at him through his virtual slumber.

"I am sorry to have to wake you, but we must leave soon," Christine explained. "I have even drawn a bath for you so that you can get cleaned up a little," she added, pointing in the direction of the bathroom. "I am sure you are now aware that you have acquired quite an odor."

Russell took a quick whiff and nodded his agreement.

Too much time cramped in the glider and then all the pedaling on the bicycle, not to mention the chickens. Under such conditions, anyone would smell.

"Thank you for preparing the bath, I'll put it to good use." Brian Russell realized it was the first time he had spoken to the intriguing woman.

"And, I believe my cousin has some old clothes in the closet which might fit you. Her husband Claude is fighting with the Free French and does not need them right now. You and Claude look to be about the same size. His clothes will make you look more like a Frenchman."

Russell thanked her and raised himself from the sofa. He took a necessary stretch and started toward the direction Christine indicated. He reached the small bathroom and looked at the old tub wondering if his athletic frame would fit into its narrow confines. Russell undressed and tenderly touched the water with his finger. It was warm and penetrating. He had slept well and actually felt quite refreshed. He stepped into the tub and enjoyed the sensation of the warm water. He allowed drops of warm liquid to cascade down his back. He closed his eyes and savored the sensation.

*   *   *

The German soldiers fanned out noiselessly, effectively surrounding the *chateau*. Von Heltscherer had given orders to proceed as silently as possible, even though there seemed to be no sign of life. As he neared the *chateau*, von Heltscherer noted the grove of trees was all apples. Their distinctive, ripened aromas cast a pungent sweetness to the air as the armed force crept through.

As the soldiers approached the house with guns drawn, Mueller pointed to several sets of tire tracks in the dirt that appeared to be recently made. Von Heltscherer acknowledged Mueller's signal and motioned the first soldiers forward. They were now alongside the *chateau*, which looked to be completely boarded up. The front and side windows were filled with various planks and the landscaping was grossly overgrown.

The possibility that this could be another wild goose chase crossed von Heltscherer's mind, but he quickly dismissed the thought . He and Hoven relaxed their guns, replaced them in their holsters, and von Heltscherer called for a meeting with the force's non-commissioned officers.

"Scharfuhrer Mueller has pointed out evidence of recent activity here," von Heltscherer began, his voice reverberating through the trees. "And I intend to find out what is going on. I want you to have your men spread out and search the surrounding area. They must take their time and miss nothing. If they do find something, they are to call you immediately before they proceed. Under no circumstances are they to investigate whatever they find themselves. Do I make myself clear?"

"Jawohl," was the group's immediate reply.

The gathering broke up and von Heltscherer's orders were quickly relayed to the waiting Wehrmacht soldiers.

* * *

Russell extracted himself from the small tub, dried off and returned to the bedroom. Christine had placed a selection of clothes on the bed for Russell to choose from. He selected a pair of under pants, slacks, shirt and coat. The clothes fit his liking and he proceeded to get dressed. Russell was a tad larger than Lucille's husband, but not enough that it was really noticeable. He glanced into the rectangular, framed mirror and satisfied himself that he was at least presentable.

Christine came back into the room and looked over her handiwork.

"There is one more addition to your wardrobe." She walked to the bedroom closet and opened it. She picked up two pair of shoes and handed them to Russell.

"Choose the pair that fits you best. These are French shoes and will make your appearance even more realistic. Your other shoes were English and are a dead giveaway."

Russell considered her point and made a mental note to mention the fact to SOE when and if he ever returned to England. He was impressed that the young woman was so thorough.

Brian Russell picked out a cordovan-colored pair and tried them on. The shoes fitted him a little tight, but he hoped that would change when he wore them more. He turned again to face Christine.

"Where is Georges?" Russell asked. He had not seen Faboul since before he dozed off.

"Georges has gone on a short errand, but should be back any moment. Georges was not nearly as exhausted as you were. He only slept a few hours. We already shared some juice and a *brioche*."

Russell's face lit up at the mention of food. He suddenly realized that he hadn't eaten in some time and that he was absolutely ravenous. He looked at Christine who had already figured out what was on his mind.

"I have set out the juice and was waiting to ask you if you wanted me to cook you some breakfast."

"The juice and some rolls will be fine," Russell answered, following her into the kitchen.

"Good. Sit down here and I will put them out for you."

Russell did as instructed and gobbled down two of the delicious *brioche*. He was just finishing the second one when Andre Faboul returned.

"I trust you had a restful sleep," Faboul teased. "All thirteen hours of it."

"I'm glad you can count so accurately," Russell retorted. "I understand why they trust you on such important missions."

Faboul grinned back. He had become fond of Russell and would be sorry when the time came for him to leave his new friend.

"I am afraid I must be leaving here within a few minutes. My train back to *Paris* departs in about three-quarters of an hour. Christine says my walk from here to the *gare* takes about fifteen minutes, so I should still have plenty of time."

Russell acknowledged Faboul's comment and saw that the Frenchman's face had turned serious.

"Before I go, I need to tell you something. Christine, can you please excuse us? It would probably be wiser for you if you did not hear what I have to say."

"I will wait out on the balcony." Christine left the room and Andre Faboul sat down in the other kitchen chair.

"My friend, I think you already know what I am going to say, but I will tell it to you anyway."

Russell sat stiffly, not at all aware of Faboul's intent.

"My country is placing a great deal of responsibility on your shoulders, *mon ami*, and I want you to be aware of certain things. I want you to realize just what our mission involves, and exactly who if affects.
The three paintings contained in your cylinder are not just great masterpieces; they are the very basis of a segment of French culture. When Francois I began collecting these masterpieces, his intention was to share them with all the people in our country. Throughout our history, many of the great kings of France have contributed and the collection has continued to grow. When the *Louvre* officially became a museum several centuries ago, it set out to become the greatest art museum in the world.

The paintings in your possession are the finest of the *Louvre's* collection and could never possibly be replaced should anything go wrong. I hope you keep some of my thoughts in the back of your mind. Also, please consider one more important thing.

From the time they are little, French children are trained to respect art and are also taught the history of the museum and of the great paintings. This is done primarily so that art and culture become part of their everyday lives. That is why your present mission is so important to so many varied individuals.

Mon ami, what I am trying to say is simple. You now hold the future of French art culture within your grasp. I wish there was some alternative way of removing the paintings from the Nazi danger, or even hiding them in France where they would be considered safe, but no one has of yet been able to come up with a plausible strategy.

As you can see, many of us in the Resistance movement are willing to risk our lives to see that no harm comes to the paintings, and I hope that you also feel that way."

Faboul paused and looked into Russell's eyes. "I just wanted you to see inside the heart of one Frenchman, so I spoke for myself as well as for my country."

Russell was moved by Faboul's earnestness and groped to find the right words.

"I most certainly understand everything you said and I am honored you chose to share your feelings with me. Even though I am not French, I certainly feel as strongly about the paintings as you do. I will do everything within my power to get them safely out of France. You have my word on that."

Russell stepped forward and embraced Faboul. He hugged him tightly for a long moment and finally stepped back.

Faboul looked around and called Christine back into the room. He addressed them both.

"I must go now or I will miss my train. *Au revoir et bonne chance.*"

"*Au revoir. A demain,*" Russell replied.

Faboul stepped forward toward Christine. He kissed each side of her face lightly and nodded affirmatively. He walked to the flat's front door, and started down the steps. Christine closed the door behind him.

She turned and looked at Russell whose concerned expression was visibly apparent.

"You look as if you lost your best friend."

"You might be right," Russell replied, his mind overflowing. "I wasn't expecting him to leave just yet. I enjoyed having his help."

Christine felt his anxiety and touched him gently on the arm. She smiled consciously, attempting to provide support.

"*I* am your helper now," she declared, matter of factly.

Russell considered her reply and attempted to alter the subject, "I am still a little hungry. Is there anything else here to eat?"

"We will have more to eat in a little while. For now, we must be on our way."

She reached for her purse and a light jacket on a table near the door. Placing the jacket over her arm, Christine opened the front door and headed for the stairwell.

"Let us go," she ordered, motioning for Russell to follow.

Once down the three flights of stairs, they exited the building and headed south, in the general direction of the *Lot* River.

* * *

It took the first German soldier, a young fresh faced schutze (private), about ten minutes to find the cave's entrance located about 150 yards to the rear of the *chateau.*

Following von Heltscherer's orders, the soldier correctly called for his unteroffizier (sergeant) to come and inspect the area. The Wehrmacht unteroffizier also properly followed his orders and decided to call SS Obersturmbannfuhrer Kurt von Heltscherer before proceeding any further.

"We have discovered a large cave, Herr Obersturmbannfuhrer. I suggest we proceed with caution. If it was used by the enemy, it could easily be booby trapped."

"Yes, I agree," von Heltscherer replied. "You did the correct thing in calling me. It is most prudent that we take our time in investigating this area." He stepped back to allow the search to continue.

SS Scharfuhrer Mueller stepped forward with a flashlight light and started into the cave. Another unteroffizier and the schutze who originally found the cave accompanied him. They had not traveled more than fifteen feet when Mueller suddenly stopped. He held up his hand. He felt down gently, to a spot immediately in front of his left leg. Something was pressing against his pants leg, right below his knee.

A tightly drawn wire was stretched across the entire mouth of the cave!

Mueller called back to von Heltscherer in a controlled tone.

"Herr Obersturmbannfuhrer, I have found something. Please come and see."

Von Heltscherer entered the cave and walked to where Mueller knelt next to the wire.

"I have found a trip wire, Herr Obersturmbannfuhrer. "

"They took precautions to secure the cave," von Heltscherer assessed, his spirits suddenly escalating. "There must be something valuable inside they wish to protect."

"Yes, Herr Obersturmbannfuhrer. It certainly appears that way."

"Well, disable this wire and let us see exactly what it is they have hidden. And Mueller, be very careful."

Mueller did not need the added guidance. He started to trace the wire to its source. He called for more lights for the inside of the cave. The lights were quickly produced from outside the cave by the unteroffizier. The effect of more lighting helped make Mueller's job much easier.

It took him five minutes until the *plastique* charges planted by the Ducrosse brothers were disconnected.

"All done," Mueller announced, "we can proceed ahead."

He stepped forward into the cave, taking short steps and feeling his way. His light glanced off the roof of the cave, which suddenly opened up into a much larger cavern.

Von Heltscherer remained close behind the three soldiers and was delighted to discover the larger subterranean room.

Mueller proceeded forward, his light dancing throughout the cavern. He was now twenty yards into the larger room when he passed a walled section that jutted out into the cavern's center, forming a partial barrier. Behind the mound of dirt and rock that formed the partition, he made a startling discovery.

"Herr Obersturmbannfuhrer, over here. Look at what I found!" His animated words reverberated throughout the cavern.

With great interest, von Heltscherer approached the spot at which Mueller had stopped.

Immediately behind the wall, a number of wooden crates rested against the sides of the cavern.

"Shine your lights over here," von Heltscherer ordered. "I want to be able to read what is written on them."

Mueller complied and leaned forward with his light.

Von Heltscherer knelt down on one knee and studied the first crate. He dusted it a bit and looked at the markings. Besides a set of numbers and letters, the word *Louvre* was plainly marked on the crate.

Von Heltscherer's spirits soared. The word *Louvre* jumped out at him like a beacon in the night. He had found the paintings from the museum! All his prayers had been answered!

"You have done well, Mueller. These definitely seem to be some of the paintings I have been looking for. I wonder how many of them are stored here." He began counting the stack nearest himself. "And send word for Herr Oberstleutnant Hoven to join us."

Containing his excitement, von Heltscherer waited until Hoven appeared a minute later. He gloated in the direction of his fellow officer.

"See Hoven, these are the paintings I told you about." He started to reach for another crate in the second pile.

"Herr Oberstrumbannfuhrer, if I may be so bold," Mueller quickly interrupted.

Von Heltscherer turned to his subordinate, and stopped.

"We do not know if there are additional explosives here, we should be careful," Mueller warned.

"Nonsense," von Heltscherer rebuffed him. "These paintings are too valuable. The enemy would never allow even one of them to be destroyed."

He crouched again and began to touch the second stack. Mueller looked incredulously as the first two crates moved forward. Von Heltscherer leaned down and searched the new crates for additional markings.

"See, I told you. There is no problem."

Von Heltscherer moved forward and reached for the third stack of crates. It was stuck so be started to pull the top crate towards him. "I cannot make out the markings on this one. Maybe if I..."

In a split second, SS Obersturmbannfuhrer Kurt von Heltscherer realized his mistake as the grenade fell dully to the floor.

A blurred white light passed across his vision as the blast resounded throughout the caves.

Chapter Twelve

Christine and Russell had little trouble locating the address in downtown *Cahors* that Andre Faboul had given her. They walked together to the *Lot* River and then along the cobbled quai on the warm, sunny morning. A light, almost humid breeze brushed their faces, and their shoes echoed in a light cadence that was only interrupted by sounds of vocal birds along the river. The walk took ten minutes and Russell and Christine engaged in small talk about the summer season until they neared their destination.

The shop they sought was a *Bar & Tabac,* nestled on a small side street not far from the river. Its location was near the *Pont Louis Philippe*, the city's southernmost bridge that entered *Cahors* and that ultimately led in the direction of much larger *Toulouse*, over 75 miles away. Upon entering the shop, they identified themselves to the proprietor who was the sole inhabitant of the bar. The Resistance's message to expect them had reached the *Bar & Tabac's* proprietor two days earlier, and he told Christine he already prepared for them. He placed a closed sign on the front door and immediately ushered them down to a basement room. The man then produced an old hand camera from an antique *armoire* in the room and motioned for them to stand next to the wall that he had painted an off shade of white.

He snapped each of their pictures individually, and asked Christine to confirm the names and addresses she wanted included in the papers. He busily scribbled a few notes and finally directed his visitors to return to the shop in about two hours. He gave his complete assurance to Christine that both sets of papers would be ready by that time.

Russell followed behind Christine as they remounted the stairs and went outside the *Bar & Tabac.* Since Christine was familiar with the area she chose a route that once again followed along the banks of the *Lot.* This part of the city was mostly residential Russell noted, but after a walk of several minutes they came upon a small hotel, complete with a modest outdoor seating area that overlooked the river.

"Now we can take care of your appetite," Christine teased Russell. "I am supposing you are still hungry?"

"Hungry, I'm practically starved," he responded in equal spirit.

"Good, we can choose something nice to eat while we wait."

They sat down at an end table and a waiter soon appeared with small, hand-written menus.

Russell pondered the choices, remembering he was back in France with its usually marvelous cuisine. Fascinated by the variety of choices the menu of even such a simple restaurant offered, he opted for a local *terrine,* a dish the waiter was quick to recommend. Christine followed Russell's lead and also ordered the *terrine,* which she knew to be one of the hotel's specialties.. Russell also chose a nice bottle of *vin du payee,* a local red country wine, to accompany the *terrine.* The attentive waiter soon brought the wine to the table and the two raised their glasses to the French Resistance and to the mission ahead.

It was an hour since they had left Christine's cousin's apartment on *Rue Clemenceau.* Several minutes passed that included some very pleasant conversations with the man introduced to her as Louis Roussell. Christine reached the conclusion that she might actually enjoy this mission a good deal more than she had first believed.

* * *

The disaster caused by the cave explosion that killed SS Obersturmbannfuhrer Kurt von Heltscherer, Wehrmacht Oberstleutnant Dieter Hoven, SS Scharfuhrer Mueller and the other German soldiers created a major uproar within the Oberkommando of the German Wehrmacht.

The military high command for France issued an immediate order to round up everyone within a one hundred miles area of *Rodez* even suspected of being a member of the French Resistance. In- country security was tightened on all major travel routes and the number of Vichy militia road guard stations was also increased.

Since von Heltscherer's mission was highly classified and the Gestapo officials knew he was working directly for Reichsmarschall Hermann Goring, the Gestapo took it upon itself to establish the specific reason why the soldiers were searching the cave. There was even talk of involving the Sicherheitsdienst or SD, the secret police within the Gestapo, to get to the bottom of the crime. It was also generally agreed amongst all German military and political factions that the use of sophisticated explosives at the cave site pointed to the fact that the explosion was the work of the French Resistance.

* * *

The idyllic lunch was delicious and satisfying and served to fulfill Russell's immediate hunger. The *vin du payee* proved to be a bright little red, grown locally around Cahors. The wine provided them both with excellent flavors and even a comfortable little buzz. Conversation between the two was insignificant during the meal; Russell preferred it that way. No need for Christine to be too well informed about their mission.

As they continued their dialogue, she imparted to Russell an insight to her charming personality, along with a few of her preferences as well as equal number preferred indifferences. She loved flowers, birds and animals, including a particular fondness for rabbits, but loathed anything that appeared insincere, unimaginative or lazy. She also hated Germans with a vengeance. While not delving too deeply, Russell concluded there were egregious reasons for her despising the Germans to such an extent. He chose not to inquire any further at this time.

He relished Christine's seemingly boundless energy and relative naïveté. Even before lunch ended, she had convinced Russell that the Allies would eventually win the war. She even brashly inquired as to whether Russell actually knew, or could guess, when the liberation of France would begin. Russell wasn't completely prepared for the degree of fervor Christine displayed. He decided against sharing with her the fact that most of the recent news and scuttlebutt he had heard in Great Britain showed the Germans mounting successful offensives on several fronts.

Russell politely avoided the subject but was nevertheless completely charmed by her abject honesty.

The meal was finally completed, and Christine reached into her pocket book and paid the bill. They left the restaurant and started back in the direction of the *Bar & Tabac*. As they left the hotel, she handed Russell a wad of French paper money.

"Here, from now on *you* carry this. Victor gave me more than enough for our journey. It will look better if you paid the bills from now on."

Russell accepted the money and placed the bills inside his pocket. He was again impressed that Christine was astute enough to notice such a small detail. Reaching the *Bar & Tabac*, they proceeded inside. The bar was empty as before as the proprietor reached under the counter and produced a wrapped package, which he handed directly to Russell.

"Here is your order, *Monsieur*."

Russell reached into his pants pocket in an attempt to pay the man for his trouble, but the proprietor shook his head.

"*Merci beau coups, Monsieur. Vive la Resistance!*" The pair nodded politely and left.

When they stepped outside onto to the *banquette*, Christine placed her hand inside Russell's elbow, as if the action was totally natural on her part. While the move surprised Russell, he was aware that it wasn't the first time she had touched him, and he found the experience quite pleasant.

Noting his mild timidity, she turned and spoke, almost teasingly.

"Well, we are supposed to be married, are we not? And this is the way married people should act, *n'est-ce pas?*"

He smiled and tightened his elbow a bit around her hand.

"It certainly is," he replied, as an expansive smile crept onto his solid face.

*   *   *

Immediately after the Wehrmacht notified Gestapo Headquarters in *Paris* of the death of SS Oberstrumbannfuhrer Kurt von Heltscherer, an official Gestapo report was immediately sent to the office of Reichsmarschall Hermann Goring.

Goring was on holiday in Holland and away from his office, so his clerk put the report on Goring's desk.

The Reichsmarschall was scheduled to return in two days, and the report was just one of numerous messages the high National Socialist official received. Besides, before he departed, Goring left special instructions that he was not to be disturbed while on holiday unless it was an emergency.

His clerk saw nothing in the text of the message that made it particularly noteworthy and placed it among the many messages awaiting the Reichsmarschall's return.

Goring would be able to read it upon his arrival.

*   *   *

Since there was ample time left before he and Christine were to return to her cousin Lucille's, Russell asked Christine to accompany him as he sought out a particular type of shop in *Cahors*' business district. Russell found the variety store he was seeking on the *Rue de la Barre*, a block down from the *Prefecture du Police*. Russell went inside the shop and browsed through a number of items that were prominently displayed throughout the store on large tables. He selected four particular items, and bought two copies of each. Russell grinned at Christine as he paid the clerk and waited for her to wrap them in brown paper. When the wrapping was completed, they departed for Lucille's apartment.

Once inside the flat, Brian Russell thought it best to discuss the proposed route of egress from France with Christine. He agreed with her contention that they follow Andre Faboul's suggestion of the City of *Lourdes* as a gateway city for his escape. The city held little in the way of military significance and was not very distant from the Spanish border in the *Pyrenees* Mountains.

Christine knew that Lourdes was a popular destination for Catholics and for people from many religions since the apparition of the Virgin nearly a century before. Even wartime restrictions failed to daunt the faithful's pilgrimages to the city and shrine of Our Lady of Lourdes. Christine confided that she was also counting on the fact that the Resistance believed that the Vichy government often overlooked minor document discrepancies for pilgrims heading towards *Lourdes,* many of whom were too old and infirmed to even have correct papers. She felt she and Russell could conveniently blend into the crowds of people headed there.

Since *Cahors* was roughly 275 miles from Lourdes, there were several routes Christine and Russell could select to get there. While a number of direct routes were available, Christine chose a circuitous route that bypassed a number of larger cities. She knew from prior experience that most roads along her proposed route were not frequently traveled.

Christine also confided in Russell that she had received a recent warning from Victor that some travelers under the Resistance's care had failed to reach their destinations. Victor was of the opinion that there was an increasing possibility of betrayal within their organization and ordered her to take as long as necessary to reach her destination.

Christine had worked out the details of her plan during Russell's long sleep. She was careful to utilize a number of Resistance contacts Victor had made her memorize before she started on the mission. Her plan called for them to leave *Cahors* and proceed south, in the general direction of *Lourdes.* They would slip off the main road early and snake through the smaller towns of *Cassou, Condom,* and into *Aire-sur-l'Adour.* If all went well, upon reaching *Aire-sur-l'Adour,* she would then choose their final route into *Lourdes.* Once they were safely in *Lourdes,* only a short distance remained before reaching their ultimate destination, the *Pyrenees* Mountains.

Her plan also relied upon the Resistance's previous experience with assisting downed airmen, refugees and others fleeing the Nazis. That prior knowledge showed that security tightened noticeably as you neared France's western and northern borders. The Resistance felt that the routes to the south were much more feasible due to the fact that security was controlled for the most part by the Vichy government.

Christine's route was designed to allow her to meet Resistance members in several towns along the way. Her original agreement with Victor as to how and when to proceed would be waiting at each stop she chose. Christine had the foresight to send a copy of her route back with Faboul to *Paris* where it was to be immediately forwarded to Victor. Within hours, each Resistance contact along her route was transmitted instructions and advised to be on the alert. While the Resistance's means of communication were sometimes complex and tedious, this infrastructure served an extensive network and usually provided its members with timely and correct information.

The stage for Christine and Russell's journey was now properly set.

* * *

The Gestapo also sent a heated directive to all offices of the *Milice*; the Vichy's government equivalent of their own despised and feared organization. It was the *Milice* who was responsible for state security within the unoccupied zone of France. The directive warned the *Milice* organization of *dire consequences* for anyone arrested involving the murders of the German soldiers near *Rodez* It also asked all aligned agencies for any information concerning any irregular or suspected Resistance activity.

The Gestapo notice also contained the revelation that a number of Wehrmacht soldiers were being sent to augment the Vichy militia's checkpoints in certain key areas throughout the unoccupied zone of France. Involved Vichy militia units were expected to provide these soldiers with any necessary help. The decision to provide additional manpower was one of the first instances on record where essential German soldiers were actually sent to prolonged duty in unoccupied France.

*   *   *

By early July, the small band of *maquisards* operating in the eastern region of *Aquitaine* had grown to well over twenty. Its members were the vanguard of expatriates from the Vichy Government's oft rumored, and soon to be announced labor draft. These were the first Frenchmen that would choose the rigors of the mountains and para-military life within the borders of France over the prospects of serving in the army Vichy would raise.

Many members of the *maquisards* objected to the very existence of the Vichy Government itself and all were uniform in their hatred of the Germans. Each became part of the overall Resistance effort to help rid their country of what they considered as dual existing enemies, the Vichy Government *and* the German Wehrmacht.

The *maquis,* as they were simply called after the French word for brush or wooded undergrowth, performed duties and operations in direct support of the Free French military forces that were located *outside* of France. In most cases *maquis* soldiers were not paid, nor were their relatives allowed to correspond with them in any manner. They existed through the generosity of the local populace who supported them with food and lodging whenever possible.

It wasn't long before everyone in France considered the *maquis* the unofficial guerrilla arm of the Resistance.

Charles Martin was 39, and before the war was known by his peers to be one of the best woodworkers in southern France. Martin would have preferred leaving France to join Charles de Gaulle's Free French force the minute France allowed Germany to cross its borders, but strong family ties prevented him from doing so. His aged, invalid mother and younger sister depended on him for their existence. In his mind, his family came first and, Charles Martin, although tempted, never seriously considered leaving their sides.

His mother lingered on until passing away in early 1942, at which time Martin made his decision. He placed his sister in the care of a nearby aunt and uncle and subsequently formed one of the first bands of *maquis* fighters in southwestern France.

The creation of his unit was even more problematic than Charles Martin could have anticipated. While many volunteers were willing to forgo the consequences and enlist with his group, Martin faced several obstructions to his success. These included a meager national organization for his band and almost total lack of regional direction. To make matters worse, Martin's men faced the most primitive living conditions imaginable,

Arms and supplies were another significant problem. Through infrequent British SOE aerial arms drops, Martin and his men were provided a small amount of weapons and ammunition.

Some arms materials were also secreted in by water through England, and even more supplies were received through small boats operating from Gibraltar, Portugal and Spain. After several months, a small amount of more complex explosives were also made available to the ragged bush fighters. Realistically, however, it was impossible for Martin to gauge the frequency of any arms or supplies drops.

Charles Martin's *marquis* fighters made sound use of anything they received. As the band's leader, Martin selected prime targets of opportunity and by and large succeeded in becoming a sharply pointed thorn in the side of Vichy government militia forces. Whenever possible, Martin's *maquisards* band appropriated weapons from its victims, thereby gradually building its limited arsenal.

All his men became proficient at hit-and-run guerrilla tactics, and planned and executed their raids carefully. Politically, neither the Nazi nor Vichy Government officially recognized the *maquisards'* existence. If any of his men were arrested, they were commonly treated as spies and immediately shot.

But Charles Martin remained unfazed by his ongoing trials and tribulations. He was the leader of a devoted group of men who were making things difficult for his country's insufferable enemy. In the minds of Martin and his men, their *maquis* results were well worth the adversity and suffering they were forced to endure.

*   *   *

As the steep hills indicating the final outskirts of *Cahors* passed behind them, Christine glanced back at Russell as the pair pedaled their cycles through the countryside. Russell was concentrating on his pedaling, for the road was still quite steep in spots and forced them to dismount and walk their cycles whenever the incline became too sheer. The road, while far from perfect, made for easy riding whenever it was level. Due to the nationwide shortage of petrol, vehicular traffic was practically non-existent. Christine found herself caught up in the passing scenery and even more the accompanying exercise. Before leaving *Cahors,* Russell had made it a point to find some lubricants and to oil both bikes for the journey. His efforts produced a discernible change in the two-wheelers; the oiling greatly reduced the invariable clicking noises and made the ride more manageable and comfortable for both of them. Russell also found several sets of canvas straps to attach the cylinder to the handlebars of his bicycle in a manner that didn't interfere with the bike's handling, a problem he had wrestled with when Andre Faboul and he were forced to pedal to *Cahors.* Even though the arrangement was somewhat unsightly, Russell preferred it to struggling to balance the cylinder as he was forced to do in the first place.

The bicycles moved along steadily, and the pair chatted amiably whenever the occasion arose. Since Christine was familiar with this particular road, she was able to direct Russell's attention to her favorite scenes and settings as they passed. Russell even took note of a brightly painted Dubonnet billboard, the first he had seen since coming back to France. On numerous occasions when he was a student at the Sorbonne, this wonderful aperitif provided him and his friends with affable memories. The signboard served to rekindle some of those good times from the past.

At around ten in the morning, angry black clouds could be seen overhead that signaled the imminent arrival of rain. Christine glanced back at Russell who was about a bike length behind and spoke in an anxious tone, "We had better find a place right away with some shelter. It really looks like it is going to rain."

Russell surveyed the impending clouds and estimated the pair had about five minutes or so before the downpour. "Right. I'll keep my eyes open."

The two continued riding and soon felt the first drops. Russell strained to see ahead but saw nothing in the distance. There were no buildings or shelter apparent that could offer them any relief.

"Maybe we should settle for some heavy trees. If the grove is tight enough, we won't get very wet."

Three hundred yards further down the road and several groves of cedar trees came into view. Russell chose the cluster that seemed to offer the most protection and the pair alighted. By then the rain was coming down quite heavily, but the space under the trees that Russell had chosen kept them both relatively dry.

"This will do quite nicely, at least for the present," Russell glanced at Christine and smiled.

She smiled back, sighed a deep breath, and said," I hope it does not last too long. The roads are wet enough anyway, and we have been going downhill for the past few miles."

"There's not much we can do about it but sit and wait out the rain."

"Yes, I know. But waiting is not one of my strong points. I always seem to want to be involved in lively things, especially when I know what I am doing is meaningful."

"And is that why you became involved with the Resistance?"

"Probably so. My parents, specifically my father, wanted me to remain in *St. Flour* and continue working in our family's watch repair business. We are actually a close family, but I had already worked in the shop for a couple of years. My mother wanted me to select a local boy, marry him and settle down with a house full of children. That prospect was more than I could handle."

"It's a little hard for me to picture you like that."

"Yes, I would certainly hope so. Over time I became quite restless and my father and I had several nasty exchanges. He thought I was quite immature and foolish to give up such security."

"So what made you finally make the decision to leave?"

"It was a combination of two things. First, when the Nazis decided to occupy our country and asked all Frenchmen to swallow their propaganda crap about a mutually beneficial treaty, I must admit I reacted badly to the idea. I could not believe that so many of my countrymen were so easily deceived. I decided at that time to do what I could to help fend off the Bosch, no matter what it took on my part."

"You said there were two reasons?"

"The other is much more personal."

Russell noted Christine's reluctance to proceed and allowed her the time. He watched her as she slowly pulled the words from her mind.

"My first cousin, Sandrine, who is the same age as me, lived with her family just outside *Paris*. She was a student at the university when the Germans came to France. We were closest friends when we were younger and spent our summers together. I always felt she was the sister I never had. Sandrine was not very political but one day happened upon a small demonstration by some other students outside the university's main building. A few of the students were sympathetic to the Germans and to Vichy, and the demonstration was designed to implicate other students who were anti-Nazi. My cousin stopped to watch and was arrested by the Gestapo along with everyone else. She was immediately taken to *Fresnes* Prison in Paris where she was interrogated for several weeks. When Sandrine was finally released, I could see that she was a different person. The experience was so traumatic that she was even unable to talk about it for months. Sandrine came to stay for a time with my family after her ordeal and I hardly recognized her. Her personality had changed as if some evil spirit had infested her soul. Sandrine will never be the same, and I am not sure that I will ever be either. It was then that I came to hate the Nazis so much and decided to join the Resistance. I have resolved to myself that I will not stop fighting them until they have left our land."

Russell saw that she was close to tears and sought to console her.

"You must realize that there are a great many who feel just as you do. The effort of the Resistance will ultimately be successful."

Christine nodded agreement with Russell's sentiment, but remained engrossed. Her thoughts were still with her cousin and Sandrine's continuing anguish.

The steady rains lasted for the better part of an hour, and Christine allowed an additional twenty minutes after the last drops had fallen for the road to dry. The warm July sun returned and produced a steamy, humid environment as the pair picked up their bicycles again and embarked on their journey.

They had pedaled evenly for two hours after the rain delay and eventually reached a more level part of the road that was dotted with several farmhouses, the first the pair encountered. Christine pulled to the side of the road and took the occasion to explain to Russell that most French farmhouses were decidedly angular in nature.

Happy for the break in pedaling, Russell listened attentively. He admitted to himself that he had always found the simple structures visually delightful. He agreed with Christine's assertion that most were constructed of stone and to his own eye seemed almost straight up in shape.

Russell also found out that Christine took great pride in the design of French farms. Most of the farms around her home utilized the abundant rocks that pockmarked the fields and mountainsides to shape stone fences out of the land.

As they started moving, Russell observed more of the stone fences and tried to estimate the area enclosed by each fence as a chore to occupy his mind. The irregular shapes and sizes soon stumped him. Some of the larger stone fences seemed to cover parcels of about a hectare, but he saw smaller ones that were irregular and of no discernable size. Moreover, as time and weather took their toll, the fences settled gradually, were covered by moss and other vegetation and lent testament to their area's natural beauty and peaceful solitude. Russell's mind returned to reality as Christine signaled to him as they approached a road sign signifying the distance to the next town. The high mileage number stated on the sign abruptly ended Russell's fascination with stone fences and French farmhouses.

Christine's first objective was to be the small town of *Puymirol*, about 14 miles east of the much larger City of *Agen*. *Agen*, in turn, was not very far from the expansive *Garonne* River. Barring any problems, Christine expected to reach *Puymirol* in two days. The first day's ride proved strenuous but uneventful, and the pair was able to make good time. Christine brought *baguettes* and *frommages* and chose to eat on the banks of a stream that they encountered near mid-afternoon. Russell drew some clear, cold water from the stream to wash down their lunch. By evening, when both felt they were too tired to push their bicycles any further, they located a clearing next to a small river.

The place seemed mostly hidden from the road and so they parked their bikes. Russell collected nearby branches and started a tiny fire; more for the light it produced than for the warmth it was able to offer. It was a soft summer night and both were thankful for the opportunity to finally rest. They laid back using blankets Christine had included when they departed from *Cahors*. Overhead, the brilliant sky danced, fueled by the illumination of the moon and many thousands of flickering stars.

"I always wanted to do this as an adult," Christine remarked as she studied the starry objects overhead.

"As an adult? I'm not sure what you mean."

"Well, when we were children we were often allowed to sleep outside under the open sky. We would always play a game where everyone had to identify a star or constellation. The most famous ones were easy, it was the lesser known ones that were the most difficult to spot."

"And everyone learned a great deal about the heavens?"

"Exactly. It was one reason my parents encouraged our sleeping outside. How about you, when you were younger, were you allowed to do something similar?"

"Sort of. My parents would take me to a planetarium in a nearby city that contained a huge telescope. I remember one of the people there lecturing about the stars and the galaxies, but I don't remember taking anything at the time very seriously."

"Really. Even when you had such a wonderful opportunity? I would have given anything for the chance to do something like that."

"It seems sort of silly to me right now to have felt that way. But, you must keep in mind that I was very young and still quite immature at the time."

"And now you finally realize what you missed out on. It is really too bad." Christine continued scouring the sky for familiar objects.

They spoke again briefly and then dozed until both were fast asleep.

The busy chirping of birds and the emergence of a warming sun caused Russell to awaken early the following morning. Christine followed a few minutes later and both washed the sleep from their faces in the cold water of the river. They resumed their ride and were able to cover a substantial number of miles until they encountered their first real problem. Just before noon, Russell's bicycle developed a flat, and the pair was forced to walk the bikes until they reached a place where it was possible to get the tire fixed. It was slow going and the intense July sun beat down relentlessly.

"This isn't the way I intend to make the rest of the trip," Russell remarked sarcastically. The two had not conversed since the flat tire had occurred.

"Me either. It is much too hot to walk the bicycles. My feet are burning up."

"Mine too, and my shoes are too tight anyway." Russell grimaced, feigning real discomfort.

Christine tried to lighten the situation. "That is the way with French bicycles. Great engineering, but no one pays any attention to the tires."

"It's different in America, our tires..."

Russell looked at Christine, who had stopped her bicycle. She stared at him awkwardly.

A long moment passed. "Just who are you?" she questioned, her tone cool and detached for the first time.

Russell immediately realized his mistake. His mind fought for the correct words as he attempted to ease the situation. The air around the two had suddenly taken on a sense of apprehensiveness.

"I only meant that I visited America before the war and…"

"I do not believe you," Christine replied forcefully. She turned away from him, her hardened eyes reaching out over the flowing fields.

Russell dropped his bicycle and started toward her. He reached for her elbow and turned her around to face him. Her eyes started to pool and Russell knew what must come next, even if it meant him compromising a part of the secrecy of the mission.

"All right, I'll tell you all about it. You certainly deserve to know."

Christine is, after all, risking her life.

Christine pushed away from him trying hard to avert his eyes.

"I'm not exactly sure where to start."

"At the beginning. It is the only way." She sat down on a large rock beside the road. Russell took a seat next to her and began.

"Okay, my real name is Brian Russell, and I'm a Captain in the United States Army. I was fortunate to have studied for years at the *Sorbonne,* which is why my French is so good. I was part of US Army Intelligence before I was selected to go to Great Britain to become part of an SOE operation. Once in England I learned I would be sent to France on an incredibly important mission that was initiated by the new leader of the French Resistance. I was taught by the Royal Air Force to fly a glider that ultimately carried me several days ago into South Central France."

Brian Russell paused looking directly at Christine. Her eyes were the widest he had ever seen.

"I brought several paintings along with me on my flight, which were duplications of the greatest masterpieces contained in the collection of the *Louvre* Museum. Once I reached France with the copies, they were exchanged for the genuine paintings that were hidden at a secret location not far from where I landed. That location used to be considered safe from the Germans, but everyone in authority is afraid the Germans will occupy the rest of France and then nothing will be safe. For your own safety, I won't tell you exactly where the remainder of the *Louvre's* paintings is kept; there's no real need for you to know. My responsibility now is to get the genuine paintings out of France to a safe hiding place until after the war."

Christine remained silent for several moments, absorbing what she had just heard.

Russell continued his explanation. "As you probably have guessed by now, the real paintings are in the cylinder I am carrying with me. Georges was sent to insure the paintings were switched correctly and to accompany me as far as *Cahors*. Now you know that your role in all this is to see that I reach Spain with the paintings in one piece. My cylinder is constructed of some secret materials, which makes it quite extraordinary. It also contains a secret lock that protects the contents at all times. Again, for your own safety, I won't show you how the inside lock works."

The young woman walked over to Russell's bicycle and carefully studied the elongated tube for several seconds. When she was satisfied, Christine switched her gaze back to Russell.

"And is that all there is to it, the whole story?" She frowned at him, unsure of what should come next.

"Yes, that's about it. I probably should also add that the safety of these paintings is exceedingly dear to the people of France. Your real leaders, including General De Gaulle, believe these paintings will be of incredible value to France if and when your country is reclaimed from the Nazis."

"*When* France is reclaimed." Christine interjected quickly. "And, all I have to do is to get you and the paintings out of France."

"The paintings are actually more important than I am," Russell stated uneasily. "If it ever comes to having to choose between my safety and that of the paintings, you must protect the paintings at all costs. Do you understand what I'm saying?"

"Of course I do, I am not a child."

"I didn't mean…"

"I know what you meant. You need not say anything else…"
Russell's revelations eased Christine's mind as to his identity and she now understood the scope and necessity for their mission. She weighed the values of risking her life and those of her Resistance cohorts for the sake of some valuable old paintings and decided her movement's leaders knew what was best for France.

Christine was also forced to re-examine her responsibility for the mission. She admitted to herself that Russell's frank disclosure placed the entire mission into a whole new perspective. Christine was now conscious of the fact that her current assignment was the first *really* important project Victor was willing to entrust to her. The gravity of the situation engulfed her thoughts and made her stop and reflect.

The more she considered it, it was possible that part of the very essence of the *entire* French nation could be affected by her actions, a humbling thought for a simple French woman. For the first time since she had joined the Resistance's fight, Christine Allard wondered if she was up to the task.

It was one thing to be asked to blow up bridges, disrupt railroad traffic or even to create havoc for the German military. She knew such actions were designed to cause the Nazi pigs worry and embarrassment. But her present mission was entirely different. A most precious commodity was at stake here and Christine willed herself the power to persevere.

She looked at Russell and signaled that she was ready to start their journey again. Seconds later, they began walking their bicycles in the same southwesterly direction as before.

Just a mile further down the road, a moderate sized farmhouse appeared after a curve in the road. The house was set back in a field of rye, the first such structure the couple had seen in hours. They approached a small dirt road that led to the dwelling and started down it. As they neared the building, it was apparent that the place was actually a combination home and barn, with a run up for the animals located to the rear. Russell approached the front door and knocked several times. After a short interval, a middle-aged man dressed in coveralls opened the door.

"*Pardon, Monsieur*, we are traveling by bicycle and have had a flat tire on my husband's bike. Yours is the first home we have encountered in some time and we were hoping we could impose on you to help us get the tire fixed."

The farmer first looked at Christine and then Russell, and smiled graciously. "Certainly, *Madame*, it would be my pleasure. We do not receive many visitors way out here."

"*Merci, Monsieur. Merci beau coups.*"

The farmer motioned them inside. He indicated an interior room to the right where his wife stood and again exclaimed how delighted they were at the prospect of having unexpected visitors. He motioned everyone to the rear of the structure where his workbench was located. As with most farms, the man seemed to have tools to fit every occasion

Russell's flat tire proved to be but a minor problem to fix. The farmer was most sympathetic, owned several bicycles of his own and started to patch the tire for Russell. While the glue he applied to the tire was drying, the farmer's wife appeared with a tray and glasses and provided everyone with freshly squeezed orange juice. After their exhausting ride in the midday heat, the beverage proved to be cool and refreshing.

After the tire was patched, Russell and Christine were invited to stay and were even offered a small lunch of *saucisson*, the incredible sweet sausage the farmer's wife had made herself, along with some freshly baked bread. Christine and Russell readily accepted the couple's hospitality and repaid their hosts by attempting to answer the pair's questions about events in France and the rest of the world. Russell was amazed that so little current news and information was available to people located in rural locations.

When the meal was completed, Christine thanked the couple and attempted to pay them for their trouble. The farmer and his wife profusely refused and walked their visitors back to the road where they wished their new friends a safe journey.

Russell and Christine remounted their bikes and were soon headed toward *Puymirol,* the next stop on their journey.

*   *   *

Senior Milice Inspector Raymond Soward was at odds with many events that occurred during his troubled existence. France's humiliating armistice with Germany served to provide him with a perfect vehicle for venting his frustrations. The Vichy government and its dismissive attitude towards human rights was the perfect cradle for Raymond Soward's demented sense of propriety.

The stocky, pie-faced man with a jagged, receding hairline had grown up wanting to be a policeman, and finally achieved that distinction in 1931. Like many others in the system, he struggled to cope with the antiquated French system of seniority within the police department. This often meant one officer must die or retire before the next in line was promoted. He vented his frustrations often, a fact that caused him animosity and ridicule from both his superiors and his fellow officers.

At an early point in his career, Soward also came to be keenly anti-Semitic.

Raymond Soward wasn't really sure when this odium first started, but he remembered an early resentment for most Jews, dating back to his youth. He could recall that his Jewish peers always had more money to spend than he did and that the Jews he knew inevitably tended to gang together in a fight. When he was seventeen, Raymond Soward found an attraction to a young Jewess and vainly tried to establish a relationship with the beautiful girl who lived in a nearby neighborhood. The process took some time and Soward was sure the girl seemed willing and open to his intentions. For his efforts, Soward was roughed up then thoroughly beaten by the young girl's brother and a group of her brother's Jewish friends. It was an early lesson that Raymond Soward would never forget.

He carried this growing hatred into adulthood. Once Soward was awarded his police commission, he was proud to boast to everyone whenever he apprehended a Jew involved in a crime or even when he confronted a Jew who simply managed to get himself into trouble. He was particularly rough with Jewish prisoners he incarcerated and took great delight in seeing even a single Jew placed behind bars.

Career-wise, the French pact with Germany was a godsend to Raymond Soward. A number of his police contemporaries soon left France to join the Free French Army, creating a plethora of immediate vacancies.

The German liaisons initially assigned to the Vichy police quickly learned of Soward's past anti-Semitism, and that factor insured him rapid promotion. Soon thereafter, his duties consisted solely of the exposure and pursuit of suspected

Jews. Since early 1942, he was able to participate in the interrogation and torture of a number of local men assumed to be helping Jews escape from France. During the ensuing torture sessions, Soward found that he also enjoyed the bizarre sensation associated with inflicting severe pain and anguish on the captives. The fact that these prisoners were usually shackled and completely unable to fight back did not bother Raymond Soward in the least.

When the Gestapo directive concerning the *Grand Vabre* murders crossed his desk, Soward decided to give special attention to anyone he encountered passing through his region. The communication indicated Resistance participation connected to the *Grand Vabre* incident, which also perked Raymond Soward's attention. Ever since the mention of the French Resistance first cropped up in official reports, Soward realized that his career's destiny was to be violently anti-Resistance. After all, the senior *Milice* inspector was convinced, along with many officials within the Vichy Government, that Jews living outside France were responsible for funding the French Resistance as a means of helping overthrow the Germans. If Jews had anything to do with the overthrow of France, Raymond Soward wanted desperately to be part of the group that brought them to justice.

Raymond Soward folded the Gestapo document and placed it inside his coat pocket. For the next few days, he firmly resolved that anyone he found traveling through his region would receive his *personal* attention.

Chapter Thirteen

Christine's plan, forwarded through Andre Faboul to the local Resistance members of Victor's network, was one of pure simplicity. After arriving in *Puymirol*, she and Russell would make their way to the small square in the middle of the town. Christine recalled seeing a kiosk in the middle of the square, neatly trimmed by small bushes, attractive flowers, and surrounded by small benches. Christine and Russell would choose a bench facing south and wait there until contacted. If the pair arrived in the morning, they would expect to be met at 11:00 am. If, in fact, they arrived during the afternoon or early evening, they would expect contact to be made at 7:00 in the evening.

Christine glanced at her wristwatch as she rode her bicycle and realized it was beginning to get late, so she motioned for Russell to quicken his pace. He did so and the pair rolled into the *Puymirol* a few minutes before 6:30. The square was deserted as she and Russell approached one of the benches that faced south.

Within a few minutes of seven o'clock, a man approached their bench and addressed Christine.

They exchanged current code words, and the Resistance contact explained to her what they should do next.

"You will follow *that* road out of *Puymirol*," he instructed, pointing to a street that led off the square. "About one mile outside of town, you will come to a stone farmhouse on the right. Go to the barn in the back and it is there that you will spend the night. Someone will meet you there and will provide you with food and further instructions. Tomorrow morning, when you start your journey again, you must be very careful when crossing the *Garonne*. The Vichy police have increased their security and for the past few days, there are also German soldiers at the main bridge. Something must have happened to tighten their security to such an extent. But, we have not been able to find out what it was."

Christine glanced over at Russell, but decided against disclosing to the local Resistance contact that it was quite possible that the increased Vichy security had something to do with herself and Russell.

After acknowledging the partisan's instructions the couple remounted their bikes. In a few minutes they had cycled out of *Puymirol* and into the surrounding country. The farm came into view shortly and the pair pulled around the rear as they had been instructed. The door to the barn was wide open and they proceeded inside. The barn's present tenants consisted of several cows, a number of chickens and an immensely rotund pig whose concentration on his feeding bin wasn't disturbed in the least by the appearance of two trespassers.

The barn's air was close and earthy, and the warm evening temperature tended to suspend the smells and sounds like a parachute covering its air mass.

Russell thought he felt a breeze develop as the sun finally set behind a large stand of trees. He situated himself near the open door where relief from the air movement was the strongest.

At the same time, Christine found herself still pondering Russell's recent disclosure of the importance of their mission. She kept mostly to herself, exchanging only essential civilities with her companion. Russell observed the overall change in her peppery manner, but marked it down to the serious nature and added pressure he had placed on her shoulders. He decided to allow her ample time to put the situation into perspective. Brian Russell felt strongly that Christine possessed the type of mettle capable of performing difficult tasks and succeeding in the face of overwhelming odds.

He asked himself again if his disclosure was best for her under the given circumstances and came away with the same answer. For some reason Russell found it difficult to lie to Christine Allard. Even though the information he imparted undoubtedly placed them both in a greater degree of danger, he felt a strange confidence that the disclosure also made their dependency on one another stronger. Once Christine realized this for herself, Russell hoped her personality would return to that of the spirited woman he had grown to know.

It was nearly half an hour after their arrival, before a comely woman dressed in simple country clothing entered the barn carrying a small basket containing an assortment of *jambon, frommages, moutarde* and *baguettes*. She placed them down on a bale of fresh straw, laid out a simple tablecloth and produced a small kitchen knife from her pocket.

"Here, help yourselves," she offered cheerily. "The *jambon* is fresh and the *frommages* ripened. I just baked the *baguettes* and they are still warm. And, feel free to use as much of the mustard as you wish; I made it myself last spring with my own recipe. I will be right back in a few moments with some wine. Before I go, is there anything else I can offer you?"

"No, merci Madame," Christine answered. "This is a great deal more than we expected. It all seems wonderful." The farmwoman blushed appreciatively and departed through the open door.

The day long exercise of pushing the bicycles up the steep hills produced enormous appetites in both Christine and Russell. The food set down in front of them by the countrywoman was the first they had tasted all day. Within minutes, the woman reappeared and offered each a glass of wine from a large jug.

"This wine is made around here and is not too bad."

"Thank you," Russell said politely, taking the small glass. "I'm sure it will be fine."

"Yes, thank you for your kindness, I am sure we will enjoy it," Christine added.

The pair sat themselves in front of the hay bale then voraciously consumed everything in front of them.

The woman returned again in a few minutes and was able to observe her visitors and their ingestion of the foods. Satisfied that the food was sufficient to meet their needs, she soon left the pair to finish their unpretentious meal.

Russell willingly washed down the last of the cheese and bread with the soft red wine. In his mind, the meal equated nicely to a picnic, discounting, of course, the fact that it was now almost night outside and the meal was consumed inside a stuffy barn. He propped his legs up on the hay bale, and savored a final sip from his wineglass. It was only a matter of minutes until the farmwoman reappeared at the door.

"I trust you found everything acceptable?"

"Oh yes, *Madame*," Christine replied, "it was much more than acceptable."

"Good, I am happy that you enjoyed it. The meal was nothing more than simple country food. Now, I need to advise you about the next part of your journey.

First, I suggest you attempt to rise early tomorrow, the earlier the better. The initial part of your trip may prove to be the most difficult. It will involve your crossing the *Garonne,* and during recent days crossing the river has suddenly become quite risky. You must be very careful, for the situation may be very perilous. In the past few weeks, a number of people have been detained at the crossings and some of them have not been heard from since. And recently, the militia has increased its security and is very carefully checking everyone trying to cross in either direction."

"And *Madame*, is there no other choice left for us to travel in a southerly direction?"

"Of course there are other choices, but I fear it will be the same everywhere. Whenever there is a main river to cross in this part of southern France, the situation becomes more difficult, and the militia is present at each bridge crossing. I must say, however, that in this case, you actually have two choices. You can go across using the large bridge near *Agen,* or, you may decide to use the smaller one not far from *Auvillar.* Both are guarded so you must choose one or the other."

"Which one would you choose?" Christine asked openly.

The woman answered without hesitation. "The smaller bridge to the south, near *Auvillar.* So far, I have not heard of anyone being detained there. I understand there are no German soldiers at that crossing, only Vichy militia. It is a bit farther, but I think a good deal safer."

"Thank you, I think we will heed your advice."

Christine glanced over at Russell who had listened attentively to the conversation between the two women.

Their Resistance benefactress left the barn and the pair gathered the remaining scraps of food and placed them on a bale of hay. Russell poured each of them another small glass of wine from the jug that the woman had placed next to Christine. A small lantern the woman had also brought provided just enough light for them to see each other.

Outside, the area was totally dark and Christine said a bit curtly, "We had better get some sleep. Tomorrow will be another long day."

She padded down a patch of hay and knelt down, arranging her surroundings. Russell watched her for a few moments, noticing her fluid movements and her slender, well-proportioned hips. She looked up unexpectedly, and caught him staring.

"Why were you watching me?' she asked inquisitively.

"I just enjoy watching you," he answered pleasantly. "Is there something wrong with that?"

"No, I guess not," she replied, somewhat unprepared for his reply. "I guess I am just really tired. I will feel better after I have had some rest."

Russell smiled at her and prepared a bed for himself in the straw. He fluffed an added amount of hay around the cylinder, which he had removed from his bicycle. After forcing it down into the straw, he decided it would make a good pillow and added more straw to soften its feel. He glanced over at Christine, but she had already curled away from him. He reached for the lantern and turned it off.

Brian Russell could not see that Christine's eyes remained wide open, affixed to a spot near the top of the barn.

* * *

Many miles to the south, a long overdue British airdrop the day before Christine and Russell's arrival in *Puymirol* brought a number of new weapons for Charles Martin and his rugged band of *maquis*. On several occasions, the British had promised to step up needed arms and supplies deliveries and Martin was delighted to finally receive the oft-expected arms and ammunition. His band was growing weekly and everyone in his group would need to be well armed to be effective. Even after the arms drop was completed, he wondered if anyone in authority within British Intelligence was actually aware of his group's lack of food and the lingering effects of such hunger. His men had hardly eaten in the past few days and to include some rations with the arms drop seemed to Martin a relatively simple task.

Two days before, Martin met with the leader of the local Resistance in *Auch*; a fortuitous meeting that provided new opportunities for his band. The local Resistance wanted the *maquis* to begin harassment of the Vichy police who were arresting and torturing local citizens much more frequently in an effort to combat Resistance activities. Martin was given the locations of several police *prefectures* within the area where the major activities of Vichy police were concentrated. He was given the freedom to attack any *prefecture* in the area that he felt comfortable his men could handle.

After leaving the meeting, Charles Martin identified at least four separate Vichy police prefectures he knew his band could easily control. He was sure that this new opportunity to harass the Vichy militia would provide his men with added enjoyment and pride. Their actions would reinforce the *maquis'* continuing role in the Resistance's ongoing struggle.

* * *

Christine followed the helpful farmwoman's advice regarding their attempt to cross the *Garonne* River by trying the smaller, less traveled bridge east of *Puymirol*. The fact that no one using that particular bridge had thus far been detained was the deciding factor in her decision.

Taking the woman's additional advice, Christine and Russell started off early in the morning and reached the road that crossed the *Garonne* by about eight. The ground and road surfaces underfoot were still slightly damp from an early morning shower, but the paved road was already dry enough by this time to allow the couple's bicycles' tires sufficient traction to proceed smoothly along its surface.

Six hundred yards ahead, a small single-lane bridge crossed the river.

Christine glanced back at Russell and motioned for him to follow behind her.

Just inside the bridge, two Vichy militia soldiers stood casually with rifles slung on their shoulders. Each smoked a cigarette, and were engaged in an informal conversation. A long stripped metal gate was positioned immediately before the bridge, prohibiting passage from either direction.

As Christine and Russell approached, the soldiers broke off their conversation and took a few steps towards their direction. One of the soldiers walked to the end of the bridge and around the metal barrier. He removed his rifle from his shoulder and motioned for them to stop. The militia soldier was extremely young and heavily scarred with acne. His greasy, wavy hair protruded from inside his shabby gray militia cap.

"Papers," he weakly commanded in a thick country accent. His militia comrade approached the group and took a position off to the side. He observed the conversation and held his rifle at the ready.

"Where are you coming from and where are you going?"

"We are from *Cahors* and we are on a pilgrimage to *Lourdes* to visit the Virgin," Russell answered.

"*Cahors*, the youth responded. "That is a good distance away from here. And, there is also a main road from *Cahors* to the south," the soldier continued, suddenly becoming suspicious. "Why did you not take it? It is much more direct."

"We attended a family wedding of a cousin two days ago near *St.-Matre*," Christine explained, having prepared herself for such a contingency. "From there, this road was nicer and certainly more convenient."

The soldier eyed Christine and then Russell. He studied the papers for a moment more and handed them back. He took a step toward Russell and inspected the cylinder resting atop Russell's bicycle and asked,

"What do you have inside the tube?"

"Some posters of the Blessed Virgin we are taking with us to have blessed," Russell answered.

"Open it," the soldier ordered, "I want to see for myself."

Russell carefully unscrewed the top and unrolled the posters he had purchased at the shop in *Cahors*. The militia soldier looked them over and motioned to his comrade who came nearer to take a closer look.

The two militias scanned the posters and handed them back to Russell, who rolled them up neatly and fitted them back inside the cylinder. When he was finished, the first soldier spoke again.

"All right, everything seems to be in order. You may proceed." He motioned to the other soldier who shouldered his rifle and raised the gate.

"*Merci*," Christine offered, as she and Russell remounted their bicycles and slowly pedaled across the *Garonne* River.

* * *

An hour later, *Milice* inspector Raymond Soward rounded a bend in the road. His automobile was finishing the short journey from the large bridge in *Agen* to the much smaller bridge 17 miles upstream near *Auvillar*. He ordered his assistant to stop the old *Peugeot* they were driving at the bridge crossing the *Garonne*. For the last month, his daily morning routine involved checking *all* the bridge crossings in his region for suspicious travelers. It was a tedious job, but Soward's long time experience in police matters made him aware that such scrupulous attention to detail could often prove rewarding.

As he approached the soldiers on guard, he spoke brusquely.

"Do you have anything to report here?"

"No sir," the scarred-face soldier in charge answered. "So far this morning, it has been very slow at our crossing. As a matter of fact, we have only had two people pass through since we came on duty at six."

"And were they from this area?" questioned Soward.

"No, sir, they were from *Cahors*. A young married couple. They were on bicycles and are on a pilgrimage to *Lourdes*. I checked their papers myself. Everything was in order."

Lourdes? Soward reflected for a moment and inquired again.

"Can you tell me anything else about them? Do you remember what they looked like?"

"Oh yes, the woman was very attractive. Black, wavy hair and a great figure. Both of us thought she was a real looker. The man was a bit larger than normal height. He was wearing a black beret."

Soward did not take time to thank the soldier. He was in a hurry to get back into his car. Soward signaled the soldiers to raise the gate, which was quickly done. He immediately prodded his assistant who stomped the clutch too hard, revving the antiquated engine to a high, irreverent whine. The driver waited a moment until the engine settled down and the *Peugeot* lurched forward across the bridge.

Soward's mind darted ahead to the road his *Peugeot* was now rapidly devouring. He fervently hoped the couple he was now pursuing had remained on this same road.

*   *   *

"**When we** were back at the bridge, I was unsure about the business with the cylinder," Christine dropped alongside Russell as they pedaled along. "I did not pay close attention when you bought the posters in *Cahors*."

"I was uncomfortable with carrying around an empty cylinder, it seemed much too suspicious to me. I thought about it after Georges and I departed from the *Chateau*. Buying the posters to help substantiate our story seemed like a good idea."

"It most certainly was. I have no idea how the militia boys would have reacted if the cylinder was empty."

"That's behind us now, I wouldn't worry about it any further."

"I was not worrying, but I guess I would have been better prepared if I had known."

"From now on, I'll tell you everything I'm thinking. Is that okay with you?"

"Fine. It will be better that way." Christine broke off the conversation and returned her attention to the road ahead.

The pair was in no particular hurry and began to feel caught up in the natural beauty of the passing countryside. At one point, Russell noticed a sign pointing in the direction of *Roquefort*, which according to the sign was 20 miles away. The town's name fondly recalled many wonderful occasions in *Paris* with his friends and some marvelous shared meals. Present at most meals was a specialty from *Roquefort*, the town that provides its name to the wonderfully pungent goat's cheese.

Another time, perhaps a different century...

A massive rock quarry materialized on the right side of the road complete with a visible number of jagged cuts that soared well over three hundred feet high. It was no wonder to Russell that every building and house they had passed in this area was built out of stone. The supply from such a place as large as this quarry seemed unlimited. He thought back to his own home in the United States where most homes and structures were built out of wood or bricks. Even though the structures were attractive and probably more economical, Brian Russell decided he preferred the rustic simplicity and natural beauty of the edifices that dotted the French countryside.

Such thoughts turned Russell's mind to the surrounding terrain that was incredibly lush and green. Patches of brightly colored wildflowers proliferated everywhere the eye could see. The morning sun was pleasant and offered little impediment to their travel. This time it was Russell who ranged up alongside Christine, who began describing in detail their next destination.

"We will next stop in the city of *Condom,* which is very famous in France," she offered. "It is where much of the wonderful *Armagnac* is produced. When the brandy is finished, the barrels are put on barges and floated down the river to *Bordeaux.*"

"I enjoy a good *Armagnac*," Russell replied, again recalling with fondness his former times in France. "How is it you know so much about the area?

"When we were small, during the summer my father took the entire family to visit family friends near here. My cousin Sandrine that I mentioned earlier was always with us. All the children would have wonderful adventures and we were always disappointed to have to return home. My father was always very careful to make sure that he took a number of bottles of the *Armagnac* back with him. I always remember the bottles clinking against each other on the return trip home."

Russell glimpsed at Christine, and thought about how much of the little girl still remained in the woman's body. He identified with her natural naïveté and found it quite engaging. He began to sense a softening of her posture toward him. He hoped the slight change signaled a new phase in the way she viewed their relationship. Russell decided that it was good that he had been patient and allowed Christine to make her own decision. Such a change would be good for the mission and for them both.

Another sign along their route announced the location of the *Lauzeite* Medieval castle and proclaimed it to be an excellent tourist site. Russell supposed the place would be closed and wondered how the advent of a wartime environment affected such historically rich locations. Each location's closing would ensure an immediate loss for both school children and also for anyone interested in such a site's history and background.

They pedaled along the road at a leisurely pace and were unaware of the slowapproach of an automobile until it was directly behind them. The old black car was the first vehicle that had passed them that morning. Russell waived it around and fell in behind Christine.

The car passed them by and Russell glimpsed a narrow faced man sitting in the right front seat next to the driver. The passenger regarded Russell carefully as the automobile crept slowly by but did not acknowledge him.

Thirty yards down the road, the car came to a sudden stop.

Both passenger and driver alighted and started back toward them.

Christine and Russell stopped their bicycles in the middle of the road.

The man from the passenger side approached and held up his hand. Raymond Soward flashed his identification and spoke to the pair with a lofty indifference.

"Inspector Soward, *Milice*. Produce your papers."

The driver took several steps backward in the direction of the tired old *Peugeot* and took up a defensive position. Russell looked up to see that the driver was now pointing a handgun in their direction.

Russell was undecided as to what to do.

I might be able to overpower one man, but...

Russell handed Soward his papers. So did Christine.

Soward examined the papers, and glanced at their bicycles. He also took note of the cylinder Russell was carrying on the bicycle.

"So you intend to ride these bicycles over 250 miles to *Lourdes,*" he leered, removing his revolver from inside his suit jacket.

Surprised by the officer's knowledge of their destination, Christine answered irately, "Yes, what is wrong with that? Is there some law that says we cannot ride our bicycles?"

"Please, *Monsieur*," Russell added, attempting to tone down the situation. "We have broken no laws and you have no right to stop us."

"You are wrong, *Monsieur*, I have every right. The duly acknowledged government of France gives me that right. And, my little friend here," referring sarcastically to his gun inside his belt, "insures that I can maintain that right."

"But, you just can't …"

"Something about this entire situation seems incorrect here. I will need to verify your papers before you can proceed any further. For the present, you will both consider yourselves under arrest and get into the back of the car and come with us. But first, I think it will be better if I take the precaution to handcuff you."

Having no magical potions at hand, Russell and Christine reluctantly complied.

"What about our bicycles?" Christine demanded.

"Do not concern yourselves about the bicycles, *Madame*. If your papers and story prove to be genuine, your bicycles will be returned to you."

Once the handcuffing was completed, Christine and Russell were pushed into the tiny, cramped back section of the *Peugeot*. The old car's motor whined again at a high pitch and the vehicle was off.

The dusty road on which the ancient *Milice Peugeot* traveled was filled with numerous bumps, a number of which had jarring effects on Russell's mind.

He couldn't believe their dreadful luck and his own lack of preparedness, the combination of which allowed him and Christine to be arrested so easily. He was also dumbfounded that the *Milice* agent hadn't as yet bothered to look in the cylinder. He tried to imagine what would happen next, but was unable to form a prudent guess. He rode silently next to Christine with his attention fixed on the police inspector in the passenger's seat.

The *Peugeot* changed roads, but continued heading southwest in the direction of *Condom,* a fact Russell gleaned when passing infrequent signs along the route. Christine also noticed the signs, and wondered what *Condom* held for them. She knew that *Condom* was the largest city in the area and was probably the nearest town where the *Milice* maintained a significant office.

The fact they were traveling toward *Condom* was not completely negative in Christine's mind, since the city was part of her original escape route to the south. She knew there would be Resistance members waiting there and silently schemed in her mind for an opportunity to contact them. She laid her head uncomfortably against the back seat cushion of the car as it sped through the verdant, bucolic countryside toward *Condom.* If only she would be provided with the chance.

Christine got Russell's attention and whispered in his ear.

"We are in *Gascony* now, and all is not lost. The *Gascons* are real fighters and the Resistance here is expecting us. If I can only find a way of contacting them."

"I will be on the lookout for something," he whispered back.

Soward turned back towards the pair when he thought he heard sounds coming from the rear seat. By the time he completed his turn, Christine and Russell had already ended their conversation.

*   *   *

At practically the same time of day, Patrice Fournay's mother sent her precocious thirteen-year-old daughter on one of the youngster's daily chores. Patrice accepted her lot cheerfully and briskly walked the mile from the Fournay house toward the center of *Condom.* She passed a number of two-story buildings that led down to the quai and crossed the *Baise* River. As she crossed the bridge, Patrice glanced up at the majestic, elongated tower that indicated the site of the *Cathedral St. Pierre,* her favorite building in the world.

Patrice had been taught in school that the *Cathedral St. Pierre* was actually more of a fortress-church whose origins dated back as early as the beginning of the 10th century. The Gothic building was ravaged several times during its history and patiently restored by reverent parishioners and local noblemen. Its last major restoration occurred during the 17th and 18th centuries when several additions were made. These included Patrice's favorite inside place, the *Chapelle Notre Dame* and a number of incredible stained glass windows as well as a major work that depicted the Crucifixion of Christ.

The cathedral 's opulent interior was a huge theater in which to worship but Patrice Fournay felt comfortable whenever she entered its ornate front doors. She chose different aspects of the *eglise* to enjoy on each visit. At times she relished the stained glass windows and on other occasions she marveled at the beauty of the elaborate wood and plaster sculptures. But Patrice's favorite pastime inside the old church was shared by many of her friends in school. The youths took great pride in being able to correctly name the numerous statues of the saints, which were placed in double rows extending outward from the altar. The scene always provided her with a deep feeling of security and pleasure as if the stone figures actually protected the altar and all those inside the church from harm.

Patrice Fournay crossed next to the *Cathedral St. Pierre*, glancing customarily at "her" building, and continued walking. She soon approached her mother's preferred *boucherie,* which was located directly across the street from the *Prefecture de Police.* Patrice enjoyed her daily visit to the shop where the proprietor always managed to provide a little *lagniappe* for her when she left. Maybe today he would offer her a piece of his prized beef jerky, which Patrice enjoyed and her mother always forbade. The thought of the appetizing jerky enlivened her as she entered the shop and politely asked for her mother's usual order.

* * *

As Soward's black *Peugeot* entered *Condom*, its driver made several turns and began slowing the vehicle as it approached the *Prefecture*. Christine was annoyed to see a number of her countrymen turn their heads as the car passed, recognizing the car and not wishing to become involved in any government business. She attempted to make eye contact with several pedestrians as the vehicle passed, but was unsuccessful in catching even one individual's attention.

The car stopped and Soward and his driver stepped out. The driver quickly darted around the front of the vehicle, dramatically drawing his pistol as he reached the *banquette.* He then proceeded to aim the weapon directly at the prisoners as Russell and Christine, still handcuffed in the narrow space, attempted to untangle themselves from the back seat of the small car.

Soward saw what was happening and realized his driver's actions would attract undue attention. He immediately yelled at his subordinate to put away his weapon. The driver flushed and promptly obliged his superior.

The gravity of the dramatic scene was not lost on Patrice Fournay who had just stepped out of the *boucherie* across the street with her mother's packages. She looked carefully at the beautiful young woman in handcuffs and also at the taller man next to her with the unusually handsome face. She alertly perceived the anguished look of desperation as she met Christine's eyes.

She would tell her father of the entire incident as soon as she returned home.

* * *

Charles Martin's men were so famished that the *maquis* leader even resolved to steal some nourishment for them in the near future if such an action became necessary.

He led his band out of the high hills and into a more populated area where he reasoned some food would be available. Martin knew he must be careful of where and of whom he asked for food. Not everyone in Vichy France was inclined to help his seedy gang of *maquis*. A number of people refused to become involved, even to the small extent of providing Martin and his men with a meal.

The group's march was interrupted by one of the *maquis* that recognized the name of the city they were approaching from a sign along the road.

"I have some relatives in *Condom*," the *maquis* fighter named Alexandre spoke up excitedly, "We are finally going to have some hot food to eat."

Martin and his men greeted the news with great enthusiasm. They were all extremely hungry and the prospect of a hot meal was even more than they could have expected.

* * *

Patrice Fournay ran part of the way to her home and rapidly related to her father the precise details concerning the young couple she had seen earlier being herded into the *Prefecture* in *Condom*. After all, such exceptional events did not occur every day in the laid back city. She described the young couple in great detail and alluded to the fact that one of the police officers waved his gun as the couple tried to get out of the *Milice* automobile. It was the first time in her life that Patrice Fournay had even seen a handgun and the memory of the experience was quite vivid.

Her father listened carefully and finally sent Patrice's older brother to fetch an old friend of his family whom he knew would be of help. Patrice was recounting the story for the third time when someone banged on the back door of the house.

Patrice's mother walked toward the door and immediately recognized the visitor. She turned back into the kitchen where the family was gathered and excitedly exclaimed, "All of you, look who is here. It is your cousin Alex. My sister's son Alex has come to pay us a visit."

*   *   *

Inside the *Prefecture du Police*, Christine and Russell were ushered into the interior of the building and immediately locked in a small, windowless room. The bleak space contained a table, several chairs and little else.

"What are we to do?" Christine asked nervously, looking directly into his face. "I tried to make eye contact with a number of people walking along the streets on our way into the city, but I do not think I was successful. If only I had a way of letting the Resistance know we are here. They might be able to help us."

Russell tied to calm her, attempting to alleviate her fears.

"I'm not quite sure of what will happen, but I will think of something. For now, I think it might be best for us to stick to our story. I don't think the inspector in charge really knows anything specific about us or has been able to put anything together. He has a good idea we're up to something, but I don't believe he knows what that is. If he knew anything factual, we would already have been charged. He will probably do what he said when he arrested us…and check our papers. Depending upon his communications, that process will probably take some time. For what it's worth, I think he's just guessing."

"All the same, we had better think of something," Christine replied, not totally convinced. Her face was masked with doubt as she continued to ponder the possibilities.

The door opened and Soward entered the small room. He surveyed the two occupants and walked around the table, saying nothing. He had not spoken directly to the pair since placing them in handcuffs.

Russell carefully observed the policeman's actions. Soward's body movements bordered on the melodramatic, as if drawn from an old spy movie, the type Russell had seen many times.

Russell figured the *Milice* inspector's silence was intended to intimidate Christine and him. That could be the only viable reason for such a performance. The man's actions were stiff and formal and bordered on the comical. It was all Brian Russell could do to suppress an urge to smile. He knew that would not be a wise move.

Soward paced back and forth, allowing additional time to pass. Finally, he turned abruptly and faced them.

He looked first at Russell, then at Christine.

"Do you both intend to stick to your ridiculous story about bicycling all the way to *Lourdes*? Do you really expect me to believe such a thing is possible? It is a long, long way to *Lourdes*."

"What we told you is true," Russell blurted out indignantly, attempting to stand.

Soward stopped his progress.

"Remain seated," he commanded, pressing Russell's shoulder downward. "I will tell you when you can rise."

Russell slumped back into his chair.

"How can we convince you?" Russell asked, bowing his head. "We were married two months ago, and we made a promise to each other at the wedding. We both felt the Blessed Mother helped bring us together and sanctified our marriage, so we made a promise to visit the Virgin's special place at *Lourdes* as soon as we could. Since we are recently married, we don't have a great deal of money, but we both felt it was important to keep our promise. This is the first opportunity we have had to make the trip. We didn't have enough money to take the train so we decided instead to travel by bicycle."

Soward listened to Russell's engaging story, but his face remained skeptical.

Christine's somber mood was buoyed by Russell's quick response and she attempted to substantiate his story.

"My husband is telling the truth," she pleaded. "Why don't you believe us? We are both good Catholics and want to do what is right." She reached for a cross, which hung around her neck and pulled it out. "The *Pere* who married us told us that the Virgin would bless our union again if we went to visit her. Is Vichy now against its citizens fulfilling their promises to the Virgin Mary?"

The hardened *Milice* agent listened to the agitated woman. Soward had heard many explanations in recent months, mostly from people bent on saving their lives. Usually, it was easy to tell those who were lying. He prided himself on being able to single out anyone whose story or explanation was unclear or unbelievable. He was also totally prepared to exert pressure on his prisoners until they eventually gave in. The couple sitting in the room with him was a bit different and their story had a ring of truth about it.

Raymond Soward was unlike many Gestapo agents who believed in physical torture as the only means to an end. Soward was an individual who believed that mental pressure on his prisoners could often act as a perfect tool with which to accomplish his job.

He looked at the pair in front of him who now held hands. Neither head was bowed and they sat squarely in the chairs. Neither seemed uneasy or unsure of themselves. It was true that both appeared scared, but that was to be expected under the circumstances. The woman was even mildly irate when initially arrested, a trait not usually associated with a guilty person. However, Soward's deepest instincts told him they were hiding something, and it was up to him to find out what. The long distance to Lourdes by bicycle bothered him, but it was not enough of a doubt to charge them..

He decided against mentioning anything about the *Grand Vabre* murders until he was able to establish a connection to the young people. No use exposing his information needlessly, there was plenty of time left for a thorough investigation.

"Why are you not working?" Soward's first question was directed at Russell.

"I was given the time off by my employer. But I do work, in an office in *Cahors*. I will give you the name and address and you can check for yourself. The owner was generous to allow me to make the trip to *Lourdes*. He said such a gesture would be a good beginning to my marriage."

Christine was delighted with Russell's bravado. If anything, his explanation might buy them additional time. She summoned her courage and added, "Yes, go ahead and check. It will be easy to prove we are telling the truth."

Soward was taken aback by Russell's intense refutation, but continued to harbor a feeling of doubt that he couldn't readily place.

Soward was also aware of the affect a night in jail could have on many prisoners. He would resume questioning the couple the following morning.

"I'm not sure that either of you possess the necessary guile to be able lie to me," he said confidently. "I wonder how you will feel after a night here in our *prefecture*. If you decide to change your story, all you need do is knock on the door. Someone will hear you and call me. Before I leave I must ask again if you are sure you want to stick to your original story? I might be willing to go easy on you if either of you will cooperate."

"But we have already told you the truth." It was Christine again, her tone deeper and even more earnest than before.

Soward shook his head negatively at the pair. He stood and walked abruptly to the door. He opened it dramatically and departed without saying another word.

When he was sure Soward was gone, Russell looked directly at Christine and burst into a wide grin. He had held it back for a long, long time.

*   *   *

Across town at the Fournay house, several events were occurring at practically the same time.

Meurice Gilles was the person summoned to the house by Patrice's brother. He finally arrived at the Fournay home and greeted Patrice's father warmly. Gilles was a trusted friend of the Fournay household, and was active in local

Resistance activities. It was the prime reason why Patrice's father wanted him to hear his daughter's story.

Meanwhile, Charles Martin was seated around a large circular table explaining to Madame Fournay his men's dire need for food. Martin had accompanied his *maquis* fighter, Alexandre, to the Fournay home both as a safety measure and to insure the message of their plight was delivered properly. Patrice's mother listened to Martin's earnest pleas and readily agreed to help. Madame Fournay immediately began to gather together a number of items for the group. She also offered the two tattered and tired soldiers a glass of her husband's favorite *Armagnac* while they waited.

Once again Patrice was asked to narrate her story for Meurice Gilles who had also taken a seat at the table. Gilles listened attentively to the details and nodded approvingly. All at once, several pieces of a puzzle fit together quite neatly for Meurice Gilles. He was one of the operatives in Victor's Resistance network who already been alerted as to the possibility of Christine and Russell's appearance in *Condom*, which he expected that same day. The reason as to why they had not yet arrived was now clear.

He addressed Patrice and placed her small hand in his palm. "You have done a wonderful job, young lady. You have been a great help to me and to your country by reporting what you saw. Your Mother and Father should be very proud."

Patrice beamed appreciably, too embarrassed to reply.

"But it is really unfortunate," his tone became more subdued. "The two prisoners Patrice observed must be very important to the Resistance. I was told to provide them with as much assistance as I could. Now, I am unsure as to what can be done. As long as they remain in the custody of the *Milice*, I cannot do a thing to help. I simply do not have enough men at my command to make a difference."

Charles Martin, who was munching on his second of Madame Fournay's warm *pain-au-chocolates*, overheard both Patrice's story and Gilles' entire reply. He stood up and stepped forward. He had heard Patrice's entire story and also Gilles reply.

"*Monsieur*, maybe it is possible that I can be of help. I have listened to what the young girl said and I believe I understand your problem. I have twenty *maquis* in my unit, all of whom are presently camped on the outskirts of *Condom*. My men are both hungry and mad. Once they are fed properly, my men and I would be happy find a release for some of our anger."

Gilles beamed approvingly. "Is it also possible you already have a plan in mind?"

"Possibly. Once I get some specific details about the *prefecture* in *Condom*, I think we can agree to a plan that will be acceptable to everyone. What I have in mind might not be so difficult after all. There cannot be that many police to contend with."

"Usually no more than five or six," Gilles offered. "The *prefecture* in *Condom* is not that large. We can go there early tomorrow and take a look. If everything seems okay, we will try to get them out. But first, my men need to be fed."

Patrice's mother was already busy seeing to that. She had already begun preparing several pots of her husband's favorite beef stew and was also in the process of boiling a large number of sweet corn ears, which had recently been cut off the family's vegetable plot.

Martin next enlisted the aid of both Patrice and her brother. The two youths accompanied their cousin Alex and carried Madame Fournay's food back to the *maquis* camp outside the city. The Fournays also generously provided the *maquis* with additional supplies of fruit, bread and even some dried beef. Martin's *maquis* unit would eat quite admirably for at least the next few days.

Before he left the Fournay home, Gilles arranged to meet Martin and his men early in the morning just outside *Condom.* He knew he would need some time to alert the remainder of his own small Resistance group so that they could also help in the action against the *Milice.*

As his daughter readied for sleep, Patrice's father gave Patrice a long, caring hug, and proudly expressed his personal feeling concerning his daughter's actions. He made sure it was clear to her that both he and his wife took deep satisfaction in her ability to recognize and identify what was happening in Condom. They were proud that Patrice had brought those things to his attention.

When he was sure that Patrice was soundly asleep, he retired to his own room and finally lay down on his bed next to his wife. He reviewed the day's happenings and realized that neither he nor his family would ever forget the events that had occurred on this particular day.

Chapter Fourteen

The nondescript little room that served as their place of confinement within the *Milice's Condom* office was, for some reason in mid-July, slightly cold and damp. This made their captivity even more unbearable than Christine and Russell could have believed. Russell surveyed the room and checked the door but found it was securely locked from the outside. The overhead light remained lit and Russell ascertained that it was also controlled from outside the room. Upon their arrival, both he and Christine were permitted to use the *prefecture's* lavatory facilities, a fact that Christine found absolutely necessary. At that time, the couple's handcuffs were removed. When they were returned to the sparse room their hands were left free.

Russell checked his watch and saw that they had now been in custody for a little more than six hours. With nothing to do, they attempted to doze sitting up in the chairs but neither was successful and soon gave up. The day's bizarre set of events had left them both disturbed and disconcerted. When added to the present uncertainty about their future status, the resultant emotions produced mutual discomfort.

Eventually, both Christine and Russell decided to attempt to stretch out on the floor, but the hard stone floor surface and lack of blankets or pillows soon proved too disagreeable to permit any sleep.

Several hours later, the door opened and another Milice officer peered in. He watched both of his prisoners for several seconds but remained silent. He checked the remainder of the room but saw nothing out of the ordinary. Satisfied nothing was amiss, he stepped back outside the room and turned the key, re-locking the door. A second later the light went out, the first good sign the pair had experienced since arriving at the *prefecture*.

As a final attempt at comfort, Russell lodged himself in one of the chairs against the wall and offered Christine a place next to him. She finally accepted, which actually meant she would be loosely cradled in his arms. Nearing the verge of exhaustion, Christine finally managed to close her eyes, but her sleep was restless at best.

Russell also managed to doze a little, but found himself awakening whenever Christine moved.

Sometime in the early morning, she shifted her weight and opened her eyes. In the darkness, she spoke quietly to Russell.

"Are you awake?"

"Yes. It's really difficult to sleep."

"What are we going to do?"

"Well, I'm afraid nothing right now. Anything we attempted tonight would be impossible. If I were sure the guard would come back on a regular schedule, I would consider jumping him the next time he stuck his head inside the door. But, it seems as if they are content to let us alone through the rest of the night. What happens tomorrow will be another story. I will think of something."

I really had better think of something, it's mostly my fault we're in this predicament.

Russell pondered his thoughts for a moment and spoke softly, referring to Soward. "I'm not sure what the little twit has in mind. If he were really convinced we were up to something I have the feeling he would have already become really nasty and roughed us up. I can tell by looking that he has a real mean streak in him. Since he has basically left us alone, I would imagine that he believes what we told him, or at least a part of it."

"Yes, I thought about that. Victor told me that most Resistance members who are captured are immediately tortured. At least that was Victor's experience with those who survived the torture."

"Christine, step back for a moment and look at the facts. The inspector doesn't have any way of knowing if we are part of the Resistance, or at least, he hasn't any proof. He didn't even bother about the false information I was willing to give him about where I worked in *Cahors*."

Christine snickered and added, "I wondered about that when you first said it. I speculated in my mind as to what you would tell him."

"I would have made up something, I was on a roll and thought it was the right thing to do.'

"That was really foolish of you. Foolish and brave at the same time."

"It would have taken him some time to check out my story. That's what I was counting on."

"I realize all that. At the time, I was amazed that you even thought of it."

"One thinks rather quickly when one is truly terrified."

"I understand. It was much the same for me. I was scared to death."

"What do you think he will do when he returns? Is there anything we can do to be prepared?"

"Maybe. I think it best that we continue to stick to our story. Until he is able to prove otherwise, and we will know *when* that happens, the story we offered him is our best bet. If the worst happens and he starts to get physical with us, then I'll try something to get us out of here.

We had better hope that they choose to transport us again. That would provide us with an excellent opportunity to overpower them and get away. In any case, everyone seems to have retired for the night. At least we can be thankful for that."

"Yes."

Neither spoke for a time, nor was either able to fall asleep.

Once again, it was Christine who broke the silence.

"When you were younger, did you ever dream of anything like this?"

"You mean like being arrested and held in jail by the *Milice*?"

Christine jabbed Russell softly with her elbow. "No, silly, I mean like being caught in some great adventure where much is at stake and horrible people chase you around trying to kill you."

"No. I guess I never gave such a thing a thought."

"I did, when I was very young. My mother used to read me stories from the Crusades, when brave knights used to go out and fight on behalf of the Church. It all seemed so romantic at the time. The only problem I could see was that I was born a girl, and girls were not allowed to go out and fight."

"What about Joan of Arc? She was a great fighter and she was a young woman."

"Yes, I admire her a great deal. All young French women do, she is our greatest national heroine."

"And now, things have changed a great deal for women haven't they? Aren't you now allowed to fight alongside men?"

"Yes. That is so. Victor tells me that there are a large number of women who are involved in the Resistance's fight. And, I even know of one woman who was captured and executed. It was in the occupied zone, and she died bravely. She would not reveal any of her Resistance activities nor give up any of her associates. She will be honored and remembered in our prayers for a long time."

Russell heard her reply but did not answer. His mind was busy attempting to find a way that would insure that Christine Allard was not added to the Resistance's list of female martyrs.

Christine also fell silent. Her active mind filled with thoughts and recollections from her youth, of knights and crusades and events she had not considered for a number of years. In the end, such righteous thoughts accompanied her as she fell asleep next to Russell. The American's tired eyes were still wide open.

* * *

Shortly before dawn, Muerice Gilles and another local Resistance member named Pampien met Charles Martin's band of *maquis* at a small park . The grounds ran along the *Baise* River right before it made its northerly turn towards *Condom's* center. Gilles had opted to bring only Pampien along this morning due to his familiarity with the *prefecture*. Martin's twenty *maquis* was ample enough firepower for the job ahead.

The *Prefecture du Police* was located about three blocks distant from the park, off the main street of the town.

Monsieur Pampien produced a rough, hand-drawn map that contained a diagram of the inside of the *prefecture*. He also informed the *maquis* that on his way to meeting them he had earlier observed a single Vichy militia soldier standing guard outside the building.

Martin studied the drawing and quickly decided on a plan of action. His idea was most basic. Some of his men would attempt to induce at least one or two more soldiers to step outside the building. Martin counted on the fact that during the early hours of morning, it seemed realistic that a minimal number of Vichy police officers or militia would be on duty.

Everyone involved listened as Martin outlined the specific function each member in his group was designated to carry out. When each fighter understood and acknowledged his individual role, Martin gave the signal for the *maquis* to start towards the building.

Gilles overheard the plan and stopped the advance. He spoke emotionally and appealed directly to Martin and his men. "Please, *mes amies*, use as little force as necessary at the *prefecture*. The *Milice* will direct reprisals for any violence directly at the people of *Condom*."

Charles Martin acknowledged Gilles' request and made sure his men understood the Resistance leader's plea. He again started towards the *prefecture* with his men.

* * *

Several hours earlier in another office inside the *prefecture,* Senior Inspector Raymond Soward's night was proving to be very unfulfilling. He had spent several hours trying to verify parts of Christine and Russell's story with his Vichy counterparts in *Cahors,* with no success.

First, the ancient telephone system in place in that part of Southwestern France simply would not cooperate. He repeatedly attempted to place the call and was informed that the lines to *Cahors* were unavailable and to place his call later. Several hours later, when Soward was finally able to reach someone in the *Milice* offices in *Cahors*, he was abruptly told to call back the following day. It seemed that the person he needed to talk with had already gone home for the evening and could not be disturbed. Soward was used to such unproductive attitudes within the *Milice*, and often questioned how his parent organization was able to function properly.

The policeman also spent several minutes examining the elongated cylinder he had taken from Russell. After some difficulty, he was finally able to open the container. He extracted a number of oversized, thickly textured, rolled sheets and laid them out on his desk. He then unfolded the pieces, smoothing them out on the flat surface of his desk. He turned each over individually and paused after the final one.

The oversized sheets were all inexpensive poster reproductions of paintings of the Virgin Mary. While he was troubled to admit it, the fact that the couple was carrying posters of the Virgin tended to substantiate their story. He glanced over the assembled papers and finally repacked them back inside the tube. He fumbled with the lock until it finally caught.

He withdrew a pocket watch from his trousers and noted the time. It was already past two and he was suddenly very tired. He had just enough time for a few hours of sleep.

* * *

Charles Martin's plan was quite straightforward but required a little imagination on the part of his men. One of his *maquis* fighters pretended to drag another soldier along with him in the direction of the *prefecture,* who Martin intended would appear wounded. Cherry juice from Madame Fournay's existing food cupboard was stained on the injured man's shirt to make the scene seem more realistic. Martin then hoped that the unfolding scenario would prompt the exterior guard to call inside the *prefecture* for additional help.

The other part of Martin's plan called for two additional *maquis* to circle around the building and up a nearby alleyway. The spot was just back of the guard on duty outside the building. If the idea worked and one or more additional militia soldiers stepped outside, the waiting *maquis* would immediately disarm them. If Martin's strategy progressed as expected, the *Maquisard* leader felt there would be no need for noise or shooting. Once the outside *militia* guards were disarmed, the whole group would then enter the *prefecture* in the guise of prisoners. With good timing and a bit of luck, the simple ruse would provide easy access to the interior of the *prefecture.*

Martin allowed his men time to reach their positions inside the alleyway and signaled his two decoys to begin. The two did as ordered, with the wounded man groaning loudly, feigning intense pain.

As they neared the *prefecture,* the militia guard saw them, immediately stiffened and raised his rifle. The Vichy soldier regarded the pair of ragged figures that approached his position. The first man was almost carrying another man who seemed to be wounded. Instinctively, the guard took a few steps backward and knocked on the door. In a moment, another man appeared in the doorway dressed in civilian clothes.

"Come, Claude, help me with these two," the Vichy guard appealed to his colleague.

The second man stepped out into the street. Observing the situation, he barked to the two *maquis,* "You two, stop where you are! What do you want?"

"My friend is wounded, and we need your help," the *maquis* fighter replied wearily.

The second *Milice* officer was about to speak when he felt the brush of cold steel against the back of his neck.

"Put up your hands or you die," another *maquis* soldier spoke from behind.

The militia guard saw what was happening and turned but was too late. The maquis approaching the prefecture quickly closed the remaining distance and grabbed the rifle from his hands.

Martin and the remainder of his men quickly joined the four men standing outside the door to the building.

"Now, here is what we will do next," Martin continued, outlining explicit instructions to the two *Vichy* men now under his control. "We are going to go inside the Prefecture and I want it to appear that we are your prisoners. But, first, I need to unload your weapons."

* * *

Raymond Soward had just entered the main office area of the *prefecture* when the outside door opened. He looked curiously as six men entered in varied types of uniforms, a number of which were tattered and torn. A militia soldier guarded the six along with a single *Milice* officer, both of whose weapons were pointed at the six men.

Something about the situation bothered Soward, but he was much too late to react. He started to reach inside his coat for the old Luger he kept there, but one of the prisoners moved first. He produced a handgun he was hiding under his tattered uniform.

"Put your hands in the air," a voice commanded, "we are..."

At the far ends of the long room, Soward's driver, who had spent the night sleeping on a mattress on the floor of the *prefecture*, pulled out his Walther Model 1938 that enjoyed an eight round capacity and began firing at the group.

His first shots bounced wildly off walls and ceilings, hitting no one, but disrupting Martin's orderly flow of events. The *maquis* took cover wherever they could find it and immediately returned the driver's fire. Soward ducked behind a nearby desk and drew his 9mm Luger M1908. Soward's driver continued firing from an open stance, an action that proved to be much braver than wise. Martin's *maquis* concentrated their fire in his general direction and hit the gunman several times. He crumpled to the floor in severe agony, groaning loudly from his fatal wounds.

"Throw out your weapons or you will all be killed," the *maquis'* voice again commanded.

Soward briefly considered his dismal options and the overwhelming number of aggressors and decided to comply.

"All right, stop shooting," he answered. "Here is my gun." He tossed the Luger onto the floor of the *prefecture*, in the direction of the *maquis*.

Martin walked over towards Soward and picked up the pistol, checking its safety.

He looked squarely at his adversary with a disdainful glare and shook his head.

"You did a wise thing, *Monsieur,* further resistance was futile."

"You and your men will pay for this, I promise you as much," Soward sneered at the intruder.

"And what makes you think you are in a position to back up that promise *Monsieur?*" Martin took Soward's own Luger and placed it directly under the *Milice* officer's throat.

Soward coughed and lowered his head. Martin smiled and turned away from the suddenly subdued *Milice* inspector. With his head, Martin motioned to his men to step forward. One of his band tugged the back of Martin's coat, wanting him to look back. There, one of Charles Martin's *maquis* lay contorted in a deadly pose, a spreading pool of crimson oozing from a wound to his temple. Martin stepped to the man and gently touched his forehead. Another brave Frenchman had given his life for his country.

Martin stood up, and quietly motioned to several of his men who rapidly produced blindfolds and ropes. Without hesitation, the bindings were quickly applied to Raymond Soward and the two other prisoners. To Charles Martin's relief, there were no other Vichy or *Milice* officers around.

With the captives sufficiently bound, Martin motioned again, and his men went about their assigned jobs. They thoroughly searched the room for any additional weapons and ammunition. Not a word was spoken as Martin stepped toward the rear of the building.

* * *

Christine was instantly awakened by the loud sounds of gunfire. She looked at Russell, but he shrugged his shoulders unknowingly. For several minutes, the place became silent.

"What is going on?" Christine inquired.

"How should I know?" Russell answered curtly. "I haven't left the room."

Christine didn't appreciate his facetiousness. "Don't joke, this is serious."

"I know it is. I was just…"

Russell's reply was cut off as footsteps sounded in the hall and stopped outside their door. Seconds later, the lock on the door clicked. A young man who appeared to be in his mid to late thirties, wearing a tattered gray uniform and a black beret, stepped inside.

"I am Charles Martin of the *maquis*. You must come with us," he said calmly, "we have come here to help you."

Russell looked at the ragged man and breathed a sigh of relief.

He practically pushed Christine out the door before him and into the hallway. They turned left and came to a larger room where Soward and two other *Milice* personnel were seated on the floor, tied up and blindfolded. Russell surveyed the room and saw the prone *maquis* fighter. From the back of the room he heard groans.

Another *maquis* in the center of the room held up his finger to his mouth as a sign of silence. He motioned for Russell and Christine to follow.

Russell nodded, held up one finger in the direction of Charles Martin, and looked about the large room. Russell's eyes roamed the area, checking everything within view. He approached each of the desks and opened the drawers. At the second desk, he finally found what he was seeking. He extracted both Christine and his own papers and handed them to her to hold.

He walked to a spot near the back wall, and found the cylinder. He examined it and unlocked the top. He checked it carefully and ascertained that the cylinder's *entire* contents were still inside, and once again locked the top. He signaled to Martin that they were now ready to leave. The *maquis* picked up the body of their dead comrade and the entire group departed

* * *

Meurice Gilles was already waiting outside with an antiquated old truck formerly used to transport Armagnac barrels. A few filled barrels were still contained in its back section, along with a number of empty barrels tied together with ropes. Russell and Christine, along with a pair of *maquis* carrying the lifeless *maquis'* body, jumped in the back and hid themselves among the barrels. The barrels exuded a marvelous, aromatic odor that permeated the air. Gilles motioned with his hand for Charles Martin to climb into the truck's cabin. In another moment, the vehicle's ancient diesel sputtered and belched out a steady stream of smelly fumes as the truck began its slow egress from *Condom*.

"I was worried," Gilles wheezed in a high tone. "When I heard the shooting..."

"The idiots started shooting first," Martin explained as he settled into the front seat. "One of my men was killed. I think we might have also killed one of them. The shooting was all so unnecessary."

Gilles sighed, hoping Martin was mistaken about the dead *Milice* agent, and turned the steering wheel. The old truck grunted again and continued its forward movement. Gilles took care to utilize a series of back roads out of *Condom* and soon the vehicle was safely out of the city heading east. Gilles took a deep breath. He knew he could only afford a few hours before he and the old truck would be missed.

*　*　*

The back of the motor vehicle was a shock for both Russell and Christine. While the vapors originating from the barrels somewhat negated the stench created by the diesel fumes, the truck was noisy to the extent that it made serious conversation nearly impossible. With a bit of difficulty, Russell was able to converse with the *maquis* fighters. They were quick to explain their distaste for the local Vichy hierarchy and the general state of affairs in their particular part of France. Russell was fascinated that the Resistance movement seemingly involved *everyone* in France, or, at least *this* particular part of France.

Gilles' intention was to drive Christine and Russell to a certain point along the road on which the truck was currently traveling. Other Resistance members would be waiting for them there. These new Resistance contacts would in turn assist the pair in their flight to reach safety.

In the meantime, Charles Martin became curious about the cylinder Russell was so careful to bring along, but decided against questioning him about it.

In such matters it was often better if one did not ask. The less he knew about it, Martin quickly decided, the better he would be.

The old truck lumbered along, vibrating as if on its final legs. The ride lasted the better part of an hour along a bumpy, country road and finally came to an end.

Meurice Gilles stopped the vehicle and alighted. He signaled to the two *maquis* in the back, and everyone got down. The *maquis* took special care in removing the now partially rigid body of their fallen comrade.

Gilles looked around, and seemed visibly disappointed. He had reached his designated meeting place but found *no* additional Resistance members waiting at the spot to meet them.

"My friends," Gilles began, gazing at Russell and Christine, "with the *maquis*' aid, we were able to rescue you from your predicament. I also planned to have additional Resistance members here to assist you even further on your journey. But, something has happened and they are not waiting here as they should be. I am unsure as to what to do next, because my local resources are extremely limited and it is vitally important that you get as far away from *Condom* as possible. I also know from past experience with the *Milice*, that your journey will soon become much more difficult.

By now, the Vichy *Milice* and militia we tied up and left back in *Condom* have probably been set free. I am sure they will do everything in their power to get you back. Your current papers will no longer prove useful to you and I am unaware of when the Resistance can provide you with fresh ones." He paused and questioned Christine. "Do you intend to return to your original escape plan?"

"We have discussed doing so, and also the alternatives. Do you have a suggestion?"

"The *Milice* have no knowledge of your route, do they?" Gilles asked, looking directly at Christine.

"No," she answered. "Not that we are aware of."

"Good. I have the capability of sending a coded radio message back to England, which will let them know you are safe. I will also inform them that you are following your original plan. They will relay the information to the correct people within the Resistance. Within a day, two at the most, the entire network will be on the lookout for you. I am uneasy about using my regular communications channels right now. "The fact my men are not here could mean we have been compromised. Is there anything else I can provide for you now?"

"No *Monsieur*, you have already helped a great deal."

"I have only done a small part. It is *Monsieur* Martin here, and his wonderful *maquis*. They are who you should be thanking."

Christine looked directly at Martin, acknowledging the *maquis'* role. Martin accepted her gesture and smiled back at her.

Meurice Gilles concluded, "Then, I suggest we all disperse in different directions. For the time being, it will not be easy for any of us around this area. The *Milice* are treacherous at best and will undoubtedly apply a great deal of pressure to find you."

He shook hands and reentered his truck. In a few moments, the truck coughed itself back into life. Gilles turned it around and headed back in the direction of *Condom*.

* * *

Reichsmarschall Hermann Goring returned to his office and sorted through the massive accumulation of mail and dispatches that were piled neatly on his desk. He took action on several of the documents he considered most important at the top of the pile and continued sorting through the remainder.

His eyes settled on the Gestapo bulletin reporting the death of SS Obersturmbannfuhrer Kurt von Heltscherer in rural France. He felt his blood pressure rise as he continued reading. Suddenly, he shouted loudly to his aide-de-camp who was working in a nearby office.

"What is this," he demanded, as he handed the bulletin to his subordinate. "Why wasn't I informed of this immediately?"

His aide-de-camp, a recently promoted SS Sturmbannfuhrer who was slowly getting used to the Reichsmarschall's frequent outbursts and erratic behavior, took the report from his superior, glancing at it.

"Herr Reichsmarschall," he stammered. "I had no way of knowing. You left specific orders not to be…"

"Sometimes I wonder about your competency," Goring ranted. "It may now be too late. Get me the Office of the Director of Abwehr Intelligence. I want to speak to Admiral Canaris personally. He will know who has responsibility for our activities in southwestern France. Do not bother me again until you have the Admiral on the line."

"Jawohl, Herr Reichsmarschall." The lesser officer saluted, turned, took a deep breath and quickly departed. Even though he was accustomed to dealing with Goring on a daily basis, he wondered if he would ever adapt himself to the repeated verbal abuse. He shook his head and picked up the receiver to place the call Goring had ordered. He also wondered why the death of this particular SS officer had driven the Reichsmarschall to such an outburst. The younger SS officer briefly considered the fate of several other SS officers and ranking members of the Nazi hierarchy who had recently been sent to the dreaded Sachsenhausen Concentration Camp. To his knowledge, all had been removed from their posts for unspecified reasons. He wondered if the Reichsmarschall was prone to such extreme measures for all subordinates who fell out of his favor. He dismissed his last thought as something completely beyond his control and returned his attention to the receiver. An Abwehr Intelligence officer picked up the other end of the line.

*　*　*

It took Soward and the other *Milice* personnel almost two hours to gain their release. Another *Milice* agent, who was away from the *prefecture* at the time of the *maquis* subterfuge, finally returned to the building and set Soward and the others in the *prefecture* free.

The first thing Soward did after being untied was to check the room where Russell and Christine had spent the night. He was not surprised to find the room empty. Their departure confirmed his earlier suspicions that the couple was not who they first appeared to be.

Soward's initial rage at the morning's events was finally subsiding. He felt vindicated that his original policeman's instinct had once again proven to be correct. Recounting the morning's proceedings in his mind, he surmised that something truly extraordinary had occurred at the *prefecture*.

He correctly concluded that the *prefecture* had been attacked by a group of men, and from their general appearance, the faction was undoubtedly a band of *maquis*. He also knew that his driver was gravely wounded and the local doctor who was called confirmed that the man would probably die in the near future from his wounds. At the center of it all, Raymond Soward now knew conclusively, were two young people supposedly on a pilgrimage to *Lourdes*.

The *Milice* Inspector also was aware that the prisoners and their liberators could not travel very far without being recognized and that a quick reaction on his part was essential if he held any chance of recapturing his prisoners.

He detailed an urgent communication to *Milice* Headquarters in *Vichy* outlining the events of the past two days. The message also contained detailed descriptions of Russell and Christine along with names and addresses contained on the papers they were carrying. He requested his message be forwarded to all similar Vichy militia and *Milice* offices. Soward was careful to urgently request help from all those agencies He also included any and all Wehrmacht military units in the area.

His primary task completed, Raymond Soward then extracted a detailed local map, which he studied for the next fifteen minutes. He made a series of marks on the map and set about developing his plan to recapture Christine and Russell. Soward hoped that he could act quickly enough to make it happen. Time was definitely his enemy and he knew his foes would make the best of it.

*   *   *

For the second time in a month Charles Martin had to bury one of his men. For him, such duty was the most unpleasant part of his responsibility, an integral part of his cause that he realized he would never become used to performing. At such times, Martin always reminded himself of his men's unyielding commitment to their ground roots organization and their willingness to die for a cause that hardly recognized them. He performed a brief eulogy over the uneven dirt and rock grave that was decorated with two crosses made from branches of nearby trees. In addition to the Christian cross, Charles Martin and others within the *maquis* always added a second marker. The additional wooden cross was the historic double *Croix du Lorraine*, the symbol of Free France. It was the *maquis'* personal representation of the depths of their feelings for their country.

Martin completed the brief ceremony and signaled his men to leave.

He approached Russell and Christine.

"So what do you do now? Where will you go?"

Christine answered for the pair.

"I intend to continue heading southwest. We will follow our original route and try to rendezvous with the Resistance further south. I see no real reason to change the plan."

Martin took note, and after Christine had finished spoke frankly to her.

"Let me be completely honest with you. If I let you set out in the direction you suggested, I must tell you the idea would not sit very well with me. *Monsieur* Gilles was correct about the *Milice* and the forces it can bring to bear. I am very familiar with the area into which you intend to travel and I think it might be best if my men and I accompany you. We would undoubtedly have to walk a good deal of the way. This would cause us slow progress, but I think you would both be much safer under our protection."

Christine turned toward Russell who was already nodding his agreement. Privately, she was also relieved to have Martin's fearless band of *maquis* around.

"Good, we all agree. Now, it is best that we begin at once. I am sure they are already out searching for us."

Martin signaled and the group started out. According to Christine's plan, their next destination and potential rendezvous was in the town of *Aire-sur-l'Adour*, about forty miles southwest of their present location. With a little luck, the group would reach the town in a little more than a day.

*   *   *

Reichsmarschall Hermann Goring was clearly adamant that an immediate investigation be started regarding the death of Kurt von Heltscherer. After a mostly unproductive conversation with the Chief of Abwehr Intelligence Admiral Wilhelm Canaris, he decided to handle the matter of von Heltscherer's death himself. He briefly considered discussing the situation with senior officers of the Oberkommando der Wehrmacht. The political and practical aspects of such an action were clouded and he decided against it.

He summoned another top level SS officer with an aggressive reputation to his office. Upon arrival, Goring instructed the SS Standartenfuhrer standing at attention in front of him to utilize the full authority of the Reichsmarschall's office to investigate the tragedy and report back to him on the status of von Heltscherer's mission. He placed all Third Reich intelligence sources at the Standartenfuhrer's disposal and demanded the development of an immediate plan of action. Goring explained that recently deceased SS Obersturmbannfuhrer Kurt von Heltscherer had been conducting a personal investigation on the Reichsmarschall's behalf into the disappearance of a number of artworks. These pieces had been illegally removed from a number of their national museums by the French. The Reichsmarschall also produced copies of several reports von Heltscherer had forwarded to Berlin prior to his death.

Goring directed that any information gleaned by the investigation be brought to him personally, no matter what hour of day or night.

The entire meeting was conducted in a manner that was irritated and imperious at the same time. Its tone sent chills down the back of the lesser officer.

Hermann Goring dismissed the SS Standartenfuhrer and returned his thoughts to the other pressing business of the Third Reich.

*　*　*

For some lingering reason, it was impossible for Soward to dismiss the notion from his mind that the City of *Lourdes* was integrally connected with the circumstances surrounding his two missing prisoners. Was it the note of sincerity both the woman and man projected when he interrogated them? Was it the fact that the tube the pair made sure to take with them on their flight from confinement in the *prefecture* contained inexpensive reproductions of the Virgin Mary? Soward wasn't sure why, but his definitive policeman's instincts continued to place the small city at the base of the *Pyrenees* in the forefront of his thoughts.

Soward prepared another dispatch regarding Christine and Russell for all regional Vichy agencies. This new alert contained a notation about *Lourdes* as a possible destination for the pair and also a brief description of the cylinder they were carrying and its contents.

Soward sent out the dispatch with the *Milice's* highest priority code. He hoped this code would attract the attention of many of his *Milice* associates.

Chapter Fifteen

The overland route the *maquis* followed was both slow and exhausting. Within hours Russell and Christine found themselves growing extremely weary. More importantly, the provisions the *maquis* were able to carry with them from *Condom* were exhausted after the first night and immediate prospects for additional food for the band didn't appear very positive. The arduous route Charles Martin chose was strictly confined to the hilly, rough countryside. Whenever a home site or buildings came into view in the distance, Martin altered his group's course around such obstacles. While the new terrain began to provide less strenuous terrain to contend with, the area was nevertheless completely overgrown and consistently difficult for Russell and Christine to transverse.

As the trek continued, Russell became more and more impressed with Charles Martin's ability as a leader. Russell even chose to share some brief details of his mission's purpose with the *maquis* chief. Without disclosing their mission's particulars, he allowed Martin to garner enough details so as to be able to appreciate the operation's importance. He also reinforced the staunch necessity for Christine and him to reach safety outside France. Since they were already in the *maquis* leader's debt for saving their lives, Russell felt his brief explanation partially helped repay the *maquis'* labors. He knew he could never *fully* repay any of them.

Russell was also pleased to observe the gradual changes taking place in the passing landscape. The terrain approaching *Aire-sur-l'Adour* slowly leveled out. The countryside's former raggedness was replaced by gently undulating fields dotted with an occasional small hill. This new area comprised a large, broad valley, and from all indications contained a vast, lush agricultural region.

A series of smallish grazing lakes began to appear that served dual usage. The lakes supplied any nearby cattle needing water. They also provided an irregular irrigation system for the nearby fields. The first major planting of wheat the pair encountered on the trip appeared on the horizon, and from its general color and appearance, the wheat was not far removed from harvest. Russell wondered how many workers were left in the local area to harvest such crops. So many Frenchmen had either fled or had been conscripted by the German and Vichy governments, it was hard to tell how many remained.

He also noted that they were now in an area of France absent of the sporadic walled cities and towns. The aging sites were testaments to the wars and strife that had plagued France for so many prior centuries. The verdant fields that presented themselves to Martin's band provided an immediate improvement from the dense underbrush and wildness of the mountains. Both Christine and Russell's shoes were now nearly totally unusable, a detail that Martin promised to attend to the next time they reached a development of any sort.

Tended crops began to pop up everywhere and the surrounding soil also experienced a gradual transformation. Left behind were the clay-rich, rocky red formations which Russell had observed all along his route from the beautiful large valley of the *Chateau de Montal.* His route from the southwest included the steep rises and craggy face of *Cahors* and then down through the more gentle slopes of *Condom.* The present soil around the *maquis* group was darker and richer, and Martin delightedly pointed out to Russell varied crops of corn, artichokes, along with an incredible amount of planted rye. Russell also thought he saw the last vestige of mustard plants that imparted a final reminder of a bountiful spring harvest for the sour tasting weed. The gentle sloping of the terrain provided a striking and remarkable facsimile of paintings and photographs. These sights were similar to ones contained in books and journals Russell remembered reading while a student at the *Sorbonne.*

The local architecture also underwent a change, from the rectangular high-topped classic French farmhouses and barns, to wider, lower styles of buildings. These edifices came complete with decidedly Spanish influenced red tile roofs.

For the first time in some hours, Russell's mind wandered, returning to his former exuberant academic times. He also considered the fates of some of his previous friends during these perilous times.

Russell wondered about his closest friend Roland Senard. Senard was the incredibly talented striker on his Sunday soccer team who was always so impassioned by events within his life. Russell recognized the extent to which he genuinely missed his old friend. He had made several attempts to contact Roland after returning to the United States, but phone service to France at the time was unreliable and Russell was forced to finally abandon his efforts. He wrote Roland a long letter but had no way of knowing if it was ever received. Brian also thought about Natalie and Renée; his friends from the *Sorbonne* who were also his unofficial guides to *Paris* and most of France. Both women insisted on accompanying Russell to the airport when he flew to Lisbon on his way home from France. The three close friends' parting proved tearful for all.

Brian Russell wished that his present assignment were more flexible, and that he had sufficient time to attempt to make contact with his old friends. He had committed each of their telephone numbers to memory but the mission's demanding schedule and the dangers of his present situation made such an idea impractical and unthinkable.

By the middle of the second day's dogged journey, the glaring, unrelenting sun finally forced the group to stop. Martin selected a small grove of trees for shade. The grove surrounded several large planted fields. He signaled his men to make camp.

"We are nearing the town of *Aire sur l'Adour,*" he reassured Russell. "I will send one of my men into the place to check. He will also gather some food for us. But first, there is something more important for us to do."

Russell was unsure of Martin's intention, but nodded his agreement. He also silently prayed that the guerrilla's return with the food would be timely and successful.

Charles Martin's reference had nothing to do with eating.

In a field adjacent to the trees Martin's *maquis* was using to camp, a twelve-foot high stone testimonial stood silently in a corner of the pasture. Upon closer examination, Russell saw that the structure was actually a crude stone and mortar altar, which contained a vaulted statue of the Virgin Mary, originally placed there by the land's owner to protect the crops from evil pests and spirits. Martin motioned his men to gather around the site. Brian Russell and Christine Allard followed close behind.

"It is time that we prayed for our fallen comrade, another patriot who has offered his life for his country and for what he believed. I regret we could not take the time when we buried him."

The *maquis* gathered around the site and removed their hats and caps. Russell and Christine also inched their way forward and stood amongst the group of fighters. Each bowed their head as Martin continued.

"Dear Lady, Mother of God, please accept the soul of our fellow partisan Robert Armantrout into your sacred presence. Help him to see the face of his Lord and share in the eternal happiness with those who have already entered Heaven. Guide our actions and help us protect our country and drive our enemies from our lands. We ask this in the name of your son, Jesus Christ, our Lord. Amen."

"Amen" the remainder of the *maquis* band joined in. Each man crossed himself and Martin gave the gesture to return to the business of setting up the camp. This took another fifteen minutes and everyone found the shadiest place to slump their tired body. It was the end to a long and difficult march through incredibly rugged and inhospitable terrain.

Russell realized that he hadn't washed himself in quite a while and that his clothes had become torn and dirtied from encounters in the wild with tree branches and bushes. It was the same story for Christine, whose neat silk outfit was now soiled and shredded. In addition to being grubby and filthy, both were hungry and tired. Even though their own physical appearance was markedly dreadful, both Christine and Russell marveled at the determination and spirit of the *maquis*, who lived completely in the wild and seldom complained about their surroundings.

The specific orders given SS Standartenfuhrer Horst Wieber by the second most powerful man in the Third Reich were very direct and to the point. The SS Colonel immediately returned to his own office and began sifting through numerous reports involving intelligence activities within the unoccupied zone of France.

Wieber was a 25-year veteran of the intelligence service whose presence in the Waffen SS was more career-oriented than political in nature. When the National Socialists rose to power in Germany during the early thirties, Wieber correctly reasoned that party members would have varying degrees of priority within the military. His career move to the Waffen SS had proven fruitful and, in his own mind, his current position was as secure as any within the German military structure.

His present assignment involving SS Obersturmbannfuhrer Kurt von Heltscherer's death was the first opportunity Wieber had to work directly under Reichsmarschall Hermann Goring's orders. He was aware that members of the Luftwaffe, directly under Goring's control, often referred to him as *"Unser Hermann"* (our Hermann). This was due to the fact that Goring was originally a highly decorated flier during the First World War. The recent tirade Wieber had endured in Goring's office and the thought of the Reichsmarschall's disproportionate personality were the traits that exasperated him. Nonetheless, SS Standartenfuhrer Horst Wieber decided to make the most of his chance. He called for his clerical assistant to bring him additional files and documents. On this occasion, Wieber wanted to insure that he covered *all* potential leads and opportunities. It would not help his career if he were to overlook anything in a case so essentially important to the Reichsmarschall.

*   *   *

Even though she knew that some of her fellow fighters considered her too young, Christine Allard was used to pressure-filled situations. She also admitted to herself that, for the first time in her life, the circumstances involving her arrest by the *Milice* outside *Condom* had actually caused her to feel real fear.

The thought that she could be so easily troubled annoyed her, and she determined to put it to the back of her mind. Christine was still comfortable with the escape route she originally planned with Victor, but given the present state of affairs, she wasn't entirely sure of what to expect from Soward and the *Milice*. The cynical police inspector would probably invoke all his powers and provide as many obstructions as possible to the completion of their journey. The trek still involved the pair traveling many miles to complete.

At the *prefecture*, Christine briefly considered ordering the killing of Soward to lessen the pair's chance of being caught, but the probable retributions to the townspeople of *Condom* outweighed such an action. If Soward were killed, who knows what those poor inhabitants of the town would have had to suffer?

Christine was suddenly sensitive to the fact that she was developing a new personal feeling that was totally unexpected and for which she was entirely unprepared.

That emotion related directly to Captain Brian Russell, USA, and the manner in which he conducted himself. As time passed, she realized her former resentment toward him had waned. The feeling was now replaced with a much stronger emotion, one that she could not realistically explain. Russell had proved to be strong, kind, and patient, the qualities she most admired in a person. He also approached most situations he encountered in a cool, detached and imperturbable manner. Christine had never found such a combination of qualities in the same man.

In Christine's estimation, Russell also possessed a strong sense of value and a witty sense of humor. This sometimes caused her mild discomfort when she was on the receiving end of one of his barbs. She enjoyed such teasing, for it usually involved insignificant matters both found were enjoyed in common. Christine also took great delight in his ability to appreciate and describe places and events. Often, their conversations were long and detailed, and provided a unique window into the personality of the man.

She looked over at him in the light of the small fire the *maquis* had started. His handsome face was outlined by the faint flames emanating from the fire. His facial attraction was also mounting daily, formed by not shaving, into the soft attractiveness of a full beard.

Christine warned herself about these feelings and about their potential consequence. It was the first time in her life she was forced to proceed cautiously about involvement with another person.

* * *

Senior Inspector Raymond Soward was having difficulty getting his Vichy superiors to approve his request for temporary duty that would allow him to proceed directly to the City of *Lourdes*. For some reason, higher-ranking *Milice* officials in Vichy were reluctant to pry him loose from his regular duties based on the evidence he documented in his reports involving the *Condom Prefecture* shooting incident.

Soward freely admitted that most of the details he had been able to piece together were basically conjecture, but the Senior *Milice* Inspector also expected his proven investigative record to work in his favor. For years, he built his reputation and prided himself on uncovering situations that were not as they appeared. His own dependable intuition strongly urged him to proceed to the vicinity of *Lourdes*. He decided not to take no for an answer and renewed his appeal to the Vichy *Milice* hierarchy. With time becoming more of a factor, he insisted that the matter be decided speedily. Raymond Soward also counted on the fact that he was the most prolific Jew hunter in his entire district and his record in supplementary matters was superior to many other police inspectors within the *Milice*. Soward continually pressed the issue until his Vichy superiors finally relented.

Permission was given to make the automobile trip to the southeast. To Soward's amazement, an hour prior to his departure, he was even assigned an assistant to drive. Papers authorizing the visit were initiated and sent to the regional *Milice* offices in *Pau*, whose jurisdiction covered all police activities in nearby *Lourdes*.

Heartened by the exceptional news, Soward and his new assistant, a fellow named Torte, whose face was marked by an oblong scar that ran the length of his cheek, set out as soon as they were able to pack some clothes. Soward was delighted that he did not have to drive the distance himself. He could now put the time to better use in figuring out how to catch his two ex-prisoners. The Senior Inspector knew the job would be most difficult.

* * *

SS Standartenfuhrer Wieber's trained eye finally settled on several items that crossed his desk.

The only bona fide facts he had to work with were the dated reports by von Heltscherer detailing his failures at *Chambord* and the *Abbey du Loc-Dieu*. In his reports, von Heltscherer was also adamant about his basic assessment that the missing artworks were still located somewhere within the specific area he was searching, the *Dordogne* Region of South Central France.

Wieber reread the report from the Wehrmacht officer in charge of investigating the explosion that killed von Heltscherer and Hoven. Reference was made to a large amount of unidentifiable debris found within the cave, and further mention identified some crated paintings that were not entirely destroyed. The investigating officer reported that subsequent investigation pointed to the fact that the paintings found inside the cave at the site of the explosion were mostly inexpensive reproductions, of little or no value.

Those factors led the SS Standartenfuhrer to the conclusion that the German officers had probably fallen into a deadly trap, and such detailed organization could only mean that the French Resistance was at the root of the bombing.

Was SS Oberstrumbannfuhrer von Heltscherer getting too close to the paintings? Was such an elaborate ruse necessary to protect them from further investigation?

Other seemingly non-related intelligence communiqués from that time period also caught Wieber's eye. First, a Luftwaffe night fighter pilot's report, filed several days prior to the cave incident, concerned an event that occurred during the pilot's night flight. The pilot was not completely positive, but both he and his radio operator thought they noticed a small aircraft either attached or in close proximity to a Lancaster bomber the Messerschmitt had strafed. The report also pointed out that the bomber's heading and the fact that a pair of British Spitfires accompanied it were both highly unusual. Wieber extrapolated the bomber's perceived heading and found that the heading pointed in the general direction of the cave where the explosions occurred. The report provided no further explanation about the occurrence.

Wieber interpreted a possible connection to what he was researching but was not able to form a plausible link.

Additionally, more recent *Milice* reports just received in Berlin covered the events involving a pair of suspected Resistance members in the City of *Condom*. A man and a woman were subsequently rescued while incarcerated at the *Condom Prefecture du Police* by paramilitary elements thought to be the members of the guerrilla *maquis*. Wieber was as yet unfamiliar with the term *maquis*, but made a mental note to locate additional information. The specific aspect of the *Milice* report that attracted Wieber's attention was a reference to several inexpensive poster copies of various paintings of the Virgin Mary, which were found inside a tube that the male suspect was carrying.

Wieber considered the possibility of such a coincidence, but the actual facts covered in the report and a possible tie to the *Grand Vabre* murders seemed to him a bit far-fetched. His alert mind conceded that the posters mentioned in the *Milice* report could be considered art. It was also true he had very little substantive information on which to prepare his report for the Reichsmarschall.

*   *   *

The *maquis* partisan that Charles Martin sent to scout *Aire-sur-l'Adour* returned to the waiting *maquis* camp with disturbing news. He reported a strong Vichy militia presence in and around the commercial section of the town, while a lesser number of Wehrmacht soldiers and military vehicles stood by the only bridge that crossed the *Adour* River.

Martin's observer kept an eye on activity at the bridge and reported that everyone crossing was thoroughly checked. Martin had expected as much after the commotion he and his men caused two days earlier in *Condom*.

The partisan did, however, manage to bring back to the waiting group a moderate quantity of fruit, breads, dried meats and even several bottles of local wine. For the first time in nearly two days, the *maquisards* sat down to a basic meal.

Martin deliberated his next move with Christine and Russell. During the past two days, Christine had quizzed him on their proposed escape route, mostly to see if Martin could offer any suggestions. At first Martin was able to provide little productive input. Much later, when his active imagination was stimulated by some much needed rest, a possible resolution to the quandary began to emerge.

Charles Martin decided he would venture into *Aire-sur-l'Adour* during the early morning hours the following day and test a plausible alternative to a possible confrontation at the *Adour* River bridge. With a modest dash of good fortune, his idea might be able to provide a means around their problem.

*   *   *

In time, Raymond Soward arrived in the City of *Pau*, the regional capital of the *Department du Grand Pyrenees*. He immediately proceeded to present his letter of authorization to the high level Vichy official in charge of police matters. Soward patiently explained the pertinent details of his assignment and was given permission to base his surveillance in *Lourdes* or in any other location Soward considered beneficial.

The Vichy bureaucrat also thought it prudent to provide Soward with a list that contained the names of several hotels in the city of *Lourdes* whose allegiance to the Vichy government was already proven. The Vichy official also decided to assign an additional *Milice* officer who was actually based in *Lourdes* to assist Soward. The female inspector so designated was completely familiar with police activities within the city and would directly support Soward in the completion of his ongoing task.

Before he left the Vichy offices, Soward asked for one additional bit of help. Soward desired to use the services of the *Pau* police department artist in producing a pair of sketches of Christine and Russell. Copies of these drawings would be distributed throughout the area. The *Pau* official quickly agreed and summoned the artist to his office.

Soward had successfully utilized similar drawings during a number of past investigations. Two hours later, with Inspector Raymond Soward working closely at his side, the police department artist was able to produce a pair of images that Soward felt closely resembled the pair of young fugitives he was pursuing.

The senior inspector soon departed *Pau*, his spirits considerably improved by the unexpected flexibility and cooperation of his fellow officer. This new turn of luck helped serve to convince Raymond Soward that, after some initial problems, he was finally on the right track.

* * *

A prudent SS Standartenfuhrer Horst Wieber took it on his own authority to write and distribute a special bulletin concerning the two individuals removed from the *Prefecture* in *Condom*. He listed all available information about the suspects and placed a high degree of urgency on the notice.

In his notice he referred to the two individuals as,

"Suspected Resistance terrorists, who are armed and considered extremely dangerous."

He attached a reward of 200 francs for any information causing their apprehension.

The notice stated that anyone coming into contact with the suspects was to immediately notify the nearest Vichy *Milice* office or any German military personnel.

Wieber also took the time to send a copy of his bulletin to Reichsmarschall Hermann Goring along with a hand written note. In it he stated it was possible that these fugitives were somehow connected to the murder of SS Obersturmbannfuhrer Klaus von Heltscherer and several Wehrmacht soldiers. He also told his superior that he would diligently pursue any additional leads he was able to develop.

* * *

Maquis leader Charles Martin awoke from his light sleep more than an hour before the sky's first signs of life. He threw some cold water from a nearby pan into his face to shake off the cobwebs and carefully made his way into *Aire-sur-l'Adour*. Martin knew the town well and used back streets and alleys to reach his destination. At length he approached the building that housed the workplace of a sympathetic baker he knew, a good hearted fellow who was always willing to share his tasty products with the *maquis*.

Martin turned a corner and was delighted to find the man in the alley immediately behind his shop, enjoying an early morning *Gitanes*.

Approaching him, Martin raised his hand as a gesture of friendship.

The baker replied with a similar gesture, and offered Martin a cigarette. Martin politely refused and followed the man inside the bakery. An incredible sensory pleasure enveloped Martin who paused to enjoy the sweet smell.

"Come in, come in my friend. At this time of the morning I always have the place to myself."

"Good, Marcel. I never get enough of your marvelous smell in here. I have enjoyed the aroma since I was a child."

"Yes. I hear many people say the same thing. I'm afraid I don't even notice any longer. Maybe my sense of smell has deteriorated."

"Maybe you just have to become used to it," Martin agreed, picking up a *pain-au-chocolate*. Realizing his degree of hunger, Martin looked at the baker.

"Go ahead, enjoy it. There is also some coffee on the table. The coffee is not the same quality as before the war, and right now it is too scarce to brew at full strength."

"Thanks, it has been quite a while since I have even had a taste."

"Charles, your words are the shame of it all. Everything is rationed and everyone gripes about it, but I do not see anyone doing anything to help the situation. I am producing a good deal more baked goods now than before the war started, but even with the rationing it is not enough. The militia come in and requisition what they want, and there's barely enough left for everyone who needs it. With the money devalued as it is, I can hardly make a living."

Martin shook his head in agreement. He hoped it would not mean a reduction in the breads and buns he was used to receiving for his men.

"What is it you want?" the baker asked, "besides your customary supply of bread. I take it that an early meeting like this with the leader of the *maquis* means that your visit is something out of the ordinary. I am correct, *n'est-ce pas?*"

"You are quite observant, my good friend, and, quite correct. This time I need some of your advice, and maybe some help."

The baker listened intently to Martin, devouring his every word. He too enjoyed the small part he was able to play in the overall Resistance effort.

It took Charles Martin the better part of thirty minutes to explain his idea to Marcel Benoit. The baker agreed with parts of the proposed plan and suggested other parts be changed. Using the timely information he gleaned from the hundreds of daily customers that frequented his bakery, Marcel Benoit made Martin aware of recent events and the necessity to alter his plan. In the end, Martin was satisfied the strategy he had developed. It was now plausible enough for Christine and Russell to attempt.

Even though Charles Martin and Marcel Benoit finally agreed on the plan's specifics, Martin knew he would need some help from other Resistance sources to carry it out. Martin left *Aire-sur-l'Adour* and made sure to return to his camp with a fresh supply of breads and pastries for his men. After a short conversation with Christine, he also decided to accompany her back into *Aire-sur-l'Adour* when she made her Resistance contact. Russell agreed that he would play no part in the meeting and decided to wait at the *maquis* camp for Christine's return.

Martin trailed Christine into the small community, remaining about thirty meters behind her. The prearranged rendezvous spot was adjacent to the small train station, which appeared deserted at this time of morning. Martin knew that the station was located on the northern edge of the city and did not require crossing the *Adour* River. He also realized the tattered condition of his uniform was a dead giveaway to his guerrilla status. His next task was to do something to remedy the uniform problem for him and his men.

According to her orders, Christine was told to appear next to the *gare* at the prearranged hour of eleven o'clock. Unless something serious occurred, she would be met there by her Resistance contact. Christine reached the railroad station on time and took a quick look around, but saw no movement of any kind. The entire area was absolutely deserted, which seemed unusual to Christine. She glanced in Charles Martin's general direction, but was unable to pick him out of the background.

She pondered the possibility that something might have gone wrong. She considered her next option if no one showed up to keep the rendezvous? As seconds passed, Christine wondered if she was being paranoid. Was it simply that there were no trains scheduled around this time of day and therefore no good reason for anyone to be around?

Christine reproached herself for such ineffectual thoughts and conceded she would simply have to remain focused. After an hour's waiting, the station area remained deserted. Christine glanced in the direction of Martin, who now emerged from behind some railroad ties where he had been hiding. He signaled for her to leave and again followed at a distance behind her as she started back in the direction of the nearby *maquis* camp.

Her return route led her through a series of groves of relatively thick cedar and willows. At one point, Christine hesitated for a moment and turned around, sensing a presence behind her. Seeing nothing, and assuming it was Martin following her, she continued on.

As Christine reached a partial open clearing in the woods, a man burst forth and excitedly confronted her. The intruder was of medium height, heavily mustached and wore a faded green beret.

Before Christine could react, the man reached for her arm, forcing her to stop.

"Please, Mademoiselle, I need to talk to you!"

"Who are you, *Monsieur*? What do you want?"

He gave the Resistance password, and Christine shrugged in disbelief.

She recalled the correct response and returned the password.

The man continued apologetically. "I am Guy LaRoche. From a distance, I saw you waiting next to the railroad station but I hesitated to approach you. For some reason, the situation just did not appear right to me. The message I received from Victor indicated there would be two of you, but you appeared by yourself. Also, you came a day later than I expected. I took a chance in even coming to the station today. It was only after you left that I was able to determine that you are alone. That's why I felt it was necessary to stop you in this manner. I trust you understand my position."

"There were some unforeseen problems that forced me to change our plan. We had a nasty encounter with the *Milice* in Condom that forced us into walking most of the way. In the end, the journey took a lot longer than we planned, which is why we are a day late. We are probably lucky to be here at all. The incidents that occurred could not be avoided." Christine took a deep breath. "You really startled me, jumping out so suddenly," she added, attempting to control her breathing.

"I did not intend…" his attention was suddenly diverted by the appearance of Charles Martin, brandishing a Walther P-38 pistol recently acquired in the *Condom* fracas. Martin had just cleared the trees behind Christine.

"Don't worry about him," Christine assured LaRoche. "He is with me. He is leader of the *maquis* around here."

LaRoche acknowledged Martin, who placed his pistol back into his pants pocket. LaRoche looked relieved and also took a deep breath.

Christine spoke again.

"As I was saying, the person I am traveling with and I experienced some problems during our journey and were arrested by the *Milice* three days ago and taken to the *Prefecture* at *Condom*. We were questioned and held overnight by a *Milice* Inspector named Soward. He suspected we were up to something, but was not sure exactly what it was. We were trying to figure a way of escaping from the *Prefecture* when *Monsieur* Martin and his daring band of *maquis* guerrillas actually broke into the building and rescued us. The Resistance in *Condom* then took us by truck to a point well outside their city, where we mutually agreed to walk the rest of the way here. *Monsieur* Martin was gracious enough to volunteer his *maquis* to protect us. For that, I thank God. That, *Monsieur* LaRoche, is the complete explanation as to why I am late for our appointment."

"I understand fully, and I thank God you are all safe. Now, how can I be of help to you?"

Martin looked directly at Christine. "With your permission…"

She nodded and he then addressed LaRoche. "I have an idea, but I need your help and advice."

"Certainly, you know I am most willing to do anything I can."

*   *   *

The lodging Raymond Soward chose to occupy was a large, sweeping hotel in downtown *Lourdes* called the *Grand Hotel de la Grotte*. The structure bore its address, 66 *rue de la Grotte,* in bold letters on its façade. The place was centrally located along a rather steep hillside and offered Soward an excellent vantage point from which to view anyone crisscrossing *Lourdes'* cobbled streets.

Soward and his driver Torte spent their first day at the city's north side *gare,* carefully checking all passengers utilizing the station. He paid particular attention to passengers alighting from incoming trains. His experience had shown him that fleeing Jews showed a marked preference for using the trains whenever possible. His close examination of documents at key departure points in his sector often proved successful in ferreting out escaping Jews.

As he waiting for another train that was scheduled to arrive in five minutes, Soward considered his present situation. If normal circumstances and surveillance permitted him to arrest a number of Jews during his present mission, it would certainly help enrich his current position within the *Milice.* Apprehending Jews while on this assignment would also be prudent since he had no assurance he would ever see his two prisoners again. With minor successes in hand, his superiors would be willing to forgive any failure were his primary mission prove unsuccessful.

With that in mind, Soward and his assistant checked the papers of hundreds of passengers taking the trains, but none looked to be suspicious or bore even the faintest resemblance to the fugitives. Soward returned to his airy room at the *Grand Hotel de la Grotte* and found himself in a most unsettled mood.

By the middle of the second day, Soward was convinced that continuing such action was ineffectual at best. He knew that he must immediately employ a drastically different approach if he was ever going to locate Christine and Brian. The police officers left the *gare* and promptly set out to contact the *Milice* agent in *Lourdes,* whose name and address had been given to Soward by his associate in *Pau.* Soward felt it critical to his task that he quickly enlists the *Milice* agent's help if he were to be successful.

* * *

From primary sources in the *Pyrenees* and western slopes of the *Massif Central,* more than twenty rivers slowly wind their ways seaward through southwestern France. A typically example is the placid *Adour* River, which twists and turns itself from its source above the town of *Bagnares-de-Bigorre* in the *Pyrenees,* through hundreds of crescents and horseshoe turns. The *Adour* finally enters the Bay of *Gascony* at its mouth, splitting the cities of *Bayonne* and *Anglet.*

For centuries, the *Ardour* had been used to carry products and goods to the sea where they were unloaded and shipped to overseas destinations. Charles Martin grew up in this environment and as a youth played along the banks of the

A*dour* and several of its smaller tributaries. He remembered the small boats plying their way upriver against the river's gentle current and then watching for them to reappear sometime later, laden with a multitude of varied goods.

For his tenth birthday, Martin recalled that his father took his favorite cousin and him on a trip up the *Adour* in a small, motorized boat. At that point, the boat trip was the most exciting event that had occurred in Charles Martin's short life. When the Martins and their cousin finally left the boat, Martin recalled they were near the city of *Tarbes,* situated less than twenty kilometers northeast of *Lourdes.* Knowing that the couple's ultimate destination was the city of Lourdes, Charles Martin felt *Tarbes* could easily provide a natural landing for anyone proceeding on to *Lourdes*.

The plan Martin developed was a complete deviation from normal routing and methods the Resistance employed. However, Martin strongly emphasized to LaRoche that Russell and Christine's mission was considered extremely critical and should be handled accordingly. Martin also asked for LaRoche to forward detailed information through Resistance channels that covered the couple's probable arrival times. Without hesitating, Guy LaRoche readily agreed.

A timetable was arranged that was practical for both Martin and LaRoche. The two men then shook hands and departed.

* * *

The female *Milice* contact Senior *Milice* Inspector Raymond Soward sought to meet in *Lourdes* turned out to be an attractive middle-aged woman. Even more surprising to the hardened policeman was that she was of German origin and who had married a Frenchman before the war.

The female *Milice* agent introduced herself as Viktoria Losse, choosing to pronounce her surname in the French manner. Soward listened to her explanation and decided that by choosing the French pronunciation, she was able to enhance her credibility within the French community. The fact that she spoke nearly accent less French and was well acquainted with the inner workings of the city of *Lourdes* made her even more valuable to the secretive *Milice*.

"Even with the war, the pilgrims still come in great numbers," Viktoria offered in retrospect, referring to the steady stream of faithful Roman Catholic worshippers arriving daily in the city.

"The Vichy government has had to turn a soft eye toward such people. There are even large numbers of individuals that still arrive from Spain having made the pilgrimage over the mountains. No one is ever turned away at the border. They mostly come and go as they wish, and the city is generally crowded. But, by far, the visitors are mostly French who come for a day or two. It is not uncommon for many of them to travel several hundred miles to make it here."

Viktoria Losse also recounted to Soward her immediate duties. Soward wasn't at all surprised to hear those responsibilities included the weeding out of fleeing Jews.

Considering himself an expert, Soward was quick to boast. "The mistake they always make," he sneered, referring to the Jews, "is that they try to bring their entire families along and even some valuables. When they do this, it is fairly easy to pick them out."

"And, if the Nazis were pursuing *you*, how would you go about escaping?" Viktoria Losse prodded her confident associate.

"I certainly would not want to attract attention. If there were more than one child in the family, I would probably take the youngest one with me and send the other with my wife. Even though it would be difficult to split up, I think there would be a better chance of both making it if the husband and wife were separated."

"And your possessions?"

"There is no question about that. What little one could carry would be inconsequential. I would put everything I owned into some rare gems. These would be easier to hide, even on one's self. Such matters are particularly easy for Jews. Most Jews I have encountered were either rabbis, bankers, or dealers in garments or gems."

Viktoria studied Raymond Soward. While she agreed that his answer contained some credence, his words was so filled with hatred and malice as to negate its effect. She knew that she would have to watch this person who had become her new associate.

Soward altered the focus of their conversation and went on to explain his presence in *Lourdes*. He produced the sketch that had been created in *Pau* that bore the renderings of both Russell and Christine.

"They are both quite attractive people," she commented, looking at the sketch. "What did they do?"

"That matter is classified, Frau Losse. I cannot tell you."

Viktoria Losse was unimpressed. She was also unused to being called frau. Maybe she had been too earnest in initially telling Soward she was German. She studied the sketch for a short while and handed it back to him.

"In that case, this is what I suggest we do." She outlined a plan of action. Soward listened and agreed.

"If they choose to travel through *Lourdes*, we will undoubtedly catch them," Viktoria Losse confided.

Soward listened, still of the basic belief that his unfailing intuition was accurate.

A number of days had passed and Bernard Masson was busy with his cheese business. He had nearly forgotten his earlier Resistance message that forecast an important upcoming mission when an urgent communication came through his normal Resistance channel. The message directed Masson to travel to the city of *Tarbes* on the following day. The coded note also advised him that a rendezvous was now scheduled in *Tarbes* that involved two Resistance operatives attempting to exit from France into Spain on a vitally important mission. The communication also made reference to Bernard's older sister, Therese, who lived in *Tarbes*.

Masson stared intently at the message, and then destroyed it. He had not had the occasion to visit his sister since before the war began. He was delighted by the fact that the proposed rendezvous would serve to reunite him with his favorite person in the entire world. He admired his older sibling with boundless fervor and missed visiting her on a regular basis. He was thrilled with the prospect of being in her company as early as tomorrow.

He made immediate arrangements to have one of his trusted workers take the recently prepared shipment of cheeses that was waiting for delivery to one of his top customers in *Biarritz*. Masson left additional instructions that would insure his business interests be carried on as usual.

Bernard Masson realized that for the next few days, his Resistance responsibilities would command his entire attention.

* * *

Guy LaRoche was able to help secure the small boat Charles Martin had requested for the trip up the *Adour* River. General apathy for anything work related caused the boat's lazy owner to initially refuse to make the journey. The owner relented when LaRoche explained that the relatively short journey up the *Adour* would only occupy but a portion of the boat owner's day. La Roche also counseled him strongly to weigh that prospect against the probability of having his boat under intensive repair in the city's dry docks.

LaRoche carefully selected a secluded spot almost a full half-mile upriver from *Aire-sur-l'Adour* for everyone to meet. After further negotiation with the boat owner, he also was able to set a time that was mutually agreeable. It was agreed that everyone involved in the plan would meet at the designated spot at nine o'clock in the morning.

Hermann Goring's entire office area shook as the distinctly burly Reichsmarschall pounded his desk.

SS Standartenfuhrer Horst Wieber nervously stood at attention, gnawing his lower lip. He had been summoned to Goring's office and was expected to present a progress report on the von Heltscherer investigation. He had handed his written report to the Reichsmarschall and Goring was quick to react to its contents.

"You mean to tell me this is all you have learned?" Goring fumed, his manner loud and abrupt.

"Herr Reichsmarschall, there is little intelligence information available on which to base any investigation. The Wehrmacht in that vicinity thoroughly combed the entire area for approximately one mile in every direction, looking for clues and information. A number of suspected local Resistance members were arrested and detained. The Gestapo was summoned and these suspects were each individually interrogated. The Gestapo was unable to unearth anyone who had any knowledge of the events involving the explosion that killed Kurt von Heltscherer and the others. The Gestapo even used scopolamine on a number of them. You know how thorough the Gestapo is in such matters. Our experts are convinced the people they were interrogating were telling the truth and, as you are also aware, our experts are quite reliable."

"And what about Abwehr?" Goring referred to the German intelligence agency's reports. "Have they not helped?"

"A little, perhaps, but nothing solid enough to begin an investigation. The only report of anything extraordinary in the entire area came from a *Milice* inspector not very far away, but there was nothing specific..."

Goring interrupted. "A *Milice* inspector's report? I did not see that in your account. Exactly what did it state?"

"Jawohl, Herr Reichsmarschall. The report stated that two bicyclists, a man and a woman on their way to *Lourdes,* were detained in *Condom* because the *Milice* inspector involved thought it odd that they would travel so great a distance by bicycle. He detained them overnight, but someone, presumably the Resistance, broke into the *Prefecture du Police* and released the prisoners. The man who had been arrested was carrying with him a tube containing several posters of the Blessed Virgin, supposedly to be blessed at *Lourdes.* At least that was the story he told the *Milice.* As you can see, there is little substance involved in the entire episode to proceed any further. I am also unable to speak of the competence of the *Milice* officer reporting the episode..."

Goring dropped his head and touched his expanded chin, deep in thought. At length, he spoke.

"Unfortunately, Wieber, I must say that this time I agree with you. I fail to see any connection between the two, and we all know that the *Milice* officers are mostly fools and idiots. The two people in question were probably Resistance members on some particular mission, which is the reason they were rescued in the first place. I agree with your assessment, you should not give this matter too much more of your time."

"Jawohl, Herr Reichsmarschall, as you wish," Wieber snapped, a look of relief covering his face. "Heil Hitler!" He gave the Nazi salute, performed an about face and walked toward the door.

Goring stopped him as he reached the door. "And Wieber, I must apologize to you for my earlier tone. This matter was important to me personally, and I wanted it finalized."

Wieber did not acknowledge the Reichsmarschall's final remark, and was unprepared for his superior's sudden turn of disposition. He saluted again, turned and hastily departed Goring's office.

*   *   *

The heavily barnacled craft LaRoche commandeered was a thirty-year-old, shallow-bottomed riverboat about fifteen feet long. It was swooped low in the center with a small bridge near the rear. In its prime, the boat was capable of towing a small barge up and down the river, but her present owner opted for shorter runs with lighter cargoes that could be conveniently stored on her deck.

The boat's owner also served as captain of the small vessel. He greeted his new visitors with a blank expression. It was obvious to everyone that the man wasn't relishing his present situation.

LaRoche helped Russell and Christine board the boat. Russell gazed around the small craft and decided on placing the cylinder upright against a wall inside the bridge area. He wanted his possession to be close by and, if necessary, easy to retrieve.

LaRoche summoned Christine away from the captain and gave her a shopping bag that contained some new clothes for both she and Russell. He also briefed her on some additional instructions.

"Your next contact will meet you at a spot I selected just before you reach *Tarbes*. If everything goes as planned, the trip should not take more than six or seven hours. The *Adour* is never patrolled in this area, so you should both be safe. By doing it this way, you miss the Vichy checkpoints at all the bridges. And since the rate of travel is so slow, I doubt if anyone will pay much attention to you on the boat. You will be given further instructions when you arrive in *Tarbes. Bon voyage.*"

"Thank you for your help, *Monsieur.*" Christine gave him a double kiss and stepped back.

Charles Martin also stood nearby in a fresh uniform La Roche had managed to secure for him.

Christine turned to him and spoke warmly. "*Monsieur* Martin, I am not sure how I can ever thank you for what you have done for us." She looked at him fighting off a tear.

Martin replied, "I think I am but one of many asked to support my country and her beliefs."

"You are a very special person *Monsieur,* I will never forget you or your men."

"Nor will they soon forget either of you *Mademoiselle. A bientot. "* He reached over and kissed her cheeks.

"*A bientot. "*

LaRoche slipped the rope mooring the boat to the dock and the tired craft started forward, its geriatric motor putting wearily as the clear water begun to pass slowly underneath. In less than five minutes, the last vestiges of *Aire-sur-l'Adour* were left behind and a superbly cobalt colored waterway unfurled before them.

Chapter Sixteen

Bernard Masson's rapid heartbeat made him realize that he was very excited. He adjusted his brisk pace to compensate for the fact that he had decided to make his way into *Tarbes* well before his visitors' anticipated arrival time. He searched around for a public telephone and stopped in front of the first outdoor booth he found. He asked the operator for the number by name and was relieved when the phone finally rang.

"*Hospices Les Soeurs de Notre Dame*, whom do you wish?"

"Sister Therese-Marie, if you will."

"And may I inform Sister Therese-Marie as to who is on the line?

"Yes, certainly. This is her brother Bernard."

"Hold the line, please..."

Masson waited for several minutes and finally a soft voice answered..

"Bernard, my dear brother. It has been quite a long time."

"Yes, too long I'm afraid."

"Where are you calling from, little brother"? It was his sister's own familiar way of describing Bernard's oversized frame.

"I am here in *Tarbes*, not too far from your hospital. I am here on some important business and I want to come by and see you. It is entirely possible that I am going to need your help!"

Sister Therese-Marie could sense her younger brother's exhilaration along with certain fervor in his voice that told her this would be no ordinary meeting.

"Well then, if it is that important to you, you should come right on over. When you get here, we can sit down and talk."

"I am no more than ten minutes away."

"Come to the front entrance. I will alert the attendant to expect you shortly."

Bernard Masson hung up the receiver and began his walk on *Tarbes'* narrow sidewalks towards the hospital. Was it his imagination or did the sidewalks seem even more cramped than usual under his feet? He felt another adrenaline rush and wondered if perhaps his heart was again beating a little too rapidly. He knew he was tense but feeling this way was a bit too much, even for Bernard Masson. He promised himself to lose some weight when he returned to *Pau*. Losing weight would certainly help and probably reduce the stress on his heart and mind. Was he now allowing his mind to control his emotions? He attempted to calm himself down as he neared the hospital.

The trip up the winding reaches of the upper *Adour* River was idyllic for both Russell and Christine. The boat gently chugged along emitting a thin wisp of smoke from its engine as its captain routinely executed the innumerable turns necessary to maintain headway upriver. A surprising number of boulders dotted the river, as if tossed at random by some heavenly force centuries before. A wide variety of waterfowl, including numerous herons and egrets were visible and also a remarkable number of smaller birds.

At one point, Russell saw gulls plying the river's thermals and wondered what natural phenomenon occasioned their flight so far from the sea. Russell also thought he spotted a wider-winged falcon circling some adjacent fields near the river, but the bird was really too far away to positively identify. Another bird species was abundantly apparent. A large number of huge black crows were clearly visible, perched on trees, fences and even some neglected ruins that the boat passed along the way. It was quite evident to Brian Russell that many different types of wildlife thrived contentedly in this rural part of southwestern France.

Immediately after boarding the vessel, Russell decided that he and Christine would remain inside the bridge of the boat, even though their combined presence made the space quite cramped. Russell felt that despite the inconvenience, he and Christine would attract the least amount of attention if they remained inside the bridge compartment. Before he said goodbye, Charles Martin had provided Brian Russell with a pistol, a weapon that he pulled from his band's meager supply of handguns. Even with his group severely under armed, it was Martin's decision that the couple have some minimal protection in the event of trouble.

Russell was no expert is small arms, but was amazed the Christine was able to identify the weapon as a .9mm short Beretta 1934 that carried a compliment of seven rounds. She had seen the same type of weapon before and pronounced it to be quite reliable at close range. She explained to Russell that in the event he fired the pistol, the gun was probably accurate at about twenty to thirty feet, but no more. Russell took her advice and recalled thanking Martin for the kind gesture. He had remarked to the *maquis* leader that he hoped he would never need to fire the weapon.

A cooling breeze rippled the air and produced a momentary hiatus for both Christine and Russell from their active events of the past few days. Russell took advantage of the situation and soon was fast asleep. Christine looked at her companion's peaceful expression and soon arched her back against the cabin wall and joined him in a restful doze.

*   *   *

As she turned the corner of the crowded hospital ward, Sister Therese-Marie spotted her brother's massive hulk through the assembled people in the hallway.

The nun was hoping to see that her brother had lost some weight in the nearly two years since they had last been together, but immediately perceived that he was much the same as when she last saw him. She carefully threaded her way through the friends and relatives of those unfortunates who happened to be confined to the hospital.

Sister Therese-Marie was a strong-willed woman had felt the Lord's calling early in her life. Along with her vocation came an equally strong responsibility towards healing and caring for the sick.

The Order of Sisters of *Notre Dame des Douleurs*, whose mother house and main hospital were located in *Tarbes*, furnished the former Therese-Marie Masson with a perfect milieu to pursue her life's work. The hospital's proximity to the nearby city of *Lourdes* and its unexplained series of miracles and cures tended to provide an extraordinary edge to the small hospital's work. A number of critical patients from the hospital itself were documented as miracles by the Catholic Church and were constantly referenced by the staff and patients.

Sister Therese-Marie regarded her younger brother whom she had not seen for nearly two years.

"Bernard, you are looking well," she spoke approaching him from the rear.

Masson turned and smiled. He prayed he had been able to calm himself down, for there was no need to alarm his beloved sister. He instantly recalled how Therese-Marie's angelic face framed within her habit always managed to produce a warm emotion within him.

"Thank you for the compliment, *Sister*." He kissed her on both sides of the face. The pair looked at each other as only a brother and sister could, and smiled.

She chided him. "I know you must want something important, or else you would not be here."

"That is not completely true, but I must admit Therese, you really do know me well." Bernard seldom took offense from his sister's remarks.

"There is something I want to talk to you about," Bernard began, becoming serious. "It all is involved with a wonderful movement I have become part of. I have not mentioned it to you until now, because I thought it best that you not be aware of my involvement."

She gazed at him inquisitively. It was the most mysterious statement her brother had ever made.

My God, it really is important!

"Therese, can we go somewhere more private and talk, perhaps to an area which is not so crowded and noisy?"

"Certainly my dear Bernard, if you think it is necessary. Follow behind me... we can use the surgery theater. At this time of day, there is no one around there."

Masson followed his sibling through the busy array of people and around several corners. They finally reached a pair of double doors that Sister Therese-Marie held open. She motioned Bernard inside.

"Will this do?" she asked.

"This is perfect." Masson regarded the room with its distinctly sterile setting. The surgery table and assembled machines sent a foreboding shiver to Bernard's spine. It was his first experience with a surgery parlor and the thought that he might one day need its usage startled him.

"As long as I never have to be here professionally." They both laughed and Masson continued.

"What I am going to say to you must never leave this room. It concerns something that has become an important aspect of my life. More than a year ago, I felt a calling to become part of the organized Resistance. I inquired around and eventually offered my services to those in control in *Pau* who immediately accepted me into the organization. Ever since that time, I have been part of a number of covert operations, most of which were quite successful. In fact, I have risen steadily in the organization. Now, I am usually asked to play what amounts to a major role in our war against Vichy and the Nazis. As our local Resistance activities have grown, I have increased the amount time I must spend on the group's behalf. I am indeed fortunate, as you might imagine, that my cheese business allows me to travel and not be missed."

"But, are not such activities quite dangerous?' Sister Therese-Marie asked plaintively, alternately proud of her brother's actions and yet concerned for his safety.

"Of course, but the end is worth all the danger. Our Resistance efforts have assisted a great many people."

"Assisted many people?"

"Yes, in most cases by providing them with escape routes out of France. Therese, you cannot believe the number of people who have been forced to leave our country." Bernard paused, not choosing to tell his sister of all his other Resistance activities. He was not sure of her reaction if she learned about his more subversive actions. These involved harassing and killing militia members of the Vichy government and, on several occasions, even soldiers of the German Wehrmacht.

Sister Therese-Marie felt the ardor emanating from her brother's words. For the first time she grasped the fact that Bernard somehow expected her to become involved in some way in his Resistance activities. The thought of such a thing perplexed her. How could she, as a member of a religious order dedicated to caring and healing, ever be able to justify such a possibility? She lowered her head for several moments and then raised them again to look deep into her brother's soft eyes.

After completing their first day's hunt for his former prisoners, Raymond Soward and Viktoria Losse were unable to show a single result for their efforts. Losse's basic concept, which Soward enthusiastically endorsed, was to mingle among the flow of pilgrims progressing towards area known as the *Cite Religieuse, Lourdes'* most significant point of interest.

For their surveillance, Losse correctly chose a particular spot adjacent to the *Pont St. Michel* spanning the *Gave de Pau* River, which served as the main crossing point for most travelers. It was also the place that anyone traveling through Lourdes on foot would need to pass on his or her way to Spain. After assessing the situation, Soward agreed with Losse. The area was sufficiently small as to be adequately covered by he and Losse. Soward then decided to send his driver to cover a second, less frequently used bridge off the *Avenue de Paradis.* Soward felt that this strategy was necessary in the unlikely event his quarry chose an alternate route to approach into the city. He also furnished Torte with several copies of the artist's sketches of Christine and Brian.

After about an hour, Losse observed several individuals she thought looked suspicious and pointed them out to Soward, who shook his head negatively. Most of the morning's participants were older and none even loosely approximated the descriptions of Brian and Christine.

"You must be patient," Soward cautioned his *Milice* colleague. "Surveillance such as this does not produce results at one's convenience. It is quite possible that we will be here for some time."

Losse did nothing to acknowledge his admonition, but fixed her attention on the steady flow of people coming and going as they crossed the bridge toward the *Cite Religieuse.*

Since today was the third straight day of his search in *Lourdes*, Soward was developing a distinct notion in the back of his mind. The experienced policeman knew this mounting premonition would cause him additional discomfort as time passed and it grew to fruition.

For the first time since the fugitive's escape, Soward wondered if maybe his sense about the fugitives' ultimate destination was wrong. He pondered the consequences if his present surveillance turned out to be a waste of time. Soward realized that if such a supposition were true, he would have a price to pay with his superiors. As a Senior Milice police Inspector, he had staked a great deal on his normally reliable sixth sense, and had committed all his resources to his beliefs. There was no way he could presently back out of the situation and retain his valued reputation. Raymond Soward knew he simply could not afford to return to his regular Milice duties empty-handed.

Christine awoke from her nap first and glanced over at Brian Russell's bent form. He slept peacefully with his back against the side of the bridge and his hands under his light beige jacket. She could also see the end of the gun Masson had given him slightly protruding from under the garment. Christine observed his unshaven face and concluded it had become even more striking with the advent of facial hair. His uneven beard set off his strong features and produced a rugged, masculine quality that Christine had always found attractive in certain men.

The light breeze blowing down the river refreshed her and Christine stood to stretch. The new clothes LaRoche had provided before the boat departed felt good on her after having worn the tattered ones for so many days. She observed the boat's captain for several moments and also the position of the sun that had now reached the first quarter of its afternoon arc. If LaRoche's time prediction was anywhere near accurate, their journey on the water was nearly half completed.

She returned her attention to Russell who was in the process of stirring and shifting his position. She wondered if his slumber permitted him the luxury of a dream. If it did, what thoughts did it conjure up? Was it possible that his dream was similar in nature to the one she experienced right before she woke up?

At that moment, Brian Russell stirred and awakened. The first thing he perceived with his still unfocused eyes was the face of Christine Allard, seated three feet across from him, staring intently in his direction.

"Did I do something wrong?" he questioned. "You look so serious."

"I was just watching you wake up, you actually sleep quite peacefully."

"Lots of practice, it's something I mastered early in life."

"You always make a joke about everything."

"It keeps everything light, and besides, joking never hurts anyone."

"No, I guess you are right. It probably does not."

Russell stood up and glanced outside the cabin. He looked around and suddenly whispered to Christine.

"Quick, stand up. Look at what I see."

Christine held out her hand and Russell helped her to stand. She turned and looked out of the cabin.

"What is it? I do not see…"

"Over there, in the distance."

"Where? Oh, yes. I see. It's so beautiful."

The boat had rounded a bend in the river and ahead to the right lay the majestic, snow-capped peaks of the Pyrenees Mountains. Russell might have seen a more grandiose sight sometime earlier in his life, but at this particular time and place, he couldn't remember ever seeing anything more beautiful.

"This is all quite incredible. I wasn't sure what to expect, but it's more beautiful than I ever thought possible," enthused Russell.

"And also quite historic. Are you aware that the English defeated the French right around here in 1814, and their leader was the Duke of Wellington?"

"No actually I wasn't. Was Napoleon leading the French?"

"No. He was still in exile on the Island of Alba. He escaped and formed a new army. Napoleon chose to meet the British and Wellington the next year, on June 18th at the Battle of Waterloo in Belgium. It was his last great battle."

"You are certainly aware of your country's history," Russell added, impressed with Christine's excellent memory. "I'm not sure I could recount all of my country's battles and dates. And my country is much younger than yours."

"History was always something I enjoyed. My teachers did not have to force me to study."

Russell again surveyed the mountains in the distance, again awed by their solemn majesty.

"I wasn't aware that Tarbes is so close to the mountains…" Russell was conscious that his statement was more of a question.

"Yes, we are quite close. The section of the *Pyrenees* in this region is rather unusual. Once you reach the base of the mountains, you go almost straight up. There are no real foothills around here to start you up slowly. And *Tarbes* itself is no more than 30 or 40 miles from the mountains."

"Well then, *Lourdes* must be very near the base. I really had no idea."

"Yes, it is remarkably close. That is the one of the main reasons *Lourdes* makes for such an excellent departure point if you are leaving France."

"This view is quite remarkable, I don't want to ever forget it."

"Perhaps you won't." Christine turned away, caught up in a wave of emotion brought on by her thoughts.

*   *   *

Bernard Masson's broad smile was a clear indication that he was pleased with his sister's initial reaction to his Resistance disclosure. He had carefully considered the consequences of asking his sister to help him, and he was fully aware that what he asked of his sister would be quite difficult for her. Bernard was even prepared for a negative contingency if Sister Therese-Marie's spiritual circumstances forced her to say no. After all, she was part of a tight religious community. Who could know what internal problems she might encounter when approaching her superiors about helping her brother's cause.

Displaying full sisterly patience, Sister Therese-Marie finished listening to all that Bernard had to say. She concluded their meeting by promising Bernard an immediate response. She showed him out through a side entrance to the hospital and told her brother to return to the same entrance in three hours. Masson agreed and spent the in-between time renewing his pleasant memories of the city of

Tarbes. He had enjoyed the place immensely in his youth and considered it the chief rival of his home city of *Pau*. Downtown *Tarbes* was bustling with activity and Bernard Masson fondly remembered several individual neighborhoods that he wanted to visit.

The three-hour interval that Sister Therese-Marie had determined passed quickly for the big man. Bernard found himself completely relaxed now; his concern regarding his disclosures to his sister was behind him. He was relieved Therese had taken his revelations so affirmatively. He started back toward the hospital and arrived shortly before four o'clock. He stopped the first person he saw in a hospital uniform and politely requested them to summon his sister. In fewer than five minutes, Sister Therese-Marie appeared in the same hallway that led to the outside door.

The habited nun bowed her head slightly and greeted her younger brother. She looked all around the area where they were standing to make sure they would not be overheard.

"My request has just been approved Bernard. Our Mother House here in *Tarbes* has given me permission to accompany you. But, I have to let you know that my superiors were not all in favor of my helping you. They were very vocal that the hospital not be directly involved in anything I do. I took it upon myself to ask for a ruling from our Mother House, and the mother in charge recognized my responsibility to a member of my birth family. Even though I am now a member of God's family, there still exists a special bond to those family members I left behind. I believe it is quite unusual for them to allow me to do whatever I feel is necessary to help you."

"Thank you Therese, I am sorry to put you into such a situation. I sincerely hope it will not affect your rapport with anyone within your order. I am really pleased it worked out for us. I am really counting on you to help me. Now, I do not have a great deal of time until my visitors arrive. I must tell you exactly what I want you to do."

Bernard Masson outlined the remainder of his plan for his older sister.

They kissed again and he hastily departed the hospital. Bernard Masson headed straight for the quai that ran alongside the river. It was a ten-minute walk to the spot below the city where he had agreed to meet his Resistance visitors. If he hurried, he would be right on time.

* * *

The *Adour* River narrowed appreciably as it approached *Tarbes*, which indicated to Russell that the *Adour* was nearing its source. Russell now understood the necessity of using a boat as small as the one on which he and

Christine were currently riding. He saw that any boat even minutely larger would not have been able to venture any further up the *Adour*.

On both sides of the river, indications signifying the outskirts of the city began appearing. On the starboard side, an overgrown and seemingly neglected rectangular pier came into view. The pier extended past the water's edge and contained a small slip, into which the captain skillfully guided the smallish boat. With fewer than ten yards remaining to the pier, the captain cut the engine and the boat silently glided to a halt. He motioned to Russell to tend the forward line and attach it to a piling at the far end of the slip.

The captain went to the stern and produced an additional rope, which he secured to another post jutting up from the water. He checked around the boat and hopped onto the dilapidated pier. Without a word, he shrugged off and disappeared behind a building.

Brian and Christine looked at each other and suddenly broke into laughter. The captain had not uttered a single word during the entire trip.

Their cheerfulness was shortly interrupted by the sudden appearance of another man, a person whose physique was much larger than the captain. The huge figure approached them from the opposite direction.

"*Bon jour,*" he announced jovially, "and welcome to *Tarbes*. I am Bernard Masson." Russell found the man's salutation extremely genial and genuine.

Masson exchanged passwords with Christine and helped both Brian and her alight from the boat. Masson noted the cylinder that Russell took great care to handle. He briefly considered asking about the object, but decided against it. He motioned for them to follow him and all three started out walking in the direction of the hospital. Due to the extra narrow sidewalks they encountered along the way, it was necessary that they walk in single file.

*   *   *

By late afternoon, the flow of the faithful on their way to the grotto of *Lourdes* was normally reduced to a trickle. Senior *Milice* Inspector Raymond Soward noticed that most of the visitors came to the place of pilgrimage during the cooler part of the day while their strength permitted. The visitors tended to be older and in many cases possessed visible maladies. Since Soward and Viktoria Losse's surveillance began early in the morning, the pair was forced to stand in the middle of the visitor stream to have the best vantage point. By mid-afternoon, the unrelenting heat of the sun made the task particularly difficult and both officers were forced to seek relief in the shade along the sides of the bridge.

Viktoria Losse turned out to be much more helpful than Soward initially anticipated. Even though both were basically exhausted after the first day's surveillance was finished, she took Soward on a looping tour of the city. Their route wound through a number of its back alleys, and ultimately into its seedy interior section. It was there that Losse knew they would confront a number of shady characters she regularly used in her work. Losse sought out a street artist she was acquainted with, a fellow who produced caricatures of the visitors to *Lourdes* for five francs each. She introduced Soward to the artist and showed him the sketches provided by the *Milice* artist in *Pau*. After about a half-hour, the artist was able to produce colored sketches of both of the fugitives, which Soward readily agreed were much more realistic than the staid, one dimensional black and white drawings he had received in *Pau*.

'We will take these with us," Viktoria explained, referring to the colored drawings. "By the time this evening's over, we will show them to enough people so that neither one could get through the city without our hearing about it."

"Brilliant, Frau Losse. I think this is a wonderful idea. The more people who work for us that see it, the better chance we have. I should have thought of it myself."

Viktoria ignored Soward's superfluous remark. As a woman in a man's environment, she was used to such ranting. Next, she took Soward to meet various members of her network of informants. To each she showed the caricatures, and offered a detailed description of Christine and Brian. She also informed each one of a two hundred francs reward being offered for any information.

Soward was again pumped with enthusiasm. With so many eyes now linked in his pursuit, he felt it practically impossible for his prey to enter *Lourdes* without being spotted.

Soward's close work with Viktoria Losse had produced another unexpected feeling in the *Milice* inspector. He began to appreciate the fact that his associate was a completely feminine woman, a woman who was also thoroughly versed in the ways of the world. At one point, while offering the caricatures to one of her informers, she touched Soward's fingers in a manner that Soward found lingering. The touch lasted a moment longer than it should and Soward turned toward her. She glanced at him for a split second before returning to her description. Soward hoped he had understood the look. Viktoria also took to calling him Raymond, rather than inspector, a familiarity that Soward immediately recognized.

Why not? He mused. After all, it had been a long time between women and his superiors could not expect him to pursue Christine and Brian every hour of the day and night. He decided that if Viktoria Losse were ever to make herself available to him, he would certainly reward himself with the opportunity.

It was soon apparent that their destination was closer to the riverfront section than Russell expected and the ensuing walk from the dock took the trio only ten minutes to complete. The small hospital was an amalgamation of several buildings, which at first glance seemed to occupy the better part of an entire block. The buildings were all single-storied, except for a solitary brick structure in the rear that was a story higher. Their construction was mostly brick with a thin sheet of plaster outside that was painted gray. On the two sides of the building that were visible from the street, several sections of the plaster had chipped away. The chipping, along with rain and the ensuing elements had combined to produce a naturally attractive aged effect on the entire premises. Russell felt it was quaint enough to be placed on a post card.

Upon arriving at the building, Russell glanced about for an identifying symbol, but saw nothing but the word *Hospices* hand-lettered on a basic sign near the front door. Also located on the sign beneath the lettering was a simple red cross. If Bernard had not mentioned their destination was a hospital, Russell would never have guessed from its looks that the simple complex was indeed a full-fledged hospital facility.

They arrived shortly after seven o'clock. It was evident that there was little activity around the hospital. Masson ordered Christine and Russell to wait outside while he went in.

"I will be right back," he mentioned. I need to find my sister."

When Bernard appeared a few minutes later with a very attractive nun in tow, and introduced her as Sister Therese-Marie, his older *sister*. Russell was completely caught off guard.

"So *your* sister is a *sister*, " Russell remarked lightly.

"Yes, and, she has been for quite some time," Masson returned the joke.

Russell decided he liked this big man. For some unknown reason, Russell felt safe in his presence.

"I am afraid I must take you around the side of the hospital," Sister Therese-Marie cautioned, "There is always a Vichy representative hanging around the front lobby. He checks on everyone coming into the hospital. It would be unwise for him to see you and for you to have to explain your presence here. It is most annoying to have people like him around."

"It's okay sister," Russell reassured her. "But do they not also check the rest of the hospital?"

"No, *Monsieur*, they are much too lazy for that. I think their actions are mostly for show, to prove to everyone involved that they are in control of the country. Several months ago, a delegation from Vichy itself came through here along with several German military officers. They caused a lot of commotion and demanded to see a number of our records. Everyone was quite upset since we are a hospital and not usually involved in politics." Sister Therese-Marie thought about her statement, glanced quickly at her brother and rolled her eyes. She returned her attention to Christine and Brian. "After they left, we never heard from them again. It was all for show, a giant charade."

Christine interjected. "It is much better for us that they do not check carefully. No one will even notice we are here."

"Yes, my staff will." Sister Therese-Marie answered. "It is just that no one from the hospital will say anything. The Germans are despised around here and the Vichy government is not much better."

"We have not encountered many citizens who support Vichy."

"Those who do so are short sighted and uninformed. But, I am not supposed to hold such opinions. As I said before, members of religious orders are supposedly non-political." This time, Sister Therese-Marie winked at her brother as they rounded a building and came to a side door.

"This is where I am going to put you for the present. It is a section of the hospital that is infrequently used. This is a ward where we put our patients who have contracted rather exotic diseases. Please do not worry, you will not catch anything." She smiled again and departed in search of some towels.

"Your sister is a most intriguing person," Christine addressed Masson. "Has she been involved in any of your prior Resistance activities?"

"No, she was not even aware of my involvement until we talked an hour ago."

"And does she approve of everything you are doing?"

"She probably approves but is not in a position to say so. She is doubtless worried about my ultimate safety, just as any older sister would be. If she were in the same position, I know I would feel the same way."

Russell nodded as Sister Therese-Marie returned with her arms full of towels and folded garments.

"It's getting late and there is very little we can accomplish tonight. For us to go into *Lourdes* at night would be foolish, for there is very little foot traffic there during the late afternoon and evening. It would be best to wait until tomorrow and work our way in with the crowds.

I have brought you some towels and there is a room where you can take a bath at the end of the corridor." She pointed in the direction of the bathroom. "I have also arranged for you to have something to eat. It is being prepared for you at this moment. I suggest you get a good night's sleep, because it might be the last really restful sleep you enjoy for quite some time. Bernard had told me of your necessity to get through *Lourdes* and over the mountains into Spain. I think what you see here will help you do just that. The clothes I have brought you," she produced two sets of black garments, "are also for you to wear tomorrow. I spoke to our Mother Superior and she authorized me to permit you to use them. When we leave tomorrow, you will disguise yourselves as a priest and nun. There are hundreds of religious people passing through *Lourdes* each day and you should attract less attention. Luckily, we keep a change of clothes on hand for a priest who visits us frequently and says Holy Mass. He is about your size," she held up the cassock next to Russell, "and will not mind at all that we lent you his frock."

"Thank you Sister, for all your kindness."

"Not at all my child. After all, this could loosely be considered God's work. I am not sure God always takes the appropriate side, but, in this case, I am not above providing Him with a little help."

"And, what about me?" Masson sensed he was all but forgotten.

"You and I have a great deal of catching up to do, little brother. You did not believe for a moment that I was going to let you get out of that did you?"

"Not really, I have known you for a long time," Masson smiled at Russell and nodded obediently to his sister.

Sister Therese-Marie also grinned and started to leave the room. Masson shrugged his shoulders and followed her out into the corridor.

Christine spoke to Brian, "She is quite a remarkable woman. We are fortunate to have her on our side."

"Yes, she reminds me of some of the nuns who taught me when I was young. With their big black habits and headdresses, many children in my class were terrified of them until they were old enough to know better. I myself do not recall ever being afraid. The nuns were there to help us and were always our friends."

"And are you also going to tell me that you were never bad as a child, and never got into mischief?"

Christine smiled again, "*Good* little girls are not supposed to get into mischief."

"Right, they always leave that for little boys."

Their conversation was interrupted as another nun came into the room, carrying a tray containing some fruit, an assortment of *charcuterie*, a small *Port Salud* cheese, a small jar of *moutarde dijonaise* and a *baguette* sliced into neat pieces.

"Good evening," she announced shyly, "I am Sister Laurentine. "I have brought this for you and I will be back in a bit with some wine for you to wash it all down. Is there anything else I can bring you right now?"

"No, thank you, Sister," Christine answered. "It all looks wonderful. We have not eaten regularly for days and this will be like a feast for us."

"Please make sure to eat as much as you desire. There is even more if you need it." She politely excused herself and left the room.

Russell surveyed the tray and nibbled at a piece of sweet *saucisson*, flavored with bits of anise.

"I certainly appreciate the quality of the cuisine and service the Resistance provides its guests," he teased.

"I was not expecting any of this. It is all Bernard's doing, or at least his sister's."

"Whoever is providing it is not important; it is incredibly nice of them to help us." He cut a piece of the *Port Salud* and fed it to Christine. He sliced another piece and put it into his mouth, enjoying its delicate flavor.

"Yes, so far I think we have been lucky." Russell remarked. "For some reason, I suspect the difficult part will come when we attempt to travel through *Lourdes"*

"Why do you say that? Do you think it was wrong for us to try to pass through *Lourdes?*"

"No, if I did I would have said something before. I don't know, it's just a feeling I have. Besides, men can also have feelings they cannot explain, right?"

Christine did not reply. She was too busy making herself a monster sandwich combining every single ingredient on the tray. She couldn't remember a time in the past when she had been this hungry.

*　*　*

As instructed, Senior *Milice* Inspector Raymond Soward checked in with his superiors in Vichy late in the afternoon and soon realized he had made a tactical mistake in doing so. His superiors were interested in the progress of his investigation and Soward reluctantly reported that there was nothing tangible to speak of. After answering a number of perfunctory questions, Soward was able to buy himself and Viktoria Losse several more days in *Lourdes*, but he knew these additional days would be his last. If he were unable to turn up anything during that period, he was ordered to return to his regular duties.

Soward accepted his fate, and determined to make the best of his increasingly gloomy situation.

He met Viktoria Losse at the *Grand Hotel de la Grotte's* small outdoor café just as the sun was setting and offered her a chair. The vista was his preferred watching spot and offered a panoramic view of the entire area. He ordered each a *pastis* and broke the silence.

"I prefer this time of the evening, it's a time when the world seems at peace."

"What a strange thing for you to say, Raymond. You appear to me to be always working, and I never see you enjoying even a little break. You seem to spend a great deal of time trying to outthink the people you are pursuing. I think you might have better results if you stepped back a bit and used the time to unwind."

"Maybe, yes, maybe you are right," Soward replied contemplating her comment. "But, even I have my lighter moments. There was even a time long ago when people considered me fun to be around."

"It must have been *very long* ago," Viktoria frowned, finger-combing her hair. She glanced over at him for a reaction.

Soward looked back, observing the feminine softness of her face. Her tousled auburn hair swooped over her left forehead, partially obscuring her left eyebrow. It was the first time he had actually taken the time to look at her as a woman. She noticed him watching her and sipped her *pastis,* all the while observing the passing activity on the street fronting the café.

"Not much is happening at this time of night. All the invalids and pilgrims have done their duty and have returned to where they came from." She glowered again and tapped her finger on the table.

"This place is actually quite punctual," Soward offered. "They come early in the morning and leave by late afternoon. I do not think I could work around here for very long. I actually find it quite boring."

"Well then, I guess it's up to us to put some life into the place. How does a decent meal and a really nice bottle of *Chateauneuf du Pape* sound to you?"

"Perfect. All that standing in the sun and extra exercise has given me a great appetite." Soward replied, rising and offering her his arm.

He placed a five-franc note on top of the check that covered their *aperitifs.* "There is a small *bistro* not far from here that I have been wanting to try. The *concierge* here at the hotel recommended the food there very highly."

"That sounds quite nice to me." Viktoria pressed slightly against his arm as the pair started off up the steep grade next to the hotel, in the direction of the restaurant.

*　*　*

Brian allowed Christine the luxury of bathing first. He sat patiently on the hospital bed, but soon realized that he was eagerly anticipating her return. He looked about the long room that was completely deserted. About thirty feet separated the bathroom area that adjoined their elongated hospital ward. There were six beds in the ward, but only three were made up with linens and pillows. Russell wondered if the three were normally made up or whether Bernard was planning to return in the near future. He studied the size of the bed and contemplated whether the oversized partisan would even fit onto it. He chuckled to himself, and silently conceded that such a trivial matter shouldn't even enter his mind. Considering the perilous nature and current status of his present mission, he had better things to occupy himself with than Bernard Masson's ability to fit onto an undersized bed.

Christine soon emerged from her time in the bathroom, her hair wrapped in a white hospital towel.

Russell gazed at her as she approached. At that moment, Christine could have easily stepped out of one of French impressionist Edouard Manet's incredibly poignant paintings. He narrowed in on her face, and realized that truly beautiful women never really possess soft eyes. That was due to the sparks of intelligence and perception that always preclude gentleness. Christine possessed both qualities and additionally, a sort of gorgeous radiation that exuded good health. She was as complete a feminine package that he had ever met and Russell delighted in what he saw.

"It is your turn now. I love the sensation a bath provides for both the skin and mind, and also the fact that it makes me feel really good. The water here is nice and hot and I was able to scrub off the dirt and filth I had accumulated."

"So you *truly* liked it?" Russell teased.

"Just to be able to have a *real* bath feels marvelous after all that time we spent in the forests. When you go in, take your time and soak a while, there is no telling when we will be able to enjoy this luxury again."

Russell nodded and headed off in the direction of the bathroom. As he reached the hallway, he glanced back and caught Christine watching him from behind. She flushed and turned away, reaching for her wineglass. The glass was still half full.

*　　*　　*

Being in his sister's presence reminded Bernard Masson of just how much he missed spending time with her. He was alternately happy and relieved to have finally shared his news with her about his ongoing Resistance activities. During the past few minutes, Sister Therese-Marie had provided him with an excellent dinner and the two enjoyed the opportunity to get caught up on the status of a number of their remaining family members.

Once the meal was completed and the everyday domestic basics were covered, Bernard intended to turn the conversation to the more serious matters at hand, namely, the continuing flight of Christine and Brian.

Before he could speak, Sister Therese-Marie broached the subject.

"Bernard, explain to me just how do you intend to get those two through *Lourdes*? You must realize that because of its very nature, *Lourdes* is always under close scrutiny. There are a number of Vichy militia checking everyone who crosses the bridges and I am sure there are probably some members of the *Milice* lurking around in the shadows."

"Yes, my dear sister. I understand all that and I think that you are right. But, I have recently embraced a new philosophy about such things, a method that has not failed me yet. It is all fairly simple. I believe that whenever one is looking for a place to hide, the best place to do so is usually *out in the open*. If we can keep that in mind planning our strategy for tomorrow, with the help of God, we will be successful."

"Well, God has already helped you, if you ask me."

"He most certainly has, and I am sincerely thankful. Now, it is up to us to make use of his gifts."

"What do you have in mind?"

Bernard was completely delighted that his sister was taking such an active interest in the scheme.

"I have thought a great deal about your idea of dressing them as priest and nun. I think that we should even take the idea a bit further. Why not make him into an invalid, one who is confined to a wheelchair. Christine can then push him. Her appearance will change remarkably once she is disguised in a nun's habit. By placing him in the wheelchair, we will also be able to cover up the long tube he is carrying, which is somehow connected to their mission and is not an easy thing to hide. The way he carries it makes me know that the cylinder's contents are vitally important to his mission. If the tube were not so essential, I would try make them leave it here."

"Bernard, we both know there are always many people passing through *Lourdes* each day. I tend to agree with you that your wheelchair idea would enhance the plan. They will blend into the crowds better. No one pays much attention to people in wheelchairs anyway. They would rather not think about the circumstances that caused such afflictions.

If we do not encounter difficulties getting across the *Pont St. Michel* and through the crowed plaza leading to the shrine itself, I believe the rest will be easy. Our friends can leave the city by the south road, the one that heads toward *Cauterets*. Once through the city, there should not be much danger. Vichy does not check many people *leaving* the city."

"What about the *gare* on the south side?" Sister Therese-Marie recalled a smaller train station not far from the *Centre Ville* on the southern side of *Lourdes*. "Why not put them on a train?"

"I believe there is too great a possibility that their papers would be examined if we attempted to use the train. After what Christine told me about the unfortunate affair in *Condom*, I would not be surprised if their descriptions were posted everywhere."

Sister Therese-Marie considered her brother's words and finally replied.

"These Resistance activities of yours are very dangerous, Bernard. You must be very careful. Even inside the hospital we keep hearing stories about the *Milice* arresting suspected Resistance members. They torture them and even execute some of them for their involvement with the organization."

"Yes, my dear Therese, I am aware of such a possibility. But working with the Resistance is a necessity for me, and also hundreds and thousands of others like me. It is something we must all do if we are ever to have our wonderful birthplace returned to us.

Therese, can you recall what France was like before all this happened? Our country was a beautiful and wonderful place in which to live. People were basically happy and there was ample food for everyone to eat. We were free to come and go as we pleased and were not forced to answer to anyone. I want all that back for myself and my family. I am prepared to do what it takes to make it happen."

"My brother, the patriot," Sister Therese-Marie uttered faintly, her words laced with a sense of quiet apprehension.

"Your brother, the Frenchman," he retorted, "and, thank God I am not willing to sit around and take what is being dished out by others. If those pukes in Vichy issue one more asinine proclamation, I think I am going to go crazy."

"I think we all feel that way Bernard. Even here in the closed atmosphere of the hospital, everyone talks about it. I do not think many people are satisfied with the state of our country's affairs."

"Anyone who *is* satisfied should be considered a sympathizer or collaborator. They should be dealt with accordingly."

"I fear there would be many such cases throughout France."

"Yes, too many. That is the reason we are in this fix right now. We act the part of sheep being led to slaughter. Too many turn their heads and refuse to get involved."

"Well, I do not think that you and I are going to alter our country's future tonight," she finalized. "I had some of our staff move the largest bed in the hospital into the room next door from here for you to stay. I hope you will be comfortable in it. You should try to get some sleep, for we should be ready to leave fairly early in the morning."

"Okay, Therese my darling. You always know what is right for me."

Chapter Seventeen

The cuisine at the *Bistro Cristsal* was better than Soward expected. It consisted of a regional collection of local specialties prepared promptly and served in a professional, unassuming manner. Soward selected a table in a corner, as much as to remove Viktoria and him from the normal flow of the restaurant, as to offer him a perfect spot to observe anyone coming and going. His prior law enforcement experience taught him to always select a seat with his back to the wall.

Viktoria also seemed to be enjoying the small place. She took great pride in ordering Soward's meal as well as her own. She also delighted in finding on the wine list, a more expensive *Cote Rotie* to replace an out of stock *Chateauneuf du Pape* to accompany their meal. Soward had been given an allowance for food and lodging that would cover such extravagance to some extent, but the cost really didn't matter to him. By the time the meal was nearing its end, Raymond Soward was more than delighted to pay whatever portion of the bill his expense allowance didn't cover. Viktoria was becoming more animated by the minute and had even touched the palm of his hand several times when ordering their meals. Her subtle expressions were not lost on Soward who suddenly hoped that the meal would end quickly and permit him and Viktoria to retire to his hotel room.

"Do you eat out often?" Viktoria asked while they waited for their entrees to be put in front of them.

"Only during the course of business," he answered casually. "On my pay, it is not usually possible to enjoy too many of the finer aspects of life. Of course, I can certainly appreciate such luxuries when the opportunity arises." He offered her his glass and they clinked lightly in a toast.

"I guess it is very different for a woman. I have a lot of chances to eat out that are seldom connected to work. And, the nice thing is that the man always pays for everything. Remember, I do not make much money either."

"Yes, women are truly fortunate in that regard. A woman has never asked me to go out with her," Raymond Soward replied truthfully. "I am not sure if I would know what to say if one ever does."

"Maybe you will get lucky one day and a woman will."

Soward nodded his agreement. He was willing to bet his good fortune would continue as early as this very evening, when Viktoria Losse agreed to come back with him to his hotel.

Seated on the bed within their rectangular room at the *Hospices Les Soeurs de Notre Dame des Douleurs*, Christine poured Brian another glass of red wine. She shifted her position closer to him and handed him his glass.

"Wine seems to be one of the few creature comforts everyone in France can afford," she said, referring to the glass in her hand. "No matter how rich or poor you are, there is always some good wine around to enjoy."

Brian took a healthy sip and stared directly at Christine. She had combed her hair back in a mini-ponytail and held it together with a blue ribbon. He reached for the ribbon and undid the knot. Her hair fell to the sides of her face as he gently cupped her head with his hands. He kissed her very softly on the sides of her face and then on the lips. Christine gradually reacted to his caress and tenderly raised her mouth to his level. She sought his mouth and pushed inside with her tongue, probing, caressing, and alternating her breathing in short gasps.

They separated for a moment and Brian spoke.

"This isn't exactly the Ritz," he said referring to their surroundings, "and, I'm not sure if Masson is coming back."

"I would not worry about him. Bernard is a Frenchman and understands the situation." Her voice was soft in tone and timbre, imparting a feeling to Brian of her willingness to continue.

He pressed her close to him, feeling the proximity of her feminine camber and breathing in a trace of the flower-scented perfume Sister Therese-Marie had handed her.

They kissed and held each other for several minutes and finally settled into the bed nearest to the one they were using for their meal. They stretched out and Brian lay alongside her, stroking her hair and slowly rubbing the nape of her neck. Even though their bodies covered the entire area of the bed, they were oblivious to its narrow confines. He kissed Christine again and felt her breath revert to short, quick gasps. He removed her blouse and began rubbing and caressing her breasts with the tip of his tongue. Brian felt Christine's nipples harden as she pulled at his hair.

A fire swept through Christine that she found startling. She paused a moment and looked directly up at Brian. He returned the look and began helping her out of the remainder of her clothes. When he was finished, he quickly undressed himself.

They embraced and the act came swiftly for each of them. The culmination of their lovemaking was two-parted and completely satisfying to each. It also provided a tenderness and release that Christine was unaccustomed to experiencing. She held Brian close to her, her eyes constricted in total surrender. He gently kissed her forehead, eyes, mouth and neck, and finally rolled off. Brian Russell settled contentedly as close as he could be to her, partially draped over one of her legs.

Neither was left with the energy or inclination to say a single word.

Even though the bottle of *Cote Rotie* cost a healthy fifteen francs, Soward decided it was well worth the money. The dinner passed by quickly and Viktoria made him aware that she was equally anxious to leave the *bistro* once the meal was finished. The pair walked two blocks back towards the *Grand Hotel de la Grotte*. They passed through the hotel's double wrought iron doors and into the lobby's black and white tiled hallway. It was highlighted by arches rounded in deco style. At this hour, the lobby hallway was dimly lit, but Soward managed to locate and press the button for the lift. He waited for a moment but received no response. Soward cursed the apparatus under his breath as he and Viktoria were forced to climb the stairs to the third floor location of his room.

When they reached the third floor landing, Soward found the switch controlling the hallway lights and flipped them on. He made his way to his room and unlocked the door, allowing Viktoria to enter first. He located the light switch on the wall and clicked it on, producing a faint overhead light. Viktoria assessed the situation and walked to another floor light and turned the switch. This time, a gentle light bathed the room. She motioned for Soward to turn off the overhead light, which he obediently did.

"You are very neat," she remarked, noting the precise rows of shirts and underwear Soward had stacked on a small table near the bed. "I am afraid you are much neater than I would be." She walked to a glass door and stepped out on the mini-balcony that protruded from the window door and surveyed the mostly blackened environment.

From the gist of her last statement, Soward wasn't sure if she intended the words as a compliment. He stepped out onto the balcony and attempted to switch the conversation.

"I thought both the meal and wine you selected were excellent. A bit rich for my taste, but tonight the government was paying for practically everything. It is the least they can do for two of their hardest working officers."

"Yes, the least." Viktoria agreed, unconcerned. She turned abruptly, went back inside the room and began unbuttoning her blouse.

Soward followed her inside and lunged at her awkwardly. She heard him coming and was partially turned toward him when he sprung at her. His mouth missed her lips and landed near her nose. Viktoria leaned back and spoke purposefully.

"Let us see if we can do better than that my dear Raymond. This time, try and go much slower and I think you will have better results."

Her remark caused him to feel a bit puerile but Soward continued on. He kissed her for a moment until she broke the embrace. Viktoria took his hand and helped him off with his coat. She led him over to the bed and turned him around to face her. Viktoria knelt in front of him. Soward was riveted by her actions and was scarcely breathing.

It had been a long time.

She pleasured him for a short while until he could no longer contain himself. He exploded with a gasp and Viktoria Losse finally released her hold.

* * *

In a larger ward adjoining the one where Brian and Christine were sleeping, Bernard Masson was finally able to relax his huge frame on the oversized bed his sister was able to provide for him. Even though he was tired, he reviewed the pros and cons of tomorrow's plan. He sought to spawn any areas of potential problems for Christine and Brian. He wrestled with several different scenarios and dismissed them all.

He realized his scheme was as safe as any such plan could be, and decided on one more important element of the scheme. He resolved in his mind to follow the pair on their trek through *Lourdes*. He felt that his presence might provide an extra element of safety that the couple might need if their situation ever became critical.

He pressed his head further down into the depths of the soft pillow and was soon fast asleep.

* * *

Christine lay close to Brian, her head lying against his hairy chest. She was completely relaxed now and was listening to his controlled breathing, wondering if he was sleeping.

Neither had spoken after their lovemaking, preferring instead to extend the wonderment of the act. She nestled closer to Brian while his breathing paused for a moment, and then resumed normally.

She chanced waking him and whispered softly, "Are you awake *mon cherie?*"

"I probably shouldn't be, but I am."

Christine turned to be able to face him. Their faces were almost touching.

"Are you sorry for what just happened?"

"No, why should I be sorry?"

"I do not really know. It is just that with the war and our mission…"

"Shush…" Brian soothed her. "It just happened. And, it was wonderful."

"Yes," she cooed, "I feel that way also. It made me feel like a young girl again."

"You are *still* a young girl," he teased, "a beautiful young French girl who just happens to fight for the Resistance."

She leaned over and kissed the corners of his mouth. He reacted at once and she bit the tip of his lip.

"So, you desire an encore," he smiled.

"I desire many encores, *Monsieur*, along with the understanding that each will be better than the last."

"I promise you they will be." Brian smiled again as he took her into his arms.

* * *

Morning came early at the *Hospices Les Soeurs de Notre Dame des Douleurs,* and Bernard Masson was among the first in the entire hospital to awaken. Once again, Sister Therese-Marie saw to it that he was provided with an ample breakfast as befitting his extensive appetite, a fact Masson found quite pleasing. In addition to a selection of warm *croissants* and muffins, several slices of fried *jambon* and a number of delicious melon slices, Masson was treated to some freshly brewed coffee, a beverage that was becoming something of a rarity these days in Southern France. He attacked his food and was finishing his second cup of coffee by the time Sister Therese-Marie finally entered the room.

"Goodness, Bernard. I am glad you were not very hungry this morning."

Masson had taken numerous similar chides before and took little offense. "You realize dear sister that a man must have the proper nourishment if he is to be able to work vigorously throughout the day."

"Yes, vigorously."

"So, have you seen to the others?"

"Certainly. They received the same breakfast as yours, only not quite as large. They are probably finished eating by now."

"Good, I want to see them and explain what it is I want them to do today. And, Therese, last evening after I went to bed, I thought that it might be helpful if we both accompanied them to *Lourdes.* There might not be that much of a necessity for you to come along, but since you are familiar with the environment, I would be more comfortable if you did."

"I do not know Bernard, for me to go would require that I get additional permission from the Mother Superior. And, then, I would have to get everyone's hospital papers changed."

"Well then, can you please see what you can to do to make it happen? If it is at all possible, I would prefer not to leave here too late in the morning."

To Sister Therese-Marie, her brother's insistence on her direct participation heightened her understanding as to his mission's importance. She went immediately to seek permission to be able to make the trip into *Lourdes*. It was the second time in two days that she would face the Mother Superior of her order.

*　　*　　*

Soward awoke and splashed some water on his face from the small sink in his room. He wondered what it was that caused Viktoria to leave so suddenly last night, but quickly dismissed the thought from his mind. He had never understood women and had no intention of starting now. He dressed himself and was careful to place his 9mm Walther P-38 pistol inside his coat pocket, in exactly the same way he did at the start of every morning of his police career.

He left his room and pressed the lift button, but was again unsuccessful in summoning the elevator. He descended the three flights of stairs and glared incredulously at the *concierge* who shrugged his shoulders in return. On the way out, he took a complimentary *croissant* from a little tray near the *concierge's* desk, an additional small frill he enjoyed each morning while working away from home.

Soward had agreed to meet Viktoria at their usual location outside the front entrance to the *Grand Hotel de la Grotte*. If Viktoria were as punctual as she had been the past two days, she would be arriving just as he stepped out of the front door of the hotel.

*　　*　　*

"I have something for you that I hope you will never need," Sister Therese-Marie explained, as she handed a small silver pistol to Brian Russell. It was an ancient 9mm Italian Glisenti M1910, but seemed to be in good condition.

He looked at the gun for a moment and turned inquisitively back to the nun.

"I have had this for several years. An older patient here at the hospital used to keep himself occupied by taking it apart and cleaning it each week. He was very proud of the gun; it was his personal weapon when he was in the Italian Army. When he finally died, he left it to me for assisting him while he was here at the hospital. It was the most important possession he had."

"But, you must keep it. It has great meaning for you."

"I will never use such a thing. I had almost forgotten I even had it. But you, Captain Russell, you might need it to help you in your escape. By the way, I checked the gun and it is fully loaded."

"But Sister, I…"

"*Monsieur*," she interrupted Brian. "I know that by necessity such extremes exist during war. War is a time when people often die. I am convinced, that, for good or bad, war is within the scope of God's ultimate design. I give the weapon to you in support of your efforts for our country, but I hope that you are never forced to fire it. Do you understand?"

Russell nodded and returned his glance to the pistol. He spun the cylinder and found it loaded as Sister Therese-Marie had said. Since he already possessed the pistol Charles Martin had given him before boarding the boat, Russell decided that he would hand over the new weapon to Christine. If trouble came, she would also have the degree of protection the gun could offer.

*   *   *

Reichsmarschall Hermann Goring peered intently at the stack of papers he held in his hand, discarding each as he finished examining it. He passed through a number of pages and finally paused at a line in one particular notice that caught his perceptive eye.

The item referred to the still unsolved murders of SS Obersturmbannfuhrer Kurt von Heltscherer and several other Wehrmacht soldiers in south central France.

Goring noted that the item was now nothing more than a postscript on the weekly Abwehr intelligence report and wasn't even included until the third page. For several moments, he reflected on the events surrounding von Heltscherer's investigation and pondered his next course of action. There were several possibilities open to him. Each involved interface with another branch of the National Socialist hierarchy, a course of action the Reichsmarschall wasn't interested in pursuing at this time.

The Nazi leader mulled over attempting to locate the French artworks again, but realized that any such operation would have to be carried out under circumstances that *he* could directly control himself. Covert operations that the Reichsmarschall was forced to share with his other Nazi associates often had a way of proving troublesome. In the case of the missing artworks, Goring was not of a mind to share with anyone.

He placed the Abwehr report back in the stack on his desk and made a mental note to someday orchestrate a new investigation similar to the one begun by Kurt von Heltscherer. He would do this the whenever his busy schedule permitted.

Brian was already finished dressing and was helping Christine fit into her habit when Bernard Masson approached the two with a huge smile. He was pushing an older wooden wheelchair, complete with wooden wheels and a wicker back. It was evident from his cheerful manner that he was enthusiastic about their upcoming course of action for the morning.

"You two look particularly pious this morning," he teased. "No one will be able to tell you from the real thing."

"I hope not," Christine replied, not as assured about their appearances as her Resistance counterpart.

"Here is what I want you to do for the present, and more importantly, how you must react when we actually reach *Lourdes,*" Bernard said, motioning to Brian. "Today, you will play the part of the sick one. We will push down the back of this wheelchair until it is almost flat. It works with this little lever." Bernard demonstrated by pulling the lever on the chair, which caused the back of the chair to almost fully recline.

"With blankets covering you, we will also be able to conceal your tube next to you without attracting attention. I believe that I have even talked Sister Therese-Marie into coming along in case we experience any trouble. She has been to *Lourdes* many times and is familiar with the way things are handled there. She will have your papers and will do all the talking."

Brian adjusted his cassock and sat in the wheelchair. Masson adjusted the position backwards and Russell secured the tube, which Christine placed next to him. To Christine and Brian's amazement, the tube was hardly noticeable. It was becoming evident to both of them that Bernard Masson's ingenious plan might just work.

*   *   *

"Sir, we've just received a transmission from the bloody French BCRA," Colonel Maurice Buckmaster announced after knocking on General Percy Barclay's door at the OSE offices. "It took them some time to get the information to us, but they've finally managed to notify us of Russell's status."

"So, go ahead man, spit it out."

"Certainly, General. It seems that Russell and the paintings are now in extreme southern France, and are trying to make it into Spain through the *Pyrenees.*"

"Any troubles?"

"The report was relatively vague. It did mention a confrontation with the Vichy *Milice*, but Russell and his Resistance companion evidently came through that in good shape."

"Well, that's all fine and good, but it seems to me as if the mission is way behind schedule. Do you agree?"

"Yes, somewhat. What we don't know is how much Russell was forced to deviate from our original plan."

"We might never know all the details. It is fortunate for us and for all concerned that Russell is the type of officer who can rely on his wits whenever he must. Such abilities will probably save his life. And, quite possibly, those same abilities will insure that Operation Angerona is ultimately successful."

"I have a feeling you might be entirely correct. I just wish we could get better intelligence."

"No need to call Jerry's attention to our man," General Barclay warned. "Until we hear to the contrary, we must assume he is doing all right for himself."

"Most certainly, General. I knew you would want to be informed."

*   *   *

Viktoria Losse was late in meeting Soward outside the *Grand Hotel de la Grotte*. Soward dispatched Torte to the second bridge crossing as he had done for the past few mornings. He thought he detected a note of disappointment from the man, who shrugged his shoulders when he was given the same assignment. Soward decided to deal with his associate later that day.

Viktoria finally appeared about twenty minutes later, which Soward duly noted by checking his watch. She stared at him in an annoyed manner for doing so, a glare that the inspector decided to ignore. Besides, in his mind Viktoria was only marginally late. And, after last night, such a minor discrepancy could certainly be overlooked.

Using his official tone, he informed her dryly, "We must be very observant today. If we do not uncover something today or tomorrow, I will be forced to call off the investigation by our superiors in Vichy. We might never see each other again."

What a complete idiot he is, Viktoria Losse thought. *I was foolish to waste my attentions on him. He is entirely self-centered and could never help my career. I must be more discerning next time...* Her gaze returned to Soward who directed her to a location across the street from where he stood.

*   *   *

The *Hospices Les Soeurs de Notre Dame des Douleurs* in *Tarbes* shared an ancient old bus with another local hospital to transport their patients whom desired to visit the shrine of the Blessed Virgin in *Lourdes*. The aged vehicle was as venerable as some of its riders and vibrated as if it were on its last legs. Its daily schedule called for it to leave the hospital at nine in the morning, but the elderly means of transportation rarely did so. A number of its special patients required meticulous handling, and by the time everyone on board was finally settled, the vehicle was always tardy in departing.

Russell was the final non-ambulatory patient loaded on board, and Sister Therese-Marie who had successfully lobbied her Order's Mother Superior to participate, saw to it that Masson's script was followed exactly. Since it was never easy to predict when a Vichy informer might be poking around, the wizened nun wasn't taking any chances. Sister Therese-Marie even saw fit to have one of her sister nuns apply some borrowed makeup to alter Russell's appearance. The makeup included a helping of mascara above his lips to give the guise of a mustache. A thin pasting of white baking powder was also applied to Russell's face providing him with an air of deathly pallor.

Sister Therese-Marie looked at Russell, as he lay semi-prone in the wheelchair, his eyes partially shut. The extra touches provided a realistic effect, even if she did say so herself. She had briefed Russell that it would be even more effective if he were to moan every so often, and Russell obliged as if on cue with a low, soulful groan. She was impressed with his effort and glanced over at her brother who sat in a seat next to Christine. Bernard glanced back, as if reading her mind, and smiled.

The trip took the ancient bus nearly forty bumpy minutes, during which the exquisite countryside leading into *Lourdes* was gracefully displayed as on a Matisse or Van Gogh canvass. The solemn majesty of the giant snow-capped Pyrenees was framed in the old bus' front windows. The city of *Lourdes* provided a fitting showplace for their pilgrimage.

Christine watched as the scenic panorama passed silently by, and hoped that her present mission would soon be coming to an end. Her tender affair the preceding night with Brian had affected her more than she wanted to admit and she suddenly found that her most serious priorities might also be changing. She realized that she had fallen deeply in love with the American and felt reasonably assured that the feeling inside him was mutual. While the Resistance mission was still vitally important to her, her new relationship now commanded a significant place in her life.

She also found that she now longed for an opportunity to talk to Brian about her feelings, but realized that such a discussion was all but impossible. Sensitive matters like these were not discussed during critical, pressure-filled times, but rather in a more tranquil environment where clear thinking and sincere feelings prevailed. Christine looked over at Brian who was in the process of emitting a groan, an act that immediately made her suppress a laugh. Out of the corner of her eye, Christine caught Sister Therese-Marie watching her, nodding negatively at her action. Christine forced herself to turn away from Brian's direction and concentrate on the outside scenery.

The bus crossed a railroad bridge and entered the outskirts of *Lourdes*. Its driver proceeded south on the *avenue Marshall Foch* and turned right onto *rue de Pau*. Several blocks later, the bus approached its drop-off point, immediately below the historic *Chateau Fort*. The *fort* was an elevated castle on a tall hill overlooking the city. The *Chateau Fort*, Christine correctly surmised, was undoubtedly the most dominant landmark in the city of *Lourdes*.

From its position high atop a mountain, the old fortress was able to provide a panoramic view of the entire area. Its massive towers heralded a time in history when such structures were a necessary protection from the onslaught of potential conquerors, but now served only as a silent reminder of the city's ancient past.

The bus finally stopped and a number of the riders and patients on the bus began their preparations for disembarking. Sister Therese-Marie motioned for her group to remain seated. Not a single person around her moved.

It was important to the experienced nun that her charges were the last ones off the bus.

*   *   *

For some unexplained reason, the flow of visitors toward the *Cite Religieuse* was heavier this particular morning than on the past two. Senior *Milice* Inspector Raymond Soward attempted to scrutinize the large number of people passing him on their way to the *grotto*. Once or twice during the past hour he glanced over at Viktoria, but she too seemed barely able to adequately handle the increased numbers of visitors. On one occasion, he noticed her stop a particular group of people. She immediately asked for all to produce their papers.

Viktoria studied the papers for several moments before returning them and eventually permitted the group to pass. Soward's own surveillance had proved fruitless to this point. He was becoming frustrated and had not even bothered to stop anyone, since he had not observed anyone even remotely resembling Christine and Brian. The lingering doubts he had pushed to the back of his mind reappeared, casting the *Milice* inspector into a state of subdued apprehension.

Viktoria Losse was also beginning to harbor uncertainties as to the wisdom of her continued surveillance. The nagging fact that neither she nor Soward had been able to uncover the slightest shred of evidence to support his theory, weighed heavily on her mind. The idea of two more days of mingling with *Lourdes'* visitors in an attempt to capture their prey brought even more reservations to the mind of the *Milice* agent. She decided to discuss the matter with Soward as soon as the day's present flow of people lightened. From the looks of the crowds, several more hours would pass until such a conversation would be possible.

*   *   *

Sister Therese-Marie had good reason for wanting her group to wait until last to alight from the hospital's bus. She placed herself at the rear of the grouping; a position that she felt would attract the least amount of attention. She assisted Christine and Bernard in lifting Brian's wheelchair to the ground and glanced around to see if anyone else was watching. When she was satisfied that their movements were unobserved, she and Christine started pushing the wooden wheelchair forward, following in the same direction as the others who had gone forward. With Russell's dead weight, the wooden wheels were difficult for the two women to push. The wheels creaked and groaned as they passed over the uneven cobblestones that composed the street.

A young boy of about ten stopped their progress. He pushed a newspaper in front of Bernard, imploring him to buy. The wheelchair and everyone concerned with it stopped.

"What is this happening?" Bernard asked his sister. "No one seems to be buying the paper. I watched the boy approach everyone who got off the bus."

"The paper he is selling is controlled by the Vichy government. No one wants to read about their lies and deceptions."

Bernard looked into the boy's eyes and produced a franc. He took the paper and the youth departed.

"Let me show you what I mean," Sister Therese-Marie offered.

She unfolded the paper and showed it to her brother. "Look here, see the white spaces? That is where the Vichy censors have decided that the article was either too critical or not to their liking. The whole paper is like that, there is almost as much white space as there is printed. It is a sad state of affairs that our newspapers are treated like that."

The procession started up again and was forced to walk at a brisk rate in order to catch up with the others from their bus. Brian pulled the end of her habit and made Christine aware that he was unable to see anything in his present prone position. Christine adjusted the wheelchair's back to allow him at least visual access to the scene unfolding before them. The route from the drop off point below the old *Chateau Fort* wound around two narrow cobblestone streets. It ended at the *Pau* River and its wide crossing bridge, the *Pont St. Michel*. A large crowd of visitors was forced to wait in line at the bridge as Vichy militia soldiers checked the papers of everyone attempting to cross.

Bernard approached his sister and whispered.

"How carefully do they check the papers here?"

"It usually depends on the number of people waiting to cross. The fewer the people the longer it takes. Today's crowd is quite large, so I don't believe the guards will be very thorough."

"That will work to our advantage."

"Yes. And, remember the papers I have with me cover the two over there and me." She pointed in the direction of Christine and Brian. "You will have to show your own papers to cross."

Bernard nodded his agreement and slipped back to a position well behind the wheelchair.

*   *   *

After leaving Soward at the *Pont St. Michel* crossing, his *Milice* driver had unhappily returned to his post at the southernmost bridge crossing. He wondered if he had crossed the line earlier that day by showing displeasure with his assigned station. It was true that he was growing tired of waiting at the less frequently traveled bridge for something to happen. He considered his situation for the third or fourth time that day and made a decision. He took it upon himself to leave his post and walk in the direction of Soward and the ostentatious woman he called the Losse woman. It seemed to Torte a good idea to approach Soward and offer his apologies for his earlier conduct. Surely his superior would accept his regrets if offered with such good intention. Once the meeting was completed, he could then return to his job.

The *Milice* officer began moving toward the spot he knew Soward and Viktoria were positioned, a distance that he judged to be about 700 yards away. As he approached Soward, he observed that the number of people pressing toward the *Cite Religieuse* had increased from prior days and for a few moments he was unable to locate either Soward or Viktoria Losse. He stopped momentarily and surveyed the crowd.

Looking to his left, he finally pinpointed Soward, whose attention was riveted on the oncoming crowd. Across from Soward, he found Viktoria Losse standing in a similar position.

He hastened toward Soward, who turned in time to see him coming.

"What are you doing here? You are supposed to be watching the other bridge up the river."

"I just wanted to offer my apology for my attitude this morning." Torte motioned towards the crowd and hoped for the best. "Since there is almost no activity at the other crossing, I thought you might be able to use my help."

"Everything here is as it should be, except that this morning there are far too many people."

"It is not the same at the other bridge. There is hardly anyone crossing there."

"That is only because it serves those coming from the South. Most of the people who come to *Lourdes* come from the North. It would be out of their way for them to use the other bridge."

"I see what you mean. Do you still want me to cover the other bridge?"

"No, you might have a good idea. It might be more useful if you were to remain with Frau Losse and me for the time being, at least until the crowd dies down a little."

"As you wish. I will remain out there in the middle of the street." He pointed to a specific spot slightly behind Soward's position. "If you need me, just make a motion and I will see it."

Soward nodded his agreement and returned his attention to the continuous flow of visitors who were exiting the Vichy militia checkpoint at the *Pont St. Michel*. He noted the large crowd still waiting to pass the checkpoint.

*   *   *

The wait to clear the checkpoint dragged on tediously for Sister Therese-Marie, Christine and Brian. They had waited for over twenty minutes and were now approaching the front of the line.

A number of Vichy militia soldiers were spread across the entrance and several others lounged behind them with rifles either slung on their shoulders or loosely gripped in their hands. A personnel carrier with distinct German lines and bearing the Vichy insignia was parked immediately adjacent to the militia's position.

Bernard Masson was stuck behind several others who were directly to the rear of his sister and the wheelchair. His trained eye surveyed the entire scene. Bernard sized up the others around him waiting to cross the bridge and found little out of the ordinary. His attention drifted to the area on the far side of the *Pont St. Michel*, noting the actions of everyone who passed within his view. He crisscrossed the street and suddenly his gaze was interrupted. He took note of two people, one on each side of the street. Each one was turned in a different direction from the passing pilgrims and each was also intently scrutinizing the oncoming crowd obviously looking for something or someone.

An alarm went off inside Bernard's massive head and he leaned forward to catch his sister's attention.

He was a moment too late, for Sister Therese-Marie, Christine and the wheelchair were already moving forward, approaching the waiting militia guard. Bernard grimaced as he looked around for another way he might stop his sister, but realized there was no answer to his immediate problem. The wheels were already in motion!

The Vichy militia soldier on duty reached for the three sets of hospital papers that Sister Therese-Marie handed to him and immediately began studying them. The young militia guard peered up from the documents and stared directly at the two nuns surrounding the elongated wheelchair in front of him.

He glanced down at the ghastly figure in the wheelchair and shook his head slightly.

Another half-dead man attempting to find a miraculous cure for his ailment? Won't such people ever learn?

The youthful soldier had seen thousands of such cases, and had often speculated with his fellow militia members as to how many of them were actually cured.

But, they still keep coming and probably will forever. For some, it is their only hope. I pray I am never in such a position.

He glanced again at the papers, recognizing the name of the hospital. He reminded himself that the place was right down the street from his family's home in *Tarbes*, and, when needed, had served as his family's hospital.

"I know your hospital well, Sister. I was once brought to the *Hospices de Notre Dame* when I was young. I had broken my arm."

"Yes, my son," Sister Therese-Marie answered. "The Lord allows us to provide care for many who are injured."

"He certainly did for me, Sister. My arm is now as good as new." He held up his arm for her to see.

"I am happy for that. Now, my son, may we pass? It is starting to get late."

"Certainly Sister, you may pass through, anytime." He smiled and handed the papers back to her. The trio started forward and proceeded through the checkpoint. Christine fought the urge to look around and kept her head lowered in an obsequious manner just as Sister Therese-Marie had instructed. The overhang of her habit's headdress kept her face hidden, exactly as Sister Therese-Marie wanted. The wise nun saw both Christine's youth and outward beauty and insisted that Christine keep her head down and covered. She emphasized such caution must be observed under *any* circumstances, and most specifically while in the city of *Lourdes* itself.

A few feet behind and still in line, Bernard realized the situation had become critical and was rapidly slipping away from him. He desperately implored an older couple in front of him to allow him to proceed ahead of them.

"Please my friends, my sister and I got separated in the lines and I need to find her. Please let me go through next. The Lord will bless you for your kindness."

Bernard's frantic look was one of pure panic and his timely reference to the Lord produced the desired effect. The old man nodded and gestured him through. Bernard stepped up to the Vichy soldier and handed his papers as his eyes looked ahead. He searched for Sister Therese-Marie and her charges and prayed that she had the good sense to slow her walk until he was in a position to catch up.

He finally located the trio as the wheelchair slowly creaked forward. To his discomfort, neither Sister Therese-Marie nor Christine turned around in his direction.

Bernard turned his attention back to the soldier and tried to calm himself. He could feel his heart pounding and his adrenaline rising. To his relief, the guard casually glanced at the picture on his papers and waved him forward. Taking the papers back, Bernard looked up but was further distressed by the fact that the wheelchair was now even farther ahead of him, still proceeding slowly forward. The wheelchair had almost crossed the river bridge, and was about to enter the plaza area that opened up and fed a pair of wide streets that lead directly to the *Basilique du Rosaire*. He increased his pace, trying to force himself not to run but still attempting to close the gap between himself and the wheelchair. He fingered the Lebel pistol he was carrying inside his jacket and cradled its handle. To his relief, he realized his pace had reduced the distance between himself and Sister Therese-Marie. Several times he successfully avoided other pilgrims headed in the same direction. At the same time, Bernard was also carefully attempting to pinpoint two individuals he had first observed while waiting in line to cross.

His present location was lower than the bridge's vista and for a moment, Bernard gasped when he failed to locate either the man or the woman he had seen just minutes before. His eyes widened their search and finally focused on the individual he was seeking. His spirits immediately dropped when he saw that the wheelchair was less than twenty yards from the man's position.

Sister Therese-Marie continued her even pace, scanning ahead for any signs of trouble. She checked Brian to insure all his blankets and cover were in place and whispered again to Christine to keep her head down.

Christine acknowledged the warning and leaned even closer to the ground, mimicking the movement of rearranging the covers on the wheelchair. Brian groaned for effect and managed to change his position slightly. Under the covers, his hand firmly gripped the pistol Charles Martin had given him as they had boarded the boat.

Chapter Eighteen

Viktoria Losse was fully occupied with crowds of people on her side of the street when a young couple came into her view. Viktoria quickly surmised that the pair was about the right age and heights and generally matched the descriptions of the couple she and Soward had been searching for during the past several days. She looked over at Soward to gain his attention but he was staring intently at a large group descending on his position. She immediately elected to take control and pushed her way through several persons, swiftly moving in the direction of the oncoming man and woman. She produced her police identification badge from a pocket and proclaimed in a loud and authoritative voice.

"You two. Stop there. *Milice!*"

The young couple stopped in their tracks, looked towards her and froze. So did practically everyone else within earshot of Viktoria Losse's chilly command.

Viktoria stepped forward placing her police identification back inside her jacket pocket. Her instinct had also caused her to draw her .9mm Walther P38 regular issue pistol that she now raised in her other hand and pointed directly at the young couple. Viktoria looked over toward Soward who had stopped his own surveillance and was cramming his neck to get a better view of the suspects whose back was now to him. He took several steps to gain a better view of the pair Viktoria was holding under gunpoint. As his angle improved, he immediately saw that the couple she was holding was not Christine and Brian, and that these people did not bear even a close resemblance to the pair they were after.

Soward also was quick to observe the affect Viktoria's raised pistol was having on the assembled pilgrims and tried to signal her to lower her weapon. The Senior Inspector nodded to her, and finally managed to make clear to his associate that these were not the people they were seeking. He wanted desperately to tell her about unnecessarily brandishing her gun, but there were too many people in between them. He tried to restore a semblance of stability and ordered the crowds to continue on their way. Within moments the flow of humanity had begun again and Soward returned his attention to the oncoming number of visitors, most of who had stopped to observe the encounter.

Soward's eyes traveled across the crowd and returned to a single figure, who was dressed in a nun's habit, but whose head was bent at an abnormal angle towards the ground. The twisted nun stood next to a wooden wheelchair and directly behind another nun. The second nun stood much straighter, with her head fixed straight ahead glued to the scene ahead of her. Another less visible person, from his size Soward judged in all probability a man, was prone in the wheelchair covered with blankets, his head hidden from view.

Viktoria also waved her arms encouraging the crowd forward again. Ten to fifteen seconds later, the nuns pushing the wheelchair neared Raymond Soward's position at the access way leading to the *Basilique du Rosaire*. He watched intently as the wheelchair passed within five yards of him. Soward leaned forward and strained to see the face of the person lying in the wheelchair. Other visitors obscured his view but Soward followed the wheelchair's progress. He continued to observe the stooped nun as the procession slowly moved away from him.

For some reason, Raymond Soward's instincts alerted him to the fact that something was not right about the wheelchair and its milieu. He had witnessed too many people in stressful situations react badly to pressure and give themselves away by the simplest mistake. To Soward, the wheelchair and the bent nun were a classic example of such a scenario. At the very least his policeman's sense dictated that he must stop and question the people involved. Soward gestured to Viktoria Losse, who was still quite near, to follow him and strained to catch the attention of his other assistant, Torte. The latter saw Soward's signal and immediately moved closer to the area towards which Soward was pointing.

Soward gestured with his arm for Torte to get ahead of the contraption. Due to the crowd and its continuing movement, the *Milice* officer found much difficulty in pushing his way through to gain such a position.

At last, Torte managed to work his way forward and was able to position himself a few yards ahead and to the right of the wheelchair. He stood at a spot where the crowd started thinning naturally.

Sister Therese-Marie saw Torte's quickened movements and sensed a problem. Her eyes had followed the man as he callously pushed his way through the crowd ahead of her. She jerked the wheelchair to alert Brian to the fact that there was a problem.

She calmly followed her jerking action with a single word.

"Police."

Soward and Viktoria finally caught up with the wheelchair and the two took up positions behind the wheelchair. Both officers were in the act of drawing their pistols as Soward shouted.

"You people pushing the wheelchair. Do not move. *Milice!*"

From several spots in the crowd, a number of women screamed loudly and people started to react to Soward's command. The crowd of hundreds, on edge from the prior encounter with Viktoria's gun brandishing episode just minutes before, broke in several directions at the same time. This caused even more people to scream and shriek loudly, adding to the general confusion.

Witnessing the unfurling scene, Soward saw that his attempt to halt the wheelchair's progress was falling to pieces. He quickly tried to improve his position and move in front of the wheelchair, but he was a moment too late. From the mass of people in the crowd behind Soward, Bernard Masson emerged with his .8mm Lebel pistol aimed and pointed in Soward's direction. The big man was in full flight and was attempting to stop his momentum to allow himself to assume a two handed grip. Bernard remembered his tedious training and squeezed the trigger evenly. This caused the pistol's barrel to rise slightly. He squeezed the trigger a second and third time. Bernard's first shot struck Senior *Milice* Inspector Raymond Soward in his right arm, shattering the humerus bone and rendering the limb totally useless. The *Milice* inspector reacted loudly to the searing pain and crumbled to the stone street, grabbing his wounded arm in agony.

Viktoria Losse, who in her two years as a *Milice* functionary had infrequently fired her weapon, found herself totally unprepared for the sequence of events that exploded before her eyes. She looked toward Bernard's oncoming figure and dropped her weapon slightly as if unsure of her next course of action. Bernard reacted quickly to the unexpected good luck, and fired his gun point blank at her head. The bullet entered her forehead below the hairline as she crumpled to the ground quickly oozing a steady stream of crimson liquid onto the cobblestones.

Brian wasn't quite so lucky. As the firing began, he was partially able to focus on the remaining Vichy agent who was in the process of drawing his own Walther. Upon hearing Masson's first shot, Brian attempted to remove his pistol from under the blanket to allow himself a shot at the man standing squarely in front of his wheelchair. His body's inclined position hindered his movement and as Brian Russell raised the pistol's barrel, it caught on the blanket covering him and he fired wildly, missing everything.

Torte also reacted to the undisciplined activity and aimed his revolver in the general direction of the wheelchair and fired two shots.

Torte's first shot struck Sister Therese-Marie on the left side of her body, about three inches below her heart. She gripped the handle of the wheelchair and began to fall to the ground. Her actions caused the chair to top just enough to alter Brian's position by several inches. Torte's second shot ripped into the fleshy part of his left arm and exited through the back wicker part of the wheelchair. Brian was still attempting to free his gun from the blanket's impediment when the bullet hit his left arm. He instinctively jerked at the pain and his natural reaction caused his finger to tighten on the trigger causing the pistol to fire. The weapon was aimed downward at the time and the shot traveled a scant two yards and entered Raymond Soward's right temple.

Meanwhile, Bernard Masson effortlessly aimed his old Lebel pistol again and dispatched the remaining *Milice* agent to his death with a quick salvo of two shots. Torte fell over backwards, mortally wounded in his lungs and heart.

The entire action had taken all of ten seconds.

Bernard Masson immediately attempted to assess the situation. Pandemonium had broken loose with the first shots and many in the crowd had turned to run back toward the *Pont St. Michel*. His height allowed him to see the Vichy guards struggling to work their way forward in the general direction of the sounds of the gunshots. Bernard silently thanked God there were still enough people between him and the bridge to make it difficult for the soldiers to get through. He saw that Christine was unhurt and was attending to Brian who seemed to be okay except for a wound to his arm, which was now bleeding moderately.

He finally turned toward his older sister and stared at her crumpled body. He sensed the worst and his entire perception of time and being came to a standstill.

Christine had finally extracted her own pistol from under her weighty habit, but saw no need for any further shooting. She realized that time was of the essence if they were going to get away from the scene alive. She pulled Brian to his feet and yelled at Bernard.

"We must all leave immediately, there is no other choice. You should leave with us."

Bernard pressed his gun into her hand. His silent, teary eyes met Christine's and told her he was unable to leave his wounded sister's side.

"You take him and get away from here. I must stay here with my sister. She is badly wounded."

Brian managed to free the cylinder from the wheelchair. He looked thoughtfully at Bernard Masson as the huge man knelt and gently cradled the head of his sister in his huge hands. He patted Bernard's shoulder and quickly moved off alongside Christine in the general direction of the southern bridge. In a moment, the crowd who had begun to return to the scene to view the tragedy swallowed up the pair.

Bernard Masson held the hand of his older sister and cradled Sister Therese-Marie's head in his lap. He looked at the bloody wound in her chest and pressed nearer to her face.

"My dearest Therese, what have I done to you?" He was in tears.

Sister Therese-Marie opened her eyes faintly, and replied weakly. "I did not do this just for you Bernard. I came because I agreed with your beliefs." She paused a moment, summoning her remaining strength. "I accompanied you for the good of our country. What has happened to me is God's will…believe in Him little brother. He will see us all through this…"

Bernard squeezed her hand as the final vestige of life departed from Sister Therese-Marie's suddenly still body.

Bernard fought to regain his senses as the first militia guards reached him.

Two young soldiers surrounded him and pointed their rifles in his direction.

"Hands up," one ordered.

"What do you mean," he retorted, feigning outrage at the suggestion. "My sister and I were on our way to visit the Blessed Virgin and suddenly everyone began shooting. We were caught in the middle."

Bernard Masson had already begun to weave the threads of his alibi.

Christine and Brian stepped into one of the first small alleyways they encountered as they quickly attempted to make their way out of the city. Both realized it was important that they discard their religious garb as soon as possible. The couple was thankful Sister Therese-Marie had insisted they wear their regular clothing underneath the religious garments. Christine tore apart a section of her habit and tied together several strips of cloth to bind Brian's wound.

"Your wound does not appear to be serious. It looks to me like a small caliber wound and I can see that the bullet has already exited the arm through the back. You are lucky, there isn't even much blood."

"Easy for you to say, you aren't the one shot," Brian retorted, only half serious.

"At times men can be such sissies, even with a little wound like this…"

Brian glared at her and Christine decided to stop teasing.

"Well, now, what do you suggest we do next?" Brian asked, as he adjusted the dressing on his wound.

"I am afraid what has just occurred does not leave us with many choices. The most difficult part is probably behind us, and we are almost out of *Lourdes*. I am also sure the militia will try to find us, but I have no idea what they will do. I do not think they will be able to piece together very much from witnesses, it was too chaotic for anyone to see anything very clearly. You and I just have to hope that none of the *Milice* who were shot are alive to tell them."

"What about Bernard? I'm sure they will question him thoroughly."

"I think Bernard Masson can take care of himself. He impressed me as an awfully clever fellow. And, he doesn't physically look like someone who would be in the Resistance. His appearance works in his favor."

"Do you think his sister is dead? She looked as if she was badly wounded."

"There wasn't any time to check, but if I had to guess, I would say she is probably dead or near death."

"If that is so, then Bernard has suffered a great loss."

"Yes, he loved his sister a great deal. She was not even supposed to be there with us."

"He wanted her to come and she felt she was right in doing so."

"Yes," Christine responded, a tiny tear welling in her eye. "Many of us feel that way."

*　　*　　*

Because there was little permanent Vichy *Milice* presence in *Lourdes*, it fell to the regional inspector's office in *Pau* to investigate the circumstances surrounding the deaths of the three *Milice* officers. Since the militia guards were untrained in police matters, and particularly homicide investigations, not a single eyewitness to the tragedy was detained from around the area in *Lourdes*. It was equally unfortunate for the *Milice* officer placed in charge of the investigation that not one nationalistic French citizen came forth to disclose what had happened in the area adjoining the *Pont St. Michel*.

A day later, a final three-page report was filed and forwarded to the *Milice* home offices in Vichy. In addition to the account of the four shooting deaths, the report made mention of only one additional person, an upstanding loyal Vichy cheese merchant from *Pau* named Bernard Masson. The report described Masson as an unusually large man related to a Sister Therese-Marie, of the order of *Les Soeurs de Notre Dame des Delours,* a hospital order located in the nearby city of *Tarbes.* Masson and the nun were on a pilgrimage to the *Basilique du Rosaire,* to pay homage to the Blessed Virgin for the goodness shown their family.

The pair's outing that particular day had been suggested by the Mother Superior of *Les Soeurs de Notre Dame des Delours* who had been personally interviewed by the reporting officer. The nun and her brother were part of a bus group that had used the religious order's hospital's normal method of transportation to reach *Lourdes.*

After crossing the *Pont St. Michel* leading to the *Cite Religieuse* section of the city, the report stated that both Masson and Sister Therese-Marie were inadvertently caught up in a *Milice* police action that ultimately resulted in the deaths of three Vichy police officers and the nun. The report pointed out that Sister Therese-Marie was killed by a stray shot fired by an unknown shooter, possibly one of the *Milice* agents. The report also alleged, due primarily to descriptions and facts contained in an old report previously submitted by the ranking dead *Milice* officer, Senior Inspector Raymond Soward, that Free French Resistance partisans were involved in the shootings, but that theory was unsubstantiated by any subsequent facts. The reporting official summarized that Masson was the only witness even interrogated during the ensuing investigation due to the fact that he was the only person identified as actually having witnessed the entire event. Masson was unsure of the specific facts relating to the shootings but thought he had seen several men shooting in the direction of the dead Vichy officers.

As a precaution, the report ordered all Vichy militia on duty between *Lourdes* and the Spanish border placed on increased alert in case the theory of Resistance involvement proved factual. Copies of the report were also forwarded to both Abwehr and Wehrmacht offices in *Paris.*

* * *

For the next part of their journey, Christine was forced to rely on her instinct to guide them the remainder of the way south into the *Haut Pyrenees.* She reasoned that the closer she and Brian got to Spain, the less likelihood there was of their being detected by Vichy government security forces. She made it a point to travel on the back streets as the pair eventually made their way out of *Lourdes* and into the countryside. After two hours walking, Christine and Brian approached a tiny hamlet named *Agos*, where they sought refuge from the afternoon sun. Christine had visited this area several years before and if her memory was correct, *Agos* served as a suburb of the larger city of *Argeles-Gazost,* her next destination on the direct route to the South.

They located a deserted stone barn with a colorful Mumm's Champagne advertisement on the side facing the road and decided to rest for the afternoon. The barn smelled of freshly cut hay and the two fluffed up a spot and lay down near an open window. Brian lightly mentioned to Christine that the barn was the type of accommodations both had recently become used to. She agreed and became silent, thinking ahead to her next move. The break also served as a useful opportunity for Christine to dress Brian's wound with fresh fabric she had saved from her discarded nun's habit.

Christine held Brian's arm tenderly and touched the area of the wound for soreness. The pair really hadn't spoken more than a few sentences to each other since their escape more than two hours before in *Lourdes*.

"Does it still hurt?"

Brian replied bravely, "Not really, I don't even realize it's there."

Christine smiled at him and finished rewinding the bandage. She purposely tied the knot a little too tight causing Brian to wince.

"Sorry," she said facetiously, "I will be more careful."

Brian looked at her and started to grin.

"We were lucky back there. If Bernard were not a crack shot, we might all be dead or in custody by now."

"Yes, it all happened so fast. There was nothing I could do. I could not even remove my pistol from under my habit."

"There was nothing anyone could do, and I almost screwed things up in a big way."

"I do not understand what you mean."

"When the shooting began," Russell explained, "I fumbled getting my gun out from under the covers. It caught on the folds and I couldn't get it out right away. That's when I got shot. I should have just fired through the blanket, but I couldn't think that fast. If I had been more alert, maybe Sister Therese-Marie wouldn't have been wounded at all."

"Do not be so hard on yourself, you acted as best you could. Besides, I think the Sister was shot first, because she fell so quickly." Christine paused and reflected. "Do you think she will live?"

"I saw a great deal of blood. That's not usually a good sign."

"I will say several prayers for her and also for Bernard. He did an incredible job of getting us through it all."

"As I told you before, Bernard will do all right for himself. It's the other part that is bothering me."

"The other part?"

"Yes, the part about the person who was that was waiting for us. Didn't you recognize him?"

"You mean the *Milice* inspector from *Condom*? I just got a quick look as we were leaving. He looked dead to me."

"I thought so too. Either he was much smarter than we first guessed, or we were incredibly convincing when we were being questioned in the *Prefecture*. I really didn't expect him to show up in *Lourdes*."

"I would guess it was probably a little bit of both, but all that is behind us now. Now, our big task is to find someone from the Resistance in the town up ahead to help us. I do not have a specific place to look, so I intend to ask around in a general sort of way."

"Do you think that anyone will admit to a perfect stranger that they are part of the Resistance?" Brian asked pointedly.

"Probably not, at least not when I first meet them," Christine admitted. "But I have the existing code words and I can be very persuasive when necessary. Besides, these are troubled times and everyone is aware that unusual things can happen."

"I wouldn't doubt your persuasiveness for a second," Brian grinned at his companion.

She caught his inflection and gently rapped him on his shoulder.

"Please be serious, you are always joking with me."

"It's the nature of most Americans to take things a bit lightly. It keeps everything we do on an even keel. When it's time to be serious, I can be *extremely* serious, I promise you that.'

"Now it's time for us to get some rest," Christine spoke abruptly, "and I do mean *rest*. I want for us to only travel at night. I cannot believe they will be searching for us after dark. "

Brian looked again and this time smiled broadly.

* * *

The evening sky darkened shortly after eight, but Christine took the added precaution of waiting an additional hour before setting out. The fewer people they encountered on the road the better, a fact that she felt lessened the chance of being discovered. It was nearly a half-hour before they reached *Argeles-Gazost*, which turned out to be a larger place than Christine remembered. *Argeles-Gazost* was a two-tiered city, with most of the older buildings located up a relatively steep hillside. The remainder of the town, located on the valley floor, included a number of smaller, individual homes and buildings that evidenced the area's recent growth.

The sign that pointed upward toward the *Centre Ville* was on a steep section of the hill. The town's streets were narrow and barely able to accommodate a wide automobile or truck. Christine observed that several hotels and a number of small business fronts dominated the main street. She decided to try the largest hotel, a four-storied angular place called the *Hotel Bernede*, which appeared to be open. As a precaution, Christine made Brian wait outside while she entered the narrow doorway leading to the hotel's interior. From a side room off the main foyer came the muffled sounds of voices. An *Edith Piaf* recording played in the background, her nasally pitch filling the air.

> *"Adieu mon Coeur*
> *On te jette au malheur*
> *Tu n'auras pas mes yeux*
> *Pour mourer…"*

The smoky room was the first bar that Christine had seen on their journey and reminded her that such intimate places still existed in wartime France.

Christine approached the hotel's counter, a tiny cubbyhole located under a stairway with a number of large keys with brass numbers filed neatly on hooks along the back wall. A slightly balding, thin-faced man stood behind the partition, intently incorporating numbers into a ledger. He looked up at Christine and produced a faint, disinterested smile.

"Yes, *Mademoiselle*, may I be of help? Do you wish a room?"

Christine phrased her response carefully; thereby insuring the Resistance code words were prominently featured.

"Possibly, *Monsieur*, if the current weather holds. However, I understand there are *thunderstorms on the way*." The Resistance code, *thunderstorms on the way*, would have to be repeated verbatim to be acceptable to another Resistance member.

"I have absolutely no idea what tomorrow's weather will offer, *Mademoiselle*," the clerk snapped back at her. "Now, do you want the room or not?" He ended his question by allowing his eyes to drift to the floor.

"No, I have changed my mind, thank you anyway." Christine walked outside the hotel to where Brian was waiting in the street next to another person, an older man in his sixties, who wore a faded pin striped suit while standing and smoking a cigarette.

Disappointed, Christine spoke to Brian. "No luck here. The clerk could not have cared less. I think this one was born without a personality. We will have to try another hotel."

The person in the background heard her statement and approached.

"Excuse me, *Mademoiselle*, but I overheard your conversation. Perhaps I can be of help."

"Yes *Monsieur?*"

"I am the *concierge* here at the hotel and I agree with you that our night clerk, August, is lacking in some basic manners. That is probably why he works mostly at night. If our accommodations were not to your liking, he should have recommended another hotel. I would be happy to help you if you would permit."

"Certainly *Monsieur*, and thank you for your concern."

"It is part of my job. The place I would recommend to you is back down the hill, and to the right, maybe less than one mile. It is the newest and in some ways, the best lodging in the entire area. If anyone doesn't like our hotel, I always refer them to the *Le Miramont.*"

"Thank you *Monsieur*, we will heed your advice."

"*Ne pas de quai, Madame.*"

Christine and Brian proceeded down the hill and eventually approached the hotel to which they had been directed, the *Le Miramont*. The two-story building was painted white, and was created in an attractive art deco manner. From its appearance, the hotel seemed brand new. Its exterior area was freshly landscaped and several huge *plantane* and pineapple trees were propped up with wooden slats to keep them from falling over. A neat striped awning accented the deco theme and led to the main door. When Christine passed through the front entrance, an older man and a younger woman stood behind the hotel's main counter to greet her.

Christine followed her script to the letter and was surprised when the female clerk announced to her co-worker that she would handle this matter herself. The man shrugged and walked away, opening a door located behind the counter.

Christine repeated her earlier phrase. "*Madame*, I understand *thunderstorms are on the way.*"

The woman behind the counter, Christine guessed to be in her early forties, replied, "That is what the weather forecast says. "*Thunderstorms are on the way, in fact I think we can expect some tomorrow.*"

After the initial exchange was completed, she spoke again to Christine.

"Now that we have disposed of the formalities, you may call me Lili. Just how can I be of help to you?"

"I am Christine. Is it okay for us to talk out here in the open?"

"Yes. There's only old Herve here besides me, and he's almost totally deaf. We are quite safe."

"I am traveling along with someone and it is imperative we get across the border into Spain. My friend is on an important mission and the Resistance has been asked to see that he gets safely out of France. We have been traveling for almost a week. We were captured several days ago in *Condo*, but escaped. The same thing happened again yesterday in *Lourdes*. We made our way out of *Lourdes* and now as far as here. I took the chance of asking around and finding someone who could help. Thank goodness the code I was given has not been changed."

Lili regarded Christine. "So you two are the ones the militia are searching for. Two soldiers came by earlier today asking questions of everyone at the hotel. They were quite vague in their descriptions and weren't even specific as to who they were trying to find. Can you believe that the soldiers actually told us to be on the lookout for anyone who acted suspicious? I almost laughed out loud. There is little chance of that happening around here. They wonder why everyone despises them."

Brian studied the woman as she spoke. While Lili was attractive, she could never be called beautiful. Her features were more rigid than soft and it was evident she had worked hard her entire life. She was neatly dressed and most professional in her manner. Women such as this were the ongoing backbone of France, Brian decided, and were one of the reasons France would never be conquered. He was brought out of his thought process when Christine asked,

"How will all that effect our being able to get across the border?"

"I do not believe it is anything that cannot be overcome. The Vichy militia in these parts is basically ineffective. It is that way throughout most of France. The government gives young country boys a uniform and puts guns into their hands. That combination is supposed to make them into soldiers. There are a few older men and even an officer or two, but few are effective. The rumor is that many Vichy militia conscripts desert their posts after a few months. I have even been told that some have even joined the *maquis* bands further up in the North. Unless you stumble onto the militia by accident, you will probably be safe."

"I assure you that we will make every attempt to be careful," Christine replied. "Lili, is it too much to ask that you provide us with a contact close to the border that can assist in getting us across?"

"But of course, *Cherie*. I already intended to do just that. But, it is already much too late tonight. I will place a call first thing tomorrow morning. In the meantime, you both can stay here tonight; your rooms will be courtesy of the Resistance. Will you need one room or two?"

"One will be fine," Christine answered, as she suppressed a faint smile.

*   *   *

Brian was impressed that the beds at the *La Miramont* were larger than most French hotel beds and that the pillows were fluffy and comfortable. He wasn't sure he would ever get used to sleeping in barns or makeshift beds. He even admitted to himself that the hospital cot he shared with Christine last night left a lot to be desired in the way of comfort. In another sense, Brian admitted that he had found the hospital cot more than adequate.

Russell also realized that this night would offer their first comfortable rest in quite some time. He determined to make the most of it. The spacious room Lili provided for them even included an accompanying bath, another rarity in many French hotels, particularly those located outside of large urban environments. Brian Russell allowed Christine the luxury of the first bath and lay down on one of the twin beds to relax while she soaked.

He had barely closed his eyes when he heard Christine's voice from the bathroom.

"Can you please come and help me?"

Brian thought he noted a implication in her expression. He rose from the bed and opened the bathroom door. Christine covered herself with her arms and leaned against the back of the tub facing the doorway.

"Somehow, I cannot reach my back, I think my arms are not long enough. Can you please help me?"

Brian grinned and accepted the washcloth she was holding in one hand. "Back washing is the first thing I was taught as an American Army officer," he responded in his spiciest tone. "It's all in the wrist and the washing motion one employs. It's always best to press clockwise first, then, when the time is right, counter clockwise."

Brian dipped the washcloth into the bath water and applied some soap, which he lathered and stroked in a soft, even manner around her back.

Christine lowered her head and closed her eyes. His fingers worked magic on her tense back and awakened a deeper, more immediate sensation between her legs.

"That is very nice," she cooed. "But it would be even nicer if you were in here with me."

That very thought had already crossed Brian Russell's mind.

*   *   *

The bathing experience extended as long as possible. Then, they finally retired and agreed to get some sleep. Brian opened the large windows that allowed a refreshing mountain breeze to creep into the room. They both lay naked and completely relaxed on top of the sheets, but neither was immediately able to settle into sleep. From outside, a mistaken cock crowed twice and broke the dead silence of the night. Christine looked at Brian and laughed. He squeezed her hand warmly and finally closed his eyes. In a matter of minutes, both he and Christine were fast asleep.

The couple slept soundly during the night and because of their state of near exhaustion remained in bed the following morning until it was nearly ten.

They were awakened by several knocks on their door of their room.

Brian rose, and quickly put on his shorts. He strode to the door and opened it about a quarter of the way.

Lili stood in the doorway with a tray of *patisseries, croissants* and juices. She regarded Brian standing partially clothed behind the doorway, pushed open the door with authority and walked in with her tray.

"Here is a little something for your *petite dejeuner.* I am sure you both could use a little nourishment. I am sorry there is no coffee, but coffee has become a rarity around here."

"This will do just fine Lili," Christine answered. "Thank you for going to so much trouble."

"It is no trouble, and I also have some good news for you."

Lili's announcement perked up both Christine and Brian. They listened attentively as she began.

"I was able to contact someone who is much nearer the Spanish border, in a little place called *Pont-d'Espagne.* It is located well beyond the City of *Cauterets* and just past *Mount Ne*, one of the tallest mountains in this section of the *Pyrenees.* This person has helped us many times before with others who were forced to flee France. He will meet you and help you cross the famous bridge for which the town is named. From there, the trip takes about two or three hours by foot, until you finally reach a point where you can leave France. That spot is called the *Port Marcadau* and once you pass through there you will be in Spain. The *Port Marcadau* is at an extremely high altitude, I believe a bit over 6,000 feet, but the climb is not too difficult. The area is quite remote, and therefore is practically impossible for the Vichy militia to patrol. The partisan will meet you and take you all the way to the *Port Marcadau.* He has contacts in Spain who he will alert to be expecting you. He will provide you with instructions as to which direction to take once you reach Spain."

"Thank you Lili, it seems as if you have thought of everything. You have been a great help."

"I do nothing that any loyal Frenchman would not do. I am just glad you found me. Now, I am going to leave and let you finish your breakfast. You might also want to take a nap sometime later during the day. After you leave tonight, there is no telling when you will get a restful sleep again."

Christine watched Lili leave and turned to Brian. The idea of an afternoon nap after a while might not be such a bad idea, but first there was a bit of unfinished business between them.

Brian acknowledged her look and took her in his arms.

*   *   *

Around seven in the evening, Lili brought another tray with food and wine. Each of them had a matching bowl that contained a *cassoulet* that the hotel's chef had produced at Lili's urging. The meal was the first hot food Brian could recall since leaving England. There were also some warm *pistolets* and an array of local mountain cheeses for after dinner. The wine was a bottle of *Chateau Fatin*, a *cru bourgeois* from the well-respected commune of *Saint Estephe* in *Bordeaux*. Upon seeing the meal, both Brian and Christine realized the factual circumstances surrounding their escape had improved a great deal. In fact, the situation was better than either could have ever expected.

"You do not have to hurry through your meal," Lili commented. "You will not be leaving here for at least an hour. I will come and get you when it is time." Lili provided the couple with an all-perceptive smile as she departed.

"She thinks we are in love," Brian remarked. "She treats us as if we were on our honeymoon."

"We *are* on a honeymoon of sorts," Christine smiled beguilingly, "And, at least *one* of us is in love."

"And, have I, my incredible little French bon-bon, done anything to indicate I'm not also in love?" Brian kissed her neck softly.

"No, and you had better not if you know what is good for you."

They both laughed and sat down to enjoy the meal. Brian poured a glass of wine and raised his glass toward Christine.

"To us."

"To us. And, to the Resistance."

"*Vive la Resistance.*"

"And, to France."

"Yes, most certainly to France. We can't forget her."

They sipped the wine and began devouring the *cassoulet*. The warm food was delicious and filled an incredible void. Brian could not remember when he had tasted such wonderful food. He broke a piece of the bread and dipped it into the *cassoulet*. A number of distinctive flavors from the creation succeeded in satisfying his most primitive needs. Another swig of the delicious well-balanced *Bordeaux* and Brian Russell knew he was not far from heaven.

* * *

A little more than an hour later, Lili reappeared and motioned for Christine and Brian to follow her. Brian grabbed the cylinder and slung it over his shoulder. The trio descended the hotel's two stairways and made their way to the rear of the hotel. At the back entrance, an old truck was waiting with its engine running but its lights out.

"You will both ride with this man in his truck," Lili instructed. "He will take you a good part of the way up into the mountains. Your contact will be waiting to meet you when you arrive up there." She handed each a jacket "to protect you from the cold…"

She kissed each of them and waved as the truck sputtered its way around a corner of the building and out of the alley behind the *La Miramont*.

The cab of the small truck was filled to capacity with the addition of Christine and Brian. The driver, an older man in his mid-fifties, said little during the short trip, which lasted slightly under an hour. Brian was relieved when the driver turned on his lights as the vehicle started its climb. The shadowy road twisted and turned, but the ancient truck took the climb in stride and eventually reached a more level part of the valley. The city of *Cauterets* appeared before them and the truck driver again cut his lights. He slowed the vehicle and proceeded on a road that curved around several turns, just missing the town. When he was convinced he was sufficiently past *Cauterets*, he turned on the lights again and continued the climb.

This part of the trip was much steeper than before and Christine glanced out the truck's window on several occasions. She carefully noted the depths and sheerness of the slopes as the truck passed. The driver was forced to shift quite often as the truck strained to meet particularly steep sections of the road. Minutes later, as they rounded a curve, a beam of light cut the vehicle's path and the old truck stopped. The driver motioned toward the light and Brian opened the door and got out. Christine followed, and a third person lowered the beam of his flashlight to their feet and politely greeted the two.

"I am Marcel," he announced resolutely, "you will please follow me."

Brian looked over at Christine and motioned for her to precede him. The old truck started up again, found sufficient room just ahead to make a turn, and started its journey back down the mountain.

Marcel followed the road for a short distance, and then set off into the dense undergrowth that comprised the thick, surrounding forest.

"At least we still have some moonlight to make it easier," he said, glancing up at the near half-moon. "If it were cloudy, our trek would be much more difficult."

The trio began to climb and both Christine and Brian found the footing slippery, a condition produced by the cooler, moist night air. They trudged along without pausing and continued for nearly two hours. Brian was saddled with the added inconvenience and weight of the cylinder, and found himself puffing to keep up. He tried to catch a glance of Christine ahead of him, and when the opportunity finally came, he saw that she, too, was laboring and struggling to keep up with Marcel's pace.

"Marcel, just a minute. Let us catch our breath."

"Sorry, I did not realize I was going so quickly. I forgot that you are unaccustomed to the thinner air up here."

"We won't need long, a few seconds will do."

"We can take longer, we have actually made excellent time."

Brian glanced at Christine whose hands were on her knees. She looked up at him and smiled.

"We do not have that much further to go. Actually, our destination is just over the next rise." He pointed at a darkened section of the mountain, which Brian judged to be about a half mile away.

"After that, it's all fairly level from there. With a little luck, we should be at *Pont d'Espagne* in about an hour."

Brian nodded his concurrence, the brief respite allowing him to catch his breath. He saw that Christine had also managed to slow her breathing appreciably.

True to Marcel's word, the three reached their destination a few minutes under an hour's time. Assembled ahead were several small buildings and homes that comprised the village of *Pont d'Espagne*. Marcel turned to his companions and assured them they were safe around the town.

"No need to worry about this place, there are relatively few people who live here and by now everyone is sleeping. There are even a few Vichy soldiers, but they will also be retired for the night. The bridge that leads to Spain is just beyond the village. Please follow me."

Christine squeezed Brian's hand and trailed Marcel through the single street that comprised the village.

About half a mile past the last building, Marcel pointed his flashlight at a darkened form in the distance.

Brian and Christine stepped a bit closer to the object and were able to make out the outline of an old, arched, stone bridge that spanned a narrow precipice.

Christine moved even closer to the bridge, motioned Brian to join her and remarked. "The bridge seems so old and beautiful. I wonder what it would look like in the daylight."

Brian took a closer glimpse. To his eye, the *Pont d'Espagne* was indeed a work of art. Large stones were cast together to form a subtle arc that produced a fairy tale effect. Vines had been allowed to grow along the sides and added greatly to the bridge's allure. Since he had not been able to make out anything but the bridge's outline when it first came under Marcel's flashlight, he was instantly pleased that Christine had stopped to admire the ancient span.

Marcel indicated that he was ready to leave and waved for Christine and Brian to start across the span. Brian started but was stopped by Christine's hand on his elbow.

"What's the matter?" he questioned, "Marcel wants to start across the bridge."

Brian Russell looked into Christine's eyes. He saw something in her incredibly beautiful eyes he knew he wasn't going to like.

"I am not going with you."

Brian Russell was totally unprepared for Christine's pronouncement.

He felt a chill down his spine as he studied her face. Her eyes were totally filled with apprehension.

"What do you mean you're not coming? After everything we've…"

Christine fought bravely for the right words. "I have thought a great deal about it, and my work for the Resistance is not finished. My country and my fellow partisans need me, there is so much more to be done. Besides, when we first started on this assignment, I had no intention of going with you."

"But, Christine, be reasonable. The *Milice* undoubtedly has your description. There's no place in France where you will be safe. You will always be looking behind your back."

"You are right my darling, and I realize it will be dangerous… but it is also something I just *must* do. I think I was born to do this, to devote my life to a cause where my efforts really matter. Besides, I can always disguise myself in a number of different ways."

"That's total nonsense. You can never disguise the fact that you are incredibly beautiful."

She approached him and gently touched his cheek.

"My dear American hero, you are much too prejudiced for your own good. I assure you, I will be all right. The *Milice* are looking for a couple and Lili confided to me that she thinks I can take a train back to *Cahors* since I will be heading in a different direction. She is also in the process of getting me some new papers. She feels that a single person heading north won't attract any attention."

"So Lili knew…"

"Yes. She also warned me to be really sure of my decision. I have thought about it for the past two nights."

"While we were making love?"

"No, silly. While we were making love all I thought about was how much I love you."

Brian let her words fade off into the silence. He realized Christine was an incredibly impassioned woman and that her decision was final. He pressed her close to him and tenderly touched his lips to her mouth. The kiss lingered and he felt himself losing control. She sensed the situation and gently pushed him away.

"So, now you need to leave," she said bravely. "You must look after your precious cargo."

Brian adjusted the cylinder and stared into the blackness of the night.

"I'll be back for you, even if it takes me a while."

"And I will always wait for you, my darling."

"How will you get back down the mountain?"

"I will wait for Marcel here. If I accompanied you any further, I might change my mind. Besides, I want the memory of this wonderful place here and this beautiful bridge to last me for a long time."

Brian kissed her again and finally pushed himself away.

He turned to Marcel and started toward the bridge.

At the top of the bridge, he stopped and turned back toward Christine. He hoped it was dark enough to obscure the tears in his eyes. He waved briefly and turned to follow Marcel.

*   *   *

Three hours later, Marcel ascended a small rise and stopped at its top.

He turned to Brian and handed him a piece of paper. He shone his flashlight and illuminated a rough hand-drawn map.

"*Monsieur*, you are now in Spain. In about a half mile, you will cross a rough road that will immediately start a descent. You will continue to follow the road whose direction is south by southwest and you will eventually come to a much larger road. You will take *that* road and continue to the southwest until you reach the Spanish town of Jaca. Fifteen miles southwest of Jaca is the Monastery of San Juan de la Pena, where help will be waiting to assist you on the remainder of your journey.

Is all this clear to you?"

Brian studied the ragged piece of paper and determined that he could find his way.

"Thank you, Marcel," Brian shook the man's rough hand. "You have been very kind to help me get this far."

"You are most welcome, *Monsieur*. I am but a small part of our effort."

"One more thing, Marcel."

"*Oui, Monsieur?*"

"When you return to the *Pont d'Espagne*, I ask you to please take special care of the lady we left behind. She means a great deal to me."

"Of course I will *Monsieur*. On that you have my word."

END

Afterword

It is most fitting that certain aspects of this novel be mentioned that significantly affect its very being. Many of the characters herein are historically accurate and have been drawn from verified historic fact. These great Resistance heroes are awe inspiring in themselves and assuredly deserve their revered places in history. Their cause was among the most just in memory and will be the subject of many works to come. They will never get old---their story is simply too true to ever forget.

For the sake of creativity, certain aspects of the great paintings of the *Louvre* were altered slightly for the sake of the story. It is my hope that the art purists of the world will be placated.

I had this particular storyline in my mind since I was a youth, when I submitted it to Hollywood in the early 1960's. I received an encouraging reply at the time but was simply unable to act upon it and see it to fruition. I sincerely hope that time and circumstance have not altered my basic premise, that being to provide a meaningful story about a period in history that I consider timeless.

Jack DuArte
Lexington, KY
2011

Just out and available on <u>all</u> eplatforms:

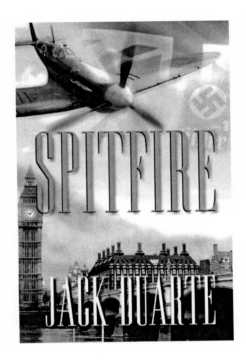

Spitfire is the third installment of Jack DuArte' World War II Series. The setting is Great Britain in 1940, immediately before and during the epic Battle of Britain. Fighting a superior number of *Luftwaffe* bombers and fighters, the valiant Royal Air Force wages a desperate air battle to save their country from certain defeat.

Flight Lieutenant Anthony Nelson and his younger brother, Fletcher, are pilots of 54 Squadron Spitfires, the great British fighter plane that is Britain's only hope for survival.

Through a suspenseful series of events, both find they are in love with the same woman. A hair-raising set of circumstances brings *Spitfire* to a spellbinding conclusion that will keep the reader glued to the final pages.

Jack DuArte is a decorated Vietnam Veteran who resides in Lexington, KY with his wife Susan, their dogs Brewster and Tucker and their miniature horse Darleigh.

CPSIA information can be obtained at www.ICGtesting.com
Printed in the USA
LVOW072029200212

269592LV00002B/3/P